OCHOCO REACH

JIM STEWART

WORD HERMIT PRESS • USA
ISBN-978-0-9908593-3-8
Library of Congress Catalog number applied for.

For Laura...

*...and for the veterans who served in Vietnam:
those who came back, those who didn't, and
those who haven't yet.*

ONE: MIKE

"Someone is watching me," she said. "I don't know who. I've also gotten several calls asking me to sell my ranch, but it isn't for sale. I think these things are related."

Her hopeful look belied the fear lurking in her heart, something my instincts should have registered but didn't. The buzz I got sitting across the desk from her was like the one I might have gotten sitting in the middle of a Balinese gong band. What else was I missing?

"Who gave you my card?"

Her mouth twisted, a lopsided smile. "Nobody. I found it in a phone book in a Prineville café. Stuck in the attorney pages."

I'd visited a Prineville café a month ago to break up a long motorcycle ride. A decent cup of coffee almost always clears road hypnosis. The Balinese gongs struck an arpeggio, and my common sense retreated further. I was convinced my stopping had been for a bigger purpose. I was supposed to meet this woman.

I scrambled to become again the consummate skeptic attorney. "Okay. You found my card and came to see me? All the way from Prineville? I mean, you could've just called."

The leather chair creaked as she shifted her weight. "I wasn't sure I wanted to get anybody involved. But when I was in Portland anyway, I just figured I'd look you up. See if you'd consider helping the proverbial damsel in distress."

Her smile was fraught with resentment. She wasn't used to being the victim.

I really wanted to help. I savored that feeling—of actually caring, without really being aware of why I should—as I leaned forward.

"Okay. Tell me about it."

TWO

I first met her on the sidewalk near my office. I had left Bucket, my Catahoula Leopard dog, asleep on the covered patio of our houseboat home. The sun backlit the usual rain, an atmosphere of quicksilver on an October Friday, and I was enjoying the magical shimmer when a voice pulled me back to the sidewalk.

"Are you okay?" A woman, maybe a few years younger than me. A dusting of freckles beneath eyes of colleen green. I must have admired those eyes a beat too long, because she folded her arms across her chest and repeated, "Really, are you okay?"

"Yes," I stammered. "I was just admiring the juxtaposition of sun and rain and…wow, you're pretty." Silently, I cursed my internal editor. A click too slow, as usual.

It was her turn to pause. Her generous mouth turned downward as she processed what I'd just said. Her lips were slightly chapped and showed just a hint of gloss. The green eyes clouded briefly and then snapped back to clear and swift, reminding me of a Montana trout stream. They wrinkled at their corners, but her arms tightened across her chest.

"You're sure," she said.

"Oh yeah. You are really pretty." I wasn't sure which foot was in my mouth. It tasted like the left.

"No. That you're all right, I mean. Your face looked like you were in some kind of pain."

I knew I should respond, but I couldn't get past those eyes. The playful curve of her cheek. I wanted to shake myself like a wet dog.

Somewhere in the vast distance between my ears I began to hear the stirring of voices. They appear from time to time, chanting in a language I don't know but understand. Usually, they come when I am in physical danger. This was different. It was more of a singing than a chanting. Sometimes, too, there are drums. The only accompaniment today was a far off wind. I shook my head to clear it.

"Yes. Really. I'm fine." My brain couldn't find a thing to say. "Can I help you?" was the best I could come up with.

"I'm looking for this address." She held up a business card.

"Sure. The address scheme can be confusing here, but it's right across the street and up the stairs. I'll show you."

"Oh, that's all right. I can find it."

"I'm sure you can, but I'm going up there anyway. It's really no problem."

When we got to the top of the stairs, I unlocked my office. She compared the number on the door with the one on her card. She became so still that I heard the drips from her raincoat to the hardwood floor.

"Aren't you coming in?" I asked.

"But…" It was her turn to stammer.

"That's my business card, and this is my office."

She watched me, her body brushing the folds of her raincoat. Stay? Or flee?

"You're about to ask me for help because that's what I do." I opened the door wider. "You wouldn't have found my card if you didn't need me."

"You're Mike Ironwood?"

I held her gaze to keep from staring at the rest of her. "At your service."

Her eyes crinkled at the corners. As she swept through my door, I breathed damp meadow and juniper. Smoothing what was left of my hair, I took her coat and switched on the brass lamp resting on my desk. The warm glow accentuated her eyes.

As the voices in my head thrummed, I motioned to a leather chair. "Please sit down."

We sat at the same time. I tried not to stare at the drape of her sweater, the shape of her legs in worn jeans. But it was her hair that captured most of my attention. It fell to her shoulders in natural waves, deeply and darkly red with highlights of gold.

To mask my attraction, I aimed for a calm, professional smile, designed to put potential clients at ease.

She chuckled. "You have the goofiest smile. I like it."

Clearly I failed at calm and professional. I switched tacks.

"Why are you here, Miss—"

"Call me Willy."

I paused at the incongruence. "Willy?"

"Short for Willimina. Willimina Hayes."

She measured me with her green eyes. I hoped my quickening heart wasn't obvious as I fumbled for a response. My voices drifted off, but stayed in the background.

She broke the silence. "Do you have anything to drink? Water? Juice? Anything like that?"

"Stronger stuff too, if you like."

"No, water's fine. But don't let me stop you."

I laughed. "Me? I keep the stronger stuff around for clients, mostly. People who seek out private detectives usually have fair reason to numb their pain a little."

"What a complete service. A private detective who sees to everything."

"Most everything." I handed her a glass of water. "How can I help you?"

She gripped the glass in both hands but didn't take a sip. "My ranch, the H-Bar-H, is a seventeen-hundred-acre spread up in the Ochoco Mountains northeast of Prineville. A good mix of range and timber. About two months ago, I noticed things in the barn were out of place. Nothing I could put my finger on. More of a feeling, I guess. It bothered me, so I set some traps. Sure enough, I caught things moving."

"Nothing stolen?"

"No. And that bothered me. Theft would be better than this vague movement, like somebody was disturbing things to mess with me. I got scared when I realized someone was watching the house. From the shop attached to the barn. One window offers a clear look, straight into my kitchen."

I hadn't been watching her tell her story. Instead, I looked at my boots. She deserved my undivided attention, and I couldn't give that to her if I tried to listen while looking at her. But now I chanced a glance.

"This vague movement. It couldn't be somebody working? A hand, maybe? Somebody with business there?"

Auburn curls framed her face when she shook her head.

"What about dogs?"

Her face pinched. "Dogs?"

"Dogs, yes. I grew up on a ranch in the Blues up out of Ukiah. I can't think of a working ranch without at least one dog."

She pulled her chair closer to my desk, her eyes alight. "Oh. We had an old Aussie shepherd, but she didn't come home…"

"When?"

"About two months ago."

Realization hit her in the stomach. Leather squeaked as she crumpled into the chair. I kept my hands in my lap to keep from reaching for her. After all, she used the word we.

Her green eyes swam. "The dog not coming back. It's a coincidence, right?"

I found myself gripping the edge of my desk. "Maybe. Maybe not. Was the dog in good health? I mean, how'd you explain it to yourself?"

"I don't know. She was a happy girl, not as active as she had been, but still feisty. I just figured she ran into something she couldn't handle."

"She probably did." I didn't believe that any more than Willy did.

I thought she might cry, but the muscles in her jaw clenched instead. "Goddamn them." She worked her hands in her lap, solid hands that knew rope and wire. The driving of nails. She wore no rings.

"You said, 'We had an old Aussie shepherd.' Who's 'we'?"

It took her a heartbeat to grasp my question. "Aurelio and Rosa Ruiz. The Ruiz family worked for my father. Since he died, we work the ranch together. If something should happen to me, I want their family to have a legal working share of the ranch."

I tried not to sound relieved. "Do you have a lawyer working on it?"

"No. I was pulling it together when this stuff started happening."

"You should call Alan Berwick. He's in Prineville. I was looking for his number when I stuck my card in the phone book. He's a good guy."

She pulled a notepad from her leather bag and scribbled his name. "Thanks. I'll give him a call."

My chair squeaked when I leaned back, like it sighed my own relief. "So, your ranch has cattle?"

"Yes. The size of the herd varies. Depends on the grass. We don't send 'em to a feedlot. They're grass fed. Nowadays, with organic markets taking off, the price stays higher."

She described moving chickens around pastures in large pens. The chickens ate larvae from the cow manure, and their guano fed nitrogen and potassium back into the grass. Passion fired her graceful gestures, her intense expression. For a few minutes, she forgot her problems. But only for a few minutes. When she stopped talking, the color drained from her face, and worry lined her eyes. She had no defenses in place.

"Mr. Ironwood, will you help me?"

To make her smile again, I'd alter the trajectory of planets. But since I couldn't, normal Mike would have to do, voices or no voices.

"Call me Mike. And yes, Willy. I'll help you. We'll figure this out."

"Can you come to the ranch? Inspect things for yourself?" She leaned forward, and another lock of auburn hair grazed her pleading green eyes. "Maybe you can come Sunday."

"Sunday it is." I made a note in my calendar.

I stood when she did. Her handshake was firm. I couldn't release her. "Let me buy you breakfast." I blurted it before I could stop myself.

THREE

We went downstairs to the Chub Town Café. My usual table clearly had been recently vacated, and the smile that Kathy, the owner, gave Willy twinkled like stars should twinkle. There was something knowing behind the smile she turned on me, but she played it cool when she spoke.

"Where's the dog?"

"When last seen," I said in my best theatrical voice, "he was asleep, twitching, on the porch. Probably chasing a rhinoceros."

"He'll miss his cookie."

"I can give it to him," I said, already knowing her answer.

"No way, José. The cookie is between him and me."

I nodded. "Kathy, Willy. Willy, Kathy."

Kathy gave me a look that said she didn't know what to think. I enjoyed it immensely.

Willy and I sat. "Everything is to die for," I said, pointing to the menu. I ordered the corned beef hash, no hashbrowns, no toast. Willy went with two eggs, over easy, with sausage and rye toast. We both ordered coffee. Kathy clucked appreciatively and went about her business.

"Did I pass?" Willy asked.

"Flying colors."

We made small talk and ate. We lingered over coffee, not wanting the meal to end.

After a sip of coffee, Willy pulled out my business card.

"What's the deal with the card? It says, *Freelance Investigator and Salvage Consultant.*"

I took my own sip. "The freelance investigator thing seems obvious. I assume you're curious about the salvage consultant bit."

She nodded.

"It's from the Travis McGee books that John D. MacDonald wrote from the sixties to the eighties. I loved those books, and when I got into this business, I decided, like McGee, that the real nature of the work is salvage. People come see me when they are confronted with problems they don't know how to solve. Sometimes they haven't even really defined the problem. Part of life has gone missing, and they want it back, be it a spouse, a child, a career, security, money, could be anything. McGee wasn't a cop or a licensed PI. He was just a guy with a knack for getting to the bottom of things and then working tirelessly as an advocate. He was tough, smart, ruthless, and stubborn as hell. He also had a romantic streak that caused him some private grief, but he hid it well. I guess it just resonates with me, so I put it on the card."

"It seems a bit Quixotic," she said.

I shrugged. "Maybe so. I do have this odd predilection for windmills."

Willy smiled and shook her head, which made me smile in return.

"So, who wants to buy your ranch?"

"At first," she said, "I received solicitations in the mail. They were from a company called Parke, with an *E*, Properties, from Tucson, telling me that they paid top dollar for Oregon acreage and that my property had been determined to be most desirable."

"Any notion of why you?"

"Not a clue. This just came out of the blue. After a couple passes, I called the number on the sheet and told them I was not interested in selling and that I never would be."

"Did you ever notice anything resembling a local connection?"

Willy frowned in thought. "I did get a phone call, after I made the refusal, from a local real estate guy. He said he'd heard a rumor that the ranch might be for sale and wanted more information."

"What did you tell him?"

"I might have been rude. I was very short—told him he'd heard wrong and hung up."

"Who was this guy?"

"Oh, I don't know. He mentioned some office in town, Schnell's, Snell's, Smell's, something like that. He had a one-syllable name, Tom, Bob, Roy, whatever. I didn't really pay attention."

"I will make some inquiries from here, but I'll do more when I get out there."

"Of course," she said.

"I'll also call my brother Daniel," I went on. "He'll discover who is visiting your barn."

Her eyes formed a question.

"Daniel is like smoke. He will watch, and then we will know."

"That's kind of creepy."

"But very useful. It will be good to actually know something."

"We've never talked about money," she said.

I resisted the urge to use my most dazzling smile—the one to add sparkle to the number, or maybe to blind the client—and just told her. Her eyes widened a little.

"Anything up front?"

"Usually, but that's up to you."

She went to her coat and handed me an envelope. "Copies of the solicitations and a small retainer."

"You're a smart lady."

"Don't confuse preparedness for brains. I'm just very methodical."

We nodded at each other slightly.

"My instincts are generally pretty good," she said through a smile.

"Be careful," I said. "Anything that doesn't look right or feel right, you call me. My brother will be up there today. You won't see him unless he wants you to. Are your guns loaded?"

"They are always loaded. What does Daniel look like?"

"A little taller than me, thinner, darker. Not quite as good-looking," I grinned. "He's half Nez Perce, or Nimi'ipuu, as he prefers."

"You don't look Indian," she smiled.

"I'm not. Daniel and I share a father, not a mother, but we grew up together." I told her I'd be in touch. We said our good-byes on the sidewalk. Grabbing my hand, she impulsively pulled me into a hug. I got the feeling it was pure impulse. It went on for a while. There was nothing sexual about it. Unidentifiable shapes moved through me, but I did not allow myself to look at them directly. I recognized the fear, but I also knew a vast warmth. The voices in my head almost purred.

"I don't usually hug my clients," I said into her hair.

She murmured something and hugged me a little tighter.

When she was done, she stepped back. There was no awkward moment. Somehow, we had become friends.

"I don't usually hug anybody," she said, "but all of a sudden it seemed exactly the right thing to do. And," she added with a sly smile, "you can learn a lot about a person during a hug."

"Well," I stammered, "I hope I didn't give too much away."

"It was just right." Her smile warmed my retinas.

She walked away, a flow that disturbed nothing along her path. My internal boulders shifted and took on an unaccustomed lightness. I knew a kinship with the people who built the pyramids and those who transported the Stonehenge monoliths. It was immense and microscopic all at the same once.

FOUR: WILLY

As I walked away from Mike, I really tried to keep my hips quiet. I knew he was watching. What surprised me was that I didn't mind. I *liked* the fact that he was watching.

My radar is spinning and picking up everything and nothing. How can that be? That hug was warm, and he took no advantage. I think he was as surprised as I was.

By the time I got to my truck, I knew that something profound had changed. I didn't know what, exactly, but it certainly involved Mike Ironwood.

Except for growing up on a ranch, we are nothing alike. He's outside my experience. He's dangerous. For all I know, he could be a thug.

My mind was racing, but I was completely calm for the first time since I began to get the uneasy feeling that I was being watched by people unknown. Knowing Mike was on my side was oddly comforting. I couldn't explain it in any more detail.

Be careful, girl. You are on a slippery slope here. The last time you felt like this ended badly. Pay attention.

FIVE: MIKE

"Oh boy, a camping trip," said Daniel. "The usual thing?"

"Mostly. We need to find out who and why, so who is a great place to start."

"So, Kemosabe, the Indian does all the work while you get to hang out with the girl?"

"Yep." I grinned into my cell phone.

"I have my own ranch to run, you know."

"Randy will handle it."

"Yeah, I know that." Daniel sighed. "I will text the GPS coordinates when I figure out where I will be."

"Rightio," I said.

"Rightio?"

"Yes. I'm reading a book about fox hunting."

"I will text you." Daniel snorted and hung up.

Daniel was born when I was three. My mother, Danielle, died from pancreatic cancer not long after I was born. Serena, Daniel's mother, had come in to cook late in Mom's illness. She stayed on, and she and Dad fell in love. She had every intention of raising me as her own, but her life was cut short by a man who wrongly figured that he could dictate her behavior at knife point. When she refused, he stabbed her. Before she died, she shot her attacker in the forehead with the .32 caliber revolver she always carried in her coat pocket. It was small consolation. It drove home the notion that just carrying a gun does not make you safe. You have to be willing to use the gun. Serena had been about two seconds late in making that decision.

Her family became ours and were willing and eager to help out at the ranch whenever they could. They made two words out of Dad's name. Iron Wood. Now, they call Daniel Iron Wood. In fact, the entire ranch is now known as Iron Wood. They call me Mike. I'm okay with that.

Our dad was never quite the same after Serena was killed. He climbed into himself and stayed there. He was a hard man before Serena died and doubly hard after. His anger and his pain kept him alive, but he took no joy in it. Daniel and I, somehow, with the help of Serena's family, made it through high school. Randy, Serena's older brother, stepped in and saved us both, by knowing how to run the ranch and by knowing that his nephew and I needed a strong, but caring, hand to get us through our rites of passage. We always looked upon Randy Two Hawks and his wife, River, as our parents. We were blessed by their unwavering devotion.

Daniel and I both ended up in the military, me on the ground in Vietnam. I trained as Special Forces and got my beret, but my inability to follow rules when combat was not in session kept me from going very far. My inability to follow rules when combat was in session kept me alive. Helping the people who lived there, learning to discover and destroy whom I believed to be the bad guys, and feeling the brotherhood with the other eleven men in my detachment were what I honored and loved about that job. I liked the operations well enough, I guess, but I had—and still do have—difficulty with accepting orders from idiots. I was lucky that, in the crucible of Vietnam, there were few of those in our bailiwick. As a group, we were misfits, as far as the army was concerned. We excelled at "unconventional warfare" and everything that suggests. I managed to hold on to my sergeant stripes, but it wasn't easy when we dealt with the regular army brass. I did two tours because that was the deal, but when my obligation was over, I was done. The war, or "conflict," as it was called, was pretty much over by that time, and the notion of continuing any relationship with the CIA didn't exactly warm my cockles. I missed the fall of Saigon, but ached anyway for the people, those whom I knew and those I didn't. It was a nasty, sad business.

The ranch life didn't satisfy my newly discovered need for adrenalin, so I joined the Oregon State Police, went through the training, and soon came to realize that my inability to follow rules with any regularity was not going to allow me a police career of any duration. The organization tried. A couple of lieutenants had seen my type in Nam and knew that I was competent and a good asset when things got to popping, but the down times were a struggle. They assigned me to various detective units to see if it would hold my interest. It helped, but I couldn't stay out of the doghouse for any length of time and resigned after only a few years. Everybody heaved a sigh of relief.

When I thought back on those days, I realized that I was one of the very fortunate few who didn't encounter any kind of lasting alcohol or drug abuse urges upon my return from Vietnam. The first year or so back, I was in Mexico with my buddy Jasper Cronk, who'd mustered out about the same time, and I was too busy remembering how wonderful life was. Sure, I drank and smoked a bit in those days, but it never got out of hand. Once I joined the Oregon State Police, I lost interest in getting high. I still drank a beer now and then. You'd be crazy not to in a town like Portland, a city that had earned the nickname Beervana.

After high school, Daniel was not enamored with the idea of mud, spiders as big as your head, snakes, punji stakes, and foot rot, as I had reported from Vietnam, so he joined the navy and became a SEAL. He had to learn to deal with mud, spiders as big as your head, snakes, punji stakes, and foot rot. His skill in the boonies and his implacable patience were second to none. In battle, his calm wrath became legendary. I was sure there were enemy soldiers who died without even knowing they'd been killed. One second they were there, and the next they were not.

Daniel stayed in the military for fifteen years, performing his duty around the world in conflicts average Americans knew nothing about. He was somewhere in Nicaragua when our father died. He was refused leave, so he missed the burial at the family plot up high on the ridge where a lone pine offered brief respite from the Eastern Oregon sun and relentless wind. Dad was laid to rest next to our mothers. It was probably the best he'd felt in years.

As soon as he could, Daniel resigned his commission. His official rank was commander, and he continued to refer to himself as Commander Spook. He received his pension, which he donated to his tribe, and was pursued for years by the various alphabet intelligence agencies who wanted his services. He was also pursued by agencies from other countries that, through close association to ours, knew of his skill.

Daniel refused them all. He was able, mostly, to put that part of his life behind him and return to the ranch, where he slowly earned the title of Iron Wood. He also took it upon himself to relearn the old ways of his people and teach the youngsters how to live on the land and to leave no mark and to move across the earth like air.

I used my share of the modest inheritance to buy a houseboat on the Willamette River in Portland. It suited my needs exactly. With Daniel's agreement, I assumed ownership of two of my father's possessions. I moved his big old desk from the house we grew up in to the front room in my houseboat. Getting it in there was quite an adventure, but with Daniel's help we got it done. The other thing I took was my dad's Colt 1861 Navy pistol, .36 caliber. It lived in the top right-hand drawer of the desk in my office. The powder was always dry. I didn't know what would happen if I ever had to shoot it in close quarters. Even "smokeless" black powder would fill the room with smoke, and the concussion might knock out a window. But I kept it there. It had been a working tool for well over a hundred years, and it just felt good to have it close.

Daniel helped me the day we moved the desk, and we told stories of our military experiences far into the night. We never spoke of them again. There was no need. Those times that nightmares came to one of us, somehow the other was aware of it. There are some scars that cannot heal. He knew this, and so did I. Just having each other in proximity helped us deal with that which cannot be forgotten or accepted in a truly meaningful way.

SIX

I spent Saturday going through the solicitations that Willy had given me. I got onto the Internet and looked for Parke Properties and didn't come up with a thing. So much for being a crack investigator.

On Sunday, Bucket and I woke up with the sun. I grabbed little roll of plastic bags, and we headed off the dock up into Oaks Park. From there we ran through the bird refuge and out along Bybee to Westmoreland Park and out through Eastmoreland Park. We circled through the neighborhoods back into Oaks Park. Bucket was supposed to be on a leash, but we had an understanding. When I called, he came. We had hand signals worked out too, and when I gave one, his whole attention changed. He knew, in his dog way, that the game changed when we went silent.

Bucket was a Catahoula Leopard Dog, named for the Catahoula Parish in Louisiana. It is not a breed recognized by the American Kennel folks, but Catahoulas have probably been in North America longer than any other breed. The truest and deepest dogs with whom I ever had the pleasure of spending time, they are working dogs, mostly shorthaired, and proudly wave a white-tipped curled tail. They were originally bred to hunt wild boar and to herd cattle. Their technique to catch a boar was to rile it up and get it to chase them back to the hunters. Their ears are designed to hear behind them as well as what's in front. True to form, Bucket loved to be chased.

Bucket was of the quad-color variety, where the colors are mottled and reminiscent of a dingo or an Australian shepherd. He was an eighty-five-pound sweetheart, and I was very glad that he was always on my side.

That morning, he was a happy boy. He knew we were going for a ride because my travel bag was packed and by the door, and he knew he was going because the Harley was still tucked in its nook in the shop.

As I slowed the pace and started to cool down, I scanned the park. We usually had it to ourselves this time of day, but this morning there was a blue Ford van parked in the lot. I couldn't read the plate from where I was, but it wasn't one of the many Oregon plates. My curiosity rose and tapped me somewhere in the medulla oblongata.

"Bucket, stay close."

He came and trailed me a couple paces on my left. I scanned the park again. Was that movement by the oak trees that ran parallel to the river? Yes. There were two guys standing in the shadows on the river side of the trees. They were looking at my house, floating there in the crook of the docks.

I went back up toward the parking lot and got close enough to jot down the license number of the van. They were California plates. Then I got closer. The hood was still warm. I rested the full poop bag against the driver's side windshield wiper and put the rest of the roll in my pocket. Bucket cocked his head at me, and I smiled.

We went upriver a ways and came back using the trees as cover. The men clearly were not terribly concerned about being seen. They were both in their thirties, maybe younger. They wore the trademarked gangbanger floppy jeans and slightly askew baseball caps. The smaller of the two wore a Yankees cap. I hated the Yankees. My father had been a Red Sox fan. I still was. It might be genetic. The other sported a Mets cap. I hated the Mets too, for the same reason. Open oversize windbreakers fluttered in the morning breeze.

Bucket snarled deep in his chest. I gave him the hand signal for quiet. I reached into my vest and pulled my Ruger .40 caliber semiauto from the holster under my armpit and let my arm hang loosely by my side. Bucket knew what the gun meant.

These two were city boys, obviously, and weren't paying enough attention to their woodcraft. I was within six feet of them before they sensed and saw me. I saw no reason to hide the gun but only showed them the smallest part of it. It was pointed at Mets Cap's chin. His eyes got big. Yankees Cap started to put his hand into his windbreaker.

"Don't be doing that," I said. "You should both keep your hands where I can see them and breathe only when you have to."

"*No hablo ingles*," said Yankees Cap.

"Bullshit."

I motioned for Bucket to cover the guy with the Mets cap. He had a unique way of holding somebody's attention. He grabbed people by the crotch with his impressive array of teeth. He knew exactly how to make it effective: just enough pressure. This time was no different. Mets Cap whimpered.

Yankees Cap stared. "*Fuerte*," he said disdainfully.

I stood ten feet from Yankees Cap. The eye of my pistol looked right into his.

"Why are you watching my house?" I asked reasonably.

"We are not watching your house. We are just out enjoying the day. The river is beautiful."

"Okay. Take out your wallets and throw them on the ground over there." I pointed.

"We have no wallets," said Yankees Cap.

"Oh, professionals. But humor me and throw them over there anyway."

Even through Yankees Cap's smoldering anger, I caught a brief notion of a carefully hidden intelligence in his dark eyes. He was starting to really tire of me. He was probably pretty good with a gun, but he knew that if he tried to go for his at this point, I would have time to shoot him. In this particular case, he was even under the dog. He couldn't stand this rare pecking order.

"Now drop your pants," I said to Yankees Cap.

He was rigid with impatience and rage.

"Do it."

He knew he had no choice. His pants went to his ankles. I smiled when the pistol clattered to the ground. I moved over and kicked it down the riverbank. His underwear was bright blue.

"*Gracias.* Now let your jacket fall off your shoulders."

He had another pistol under his left armpit. I took it from him and tossed it after the first.

"Now lie down on your belly and wait."

"I will kill you for this," said Yankees Cap.

I laughed. "No, you won't."

I told Bucket to let go, and Mets Cap nearly fell to his knees. We repeated the Yankees Cap routine. Soon, they were both lying in the cool grass, beside each other head to foot.

Bucket's eyes were on me.

"Truck. Rope. Go."

I could've probably taught him this behavior with one word, but I thought it sounded vastly more impressive as three words. He trotted off. The ridge along his backbone was up. He loved this stuff. When he came back with the coil of rope in his mouth, I swore he was grinning.

"Good boy," I said and gave him a small piece of jerky. I always had some in my pocket for when he was especially competent.

When the two baseball fans were trussed up, I studied their IDs, which didn't tell me much. Yankees Cap was Jesús María Chavez, and Mets Cap was Frederico Angel Ruiz. They were in their late twenties. Their licenses said they both were from Oakland.

I squatted by Mets Cap. His name nagged at me. After my tours in Vietnam, I spent quite a bit of time in Mexico decompressing and relearning that not all problems are solved with deadly force. I still have good friends there. My Spanish was probably rusty, but I tried it anyway.

"*¿Hola, Freddie, cómo está usted relacionado a Aurelio Ruiz?*"

"*No le dices una cosa, jodido,*" said Yankees Cap.

I caught Bucket's attention, spread my fingers, and then formed a fist.

He went over to Yankees Cap and put both front feet in the small of his back. He growled for good measure.

I made the fist again. He laid his ears back and gave me his dog grin.

"Freddie?"

He let out a long shuddering sigh. "*Él es el segundo primo de mi madre,*" he whispered.

"*Pendejo,*" hissed Yankees Cap.

"Jesús, shut the fuck up."

Freddie knew he was in deep shit. Aurelio Ruiz was his second cousin on his mother's side. Part of the puzzle was solved.

"Gracias," I said.

I rechecked the bindings and patted the men down thoroughly. Ruiz had a switchblade knife, which I put with his wallet. Chavez did not carry a blade. I took their cell phones. I was satisfied that it would take them a good hour to free themselves, if they knew what they were doing. That should give the cops plenty of time to get there.

"C'mon Bucket," I called.

He bounced his two front feet off of Yankees Cap, who winced.

"Good boy," I said and gave him another little piece of jerky. He was having a fine day.

I stashed the wallets and other stuff in the shop, took a quick shower, and pulled my maroon 1950 five-window Chevy pickup up to where I could see my two new pals. Yankees Cap had flipped over onto his back and was now lying on both his arms, which had been bound tightly behind him. He looked busy—making everything tighter. Good for him.

I called Detective Tom Hannarty's cell phone. Tom might have had a good career as an NFL wide receiver, if not for ripping his knee against Montana State in 1976. He and I met while he was recovering from that. I was an Oregon State cop then, and Tom claimed that it was our meeting that steered him into police work. He became a cop for all the right reasons. He certainly wasn't the first black cop on the Portland Police Bureau, but he was among the first to make it to detective. He was now a lead in the homicide squad.

"Hannarty," he answered.

"You done with your doughnuts yet?"

He sighed. "Yes. I'm just beginning my daily search for someone to brutalize."

"You guys just can't seem to escape the clichés."

"What's up?"

I told him.

"They can't be clean," I said. "Maybe you can get something useful, like maybe match a gun to something. The guns, wallets, and cell phones are under the drill press table in the shop."

"This something you're working on?"

I could almost see his dark brown eyes snap into focus.

"Probably. Next time we hook up, I'll fill you in a little."

Hannarty laughed. "And I know you're not kidding when you say 'a little.'"

"Priorities," I said.

I felt him nod. "Be careful."

Now it was my turn to laugh.

"I mean it," he said. "The bureau is hot and heavy on something right now, and it involves Mexican drug cartels. Those guys kill you first and ask never."

I thought of Yankees Cap, Jesús Chavez. I also thought of Willy. And of Daniel.

"That might fit. Who's the alphabet guy on this?" referring to the FBI.

"Jepps," Hannarty said. "Arthur Jepps."

"Could be worse. See ya."

Curiouser and curiouser.

SEVEN

Bucket and I drove across town, caught I-205 south very briefly, and hopped over onto Highway 224 toward Boring. There were probably as many snapshots of people standing under the Welcome to Boring sign as there were of those in Hell, California, but probably not as many as Fucking, Germany. When I drove past, there was nobody posing. A slow tourist day.

The old Chevy was one my most prized possessions. The only thing on it that wasn't stock was the steering and suspension. I put new equipment in there because I wanted the old look and feel and some driving performance. I still had the 235 straight-six engine, as reliable an engine as any ever built. It certainly wasn't a show car. Like my Harley, it was sturdy and well cared for. The Harley was something of a no-big-deal hotrod, but not the truck. It was just a truck.

Bucket sprawled out on the bench seat in his usual position. If not for going sixty, I could've probably heard his soft snoring. I called him Bucket after the hero in Jack London's *Call of the Wild* and also after Charles Dickens's Inspector Bucket. It just fit his laconic yet detail-oriented personality.

He was a dog, and I treated him as such. Dogs are not little people in fur coats. But I still talked to him all the time and shared my thoughts, things I wouldn't share with anybody else, except maybe Daniel. I wanted to talk about Willy, but I wasn't ready to share any of that yet, not even with Bucket.

Over the southwestern shoulder of Mt. Hood we went, down the long hill where the land changes from alpine to high desert. Most everywhere outside the Willamette Valley in Oregon is ranch country. Real cowboys work the fences, the creek bottoms, and the high grazing land every day, rain and shine, heat and bitter cold.

We were about a mile from where the Mill Creek bridge spans a deep gnarly canyon when my cell phone buzzed. I hit the hands-free button.

"Speak."

"Can't you just answer a phone like everybody else?" Hannarty said.

I chuckled. "Sorry, Tom, I was just feeling expansive."

"Well, cowboy, rein yourself in because you're not going to like this."

He paused. I didn't say anything. I was too busy pulling into the parking area on the south side of the Mill Creek bridge. I leaned across the cab and opened the door to let Bucket out. He had that needy look.

"Which of your guys had which hat and who had which guns?" Hannarty said.

"The guy with the Yankees hat, Chavez, had two," I said. "Some kind of .38, Brazilian I think, probably his throwaway, and a Glock in his armpit. The guy with the Mets cap, Ruiz, had a no-name nine stuck in his pants. The guns are with the wallets and cell phones under the drill-press table in the shop. You know where the key is. What did you find in the van?"

"There was no van," Hannarty said. "There was one guy, Ruiz, apparently, and he was dead. Somebody broke his neck and left him there, trussed up. The other guy is gone, but the grass was all torn up where he'd been. We have the license number you gave us and the word is out, statewide, Washington too. Where are you?"

That Yankees Cap had been able to get himself free in such a short time left me taut with anger. I shook my head and didn't look at myself in the mirror. I thought again of the intelligence I'd seen in his eyes.

"Mike?" Hannarty was impatient.

"On my way to the Ochocos out of Prineville. I'm not sure when I'll be back. Probably tomorrow."

After a few heartbeats, Hannarty said, "Stay in touch."

The connection broke.

Bucket hopped back up into the truck and stretched. He turned around and lay back down with his chin resting on my leg. I ruffled his ears.

"I fucked up."

He sighed and licked my hand. I wondered who else would die because I had underestimated a stone-cold killer. I also knew that I was number one on the Yankees Cap hit parade. That settled me down. There's nothing like imminent death to sharpen a guy's outlook.

The cell phone buzzed again, but this was the text message buzz. The little screen told me the coordinates of Daniel's camp. But it also said, Get here now.

Swearing softly, I put the Chevy in gear and dropped the hammer. The door slammed shut. The rubber and the road began singing their song.

EIGHT

We blew through Warm Springs at a pace that might have been ticket-worthy. Madras came and went. We hummed along past a mix of ranches, industry, and roadside attractions. The Cascades were behind me now as I headed east. The sky was a brilliant blue. My phone buzzed again. It was Willy.

"Where are you?"

"Twenty minutes from Prineville."

"Don't come to the ranch—go to the hospital. I'll meet you there." She told me where it was.

"What's going on?"

"Somebody shot Aurelio."

"How badly?"

"He'll live, I think. Gotta go."

She hung up before I could ask about Daniel.

I tried to piece together what I knew of this rapidly escalating series of events. Less than forty-eight hours ago Willy and I met on a corner in Multnomah Village. So far, there was a dead gangbanger and her trusted ranch hand was in the hospital with at least one bullet in him. My usual methods when faced with needing information all involved stirring the pot until things began to happen, took shape, and started to become apparent. This particular case certainly hadn't required much stirring. Hannarty's caution about the drug cartel was buzzing around in me. I decided to call Agent Jepps at my next opportunity. I really didn't like initiating contact with any entity having *federal* in its description, but I was ready to make an exception.

I parked on Elm Street and hoofed it to Emergency. Daniel was waiting outside. He was wearing what he called his buckskin surveillance suit and a gray wool hat. The air was brisk.

"I do not know what you are into, brother, but it is not good," he said. "My infallible Indian Sense tells me that more European violence will befall me as it has befallen the gentleman inside."

"I beg to differ—the guy who did the shooting probably has a lot of Indian in him."

"Well," said Daniel, "his handlers probably do, but the guy who actually pulled the trigger is a white kid named Jerry from The Dalles. He also has a serious methamphetamine issue."

"A tweaker?"

"I think that is probably why Mr. Ruiz is still alive. The kid cannot shoot when startled. I startled him pretty good. He told me way more than he should have, so he probably will not survive the day, given who I think his bosses are."

"How'd you get him to talk?"

"We savages can be very persuasive." He grinned. "I told him I was going to bury him alive in an ant hill and put wasps in his ears."

"You sure that didn't come from your Irish half?"

"Pretty sure."

"Where's this kid now?"

"With your old pal from the OSP, Thad Krieger."

"You work fast."

"Comes with practice."

"What now?" I said.

He adjusted his hat. "By your leave, sir, I will reestablish my position."

His grin was infectious.

"I'm thinking of calling Jepps," I said and filled him in on what Hannarty had told me.

"Let me call Jepps," said Daniel. "He owes me a couple of favors, and I really should collect an installment."

"Does this involve that business a couple years ago?" I asked.

Daniel had been instrumental in saving the lives of several people in a bank hostage situation a few years back. Agent Jepps's daughter had been among them.

Daniel smiled.

"I will be in touch," he said and was gone. He didn't just walk away—he vanished. I will never understand how he does it. A friend of ours, Isao Arai, who is of Japanese descent but speaks with a South Carolina drawl, says that Daniel is a true ninja, a historical throwback, who has one foot in this world and one foot in a place that we can't comprehend. Daniel scoffs at this. He says that he's just found a way to be an old-school Nimi'ipuu warrior.

NINE

"What is happening?" Willy's face and voice cracked with worry.

Notions flew about between my ears, to be sure, but nothing that I could articulate. The question of motive had no answer, nothing to help understand the escalation we were grappling with.

"I don't know what to tell you, yet. But I will figure this out and stop it. It's what I do."

We stood in a sun-washed waiting area, bright, but not warm. Her friend and ranch companion Aurelio Ruiz was in surgery, having a bullet removed from his upper chest. She gripped her elbows.

"I just don't understand this at all." She walked to the window, ponytail swinging across her back, and stared out at the oddly normal-looking day. I stood next to her. I wanted to touch her, to reassure her somehow, but I kept my hands to myself. Instead, I told her about my morning and of the two gang-bangers watching my house. I told her about Señor Ruiz's second cousin. She listened intently. When I was done, she turned on her heel and strode toward the door.

"Come on," she said over her shoulder.

We turned into another, smaller, waiting area. The light was dim and the walls a pale green. Seated by herself, her head in her hands, was a woman dressed in jeans and boots, her well-worn corduroy shearling jacket open. Her long black hair needed a brush and showed streaks of silver at her broad temples. A beat-up brown cowboy hat sat on the magazine table in front of her. Her eyes were wet.

"Oh, Willimina," she said in a husky contralto. "Why would somebody do this?"

That seemed to be the question of the hour. I would not admit to being baffled because the seed of an idea had taken root in the stubblefield of my mind. But I wasn't quite ready to commit to a vague theory until I had some more information.

Willy sat down next to her and took her hand. "Rosa, he's going to be okay."

"Sí, but who would do such a thing? Aurelio has never hurt anyone."

Willy took a deep breath. "Rosa, this is Mike Ironwood. He is here to help us."

They both leaned forward with expectation. "I have a couple of ideas, but nothing concrete. I don't want to say anything until I know more."

I silently chastised myself for such a lame statement.

"Rosa," I said, sitting, "do you know a young man named Frederico Ruiz?"

It was if I'd hissed an obscenity in her face. She actually recoiled. She hooded her eyes and became strangely distant. Willy just sighed.

"Yes, señor," she said carefully. "He is the nephew of Aurelio's oldest sister."

I waited through a profound silence.

"He is a very bad young man," she added finally.

"He is also very dead," I said.

They both stared at me, mouths open.

"Would he have reason to hurt you?"

Rosa pursed her lips, considering.

"Not that I know. But he is a disgrace." This was more to Willy than to me. "He is in a gang, and they work for the cartel in Western Mexico. He always brags that he is going to buy California and throw all the *gringos* out, but I don't know how he is going to do that since he spends all his money on cocaine and *putas.*"

"Not anymore," I reminded her.

Rosa sighed. "*Sí.* Out of respect for Aurelio's family, a couple years ago we offered him work, to get him out of his life and into something that would make him strong. He came and spent a few days but did no work. He laughed and said he could make more money in one afternoon in his old life than he could working a month on the ranch. He stole our grocery money, a rifle, and left."

I held out my hand, and Rosa took it. Her skin was dry and warm.

"Did he have something to do with Aurelio getting shot?" she asked.

"Yes," I said. "He probably convinced somebody that the ranch would make a good place to store or make drugs, most likely meth."

Willy's eyes went wide. "Are you sure of this?"

"No, I'm not sure, but it makes sense."

Rosa's hand tightened in mine. I gave it a gentle squeeze, let go, and stood up.

"How did Frederico die?" she asked.

I told her.

"It is the way he lived."

"Yes," I said.

Her eyes found their way past mine, into my core. "Will you kill the man who killed Frederico?" she asked.

"If I must. That will be his choice, I think."

She looked away. "He will want to kill you."

"That is usually how it goes."

TEN

We left Rosa in the small waiting room. I followed Willy down the hall and back to the sun-washed lobby. I had my hands in my pockets and chewed on my lip. The notion that our adversaries were professional drug people had been rattling around in my head and seemed to make sense, but there were logistical issues that I couldn't quite drag together. If Yankees Cap, Jesús Chavez, was on the lam in Portland, where was the van, and how did this kid from The Dalles show up and try to kill Aurelio? And gunslingers don't usually care about property values, so who was working it on the real estate end? Trying to put myself in the shoes of the enemy and understand the why of it was not coming together as I wanted it to. Tom Hannarty had said that the FBI was involved and that there might be Mexican cartels in the mix. What that said to me was that there were probably other federal outfits involved, like the DEA, maybe even the CIA. There were certainly people involved that I could not yet see. That bothered me. What also bothered me was that if all this alphabet soup was bubbling, the legendary lack of cooperation between the FBI and CIA was bound to be a problem. The FBI and the DEA had been known to pool resources. What the hell had I stumbled into?

Willy was saying something, and I came up out of myself.

"Huh?"

She smiled. "You were working, I think. At first I thought your face looked indescribably sad. Then, I realized that it is just how you look when you're concentrating. Where did you go?"

"I'm just trying to fill in all the blanks and can't. We need more information. Have you remembered anything about that real estate guy who called you?"

Willy frowned. "No, but I could probably recognize it if I saw it. Let's go find a phone book." She winked. "There's one up the street in a café."

"Ah, the famous phone book," I said. This reminded me that I still needed to look up my old friend Alan Berwick, the attorney who had, quite inadvertently, started this whole situation. He would certainly appreciate the irony.

I went to the truck and liberated Bucket. "Stay close," I said, and he dropped to the sidewalk and stretched, long and deep, tail in the air.

He regarded Willy with interest. She let him sniff, and he was mostly polite about it. His tail wagged, and he licked her hand. She ruffled his ears, almost exactly the way I do. That pleased me to no end. I think it pleased Bucket too.

As we walked, a helicopter flew over, loud and low. Helicopters always scratched a nerve in me. Those machines held an odd place in my psyche. On the one hand, they brought help and support during my time on the ground in Vietnam. On the other, they stirred up memories that I was in a situation where I needed help and support. The whup-whup-whup of those relentless blades put me past the razor.

It powered out of sight with a churning throb. I couldn't make out any markings. A little flashbulb popped as my curiosity stirred.

"Stay," I said to Bucket as we reached the café, and he settled down next to a small flower bed that brightened the entrance even in the winter, with its mossy greens.

Word travels fast in a town the size of Prineville, and Willy reassured everyone that Aurelio would be okay. We sat at the counter while she flipped through the realty pages. The coffee was as good as I remembered.

"That's it right there," she said, pointing to the ad for Sawtell Properties.

"How far it is it?"

"Not far. Let's go."

Before I got up, I flipped back to the attorneys pages and found Alan. I punched his number into my phone and saved it. I also memorized the address.

Willy led me, with Bucket trailing, back to Elm Street and then north, past Ochoco Creek Park and onto Fourth Street. Sawtell Properties was in a converted old house, a study in browns and yellows. At the top of the steps, Bucket growled.

"Stay," I said. Out of all the commands Bucket knew, this was his least favorite. And now I was using it twice in under an hour. He sat on the front steps, but the growl was still in his throat.

A bell on the door tinkled as we went in. I unzipped my leather jacket.

The room we stepped in to, a reception area, was empty. My watch told me it was one forty-three. Too late for lunch, I would think. As my ears adjusted to the inside, I could hear an insistent beeping. The hair on the back of my neck bristled. I touched Willy on the arm.

"Wait here," I said and stepped quietly ahead of her and looked into the back office.

The desk chair was toppled backward, and the arms of the man still in it were flung wide open against the floor. One of his eyes was misshapen, and there was a wide smear of red pooled at the head of the overturned chair. He still looked surprised.

A brass and mahogany nameplate announcing *Bob Fraley* sat at the front of the desk. Right next to it was the little blue bag I'd left on the van's windshield this morning.

I caught Willy's scent. I turned to her and put my hands on her shoulders.

"Don't come in here. Call 911 right now."

She tried to crane her neck and peek over my shoulder, but I was too tall and too wide. The fear in Willy's eyes was vibrant, but she didn't panic and turned to the phone on the front desk.

"Use your cell," I said. "Tell them we found a body and that there's no need for immediate care. I'll meet you outside."

While she made the call, I stepped back into the room and very gingerly picked up the little plastic bag and put it in my pocket. It had been left for me anyway, and there was not a single reason I could think of to leave it in place. I left the beeping phone receiver where it was on the desk.

I sat on the front steps with Willy and Bucket listening to the sirens coming and wondered how that kid with the Yankees cap could be one step ahead of me so soon after I'd left him tied up like a rump roast 150 miles away. I shook my head and sighed. Willy's eyes were wide, but she said nothing. Bucket watched a squirrel across the street and yawned. The air was cold, and the sky carried a threat of snow.

My cell phone burbled. It was Daniel. "This just keeps getting weirder and weirder," he said.

"Tell me about it. We just found a dead real estate guy."

Daniel whistled. "Wow. Well, I do not want to go into what I've got until I see you, but the sooner you can get to the H-Bar-H, the better. You will be flat-out blown away when I tell you what just went down."

"Did it involve a helicopter?"

Daniel laughed, a short bark I was very familiar with. He was both surprised and pleased.

"I have talked with Jepps, too, and that is just icing on this cake. Have you ever heard of a DEA guy named Deems?"

"Nope."

"Well, you will when you get out here."

"Okay. I'll let you know when we're on our way."

I shut the phone and caught Willy's eye. Her eyebrows were up in her hair.

"Apparently, Alice, we've left reality and have crossed over into Wonderland."

Her eyes glinted green sparks in the afternoon light.

"You're telling me."

ELEVEN

The first set of flashing lights to arrive belonged to one of Prineville's finest. She was crisp and all in blue and all business. Willy and I stood up.

"Where's the body?" she asked me while she nodded at Willy in recognition. Willy nodded back.

I flashed a thumb over my shoulder.

"In the back," I said.

"Did you touch anything at all in there?" she called as she walked back to her car's trunk.

"No, ma'am. Our footprints may show in the main office. I was the only one to go into the back office. I did not stay in there longer than ten or fifteen seconds, tops."

She lugged her crime scene kit in its big aluminum suitcase. "I'm Detective Kelso," she said, offering her hand.

I shook Detective Kelso's hand. Her grip was firm without being masculine.

"Mike Ironwood," I said.

Willy nodded to her and they shook hands too.

"Nice to see you, Willy," said Kelso.

"Nancy," Willy nodded back.

An Oregon State Police car cruised in, lights flashing, and came to a stop. It was my old friend Thad Krieger. He and I had gone through training together and stayed in touch. We were definitely closer now than we had been when I was wearing that uniform. He shook my hand and went inside. After about five minutes, he came back out.

"We have a double homicide in here."

That snapped my head around. Thad beckoned me to follow him.

I touched Willy on the shoulder. "Stay here with Bucket," I said. "If anybody gets stupid, tell Bucket 'down' and motion downward with your open palm." I showed her. "It will take an act of Congress to move him. It'll just keep him out of trouble."

"How would I release him?"

I crossed my eyes. "With 'up.'"

She laughed in spite of the grimness of the day. I squeezed her shoulder and followed Thad.

He led me into the back office. The guy in the chair was still open armed and just as dead, maybe deader. Nancy Kelso was crouched on one knee at the far end of the room, by a back door, pointing her camera through it. Thad stopped behind her, and I looked over his shoulder. A young woman was huddled between the commode and the wall, knees to her chest. Her head was at an odd angle. Her clasped hands made her look like supplicant, a testimonial to her last seconds.

"Mr. Ironwood," said Detective Kelso without stopping her work, "Thad tells me that you two used to work together and that you were almost a very good cop."

I nodded until I remembered that she wasn't looking at me. "Depends on how you define almost. I guess I still feel like I'm a cop. I just don't have to take orders when there's nothing going on. And I can nap when I want to."

"Thad also tells me that you're working on something that might be a part of this." I was relieved to hear a smile in her voice.

"Yes. I know who killed these people."

They both turned around and stared at me. I sure knew how to become the center of attention.

"If I were a betting man, and I am, I would bet that a gang shooter out of Oakland and, probably, points farther south is your killer. His name's Jesús Chavez, and I have no idea how he's getting around, but he is very mobile and"—my voice trailed off for a second—"very deadly. If I'd done my job better this morning, these people and another would probably still be alive right now."

I felt the acid of that in my guts.

Thad's eyes showed a questioning stare. I filled them in on this morning's adventure, but left out the part about the well-traveled baggie of dog poo.

"Tom Hannarty of the PPB has details on the guy," I added.

"How do you know this?" Kelso asked.

"Reasonable question." I was buying time. "Let's just say there's a signature here I recognize." It wasn't a complete lie, more of a creative fib.

I asked Thad about the kid he busted with Daniel.

"He's a few blocks away," he said, pointing southwest, "at the county jail. You want to talk to him?"

"Yeah, but it can wait."

We were interrupted by a large, heavy-eyebrowed gentleman hollering from the doorway. "Kelso, are you done with this guy?"

Nancy stood up, brushed the dust from her knees, and hollered back. "Hell no. Hold your water, Sully. Go get some coffee. Give me another hour."

My memory clicked. Ed Sullivan, the Crook County coroner. He had held that job for as long as anybody could remember. He was smart and suffered fools not at all. When I was a state cop, he was always free with information and always told you straight, even when reality was the last thing you wanted to hear.

All these uniforms around, I caught myself getting antsy. I said my good-byes and started to slide out the back door.

"Mr. Ironwood," said Detective Kelso, "I'm very glad you won't be leaving town without first providing a detailed statement. I know you think this is solved, but please humor me until I'm convinced too."

Thad made a phone motion.

"Yes, ma'am."

It had started to snow. I whistled for Bucket, who was around the corner of the building in less than three seconds. Willy was right behind him.

"Boy, you really are pack leader, aren't you?"

"Yep. Bucket knows we're working. He's very on top of that."

I squatted down and he sat, looking at me expectantly. I reached into my pocket and showed him the small plastic bag. He sniffed it.

"Find it," I said. I stood, walked over to the back steps, and tapped them with my hand. "Find it," I repeated. A brief thought of him pointing his nose at his own butt almost made me laugh. But he was smarter than that.

Bucket sniffed back and forth on the steps and found a thread of something that was also on the bag. With his nose on the ground, he led us south, through the park and to Third Street, the main drag, which was also Highway 26. The trail disappeared there.

"That was pretty obvious," I said, giving Bucket a bit of jerky. "But the car was, most likely, pointed west, and I'm guessing that he took off that way."

"Let's go back to the hospital and check on Aurelio," Willy said. "Then, you can follow me out to the ranch."

"'Through bog, through bush, through brake, through brier…'"

"It's not midsummer." Willy smiled, looking at the snow.

Damn. She knew Shakespeare too.

TWELVE

Even under the remaining influence of the anesthesia, Aurelio's eyes snapped with energy and purpose. They softened when they saw Willy.

"I am fine," he said with conviction when he saw her worried face. "I'm told I will recover fully and have a nice scar. My beloved," he continued, reaching out a hand for Rosa, "will kiss it to help it heal."

Rosa's eyes shone. "I will pinch it when you leave your socks in the bathroom."

We all laughed, which made Aurelio wince. "Introduce me to your friend," he said to Willy while looking at me.

"This is Mike Ironwood. He's helping us stop this insanity."

"As quickly as I can," I added.

Aurelio's right arm was taped across his chest, so he took his left hand from Rosa's and reached it across his body toward me. I used my left, and we shook.

"I have met your brother," Aurelio said. "He appears to be an extraordinary man."

"In many ways."

We said good-bye, and Willy led Bucket and me to her truck, a 1962 Chevy Apache. I whistled.

"I like old trucks."

"Me too."

Our eyes locked briefly.

"Where's your car?" she asked.

I pointed over my shoulder.

"We're going to turn right at the light. I'll wait for you there. What are you driving?"

"You'll figure it out."

Bucket didn't follow me. Without consulting anybody, he went to the back of Willy's pickup and vaulted up over the tailgate and into the bed. He showed me his unmistakable dog grin.

"Impressive," I said.

He lolled his tongue at me as I went to my truck.

We went north out of town into the Ochoco Mountains. We reached a small sign that said, *H—H*.

By the end of winter, the road to the ranch would probably develop a washboard, but this early in the season, it was in good shape. The fence lines were taut and straight. I knew what it took to make that happen.

The country was also fine. Range land rolled away on both sides of the road, which also passed through stands of timber, ponderosa, and lodgepole pine. The air smelled of juniper. I could see timber in the draws between the hills and ridges, where the water ran and collected in springs, seeps, and creeks. My admiration for Willimina Hayes grew with every bit of maintained land I saw. Up ahead I saw Bucket through the swirling snow perched in the bed of Willy's pickup. He faced off to the left, which would be north from this angle, head up and tail out straight. He was pointing. At what I had no idea. Could be anything. But my gut registered it and wondered.

The house looked like it had grown from the earth, low slung and neat. A huge kitchen dominated the east end and the big old stove was fueled by both propane and wood. The pantry was as big as my bedroom. A young pretty woman named Inez had coffee going and was mixing a batter with a wooden spoon in a large blue bowl. Her eyes sparked warmly when Willy walked in and regarded me coolly when I was introduced.

"There is a big dog outside, Inez," Willy said. "He is a good boy."

Inez did not seem overjoyed by this but nodded.

"When you get a chance, please go out and give him one of Maggie's biscuits."

The girl frowned but nodded again. "I will."

"His name is Bucket."

Inez giggled.

Willy and I walked Bucket around the house as a start to our tour. When I was satisfied that he understood the area he was responsible for, I held my arms out wide and said, "Stay." He went around to midway between the shop and the house and lay down in a spot that the wind kept clear of snow.

"Good boy," I said.

The shop was well equipped and even had a tire-changing machine, which made me jealous as hell. Someone was working on a newer Ford F-150, clean but worn as only a ranch truck can be.

"I talked to Mama," the man said to Willy. "She says Papa will be home tomorrow."

"He is a tough *hombre*," I said.

The young man nodded thoughtfully. I guessed him to be in his late twenties.

"Mike, this is David." She pronounced it Dah-veed. Putting a hand on my shoulder she said to David: "He is a private investigator."

He wiped his hands on a rag and shook my hand. His grip was strong. "Anything I can do to help, just let me know."

"At some point in all this, I will gladly accept your offer. Thanks."

He seemed satisfied with that and went back to his work.

After showing me around the barn, Willy brought her truck around. "Hop in. I'll show you the good stuff."

We headed up a steep hill and around a long curve. It was no longer snowing, but an inch of the stuff lay nestled into the tall grass. The road was white with it. Just as the house disappeared from view behind us, a man stepped out of the woods in front of us.

"What the hell...?" Willy slowed.

It was Daniel.

THIRTEEN

He'd thrown a deep-green twill shirt over his plain buckskin. Thick moccasins stopped at midcalf. A Bowie knife rested easily at his left hip. I knew that his pistol was hidden under his shirt at his right hip. He stood, quite nonchalant, flipping a small silver disc in his hand like a coin. He said to me once that the best thing about no longer being a SEAL was that he could grow his hair, and he wore it in a long black braid. He always teased me because my hair didn't grow—it just fell out.

Willy pulled up alongside of him and rolled down her window. The air bit at us.

Daniel stopped flipping the disc and extended his hand.

"Daniel Ironwood," he said. "You are giving my big brother, there, a ride. You should be very careful around him. He is crazy."

His smooth brown face was inscrutable.

Willy didn't blink. She shook his hand.

"Willimina Hayes," she said. "Thanks for the warning, but I've learned that *crazy* is a relative term."

Daniel flashed a surprised smile at the clever pun and looked past Willy to me. I responded to his pleasure with delight.

"Park this thing and follow me. Showing you will help me explain."

"What the hell are you talking about?" asked Willy as we got out of the truck and followed Daniel into the woods. Somewhere a steer bawled. About a hundred yards in, out of sight of the road, was a neat pile of stuffed plastic bags.

"Ten kilos of cocaine, twenty kilos of crystal meth, and thirty-five thousand dollars in cash," he said and held up the small silver disc. "With a locator. It was stashed in the tool shed at the edge of that lower pasture. Delivered by three guys in a helicopter, a pilot and two mules. There were no markings on the helicopter."

Willy's face darkened. "What the hell is going on here?"

"We think somebody wants your ranch as a place to move dope and, probably, launder money. The really strange thing is—"

Daniel interrupted. "That it appears to be an official government agency doing it."

"DEA?" I asked, looking at my brother.

"When I talked with Jepps, our FBI associate"—he nodded at Willy—"told me that a hot-shot DEA agent named Deems has a big deal going on but that he has been trying to keep it quiet, which is really, I guess, out of character. Enough so that there has been a small flag raised in Jepps's office."

"And I'm stuck in the middle of this nightmare," Willy said.

"I am afraid so."

"Son of a bitch," she said.

"My best guess," said Daniel, "is that these guys will be back at oh-dark-thirty tomorrow to bust you red-handed as the state's newest drug queen. Then, with you out of the way, they can do whatever they want with your ranch."

"They can just do that?" Willy was aghast. There was worry in her voice but no panic.

"Well," I said, "not if we have anything to say about it."

I nodded at Daniel's hand.

"Where were you thinking of putting that thing?

"The weather is getting cold." He smiled. "The snakes are looking to wrap themselves together in a big wad." He nodded at Willy. "Do you have a notion about a good place to look?"

"I like the way you think," she said and told him where she thought they might be.

"Does Jepps know about this whole scam?" I asked Daniel.

"He's on his way here. I think he wants to abscond with the evidence."

As if on cue, Daniel's cell phone buzzed. He looked at the display. "Jepps. He's here."

FOURTEEN

"This is unprecedented. This is weird," Jepps said. "This is so blatant that I can't figure it out. My superiors are telling me to keep a lid on it, don't let anybody know anything." His eyes flickered at us.

As Daniel told him how he'd found the drugs, he didn't say a word about the tracking device. I knew this meant Daniel had decided that he was fully engaged. That also meant that whoever was on the other side had no idea what they were in for. That was true for us as well, but understanding that Daniel had committed was a good feeling.

Daniel's view of the FBI was jaundiced because of the agency's history of abuse of American Indian rights, but his personal views did not fuel any form of bigotry toward individuals in the FBI. He was above that, part of what made him a good guy.

Jepps turned from Daniel to talk in a low, earnest tone with Willy. Her face registered an odd mix of horror and reassurance.

The young agent who had arrived with Jepps leaned against the car they'd come in, looking bored but really studying the layout. I took an automatic dislike to him. He felt wrong. There was something out of place in his face. I filed that away to think about, talk with Daniel about, later. For now, I was most concerned about getting the tracking disc hidden.

"You going to show Jepps the pile?" I murmured, not looking at Daniel in case the agent was looking at us.

"Yep."

"Then give me the disc. I'll get Willy to show me where those snakes might be."

"It is already in your jeans pocket, next to that little box you call a wallet."

I put my hand in my pocket, and there it was. "Don't *do* that."

"Got to keep my skills sharp."

Jepps came over, interrupting our moment. "Show me what they left, and I'll get it out of here."

Daniel nodded and looked at Jepps's buddy. His sidelong glance at me let me know that he didn't like him either.

"Let us proceed," he said.

As the FBI van pulled out and up the road, I touched Willy's elbow. "Let's continue the tour."

She nodded, distracted.

Willy took me the other way from which we'd come.

"The roads on the H-Bar-H basically form a big loop," she told me. "There is a mountain in the middle that has two peaks. They aren't very tall, but they make for great pasture and good stands of timber. The slopes on the west side get pretty steep, and there's a canyon there that gets a lot of southern sun in the wintertime. It's where the snakes go this time of year."

The western rattlesnake is not aggressive but will strike a person if surprised or threatened with a nasty toxin that destroys tissue and internal organs and interferes with blood clotting. It lacks the elegance of, say, a black mamba, whose venom will kill you inside of an hour by paralyzing your muscles so that your systems shut down and you suffocate. The western rattlesnake might kill you too, but it's more of a slow rot and very painful.

Willy turned her Chevy from the main road onto a less-traveled track that headed up into the timber. After a couple miles, she stopped the truck. "C'mon."

The shadows were growing long as we hiked up through a stand of lodge-pole pine and scattered juniper. When we broke out, backs to the fading sun, there was the narrow rocky canyon.

Willy led me up a steep track to the top of a ridge that ran into the gaping crack. "Right down in there." She pointed.

I carefully wiped the small disc on my shirtsleeve and flipped it down into the fissure. It struck me, as I stared down into the inky gloom, that this crevasse and its presumed population of somnolent vipers formed a pretty good metaphor for what I'd grown expert at ignoring about myself. Somewhere in the labyrinth of who I was lay a sleeping knot formed by my history. I had been the last person seen by many whom I'd identified as the enemy. Some of them never even saw me. All I could feel about what was behind the internal wall I'd subconsciously constructed was a cold wind. As I felt a stirring of rising voices, I stood up from where I'd been squatting and brushed my hands together.

"That's that," I said, looking at Willy who watched me with a strange light in her eyes. We were silent as we walked back to her truck.

"I'm not sure why we did this," she finally said. "I like the defiance of it, but it'll just antagonize them."

Everything she had was as stake here. I was just a hired gun, quite literally, and my involvement was, theoretically, strictly professional. I had to keep reminding myself of that. If Willy and her ranch got swallowed up by a voracious corruption, what was it to me?

That was a very powerful question. What was it to me? I was cautiously excited to find out.

"Yes, it will antagonize them. When I signed on to help you, you got all of me. They"—I jerked my head at the sky—"are the enemy. I will antagonize them at every opportunity. If I can make them angry enough and stay calm myself, they will make a mistake, and I will take advantage."

"*The Art of War*," said Willy.

"Bingo."

She smiled a slow smile that put a wrinkle in my heart. "I like the way you think," she said.

Her scrutiny stood up the hairs on my wrists. A wave of responsibility washed over me. It was a new feeling. It was very personal. My heart quickened. I think I liked it, but held it at arm's length.

The ride back to the house was relatively quiet. The sun had dipped behind the Cascades and framed their sharp silhouette with a blush of warm peach that belied the temperature drop. The snow was mostly gone. It was cold, but only the shadows were cold enough to maintain any flakes. High cirrus clouds glowed a bright silver, with their leading edges stained a dark purple. The contrast was stark. At the same time, Willy and I sighed in appreciation. That shared sound loosened something in me.

"The only thing out here prettier than that is you," I said.

She laughed. "Nice try, cowboy. I'm immune to that sort of stuff."

I grinned. "No, you're not. Not when it's heartfelt."

She shook her head in a good-natured way, and focused on her driving. "You're welcome to stay in the guest room," Willy said when we got back to the house. "The sheets are clean."

I answered too quickly. I couldn't bear to stay in the guest room. "Thanks, but I need to spend some time with Daniel. I need his take on what happened and what our buddy Jepps is thinking. The political ramifications of this are huge. The fact that the FBI has secretly stepped into the middle of what appears to be a DEA operation is not terribly common."

"But where is Daniel?"

"Somewhere up there." I pointed. "Not far, would be my thinking."

"You can find him?"

"Since we were kids. Bucket will stay near the house."

"Okay," she said. "If you want breakfast, it's at 6:30. Do you need anything? Supper? Anything?"

I shook my head. "*Nada.*"

"See you in the morning." She turned to the house.

I started to say, "Looking forward to it," but caught myself. She walked to the door and disappeared without looking back.

I ruffled Bucket's ears, told him to stay, and went to my truck. Tires crunching on the gravel, I drove slowly up the hill toward where Daniel had shown us the impressive pile of DEA dope and money. I parked the truck at a gate in the fencing and found evidence of him fairly quickly from the GPS coordinates he'd sent me earlier in the day. When I walked into his camp, he was nowhere to be seen. I paid that no mind and helped myself to some of the rice flecked with something pink he had on his little propane stove. There was no campfire. We wouldn't be visible to any vehicle coming or going to the main road, but I guessed it would be to us.

"Man," I said into the darkness, "this is great. Is it salmon or steelhead in with the rice?"

Daniel walked into my vision and sat. "Steelhead. You want some coffee?"

"That would be good. Thanks."

As Daniel set about his task, his eyes regarded me pointedly.

"She is an extraordinary woman," he said, "and beautiful. You left Bucket to watch the house and compound?"

I nodded at the shape of him in the darkness. As the stove flared, his eyes were just black obsidian.

"Yes," I said and offered nothing further into the comfortable silence.

When the water started to boil, he spoke again. "Jepps is very concerned about our involvement in this. He thinks Deems, the DEA guy, is going after one of the bigger Mexican cartels. That is a very dangerous business."

I let him focus on his little French press.

"The guy I tied up this morning killed three people today—that I know about. I'm guessing he is not doing it on his own. Well"—I paused—"maybe the Ruiz kid this morning, but the other two, somebody probably told him to. I don't understand why a cartel would want to kill a small-time realty guy and his receptionist in Prineville, Oregon."

"Removing witnesses?"

"But how could they possibly hurt a big-time Mexican drug outfit? Nah," I said, "there has to be a local angle. And if somebody local is pushing this shooter's buttons, who the hell could it be?"

"All the signs point to a very odd source," Daniel said.

This silence wasn't entirely comfortable any longer, but it was still companionable.

"This is going to be dangerous," he said happily.

I regarded his shadow. "Okay. What else is going on?"

"I got a call today from one of my old contacts. He wants me to do a job for a third party."

"Uh-huh..."

"They want me to assassinate one of the drug lords in Western Mexico, real high-tech long-range stuff, fifty-caliber from a mile away."

"Who is this third party, and how can that have anything to do with actual national security?" I asked. "Or are they calling you for political jobs now?"

"They are all political, but your point is well taken. I do not know who asked the contact to find me. There is something happening on a very large scale and somehow"—he paused to press the coffee grounds to the bottom of the pot—"the Ironwoods have tumbled, once again, into the briar patch."

"Just lucky, I guess." I accepted a cup of hot coffee. I took a deep breath and sipped. Bells clanged beautifully.

"You going to accept this job offer?"

"I do not know yet. As far as I know, I do not owe whoever is behind this. But if you look up in the fairly near future and I am gone, you should be able to guess at my whereabouts."

"So, this is just for large dollars?"

"And keeping the weapon itself, with all the bells and whistles."

"That's a hard one, to kill a guy just for money."

"I am going to research him. It may be that I would be doing the world a service."

"Maybe, but a new boss will take the helm and may be even worse. You going to kill them all?"

"It is an interesting thought."

His comment mixed with the coffee, souring my stomach. Daniel and I share a business philosophy with the bad guys, though we rationalized that away because we were the good guys. Right? It was true that neither of us did what we did just for the money—we had what we considered to be noble motives—but the end result was often that people died.

My thoughts trailed off as we both heard the low whine of a helicopter.

Daniel and I sprinted up to where the road skirted the hillside and vaulted the fence. I went to my truck and jacked a round into the chamber of my .40

caliber Ruger. Daniel kept heading uphill. He paused briefly.

"Try not to kill anybody wearing a badge," he said.

"That's about the only plan I have," I said as clambered into my truck and launched it down the hill toward the darkened house.

Rather than rouse everybody within ten miles, I sat in my truck at the end of the long, well-kept driveway. If this was to be a large bust, there would be at least ten cars speeding up from the main road. There was nothing. I got out of the truck to listen.

I still heard the whup-whup, but it was faint, and coming from up where Willy and I had been at dusk. They must be tracking their locator. I smiled, put the safety back on, and holstered my pistol.

Pretty soon, the helicopter noise shot straight up, turned sharply, and disappeared to the northwest. It sounded angry.

I went to the truck and pulled a blanket from behind the seat. Once the dog and I climbed in, I wrapped the warm wool around me and thought of Willy, asleep somewhere in the house.

FIFTEEN

Bucket woke me up by standing on me and wagging his tail. Outside my window, Willy, framed by the house lights, held a steaming cup.

I rolled the window down all the way and took the coffee. I'm pretty sure I mumbled thanks.

"Didn't you freeze?" Her voice had a "men are crazy" lilt to it.

I stretched. Her head was on fire. I could not see her face. I guessed it to be about six o'clock.

"No, it was only a one-dog night." I scratched the top of Bucket's head. He yawned and did his morning stretch. I know exactly from where the name for the yoga pose called downward-facing dog comes.

I told Willy about the helicopter. "I don't think we'll get visitors today," I said. I think they'll go to Plan B."

"Whatever that is. Come on and sit in a warm kitchen."

I liked the sound of that. I got out of the truck, and Bucket hopped to the ground. He trotted off to take care of his morning business. I followed Willy.

When we got to the kitchen, the smell of bacon and coffee made my mouth water. Willy tossed me a towel. "Go wash your face. You've been drooling on yourself."

I laughed a short bark. "Flattery is your second-best feature," I said and found the bathroom, down the hall, first door on the left.

When I came back, Willy was draining bacon and flipping eggs. High on the wall next to the massive wood stove was a photograph of a man, probably in his fifties, with a smile creasing his angular face. He wore a plain Resistol cowboy hat.

"Your dad?"

"Yes. He was my best friend. I owe him everything that's worth anything."

"Breakfast smells wonderful."

"Inez does this most of the time, but she's visiting Aurelio—oh! Who's probably going to be released this afternoon."

"That's wonderful news."

Over the brim of my blue cup, I admired the way her faded maroon sweat-shirt and work jeans fit her curves.

"You checking me out?" she asked with a smile as she set down a plate of sourdough toast.

"You bet."

"I haven't felt that scrutiny in quite a while. Most times it's annoying, but from you it seems natural, somehow."

"Thank you. There's a big difference between lechery and admiration."

"How much bacon?" she asked.

"All of it."

I think she blushed but couldn't be sure. She recovered quickly. "I have to work that high pasture today. You're welcome to come help."

"I would love to, and I hope you truly believe that. But I have to work the Federal Building in Portland today."

Willy sipped her coffee. "I'm sorry."

"When this is all resolved," I teased, "I promise that I will come ride the ranges with you and pretend I'm your top hand. Bucket is even a passable herd-er. This is a beautiful place, and you manage it well. In fact—I would like to reciprocate and show you Daniel's place, where he and I both grew up."

"I'd like that, but isn't it your place too?"

"Yes, of course, but I have made my home on the river in Portland. The ranch really belongs to Daniel and his family. They raise bison rather than cat-tle. They have done so much more with it than I ever would have. They don't look at it as ownership. More like stewardship. I get the feeling you're doing much the same thing here."

"We're really lucky here. The bank doesn't own anything. Every once in a while, cash flow being what it is, I have to borrow a few thousand dollars, but it's always paid off in as short a time as possible. I don't like making money with other peoples' money unless it's very short-term. Some folks think I'm abso-lutely crazy, but I don't like owing anybody anything. Too much Scotch-Irish in me, I guess."

I nodded. "We never had much. Dad was not an extravagant man. But he worked with purpose and was beholding to no one. His relationship with the Nimi'ipuu arose out of circumstance, but fit him like a roping glove. He started raising bison long before it became fashionable. His notions of owner-ship changed over the years. When Daniel's mother was killed, my father might have died too, if not for the support of her family. He had accepted them when he'd married and earned their respect. When he was widowed, they held him up and ended up raising both Daniel and me."

"So you never really knew your mother?"

"I have the foggiest recollections. I don't remember what she looked like and I'm not sure I really remember anything. When I think of her I remember more of a visceral feeling, maybe something like a smell. I remember Daniel's mother a little bit. She had a very musical voice. She could make my father laugh, I remember that. I remember his smile when she got him going. That smile was a rare thing."

Willy listened. Ease wrapped us both. I cleared the plates and began to wash them.

"What's my best feature?" she asked playfully.

I laughed. "Your heart."

I turned and saw she was looking at me thoughtfully. She smiled. I'm pretty sure I smiled too, but I think my brain may have been upside down.

"Excuse me a minute," she said.

I nodded and continued to wash. Looking out the window over the sink, I saw Bucket trot to the long shadows by the barn and shop. He was wagging his tail.

I walked quickly through the living room and let myself out the front door, making little sound. I stayed in the shadows along the west side of the house, keeping as low as I could. I carefully peered around the corner of the house, trying to see where Daniel might be.

We had played this game all of our lives. This particular episode was over when a pebble bounced off the back of my head.

"You army guys are just too direct," he said, laughing.

My lips tightened into a thin line. Being killed is never any fun. Bucket came around the corner and looked at me with reproach. I hung my head in mock shame.

"I'm on a pretty bad losing streak."

Daniel stretched his long ropy arms to the sky. "Not when it really counts." He dropped his arms. "And you are not easy—I just know you too well."

"Good morning, Daniel," I heard Willy say, and I turned to see she'd added a thick Pendleton jacket that came down to the pockets of her jeans. A well-worn hat covered her hair, which she'd gathered into a ponytail. She carried a lever-action rifle. "What are you guys doing?"

"He just killed me. And the dog helped," I finished accusingly.

Bucket was suddenly interested in a bug by his left front foot.

We all laughed.

When the moment passed, I told Daniel my plan was to go to the Fed Building in Portland and meet Mr. Deems.

"Do you think that is direct enough?"

"You got a better idea?"

He pretended to think about it and shook his head. "One thing. Call Jepps and tell him where you are going. I know you do not have a real plan and will just stir the pot to see what boils over, but Jepps needs to know so that if you magically disappear, he will have a time frame."

"Magically disappear?" Willy asked.

My heart clapped once, sharply, when I heard the concern in her voice.

Daniel smiled. "One thing you will have to accept about our buddy here is that he is willing to confront nearly any problem with small regard for his own safety. I used to worry about it when we were younger until I realized that his technique was almost always effective and that the problem he was facing was suddenly short-lived."

Willy's eyes flashed back and forth between us brothers. Finally, she said, "I have work to do." She smiled at Daniel. "It was good to meet you. Are you going to continue your surveillance?"

"Not immediately. I have your number and will call you if I am going to be skulking around, just so you know."

She turned to me. "Call me when you can," was all she said. Her lids were open, but her eyes were closed.

With that, she walked off to the barn.

"Nice rifle," I called.

"Browning .243," she said, raising it a little. "It shoots really straight. You'll have to try it sometime."

"Can't wait."

SIXTEEN

First things first. I owed the Prineville police a statement and the locked-up tweaker a visit. Prineville welcomed me with little traffic. Storefronts alternated, some vibrant and some tired.

As I stepped into the station's small lobby, Bucket left waiting in a patch of sunshine for me, I saw Nancy Kelso talking with a small man in a suit. He might as well have been carrying a neon sign that flashed *Fed* in big letters. I was very curious to learn which agency he called home. Kelso did not look happy as she talked with him but brightened when she saw me. She waved me over.

"Speak of the devil," she said.

The man's narrow face held eyes that stared out at me like lasers. I felt the hair on the back of my neck stand up, and my breathing deepened. I took a chance.

"Mr. Deems. We finally meet."

He was taken aback but recovered quickly. "What do you mean, 'finally'?"

"I mean, you were on my mind much of yesterday. Arthur Jepps mentioned you during a meeting we had."

"Who is Arthur Jepps?" It was almost a snarl.

Kelso's eyes widened, and she took a step forward, as though to block one or the other or both of us. Somewhere, it registered in me that she was a really good cop.

"Why, Mr. Deems," I said, "surely you know the senior FBI agent in Portland? He's been in that office for damn near twenty years."

Deems balked a little. "I'm fairly new here," he conceded. But then he turned up the heat again. "But I suppose I could speak of us *finally* meeting too—I've been meaning to look you up. You may have some information we need."

"I can't imagine why the DEA would be interested in me," I said, "but stranger things have happened. Will you be in your office this afternoon?"

He nodded carefully.

"See you about three." I turned to Kelso. "Who should I see about giving a statement about yesterday? Also, we should continue our conversation."

"The form is waiting at reception. Then come see me at my desk." She pointed to the bullpen. Her look told me that she couldn't wait to talk to me.

I took a step toward the young woman at reception. "Oh," I said, turning to Deems once more, "I'd like to offer you a heads-up about a shooter named Jesús Chavez. I believe he's a real danger to the community. I also believe he has cartel connections. But we can talk about that this afternoon when we exchange information. I know you can't really say anything"—I winked—"but I really think you're onto something if you're following Chavez around. Stone-cold killer." I relished watching the color drain from Deems's face. I should have left it there, but couldn't. "I'm sure the DEA is very familiar with Señor Chavez. Are you in Prineville on business or just for the fishing?"

Kelso's eyes snapped wide.

Deems looked like he wanted to shoot me right in the forehead. But he stayed cool, I'll give him that. "Enforcing the law," he said with a small smile, "and you'll read about the rest of it in the papers, I'm sure." Nodding to Kelso, he turned and walked toward the door.

Now it was my turn be chilled. I followed him outside, to the top of the stairway.

"Mr. Deems. I am a little tougher to kill than a small-town realtor and his nineteen-year-old receptionist."

He turned. His eyes were hard diamonds. "I sense a threat directed my way, eh, Ironwood? That would be a very serious mistake."

I smiled at him. "No, sir. I'm just sharing information."

I stepped back into the police station but watched him through the window. He walked to a pale-green Explorer parked at the curb. He got into the passenger seat and slammed the door. That made me smile, but I wasn't kidding myself. Deems was more dangerous than an outhouse rattlesnake, and I was going to have to be very careful. I'd already given him too much information. This was big-league trouble.

The thing I noticed first about Nancy Kelso's desk was that one of my business cards was propped on her phone. Thad must have given it to her. As I started to sit, she stood. Her uniform was immaculate. Her short blond hair was brushed back behind her ears. He forearms were muscular, and her Glock rested at her left hip. A simple white-gold wedding band gleamed on her left hand.

She skipped any greeting and launched into it. "Deems grilled me about Willy Hayes. When you came in, he was grilling me about you. I know Willy. I don't know you, so I had nothing to say. But he certainly is an arrogant little prick."

I tried to keep my face nonchalant.

"Let's step outside," she said. There were a couple of other cops working in the open squad room, tapping out the never-ending reports that are the back-bone of police work.

The sun was finally coming through on its earlier promise of warmth. The Ochocos rolled off into the distance, green and golden, tipped in white. Kelso got her American Spirit cigarette going and sighed. She offered me one and I shook my head.

"Gave it up when I became a civilian."

"I love this time of year," she said.

"Me too. It's my favorite, I think."

After exhaling a long plume of smoke, she leaned against the railing and regarded me. "What kind of gun do you carry?"

The question surprised me until I remembered that I wasn't the only one working.

"It depends. The comfortable gun is a Ruger .40 caliber. It just fits. When I'm really working I carry a Glock-19 nine because the clips hold fifteen rounds, and the gun handles abuse better than anything else I've found. Sometimes I carry a .357, and sometimes I carry all three."

"And what are you carrying this trip?"

"The Ruger .40. I have the cannon," I said, referring to the .357, "in the truck, along with a shotgun and a 7mm magnum rifle."

"No nine?" she asked.

"No, ma'am."

"I will believe you," she said, "because Thad says I can and should. You are officially removed from the suspect list."

"That's a relief," I meant it.

"But remember, Mr. Ironwood," she flicked the ash from her cigarette, "if you shoot somebody in Prineville, I will be all over you like ants on a picnic."

"As you should."

She nodded and smiled. I'd given her exactly the right answer. "Some of your file," she said, "requires an impressive security clearance to see. I don't have that clearance."

"You can ask me anything, and I'll answer honestly." Here I paused. "Most-ly," I finished.

"What do you know about this guy Deems?"

"What I know about Mr. Deems," I said after a couple heartbeats, "is mostly nothing. He's DEA, he's ambitious, and he's working on something that the FBI finds very interesting. Now," I continued, "the FBI and the DEA usually work very closely together. They almost merged not too long ago. The FBI guy I know pretty well has been very tight-lipped about it, but there's something odd going on."

Kelso sighed. "I'm not going to ask what you're not telling me. But please let me know if you come across any information about this guy Chavez, the guy you think did these murders." She drew in a long breath. "I've been in touch with Hannarty in Portland. I have a blurry scan of the driver's license. But the really strange thing is that he's not in the system. Anywhere. How can that be?"

It was a rhetorical question but a really good one. It added some weight to my personal theory, which was forming a clump at a time. Chavez was working for Deems. I had no proof, but my gut was certain of it. If I could find the van Chavez has used, I might be closer to the truth.

"How well do you know Willy Hayes?" Kelso asked and chuckled. "That look just told me more than I'd asked for."

I studied my right boot for a second. Why do people find it amusing when they see that your life might be upside down?

"I don't really know her at all," I said. "She came to see me in Portland and asked for my help. I accepted her as a client. That's all I can tell you."

"Willy was three years ahead of me in school. She's extended family, so I have to wonder anytime someone I don't know takes an interest in her. Especially when other things, terrible things, start happening." I felt my mouth open, but before I could figure out what to say in defense, Kelso continued. "I'll tell you a story about Willy. There is a bigoted moron named Bryant whose spread is just downhill of the H-Bar-H. He was making loud about the Mexicans and how they didn't belong here, and Willy got wind of it. She saddled that big mare of hers and rode right into Bryant's front yard. Gave him hell. He gave her hell right back.

"When Willy got home, she fired up the tractor and dammed the creek that flows from her place onto Bryant's. Well"—she shook her head—"it was World War Three. Bryant went ballistic and filed suit against her. It turned out that he did have a leg to stand on, but Willy said that she would restore the creek to what it was only after Bryant felt the pinch of it. Oh hell. It was a mess. The state got involved, the county threatened her, but she just stared back, hard-eyed, until she decided Bryant had been properly chastised. There were environmental charges filed against her, but they were dropped. I'm pretty sure she had to pay a hefty fine for messing with the creek."

"That doesn't surprise me," I said.

"But it gets better," said Kelso. "The following winter was something out of Norse mythology. It hit Bryant extremely hard. He left his cattle too high too long and lost a lot of them. Willy donated the services of one of her bulls to help him get back on his feet. She and the Ruizes helped rebuild a mile of fence that had come down under the weight of the snow."

"From what little I've learned," I said, "that doesn't surprise me either."

"And for Bryant's part," she went on, "he thanked her profusely and apologized for his past behavior. He must've been sincere because that would have been very hard for him to do. He also dropped the lawsuit, much to his lawyer's disgust."

We leaned there on the porch for another couple of minutes, enjoying the morning. "That DEA guy is spooky," Kelso said. "He told me that he wanted my full cooperation when they 'made their move.'" She made quote marks with her fingers.

I nodded. "Yes. I felt the same thing. He reminds me of those guys in Nam, the ones who couldn't wait until it got dark." I was starting to think out loud, which was my cue to shut up. I could do that with Daniel. I might be able to do that with Nancy Kelso, but I didn't know that yet. It would take time to develop that trust.

"I know there's a lot more going on than you're willing to share, Mr. Ironwood." She smiled. "But please keep me in the loop."

"Call me Mike. I will keep you as informed as I can. I operate a lot on guesswork and hunch and I don't share much theory until it pans out. If it doesn't, which happens a lot, I haven't confused anybody if I've kept it to myself."

"And you look smarter."

"My secret is out."

"Don't worry," she said. "It's safe with me."

Bucket stayed in the bed of the truck while I motored over to the county jail. In the mirror I could see that he was a happy boy. Suddenly, so was I. That lasted for another couple minutes.

When I got inside the jail, I asked to see the kid Jerry Thad Krieger had run in the day before.

"He's a popular kid this morning," the deputy drawled.

"What?"

My thin smile put him on the defensive.

"The feds, DEA, came in and took him, said it was part of a larger investigation."

"Did you call Thad Krieger at the OSP?" I asked, incredulous.

"No. Showed me his badge and the transfer papers. The kid looked oddly happy about the whole thing."

"Good to know," I said. "Thanks. Call Thad Krieger at OSP."

I did not let the door hit my butt on the way out.

I called Willy and left her a message, telling her that I was on my way home and that I'd see her when I saw her. I told her I hoped to see her on Wednesday, the day after tomorrow. I didn't mention meeting Deems.

Next, I called Daniel.

"Deems is a nasty little man," I said.

Daniel chuckled. "And you expected, what, a nasty big man?"

"I didn't expect to see him at the Prineville Police station talking to Nancy Kelso."

I almost heard his eyebrows shoot up. "Really," he said. "Hmm."

"I'm headed back to Portland. But I'm going to blow Deems off and just let him wonder. Let me know, in your inscrutable Indian way, if you're going to war."

"I think we are both going to war." He hung up.

All of my instincts told me he was probably right. As usual, Bucket was already asleep on the seat next to me.

"Glad to see you're resting up," I muttered. "We'll need it."

SEVENTEEN

I'd spent Tuesday morning and early afternoon in a fruitless search for the blue van and was trying to relieve frustration by doing my routine of pushups and core exercises when Bucket let me know somebody was coming to the door. I threw a shirt on and went into the kitchen so I could see the porch and entryway. It was Willy. Not wanting to startle her, I let her knock before opening the door.

"Hey," I said.

She stood in the shadow of the house. As usual, her hair seemed to have a light of its own as it swept back from her face and brushed at her shoulders. The pit of my stomach started falling away again.

"Hey." She ran her fingers through her hair. It was a nervous gesture and made me curious.

I was pretty sure I had a sappy smile plastered on my face. "I was going to head back to your place tomorrow. This is a very nice surprise."

"I decided to show up here, instead," she said. "After moving the big chicken pen this morning, I was restless and wanted to drive. With all that's going on, I just can't seem to relax."

I nodded and ushered her into the living room. Bucket was very polite as he sniffed her feet and legs. She held out her hands for inspection too. When he was satisfied, Bucket went over to his spot by the slider that went out onto the deck that ran around the house. He plopped down and watched the river, making sure it wasn't going to do anything other than flow north to the Columbia.

Willy watched the river too. She took in the whole panorama, from the old span of the Sellwood Bridge to her left and then downriver to Ross Island, the skyline, and the bridges beyond. The sun was a couple hours from disappearing behind the rise of hill that held Riverview Cemetery, but was still lighting the clouds overhead with a brilliant display.

"This is really nice," she said. "No wonder you like it."

"It fits. I really feel at home in this spot. Can I get you something? Water? Juice? Beer? Glass of wine?"

"A beer would be good."

"Light? Dark? Wheat? IPA?" Like I said, Portland is beer heaven.

She settled on a Widmer Heffeweissen, no glass, and I grabbed a Bridge-port IPA, my current favorite. When I came back into the front room, she was leaning against the edge of the big old desk, coiled like a spring. If I'd tapped her on the arm, I was pretty sure she'd have rung like a bell. I handed her the cold bottle and watched her take a sip, swallow, and close her eyes.

"That's good," she said.

Her shoulders dropped about an inch. I didn't think it was the beer, al-though that familiarity probably helped. I thought she'd accepted that she was in my front room and that she was safe there. She still had an edge to her, but it was not the tautness of a few moments before.

"How's Aurelio?" I asked.

"He's okay. They're a little worried about infection from the jacket material in the wound, but he's as good as can be expected. His spirits are strong."

"Did the cops spend a lot of time with him?"

"Not really. He made a statement and identified a photo of the guy who shot him. Apparently, the guy who shot him wants to press charges against the guy who hit him with a rock."

I almost snorted my beer. "I don't think he ever really saw Daniel," I said. I decided not tell her that the DEA now had custody of the kid who shot Aurelio. He'd become a loose end, and I didn't like loose ends. With all she had on her mind, Willy didn't need to care about Jerry from The Dalles.

"No. And Aurelio saw very little," she said. "But he did say that Daniel saved his life."

"Yep. That's my brother. And if I know my buddy Thad, the OSP guy, he won't offer much information about how he wound up with the arrest."

Willy took another sip of beer. "You guys are quite the pair."

My intuition screen was blank, but I was still picking up a vague uneasi-ness. I hoped I could figure it out later.

"C'mon," I said. "I'll give you the nickel tour."

I led her outside through the sliding door, and we stood in the chilly breeze.

"Ah," I breathed, watching the plume come from my mouth, "how refresh-ing."

Willy laughed. "You're nuts," she said, pushing at my arm. "Show me some-thing warmer."

I showed her what I called the covered patio, where the charcoal barbeque sat on its metal sheeting, and the table where I watched the world go by on warm summer days. We went around to the other sliding door, which led into my bedroom, which was clean but rumpled. Her eyes lingered on the gun hanging from the left-side bedpost. It was the nine that Nancy Kelso had wondered about.

She hurried through without comment. The guest room was right across the narrow hall. I opened the door and went in.

"Here's your space," I said lightly.

It was simple room with a queen bed and cream-colored walls. A small bureau sat in the corner beneath one of the two windows that looked at the park out past the dock. There was a framed picture of a German shorthair pointer pointing at a pheasant. The curtains were red.

"My space?" Her eyebrows were up, but she was smiling.

Now it was my turn to be distinctly uneasy. I stammered something nonchalant. Willy laughed.

"I appreciate the thought, but I'll probably stay where I usually do, downtown at the Viscount."

"I didn't mean to presume...I meant that you're welcome here. If you want."

"What if I wanted to stay in there?" She pointed toward my bed. "How would I go about that?" she asked.

Her eyes still danced. There was an ocean in them.

I didn't know what else to do or say so I kissed her. I thought I knew how to kiss. It turned out I hadn't known much of anything about it.

"I think we should lie down," Willy said, "because if we don't, I think I will fall down."

"I will never let you fall."

She shook her head, smiled, and kissed me. It was back to square one on the learning curve. Somehow, with help from each other, we managed to get undressed and collapse on the guest room bed. I ran my right hand along her side and then rested it on her hip. She put a hand to the side of my face. Our lips parted and met again. This time there was no coming up for air. We became sea creatures and let the tides tumble us until we were polished and gleaming, an emerald and a sapphire, washed by late afternoon sun.

EIGHTEEN

The world seemed an entirely different place when our hearts slowed, and we rested comfortable and warm. Willy traced a fingernail across my chest. I ran a finger along the top of her ear.

"I think that's why this is called 'making love,'" I said.

Willy giggled—did I say she had a wonderful giggle?—but she didn't seem to really mind me being silly. "Pop quiz time," she said.

I cocked an eyebrow. "Shoot."

"You are an absolutely gorgeous man," she said, "a little on the rough-and-tumble side, perhaps, but I am amazed that there doesn't seem to be a woman in your life. How is that possible? Am I to assume, then, that there are lots of women in your life?"

"That question is a two-way street."

"Okay," she said, "but you first."

She was tousled and more beautiful than anything or anybody I had ever seen. I really hoped that what I had to tell her didn't scare her too much. It scared me, but over time I have proven that I am very good at managing my fear.

"I've had brief flings from time to time. I'm as human as the next guy, but they have been all heat and no real warmth, if you know what I mean."

She nodded.

"I never lead anybody on. Ever. I have"—here I paused—"been waiting for The One."

"The One," Willy said, "with capital letters?"

"Yes," I said, "with capital letters. I have always known she is out there. Never doubted it. Absolutely sure. It's just a matter of time. I know it like I know my own name."

Willy was very quiet. The light in her glowed like a furnace.

"Tag." I tapped my finger on her nose, "you're it."

Her breath caught.

"Enough about me," I rushed to say. "What's your story?"

She rolled over, arched her back, and stretched herself taut until she shook. She went slack and took a deep breath. When she moved back to her side, she gave me a small, steady grin rivaling the power of the river beneath us.

"I was married for ten years and in another serious relationship for two. They were both wonderful, and ended painfully. Both of them…died. My husband was killed in a tractor accident on our ranch down in Bakersfield. Jack died in a plane crash on his way to help rebuild a Guatemalan village that had been wiped out in a flood. I've spent the last decade by myself and have come to like it very much. So, as incredible as this just was," she went on as she smoothed the wild tangle of her hair, "I'm not going to rush into anything."

"Well," I said. "We've known each other for an entire six days."

She punched my chest.

"Ow," I said.

This time she snickered. "You know what I mean."

I couldn't decide if I was more enamored of her giggle or her snicker. It would require more research.

I rose up on my elbow. "I know exactly what you mean. I don't know what I'm doing, really. I'm also just following my instincts, and every instinct is telling me to go slowly and pay very close attention."

"I like it when you go slowly and pay attention." The tip of her tongue touched her upper lip.

"You certainly have my attention. I might be able to go even slower."

"A splendid idea," Willy said, taking my hand. "Let's." She stood up and led me into my bedroom to fling back the rumpled covers. "Your bed."

"Yes," I said.

"Does that thing have to stay where it is?" she asked, pointing at the pistol.

"Yes," I said again.

After a long while she said: "This is crazy."

I must have made an agreeable noise because she wrapped me up in her arms and legs and squeezed until my eyes bulged.

"Good to know," I said.

"What?" Her lips curled on my cheek.

"You're even stronger than you look."

"You better believe it, buster," she whispered fiercely into my left ear as she reapplied pressure.

"Hard not to," I gasped.

NINETEEN

When we got out of bed, Bucket came and sniffed us both with interest and appreciation. Even my human nose could smell us, so I figured that his dog nose was in overdrive. Finally, he snorted. Willy and I both laughed. Snorting is also his way of asking to be let out. I obliged him. The street lights were just starting to come on.

I built a fire while Willy made coffee.

"How long have you been a PI?"

"About twelve years." I paused, watching the flames lick through the kindling. I'd answered what she'd asked, but maybe I could give her a little more. "But in all that time, I've only worked a couple of divorces, which seems to be a lot of the work out there. When I started, I swore to myself that I would never be the guy in the tree taking graphic photos of infidelities."

Willy came out of the kitchen with two mugs and put them on the low table in front of the long leather couch. She took the end of the couch closest to the fire and tucked her long legs under her. She wore one of my T-shirts that fit her like a nightgown.

"Why not?"

"Umm." Every time I looked at her, another little bit of me wandered off, mumbling. "I guess, I seem to be inexorably compelled to do what I think is the right thing to do, and that kind of spying rarely seems right."

"Are you telling me that you're a hopeless idealist?"

I grinned at her. "Reckon so."

"I can live with that."

That had a nice ring to it, in a scary sort of way. I put more wood on the fire. Willy sat up and regarded me seriously.

"I'm not going to ask you how many people you have killed because that's really none of anybody's business. What I want to know is how you deal with it."

I found the green of her eyes, and she didn't look away. Her lips, swollen a little from our kissing, were slightly parted. Her hands gripped her knees.

Her hair, now only in mild disarray, was smoothed back from her forehead. There was no glamour in her. A deep part of me registered a bond there, not as a lover, or a couple, or anything having to do with romance. She was a boon companion, something more, quite likely, but certainly nothing less. She was a rock with connections to the center of the earth.

"It seems glib," I began, "to call that part of it an occupational hazard, but it's true nonetheless."

Here I paused, considering. I turned. The fire was doing nicely.

"I don't know, Willy, I'm not really sure I deal with it at all. My time in the Special Forces was intense, and I've let as much of that go as I can. Dreams come sometimes, and I don't react well, but I understand that those memories are a part of me. I can ignore them most of the time. When I can't ignore them, I have Daniel, who has many of the same dreams. But my life since then has been spent as what I call a protector. I take that very seriously. If I had a better relationship with authority, I'd probably still be a cop, or maybe even still in the military."

I nodded to where my beret was hanging on the wall behind the big desk.

"I don't wear that hat any more, but I'm proud of the service I gave, even if the big picture was horribly misguided and cruel. It's always the regular people who suffer the most in a war. Soldiers have a job, and it keeps them on some kind of a track, however tenuous. The general population doesn't have squat in a war zone. They're just in the way, and they die, often simply at the whim of fate."

I moved to the couch and picked up my coffee. Willy turned slightly toward me and waited.

I was treading water in an uncharted sea.

"I think," I went on, "there is a warrior class in the human family. In that are good guys and bad guys. Daniel and I are part of the good guys, at least by our own reckoning. We are both very good at violence, at staying calm when others panic. Would the world be a better place without us? I don't know. I suppose it's a question worth asking, but for me, it is what it is. I am a warrior, and I accept what that means. I am grateful for the awareness of it, just as I am grateful for the breath I draw. I don't think I can articulate it any better than that. Answer your question?"

She sat back sipping her coffee, the T-shirt riding up her thighs a little. Her eyes were not smiling, but they were open. Her face was composed.

"Not exactly"—here she smiled at herself—"but I'm glad it is a gray area for you. Character counts, and you are one. I hope," she continued, "that we have this conversation many times. I am interested to see how it turns out."

I leaned over and kissed her on the ear and then leaned back. "I like you."

"I know you do. And I am utterly infatuated with you, which is very interesting. My intuition tells me that's okay, but my brain is very leery. So, I'm just going to let whatever happens, happen."

"Great plan. I think I'll tag along."

She slid over to my end of the couch and snuggled into the crook of my arm.

"Mind if I stay here tonight?"

"You are such a comedian."

"My stuff is still in my truck, and I'm not really dressed to go get it."

"I'm really not either."

"But you're a man." She moved my sweatshirt. "See?"

"Would you put clothes on if I went and got your stuff?"

"Maybe."

"Well then, your bag can stay right where it is. Shall we move to the bedroom?"

"What's wrong with right here?" Her voice was thick.

"I like the way you think."

Between the fire and us, the leather on that couch got really warm.

It was fully dark, and the city skyline was aglow when she spoke again. A light rain had started. We may have dozed a little. I was hoping that Bucket was not insulted. He was still outside.

"Now will you please go get my bag?" she asked. "I really do want to clean up a little and need my girl stuff."

I kissed her like we'd been doing it for years and got up and stretched. I could just barely get my fingers to the beams that held the houseboat together.

"You really are a big boy, aren't you?" she said. "How tall are you?"

"Six-four, two-twenty," I said. "But right now I'm probably ten feet tall and weigh maybe a hundred pounds."

She laughed. "Go get my bag. Flattery is your third best feature."

TWENTY

I awoke when Willy got out of bed. I was hoping that she'd just go to the bathroom and come back, but the shower started. The sky was watery and opaque. It felt like six o'clock. I got up and went into the bathroom.

"Hey, mind if I get in there with you?"

"It's certainly big enough. This the biggest shower I think I've ever been in."

I turned the second showerhead on and tensed a little until the water was fully warm. She had her eyes screwed shut as she rinsed her hair. I wanted to be objective. She was lean but round where she should be round. Her arms and face were deeply tanned. Her breasts were proud and pointed in slightly different directions. Her torso and legs were the golden color of rich cream. Her shoulders and upper arms were strong from a lifetime of ranch work. She was beautiful and comfortable with it. The word that came to me and stuck was *formidable*. Yes. Formidable.

She squinted through the water cascading over her face.

"You checkin' me out?" she asked.

I grinned at her. "Yes, ma'am, I am definitely checkin' you out. I will never tire of it."

"Good."

"I think the guy who built this house liked to have parties," I said. "Huge deck, giant shower, large kitchen. I really bought it because of where it sits, but the rest of it has really grown on me."

"Well, it fits you. And"—I could see her choose her words carefully—"if you have a party, I want to be here."

"No parties," I said, "unless you're here?" I pretended to decide. "Okay, that's a deal."

She kissed me lightly as she got out of the shower.

I scrambled some eggs, folded in a couple ounces of Tillamook pepperjack, and finished it off with some smoky salt.

"You're quite the chef," said Willy.

I suspect my face showed a pained expression.

"Scrambled eggs? Chef? You must not get out much."

She took a bite and pretended to swoon.

"That salt is divine, but these are not ranch eggs."

"Whiner."

"Next time you come to see me, I'll send you home with some real eggs."

"Depending on what happens later today, I'm thinking I'll head your way Saturday."

"You could come tomorrow night," she said hopefully.

I smiled. "Please don't tempt me. I should be working, you know."

After a long hug by the front door, she picked up her bag and walked off the dock to her truck. Watching her drive up the hill and out of sight, I let out the longest sigh of my life. For something we were going to take our time with, this was happening pretty damn fast.

Bucket stood next to me and yawned. He probably knew what was going on better than I did.

"Is she the One?" I asked him.

He cocked his head and eyed me like I was an idiot.

TWENTY-ONE

I spent most of Thursday morning looking for my brain. I went to the office and read online everything I could find about Mexican drug cartels. I didn't really learn anything useful, other than that the murder rate associated with them on both sides of the border had skyrocketed during the decade. The cartels were at war with everybody: each other, governments, law enforcement, you name it. The money flowing into their coffers made most multinational corporations seem like people on street corners selling pencils. It was obvious to me that the recreational drug market was reaping huge benefits from the "just say no" mindset. If half the money being harvested by the bad guys was pumped into the Mexican economy where regular people would benefit, the waves of people coming across the border would slow to a trickle.

I kind of dragged around on Friday, wondering at the entirely new wrinkle in my life. To say I was preoccupied was understating the obvious. There were several things I could be doing as background work on Willy's behalf, but I'd catch myself staring off into space and wonder where I'd been. I understood what was happening. My focus was completely torn asunder. Understanding it didn't mean I liked it. The plain and simple of it was that I'd become deeply infatuated. I was in a wrestling match with a whirlwind. On one side, I'd fallen into an abyss where I was struggling to find equilibrium. One the other, I was flying in some very rare air. I'd never been convinced before that I was in love. I had yet to put a label on what I felt about Willy. All I really knew was that being with her made me feel like all things were possible. I wanted to embrace the tenderness of it. I knew it made me vulnerable, but I didn't care. It felt absolutely right. My pet voices kept humming when I thought of her, which was most of the time. I sensed great approval. Shaking my head to clear it began to sound like rattling change in a glass jar.

At about two o'clock, I finally gave up on going through the motions and loaded a small travel bag. Bucket gave me a look that said, "It's about time, Idiot Boy," and jumped up into the cab of the truck, where he immediately made himself comfortable. If this kept up, I would soon know the road to Prineville as well as I knew the walk from my bed to the bathroom.

One of the many things that I love about driving or riding a motorcycle is that it gives your body and that part of your brain responsible for keeping you alive something very important to do while the creative part of your mind is free to roam. As I left the city, I forced my creative side away from my almost mooning thoughts of Willy and tried to climb onto the task at hand. I needed to figure out what was going on in the interagency and drug cartel smorgasbord that was scattered all around me. I tried to make a list of what I knew, but it was woefully short. I knew that Jesús Chavez was a bad guy, and I was pretty sure Mr. Deems was too. When I'd met Deems at the police station in Prineville, my barb about the murder of Bob Fraley and his receptionist had struck him. I had no idea where Yankees Cap was or how he continued to elude everyone who was looking for him. Hell, he could be in Thailand, for all I knew. But I doubted that. He was probably still too close for comfort. I wondered if he was thinking about me as I thought about him. A part of me never wanted to see him again, but there was another part that wanted another few moments of up-close-and-personal.

I had to admit that Willy was still at risk. These people had tried to lay some serious trouble on her and had not been able to. I figured it was probably naïve to assume that they would just forget about her and the ranch. If it was worth killing two people to cover their tracks, it was worth coming up with a new plan to achieve their aim.

What was their aim? Was it as simple as wanting the property to use as a depot and manufacturing site? Or was there some other purpose to it? Not knowing tied a knot in me where I didn't like to have knots.

Suddenly, I wondered if Willy had told me everything I needed to know. She seemed so guileless with me that I couldn't believe she would keep something pertinent to herself. Maybe she knew something but just didn't connect it with all that was going on. My infatuation with her had shifted my perceptions. I wanted to get to know her, and there were probably questions I should have asked that I hadn't asked because I'd been too involved with my own personal desire.

I knew that she deserved better from my working self. As I dropped down into Madras, I resolved to back up a little bit and refocus on doing my job she'd hired me to do. The other stuff was definitely in motion and would move at its own pace. Right now, she didn't need Mike Ironwood, lover boy—she needed Mike Ironwood, salvage consultant. A bit ruefully, I admitted there were many Mike Ironwoods. I hoped that, over the course of time, she would meet and like most of them. Even I didn't like all of them, but it was the package I lived with.

I didn't stop in Prineville. I went straight to the H-Bar-H. As I drove up the long access road, the sky was a high pale blue, and I could see clouds, a line of wild-mane mustangs leaping over the Sisters and Mount Bachelor, building to the south and west and bringing a promise of rain, maybe snow. Willy's truck wasn't in the dusty yard. I got out and knocked on the door of the house. No answer. I peered in the window and saw a piece of note paper on the counter by the refrigerator. The door was unlocked.

The note said: *Hurt calf in the middle pasture.* There was no signature and no time. I thought it strange because it was the wrong time of year for calves, but it happened sometimes. I left the note where it was and went back outside.

Bucket was in the yard worrying about something. He sniffed around the door, swiveling his ears and whining at me. He was trying to tell me something. I was positive that I wouldn't like it.

We hopped back in the truck and went up the northeast fork of the road. What I estimated to be a couple hundred head of cattle ranged across the lower pasture. After a while I saw the glint of sun coming off of what I assumed to be Willy's truck. It was. I parked behind it and got out. The driver's side door stood ajar. Her Browning rifle was in the window rack. The ground on that side told me where she'd left the cab and headed for the fence gate, which was also open. I saw a small cow lying in the grass about 150 yards ahead of me. I started trotting. Bucket ranged ahead of me. I was certain he was following Willy's track.

The cow, a young Hereford steer, had been shot in the head. Willy's medical kit was lying on its side next to the body. It hadn't been opened. There were no other cattle I could see, but I could hear them in the lower pasture from time to time. More important, there was no sign of Willy. Wind swirled and tried to lift the brim of my Mariners cap. I yanked it off and put it on backward.

Bucket and I ran back to where the trucks were parked. I fully opened Willy's door and ran my hand briskly over the seat. I put my hand under Bucket's nose.

"Find," I said.

Bucket whined once and retraced our path to the cow. I was right behind him. I held my hand out once more.

"Find," I said again.

He circled once and took off for the crest of the hill to our right. I put myself into an easy gait and followed. When I caught up with him on the downhill side of the crest, he was circling, as if the trail ended abruptly in the middle of the expanse of grass. It might have been a mystery to him, but it was not to me. I could see the unmistakable evidence of where rotary blades and a lot of horsepower had flattened the grass. It was no wonder Bucket had lost Willy's scent. She'd gone straight up, leaving no trail at all.

The full impact of it slowly dawned on me. Willy was gone and in grave danger. The guy who had driven to the H-Bar-H and up to this pasture was off somewhere, wondering when he could come back. The guy in his place, the one feeling my heart beat and my slow, deep breathing, didn't wonder much about anything. He was completely results-oriented. He was completely committed to his own survival and to the survival of his mission. His mission, in a nutshell, was to touch the skin of Willimina Hayes and to ensure her survival, even if it meant offering up his own in trade.

I locked eyes with Bucket briefly until he looked away. He dipped his head and put his ears back. He was living for me to tell him what to do. It was a relationship that stretched back fifteen thousand years to a distant meadow at the edge of a wood, two creatures agreeing to do their best to keep each other alive in a hostile world. I also sensed an eagerness about him that fit with my own. Warriors will be what they are whenever they get the chance.

I knew that the next few days would change several lives. For some, those changes would be endings.

"C'mon, Buck," I said. "Stay close."

I closed the gate behind us and Willy's truck door too. We jumped in my truck and went straight to see Aurelio and Rosa. They were distraught at my news about Willy, but we shared a practical side, and we could also focus on the fact that the ranch needed to continue to run.

"Will you need help?" I asked, looking at Aurelio's shoulder.

His face was a mask of alarm and worry, but he was man enough to be honest.

"Sí. We have to work above the high pastures and get the last of the strays out of the breaks and canyons. Willy does the work of two men, and I am reduced by half."

"Men will arrive," I said, thinking of Daniel's friends and family, "tomorrow, with their own horses. I will tell them what's going on."

Aurelio's good hand combed through his shock of black hair. He had gone even paler than when I'd seen him in the hospital. His eyes were points of pain.

I was turned to my truck when Rosa's voice stopped me. "Miguel," she said. "You are different now because you are frightened and angry and ready to fight. But there is a calmness I see, and that is good. Remember that mercy is not a sign of weakness but strength."

In her eyes I saw my own mother and Daniel's mother and the mother of all of us who have been lonely and who have wandered without deep comfort. I couldn't trust myself to say a single word. All I could manage was a grateful nod.

She came to me and touched my arm. "*Vaya con dios.*"

"*Gracias*," I said. I nodded to Aurelio, turned to my truck, got in, and drove. I thought about mercy all the way back to Portland. I came to no conclusions. I did, however, understand that the people who I was up against would show me no mercy whatsoever.

Daniel did not answer his phone. I broke the connection and called again. Still no answer. This time I let it go to his voice mail.

"The bastards have Willy," I said and hung up. At least he would be compelled to call back.

Arriving in Portland, I went straight downtown. The large, nondescript Federal Building sits at Portland at Southwest Third and Madison, where it occupies a full city block. I parked up on Fourth and left Bucket with the truck. I stood in the middle of Chapman Square, a nice half-block of lawn and statuary, looking up at the building. The iron elk in the middle of Main Street watched me. I called Arthur Jepps.

His hello was curt.

"This is Mike Ironwood." I paused just long enough for that to register. "How close are you working the DEA thing Daniel and I stumbled into?"

"Where are you?" he asked.

I told him, and he sighed. "I'll be right down," he said.

When he sat on the park bench next to me I thought of all the movies I'd seen where the two spies met in a park to share information. At another time I might have enjoyed the slice of life imitating art.

I told Agent Jepps that Willy had been kidnapped and that the vehicle used had been a helicopter. He seemed skeptical. "Kidnapped is a pretty strong word, Mike," he said. "Maybe he had her arrested, just to keep her on ice, so to speak."

I considered this. My gut yelled no.

"You can call it whatever works for you," I said. "False arrest, detention, I don't care. There is no legal reason that says he can fly onto her property, shoot one of her cows, and force her to get into a helicopter. As far as I'm concerned, that's kidnapping, plain and simple."

"Mike," Jepps said, "he's running a very sensitive operation against one of the most powerful cartels in Mexico."

"So what?" I said. "In his case, I'm not convinced that he has the best interests of the United States as his primary directive."

"What? You're saying he's working both sides of the fence?"

I nodded. "Have you identified which evidence group the dope you confiscated came from? Have you figured out whose money was with it?"

Jepps was noncommittal.

"If you can get me into the vehicle pool area, I'm pretty sure I can prove it to you," I said.

Jepps held my gaze for a long time, trying to decide if he was insulted by my tacit accusation of one of his colleagues. He had the dope and the money with which they tried to set up Willy. He had to know something hinky was going on, but now it was truly staring him in the face. Maybe he was well aware of it and was just appalled that an outsider had lifted the curtain on it a little. I was getting impatient.

"C'mon, Arthur," I said. "Willy could be halfway to anywhere by now."

"Mike," he said, "you know how this works. I'm working my own side of this thing, and it is much bigger than you can imagine. I can't let you in on much of it."

He stared down toward the river. "I have my doubts about Deems," he said, almost to himself and turned to me. "You say you can prove to me that he's on the wrong side of this? If he is, it would explain a couple things that I can't quite put together."

I stood up. My heart was not calm. I exhaled and slowed down. "Get me into the motor pool parking area, and I'll know for sure."

He sighed and stood. "Let's go," he said.

We walked from the park to the Federal Building.

"Are you packing?" he asked.

I nodded. The pistol was in my armpit.

"Jesus," he said and tugged at his ear. He gave a small smile. "C'mon."

He got me signed in. The uniform gave me a Special Visitor badge, and Jepps led me around the metal detector.

When we reached the elevator, I looked at him. "Thanks," I said.

"You owe me, Ironwood. Big time."

The elevator door opened to an array of nondescript vehicles. There were sedans, SUVs, four-doors, and vans. I was looking for a van.

"Where would you park a rig in here to hide it in plain sight?" I asked.

Jepps led me down a row and turned a corner. "Probably along that wall." He pointed.

It didn't take long to find. Parked third from the end along the wall was the blue Ford van that I had seen in the parking lot above my house. The plates were different, but it was the same van, I just knew it.

I said as much to Jepps. "Tom Hannarty of the PPB will need to know this too," I added.

Arthur Jepps was not a happy guy. He may have felt vindicated a little bit that this realization sewed up a couple of flapping theory ends, but if the story got out, the damage it would do would give all of the hard-working, straight-shooting, federal law enforcement people a black eye they didn't deserve.

Jepps stood with his head down, chin in hand, and his brow knitted in macramé knots. When he spoke, his voice was tight. "You have no doubt that this is the van those gangbangers were using?"

"None."

"Well then," he said with a small grim smile, "let's see what else falls into place. C'mon."

We walked quickly to the elevator. The ride up to his office was silent. I tried sending Willy some comfort by way of the spirit lines that Daniel had always told me are very real and connect all creatures. Daniel, who was absolutely pragmatic, called this belief "strong medicine," and I had to respect that. Daniel was absolutely convinced that those mysterious invisible lines kept him alive on several occasions. He told me that I was also alive because of them. On the occasions we fought side-by-side, in the heat and chaos, Daniel looked at me and said, "Stay open, Michael." My intellect scoffed, but my body didn't. In times of extreme duress, anything that may help was okay with me.

To underscore my thoughts, the voices in my head launched a brief chant.

Once in the FBI offices, Jepps was brisk. He introduced me to a lovely woman, petite and blond, whose calm demeanor belied the steel I sensed in her. Her nametag said Amanda Wilson and she wore a trim gray business suit that fit her well. I wanted to smile, but it died somewhere before reaching my face.

"Mike's working on something that's of help to us. If he asks for anything, please accommodate him as best you can."

"Just don't ask me for coffee," she said. "That you can get yourself. It's in the break room down the hall."

It wasn't that funny, especially considering the culture of sexism in law enforcement, which meant Amanda probably did get asked to fetch coffee, but from her smile, I knew she meant the comment to coax my own smile out. I laughed in spite of myself and felt my shoulders relax. "I promise."

"She's one of the best agents we have," Arthur said.

He ushered me into his office and pointed at a chair. His desk was mostly clear, but pictures of his family, like a protective shield, surrounded the perimeter.

"Let's check on Mr. Deems's whereabouts," he said as he typed on his computer.

The toe of my boot began to tap the light-green carpet of its own accord, and I stood up because I could no longer sit. Perhaps my antsy spirit line was indeed open, because just then my phone line warbled. It was Daniel.

"Okay," I said to him, walking out of Arthur's office and into an empty conference room. "Here's the deal. Willy got snatched by a helicopter in the northeast pasture one ridge up from the house. I don't know where she is, but I'm working on that with Jepps. I'm starting to think that your other phone call, the one we talked about the other night, and this may be oddly related, but that's just my gut. I don't know anything for sure."

"My consulting gig will start late this evening," Daniel said, "and you have been recruited. I might have known about Willy before you did. I think your gut is right on the beam, as usual." He chuckled grimly. "I have other news as well that I cannot mention here. Meet me at Willy's house as soon as you can."

"Got it. Are you feeling like your job and mine are connected? How could that be? Oh, and another thing. Aurelio needs help getting the strays out of the high pastures. Can you and Randy spare a couple guys, with horses?"

Daniel paused briefly. "Sure," he said. "Our jobs have merged, I think. And bring your rain gear. It is going to be wet. *Hoka Hey.*"

The connection ended. I stared at my phone before putting it back in my pocket. For the first time since the pasture this morning, I felt something like hope.

Daniel had just told me to show up fully armed and ready to fight. His last words told me that we should get after it with all we had.

Jepps's office door was closed, but he beckoned me in as soon as I knocked.

"I just got off the phone. The intel," he began, "is very guarded. There is stuff going on that is so far above my level…I am on a short string. I do know that Deems left about three hours ago on official business"—he made quote signs with his fingers—"in a very fast airplane. They are headed for Mexico, but I don't know where in Mexico. If I can, I promise you that I will tell you where, as soon as I know. And"—here, he paused—"he had traveling companions: a woman and two men, probably Mexicans. The woman had red hair."

Jepps's eyes bored into mine. I returned the favor.

"Mike," he continued, "this is a really big deal. I'm not sure you should go gallivanting off on any kind of rescue. You'll probably regret it profoundly."

"Arthur, I am already involved in so many ways. I respect your authority, and I respect your position, but I will do whatever I must do. You know that."

"I won't be able to help you at all if"—he amended himself—"when the shit hits the fan."

TWENTY-TWO

Bucket whined happily as he stretched. The side windows were streaked with nose marks.

"I'm going to have to teach you to wash windows."

He nodded and sat contentedly and as I negotiated my way toward the Sellwood Bridge and home.

It was a brief stop. I put the .40 and its holster in my gun safe, grabbed the gear I always have ready, added the .357 revolver, the Glock-19, and the disassembled CAR-15. I stowed the pack on the passenger-side floor of the Chevy. To it, I added a bag of food for Bucket. He wasn't going to like it when I left him with Aurelio and Rosa, but he couldn't go on this one. I would make sure he knew that he was working when I left. It would be small consolation but could not be helped.

I was at the top of my short driveway when Tom Hannarty's unmarked Monte Carlo pulled in next to me. His window was open, as was mine. He didn't look particularly happy, but then he rarely did. As usual, he was dressed in a starched white shirt and a crisp blue tie. It was always a pleasant contrast against his mahogany skin. I could see his sport coat laid carefully in the back seat.

"Off on an adventure?" he asked.

"Something like that."

"Okay," he said. "I get it. Sort of. I have not made much progress on tracking that van, and the banger has just flat disappeared. His gun is a different story. The Glock ballistic tests generated a couple hits from the Bay Area. I have yet to hear back any details."

"The van mystery," I said, "will be cleared up shortly, I think. At least, I hope so. Jepps is working that angle too, and he made noises this morning about something soon to break."

Hannarty's eyes locked into mine. "Jesus Christ," he said. "You have that look."

"I guess I'll have to brush up on my thespian skills."

Hannarty sighed and put his gaze on the river. He ran a long-fingered hand across his short black hair. "I'll ask the patrol guys to keep your house in mind," he said.

I put the Chevy in gear and pointed myself south and east. In my side mirror I saw Hannarty talking into his radio microphone. Good man, Tom Hannarty.

TWENTY-THREE: WILLY

The sky was high and white-blue. Weather was starting to boil over the Cascades behind me. It would probably snow before morning. There were a couple of late calves in the herd up high. They were mostly all out of the timber and the creek bottoms, but we still needed to bring about fifty head to the lower pastures for the winter. I wished I could persuade Mike to help with it.

At the thought of him, I felt myself flush. *Dammit, I am not a schoolgirl. With Aurelio hurt, I don't have time for that nonsense. What am I thinking? There's just too much going on. Mike will help sort out the problems, but I don't want him to become one.* My hands gripped the wheel more tightly. The note I'd found on the kitchen counter, *hurt calf, middle pasture,* had probably been written by Aurelio's left hand. His right was still in the sling. I'd hurried through the mud room, grabbed the medical kit and hopped into the truck. I was getting close and I didn't see Aurelio's truck. *Maybe he's already taken care of it.* Maybe I can get back to the repair job I'd been doing before I saw the note. *There is always more to do than I have time for.*

I got to the fence gate, shut off the motor, grabbed the medical kit, and got out. The wind bit at my cheeks. *No sign of Aurelio.* I could see the top of a cow lying in the grass. It was too big to be a calf. *I don't like this. This is weird.* I opened the gate and began trotting up the hill. I caught myself again wishing Mike were here, and the thought almost stopped me in my tracks.

That's absurd. I don't need anybody to help me take care of this.

The cow was dead. It was a young steer. Somebody had shot it in the head. A cold rage vibrated in me, putting me in a place that grew even colder when I heard a calm voice behind me.

"Be very still, *señora.* You will not be harmed, but you must do exactly as I say. If you do not"—the voice seemed to shrug—"we will be forced to use different methods. Turn around very slowly."

There were two men standing about six feet apart. One held a rifle, and one had a black pistol. Both weapons were pointed at my chest. *I'd be shot in two steps if I made for the truck. There is no outrunning a bullet.*

The one with the pistol was the smaller of the two and very calm, his dark eyes snapping with intent as he held himself with an arrogant, fluid grace.

"Drop the box," he said.

That first lick of deep fear iced my heart. I dropped the medical kit. It rolled, clattering.

The second man wasn't particularly tall, but he was thick, with a muscular neck. But he was hunched against the weather. His face was broad and pinched with cold, but it couldn't hide the leer as his eyes raked across me. There was something odd about his rifle, but I couldn't decide what it was.

I was numb. *Gather. Do not show fear. Breathe.*

The smaller man motioned with his pistol.

"Walk," he said.

I followed a trail in the tall grass and cursed myself for not seeing it earlier. I cursed myself, too, for not having my rifle, but these guys were professionals, the ones Mike called the Bad Guys. Having the rifle might have gotten me killed. *Oh, Mike, now I really do wish you were here.*

As I summited the hill, the black unmarked helicopter came into view, its rotors drooping like rubber sabers. As soon as the pilot saw us, the motor began chugging to life. It was probably the same one that delivered the dope that Daniel found and the FBI now had. My heart went ragged. Once I was in that helicopter, my chances—of escaping, certainly of being rescued—dropped. Panic was a tempting indulgence, but I kept it at bay, a gloom somewhere out at the edge of who I was. *Breathe.*

The man with the rifle moved ahead of me to open the small door that led to the two cramped seats in the back of the cabin. He motioned me in with the rifle barrel. The man with the pistol, in a crouch, went around to the far side to get in the front. As I reached forward and ducked to get through the door, a hand grabbed my right breast and squeezed. That straightened me up so fast that I hit my head on the fuselage.

"You son of a bitch." I took a wild swing at the rifleman's leering face.

My fist connected with his temple. The only effect it seemed to have was to enrage him. He chopped the rifle barrel against my right shoulder. My entire arm went numb. He shoved me roughly into the helicopter, across the two seats. My head slammed against the far door. As I struggled to right myself, his hands grabbed and pushed on my butt. Without thinking, I instinctively twisted, lashed out with my legs, and caught him full in the chest, knocking him backward. He dropped his rifle. Before I could do anything with this, the man with the pistol was back around the side of the machine, but he was pointing his pistol at the enraged face of the man who'd had the rifle.

"*Pendejo!*" he hissed. "*Sientese en frente.*"

The man was sullen but moved around the craft to get into the front, next to the pilot. The man with the pistol picked up the rifle and lashed it to an outside compartment. Having a chance to study it up close, I understood why the rifle looked different. It was a dart shooter, usually used to bring down game without killing it. If I'd run, it would've been me. *That means they want me alive. For what?*

The guy with the pistol climbed in and took the seat next to me. His face seemed genuinely apologetic.

"Are you okay?" His eyes were clear.

I nodded slightly, still seething. My hands clenched.

"I am Jesús," he said, "Jesús Chavez."

His face was taut with concern. I nodded, once. I could think of nothing to say.

"That will not happen again," he said, raising his voice so the man in front could hear over the rising noise of the turbine.

I doubted that as my neck, arm, and boob throbbed.

No one spoke as the helicopter flew us to the back side of the airport in Redmond, where we were met by a light-green SUV. A small man with close-cropped hair was driving. Chavez opened the passenger door for me. I got in because there was nothing else to do. He and the other man got in the backseat.

"It's a pleasure to finally meet you, Miss Hayes," said the driver. "My name is Howard Deems."

He offered his hand. I ignored it. His eyes undressed me, his gaze much like the man in the middle pasture earlier—full of power and lust. *Let them look.* Mike's comment in the kitchen a few days before, about the difference between lechery and honest admiration, came to me. It hadn't been a revelation then, and it certainly wasn't now. *This sure isn't admiration.*

Deems drove us across the taxiway, where we quickly boarded a black private jet. Deems boarded first, followed by the groper. I went up the short stairs after him, and Chavez came on board last.

There were four individual seats on each side of the cabin, facing each other across short tables. A bench seat ran along the starboard bulkhead toward the aft of the airplane. A lone seat facing the back of the craft was across the aisle from the four facing seats. Deems dropped into the first seat with a table, and the man who'd hurt me went back to the bench, where he stretched out. Deems pointed to the seat across the narrow aisle from him.

"Sit here," he said.

I sat. I was suddenly excruciatingly tired. My fear and anger fed each other, keeping each other at bay. *No way I'm going to sleep. No way.* I wanted to scream, I wanted to cry, I wanted to sleep, but I sat, cold-eyed and calm.

"Where are we going?" I asked. *And why?*

Deems's mouth stretched to a pale thin line. "South."

After closing the aircraft door, Chavez took the seat across the small table from Deems. He did not look at me, but I could feel the weight of his thoughts. Unlike the other two men, I felt no lust emanating from him, but being in his presence was oddly intimate, like sharing a small space with a cobra. *No sudden moves. Stay calm. Pay attention.*

I was puzzled by my reaction to him. It was, somehow, all knotted up with my feelings for Mike. I think I knew the answer, but it circled, wraithlike, beyond the sky of my awareness. It was almost an anticipation, like awaiting the Sunday crossword. I hoped the solution would not be written in blood, but it seemed inevitable, almost ordained, that it would be. Chavez was certainly not Mike, but there was a hint of similar energy and quiet strength. *Maybe, two sides of the same coin?*

The jet revved up, taxied quickly, and took off. As Deems had said, it banked in a tight arc and headed south. I watched through my portside window, looking east and to the familiar shape of the Ochocos, bathed green and golden in the afternoon sun. A fierce pride arose in me and with it a diamond hardness that surprised me. There would be no compromise with these men. *Mike will come find me and, if nothing else, bring my body home. Maybe I can escape on my own. Stay calm. Pay attention.* I was outside myself, a place I'd never experienced, but it seemed as familiar as the boots on my feet. The plane's white noise lulled me into a state where my constant dread receded to a dull hiss.

The cabin grew darker. I fought sleep, but I probably dozed. The groper snored softly. Deems leaned against his window with his arms folded tightly at his chest. Chavez's face was empty, almost like he was in a trance, but his eyes were open. I stretched and yawned. My guess was that we'd been airborne for over three hours. Suddenly, a scratchy loudspeaker voice startled me into full wakefulness.

"Descent in twenty minutes," it said.

Deems stirred, stretched, yawned, and stood. He made his way, a bit unsteadily after sitting so long, to the front of the aircraft. I heard a door open and close.

When Deems came back, he put a hand on the back of my seat, near my left ear. *Touch me and I'll hurt you, no matter the cost.*

"If you want to freshen up, now is the time," he said.

That's funny. Like we're on vacation? But I really do have to pee.

In the cramped restroom, I searched in vain for something I could fashion into a weapon. Impulsively, I grabbed the small cake of soap and put it in my pocket. It was nothing, but it made me feel better.

I opened the door and there stood the groper. He smirked and gave me very little room to pass. I stared into his eyes, snapped both hands to his chest, and shoved him backward into the bulkhead. He raised his hand to strike, but Chavez was there. His eyes were brilliant.

"*Si toca otra vez, te mataré.*"

The man sneered and went into the restroom.

"*Gracias,*" I said. I meant it.

Chavez's eyes gleamed, but did not smile. He nodded almost imperceptibly.

The landing was smooth. The scene through the windows was bright with late-afternoon sun. Out the window, airport personnel were in their shirt-sleeves.

As the plane rolled to a stop, a black Lincoln Town Car appeared and came to a stop under the left wing. Chavez went forward in the cabin. The aircraft door whooshed open, and I watched the stairway descend.

As I walked carefully down the stairs, the air was warm and soft in a way unique to the tropics. *This is Mexico. Has to be. The cartel Mike and Daniel mentioned is Mexican.* When my foot touched the tarmac, Deems tried to take me by the elbow and steer me to the waiting car. I jerked my arm free. Chavez watched me. *What is he thinking? Why do I care?* I took a deep breath.

When we got to the car, Deems, with a tight-lipped smile, went around to the passenger side and got in the front. Chavez and the other man had disappeared. A uniformed driver was waiting for me and opened the rear door. I ducked and slid into the broad backseat.

The air conditioner was running, and inside of the limo it was cool. My eyes adjusted to the dim light. A man was sitting there, his face familiar, but I couldn't place it. He was smiling.

"Good afternoon, Willimina," he said. "It has been a long time since Guatemala. You are still as beautiful as I remember, perhaps more so."

Suddenly, it was a decade ago. You! You were there when I went to Guatemala. You're the one who released Jack's body to me so I could fly him home. You are why I'm here? You bastard!

TWENTY-FOUR: MIKE

When I pulled into Willy's yard at dusk, I saw Daniel talking with Aurelio. I parked my tired truck next to Willy's, which had been washed and was gleaming in the fading light. Bucket jumped out and sniffed Daniel's knees. He then sniffed Aurelio's boots. Satisfied, he trotted off around the house. I let him go.

Daniel came over to me and put his hand on my shoulder. "Best hand-to-hand fighter I have ever seen," he said to Aurelio, whose eyes grew wide.

"Don't let him kid you," I said. "He's the best," I pointed at Daniel.

Aurelio laughed, though it clearly still pained him to do so. "Nobody is the best at anything for very long. There is always somebody who can beat you. The magic is in avoidance."

"We cannot avoid anyone," Daniel said. "If it comes to *mano a mano*, there is no avoidance, and there is no sport."

Aurelio nodded. "*Sí. Entiendo.*"

"So, what have you got?" I said to Daniel.

"Let us go in the house."

Aurelio excused himself and went back toward his house. Bucket trotted out of the shadows and startled him, but he recovered quickly and put out a fist for the dog to sniff. He scratched Bucket on the head, right between his ears.

"Good boy," I heard him say.

Bucket came over and laid down to the right of Willy's door. Now it was my turn to tell him he was a good boy.

"Work," I added.

He already knew we were working. I just wanted to reiterate it. His rich brown eyes fixed on me very briefly and looked away. He was on top of things. Whatever he could control, he would. Whatever he could not, he would let me know.

"The dog cannot go," said Daniel as we settled into the chairs where Willy and I had eaten breakfast a couple days earlier.

I nodded. "Let me tell him. His feelings will be hurt, and I'm much more sensitive than you are."

The corner of Daniel's mouth twitched. "He would be a liability," Daniel said.

"I know. Mexico is a big country."

He raised an eyebrow. "That is a good guess."

"No guess. Jepps said Deems is on his way there—he just didn't have a final destination. He also confirmed that Willy and two men are traveling with him. Maybe Chavez is one of them."

Daniel nodded and sat quietly for a moment.

"I will tell you what I have learned from the people who have hired me. I promised them I would not tell you who they are unless you really needed to know."

I nodded. "Fair enough. I'm not sure I give a damn who they are. At some point in this, I may want to thank them, but I'm pretty sure that would be pointless. The only reason they've agreed to have me along on this little lark is they have a purpose for me. Otherwise, I'd be S-O-L."

"That is true," Daniel agreed. "We are leaving here," he glanced at his watch, "in a couple hours and will be driven to the National Guard airbase in Klamath Falls. From there, we fly to an airstrip outside of Tucson and walk into Mexico, carefully and quietly, carrying a whole bunch of stuff that would be severely frowned upon were we to be discovered. When we get to a wide spot in the road called Microondas, we will be met by a *federale* named Montoya, who will brief us on the next leg of our journey, which will begin almost immediately. Allegedly, he is, right now, figuring out how to fly us to the small beach town of San Blas."

"I know San Blas," I said but gave him a quizzical look.

"Up in the hills above San Blas is a large villa that has been acquired by one Gustavo Flores, who uses it as his fortress and lavish party palace. And in case you did not know, Señor Flores is *el jeffe*, head honcho, *le gros fromage*, *numero uno* dude in the cartel we are targeting."

"He's the guy you're going to take out from a mile away?"

"If everything goes right, yes."

My pocket made its phone noise. It was Jepps. I motioned to Daniel and answered.

"The flight plan looks like they're going to Tepic."

"Thanks. Gotta go."

Jepps grunted and hung up.

"They're landing at Tepic," I said. "If memory serves me right, that's about thirty-five miles inland from San Blas."

Daniel nodded. "Yes. But we are going to San Blas, I think. It all depends on what Señor Montoya can put together."

"So what's my angle in all this? Right now, I'm just handsome window dressing."

"You are along to create a diversion after my bullet, or bullets, if I am worth my salt, strike Señor Flores. This allows the true undercover guy to get the hell out of there with his life and an incredible array of intelligence data."

I sat for a minute, letting the dusky scene outside the window move in and out of focus. "This undercover guy is not Agent Deems, I presume."

"No. It is one of those oddly convoluted and nasty double-cross deals. Deems is supposed to be undercover, but he is really working the other way. He is a jewel in Flores's crown of power, and a senior DEA guy on the wrong side is quite a weapon."

I nodded. It was quite the understatement. "So let's review and simplify. We end up in the woods above San Blas, you get set up, and I, somehow, get through the inevitably sophisticated security system at this fortress, where I wait until you put a couple of high-tech .50-caliber slugs into one of the most powerful men in this hemisphere before initiating an attention-grabbing scenario that allows a valuable asset to escape and make his way to relative safety."

Daniel nodded. "In a nutshell, you got it."

"And in my spare time, I get to rescue the girl and live happily ever after."

Daniel shrugged. "To the people driving this, whatever you do in your spare time is up to you."

"Jesus Christ," I said. "What could possibly go wrong?"

"There is one more thing."

"You're shitting me." My eyebrows went up under my hat brim.

Daniel's eyes slid away briefly. "You will have to find your own way back into this country. Or at least to where Señor Montoya can help you."

"Because this alleged valuable asset is taking my seat?"

Daniel nodded and gave me a wan smile. "I do not care what your teachers used to say, Mike—you are as sharp as the knife in your boot. This is the only way it can work. There would not be enough room for Willy anyway."

"Jesus Christ," I said again. "That's a hell of a plan. Do I get anything else out of this? I mean, other than getting to rescue the girl?"

Daniel shook his head. "In the big picture of all this, you do not even exist."

I sighed. "Y'know, I am truly grateful for that. And I really appreciate you going to the well for me on this. I'm sure it was nearly impossible to convince them to get me down there, and so quickly too."

"Actually," he said, "it was pretty easy to get them to agree to your one-way ticket. I just told them that it was all or nothing. You and me or nothing."

"What I'm trying to figure out is why they snatched her in the first place and why they were in such a hurry to fly her into this mess."

"I can shed a little light on that," Daniel said. "It seems that an order came down from the top, maybe Flores himself, to grab Willy and bring her to San Blas. That does not make any sense to me, but there it is."

"This is according to the guy inside?"

Daniel nodded.

"You got a picture of this Flores?" I asked.

Daniel went to his pack and brought back a thick manila folder. He opened it on the table and spread out the contents. After some rummaging around, he tapped a photograph of a good-looking Hispanic man, about thirty-five, with lots of wavy black hair. He was not fat but looked fleshy, like he could use some exercise.

"How recent is this?"

"Within the last month or so," Daniel said.

I memorized the face and then picked up the stats sheet.

"Born in Guatemala," I said, "in 1960."

A little bell went off in my head. I read further.

"He actually worked for the Guatemalan State Department until about twelve years ago."

Daniel shrugged. "He has been involved with the cartel since he was a teenager. His dossier goes on to demonstrate how he used that state department gig to emasculate the entire Guatemalan law enforcement arm that oversaw the control and movement of drugs and money. His political skill and his ruthlessness are how he got to where he is today. He fancies himself to be the head of state in his own imaginary country. In fact, the people I am working for suspect that he has gone, as Dad used to say, 'a bubble or two out of plumb.' His behavior has become more erratic. The murders the cartel is committing are horrendous—beheadings, torture—all of the worst stuff you can think of and probably some you cannot. It is an unprecedented escalation of violence."

"So this is why you're involved?" I asked.

"I think so," said Daniel. "It has become politically expedient to take the guy out."

"How much time until our ride shows up?"

Daniel glanced at his watch. "About an hour and a half."

"It's about time I slipped back into my crack investigator disguise."

"More like cracked investigator."

I nodded absently and moved quietly down the hall.

Willy's bedroom, which I determined was hers from the travel bag she'd had at my place, was quite simple, with a queen bed, a nightstand, an old oak dresser, and an attached bathroom. I had to ignore the emotion that arose from catching her scent. On the dresser was a photograph of a young Willy and a dark-haired man wearing a cowboy hat and a pearl-button shirt. They were arm-in-arm, and she had her left hand resting against his flat stomach. There was a gold band on her finger. They both looked like they were too young to be driving, let alone be married. But they looked happy. Willy's hair was lighter and there were no worry lines around those amazing green eyes.

In the bathroom, another dark-haired young man, maybe ten years older than the couple in the first picture, stared at me from a four-by-six frame on the wall. He had a faint scar along his hairline, but he looked into the camera with such open affection that my heart went out to him. He would be the second love of her life who had the gall to die on her.

I opened the medicine cabinet to the usual kinds of stuff: lotion, aspirin, toothpaste, probably fewer makeup supplies than someone else would have. What was tugging at me was not in the bathroom. I moved back through the bedroom and stuck my head into the room right across the hall. It was a study. I turned on the light and sat down at the desk. Nothing in the desk drawers spoke to me. I went to the closet and slid the left-side door open. Boxes were stacked. I dragged one out into the light.

It was a box of photographs, hundreds of them. I sifted through them quickly, looking for the right time period. When I got to that layer, I slowed down. I saw pictures of her and the second young guy.

Suddenly, there were pictures of jungle and of devastated houses, dead donkeys, and piles of debris. It was in that packet that I found a picture of Willy, red-eyed and distraught, looking blankly into the camera. Behind her was a heavy cardboard air freight coffin. Behind the coffin, looking at Willy with undisguised interest, almost with what could be taken as unbridled lust, was a younger Hispanic man whose face could very well be that of Daniel's target, Señor Gustavo Flores.

I took the photo out to the kitchen and put it on the table in front of Daniel.

"Whaddya think?" I said.

Daniel whistled under his breath. He got out the photo from the Flores dossier and put it next to the one I found. "I do not know how this stuff comes to you, Mike, but that is the guy."

"That's what I thought too. Just another silly wild-ass guess."

"You are the profiler in the family," Daniel said. "What does this mean?"

"I'm clueless, unless the guy has harbored a closet infatuation all these years and is finally getting out-there enough to start thinking she's felt the same way all this time. In fact"—I warmed to the thread—"if he became aware of her by coincidence through Deems and recognized her, he might be thinking it was fate working on his behalf. That, I think, would be pretty powerful."

"Yikes," said Daniel. "Where do you come up with this stuff?"

"I dunno." I shrugged. "The tide goes in; the tide goes out. Sometimes it's nonsense, and sometimes it's not. I just take the first thing that pops into my head and then try and talk myself out of it. After cycling though that for a while, I usually end up with a pretty fair picture."

"You would make a great shaman," Daniel said.

"Wrong mother."

We laughed. Especially given the circumstances, it was a nice sound to hear.

Tires on gravel made us both turn to the window. A Humvee had pulled into the yard. Bucket was between it and the house, staring it down.

I put the picture back where I'd found it. On the way back to the kitchen, I stopped in Willy's bedroom. Her running shoes were sitting out, by her overnight bag, but guilt dogged me as I rummaged through her bureau. I found a pair of socks and some underwear. I shoved them into the toes of the shoes. She and I would have to cover some country, and I wasn't sure the boots she'd been kidnapped in would be up to the task.

Our driver looked out the window at Bucket, who was growling at him.

"Bucket," I said. "Take off."

He trotted away toward the Ruiz's.

"Good riddance," said the driver.

"You'd want that dog on your side," Daniel said.

I didn't say anything. The driver rolled his eyes.

We loaded our stuff into the back of an armored Humvee. When I was done, I trotted to my truck and rummaged in the glove box. I carried the envelope I found inside, opened it in Willy's kitchen, took out her retainer check, and ripped it neatly into four pieces. I put the pieces back in the envelope and leaned it against the toaster.

I looked up into her father's faded eyes in the framed picture on the wall.

"This is all personal now. I will do my best to bring her home."

The picture said nothing, but might have blinked.

The next part was much harder. I went back outside and whistled for Bucket. He was there in a flash.

"C'mon," I said and walked around the corner of the house. I heard Daniel call my name, but I ignored him. Bucket and I walked out to the fence that protected the garden. I peed on a fence post. Bucket did the same.

I walked down toward the Ruiz house. Aurelio was out in the front, smoking a thin cigar. He watched Bucket and me.

I knelt onto my left knee and Bucket came in close, putting the top of his head against my solar-plexus. I put my hands on his shoulders and kissed his head.

"Good boy," I said. "You are such a good boy."

He pushed his head against me.

"Work," I said. And now the hard part. "Stay."

I repeated myself and felt him accept it. Standing up, I shook Aurelio's good hand, turned, and jogged to the black Humvee that was idling in Willy's yard. I never looked back, but I knew that Bucket was sitting by Aurelio watching me go.

"How touching."

At the driver's voice, I looked up to meet his gaze in the rear-view mirror. I wasn't sure I'd heard right. "Pardon me?"

"How touching," the driver repeated, his voice dripping with sarcasm. "Saying good-bye to the nice doggie."

"Fuck you," I said agreeably.

The driver's eyes snapped up into the rear-view mirror again. "What did you say?" The car slowed a little.

I looked back. Daniel put his hand on my knee. I brushed it off. "You deaf?" I turned to Daniel. "Where did they get this asshole?" I asked. "Ted Mack's Driver Service?" I turned back to the driver. "Oh, what I said was 'fuck you,' and," I added, "fuck your sister too."

"Oh shit," said Daniel as the Humvee came to a screeching halt, and the driver vaulted out of his door. When he got to my side, I was waiting for him in the road.

"You're not really cut out for this kind of work, are you?" I said as he unloaded his swing at me. All he got was air.

I hit him twice, once with each fist. For good measure, I added my right knee as he went down. He stayed down, bleeding from his nose and mouth.

"Shit, Michael," Daniel said. "We do not have time for this. He was upset because we were ten minutes late in leaving."

I was unmoved. "He's an asshole."

I picked his large form up and stuffed it in the backseat. I didn't care what he bled on. I also relieved him of his gun and wallet. His NSA ID card told me that his name was William Oskarsson.

Daniel had moved to the front seat and was going through the storage compartment under the dashboard. He produced a pair of handcuffs. "Put these on him," he said. "When he wakes up, he will not be happy." My brother was still angry at me.

"Just making sure my edge is on," I explained. I jumped into the driver's seat. "Hang on," I said. "We have time to make up."

We were singing down Highway 97 at about seventy-five when Daniel made a phone call.

"Your driver is a moron," he said into the phone. "He may need medical attention. Our ETA is a bit ahead of schedule."

I looked at him and grinned. I knew he didn't want to, but he couldn't help himself and smiled back.

TWENTY-FIVE: WILLY

"Why are you doing this?" I asked my obvious question.

His dark eyes drank me in like I was some fabulously presented dessert. I was disheveled, scared to death. I probably stank of fear, and still those eyes pulled at me. Heat came off of him, crowding the backseat. *Good lord, girl, you are in far more trouble than you thought.* I was speechless.

Flores put out his hands and gently cupped my face. I willed myself to climb out of my body so I would not feel his dry skin or smell the soap on his fingers. He ran his thumbs easily along my cheekbones and took a deep breath, his eyes searching mine. I stared above his pupils, at his eyelids. Leaning back, I put my hands on his wrists to push his hands away.

"Please don't touch me," I said. Crazy fear churned in my belly. Chavez would not help with this. *This was why he brought me here. I am on my own.*

Flores smiled warmly and dropped his hands, but not before resting them briefly on my right thigh.

"Please don't touch me," I repeated and found his eyes with mine. "We are not long-lost friends. I am here against my will, and I demand that you allow me to return to my home."

"Give me a few days," he said. "I will try and change your mind." After a pause, he continued. "I can be very persuasive. In the meantime, enjoy your stay as my guest."

I think he meant his face to look open and honest, but he would win no award for such a shallow performance. He reminded me of a rattlesnake trying to smile. I wanted to laugh, but knew that would be a very bad move.

"Good luck with that," was all I said, and I turned away from him.

Flores did not speak to me for the remainder of the ride. *I've made him uncomfortable. Good.* He spoke softly with Deems. Flores stiffened slightly near the end of the conversation.

"*Él es un hombre muerto,*" Flores said under his breath.

I did not like the sound of that.

The rest of the ride was quiet. The town car rolled smoothly north until turning west. We moved through farmland and forest, passing small towns and villages, until the vegetation turned to what I would call jungle. Finally, we came down a long sweeping hill and turned left into a broad driveway with a gate and a guard shack.

The driver buzzed his window down. The guard lost his bored look as the car passed through the gate into a large garage.

Past the large commercial-looking kitchen and up a short flight of stairs, Gustavo Flores showed me my room. It was a spacious suite with a large window overlooking a patio below. *Could I get down there with a knotted bed sheet?* The queen bed looked freshly made.

"I trust you will comfortable." He smiled. "Rest now. I will send somebody around six o'clock to see about some clothes for you. Dinner will be at eight."

"But…" I started to say, but Flores put his finger to his lips.

"Hush. Rest. I will see you later." He made as if to pat me on the shoulder, but I moved back. When he closed the door behind him, his eyes were slightly disappointed. I heard the lock engage. So much for being a "guest."

I sat on the bed, allowed myself a single quiet sob, and stood again, angry. *I hate feeling like a sparrow in a hurricane. I am an independent human being. I've taken care of myself and overcome things where other people, other women, would have let go and given up. I oversee a successful ranch. How the hell do I get out of this? Mike will come, but I hate being a damsel in waiting. This is ridiculous!*

In the bathroom, I ran a cold washcloth over my face and stared into the mirror for a long while. *You will be okay, girl. You will get through this. You have to. There is no other option.* I heard Mike call my name and turned back to the bedroom,. It scared me anew, but a warmth spread across my chest. It was like hearing him mumble in his sleep.

I crawled onto the bed and was totally out in seconds, boots on.

Bucket came into the room and sat at the foot of the bed. Mike was calling for me and for Bucket, alternating our names. I tried to tell him Bucket was with me, but he couldn't hear. Frustrated, I snapped my fingers to get his attention.

The click of the lock woke me up. I was swinging my legs to the floor when the door opened and a pretty Mexican woman came into the room, carrying a tray with a covered dish and a stainless steel pitcher. She put the tray on the dresser along the wall opposite from where I sat trying desperately to come awake.

I think my face was on sideways, but the woman smiled. Her eyes seemed friendly, but there was something else there that I couldn't identify. *She is afraid of me. Why?*

"I am Angel," she said with just the trace of an accent. It came out as "Ann Hell."

I filed that away to enjoy the irony later. At least, I hoped I could enjoy the irony. *I hope there is a later.* I sat on the bed not knowing how to respond or what to say.

"There is fruit and coffee on the tray," Angel said. "If you want to eat and take a shower, you are welcome. I will bring some clothes."

A shower sounded wonderful. "Thank you. I don't think I will need any clothes."

"But you must dress for dinner!" Angel said, looking worried. "People are dying to meet you."

That might be entirely too true.

"Something simple and plain, then."

Angel brightened. "Yes. That is probably best."

As the door opened and closed, I saw a man standing in the hall outside. I assumed him to be a guard. He did not turn to look at me. The door closed, and the lock clicked again.

I let the warm water cascade over me, and the fluttering in my stomach almost stopped. I stood under the water for what seemed a long time. I was drying myself, surprised to actually feel a little better, when a gentle knock on the door preceded the sound of a key in the lock. *Yikes!* The door opened, but it was Angel with clothes, which she laid on the bed as I covered as much as I could with the towel.

Angel's eyes flashed wide. "What happened?" Her voice shook with outrage.

At first, I didn't have a clue what she was talking about, but then Angel's eyes told me it was the bruises on my right ribcage and breast.

"One of the men who kidnapped me, grabbed me. I got to hit him once, but once was not enough."

"Oh, *señora*, that is terrible. Who did this?" If she wasn't sincere, she was very convincing.

"Not the pilot, not Chavez, not Deems, the other one."

A knowing crept across Angel's face.

"Ah, Señor Guzman. That is not very surprising. I am glad you got to hit him. I will tell Señor Flores."

I considered this. "If you must."

"Oh, *sí*, I must." Her eyes wandered away to somewhere inside herself.

I adjusted the towel and felt drops still running down the backs of my legs. My shift brought Angel back to the present.

She shook her head. "I brought two dresses. You can decide which fits best. Please be ready by seven thirty."

She nodded politely and was gone. The damn lock clicked once more.

TWENTY-SIX: MIKE

Daniel's contact at the air base in Klamath Falls, a major named Lewis, studied the sullen Mr. Oskarsson with pursed lips.

"You are in a world of hurt," he said, stating the obvious.

Oskarsson sat smoldering. He wouldn't look at me. It was probably the first time in his twenty-eight years that he had ever been physically dismissed, and his pride and ego had been damaged. That probably hurt far worse than what my hands and knee had done to him. His jaw was swollen, and his snappy white shirt was covered with dried blood.

I knelt in front of him, trying to force him to look at me. He pulled his head back and shifted his eyes to somewhere near my shoulder.

"Look at me."

His eyes snapped to mine, and there was anger there, of course, but fear too. There was also a faint glimmer of curiosity. I appealed to that.

"You may not realize it right now, but you are a lucky young man. We both are, because I could have killed you. I'm glad I didn't. Your comment about my attachment to my dog really pissed me off. Neither of us acted professionally, and I apologize for my part, I really do. But you can't just fly off like that. You had no idea who I was, and you could've put this whole operation into disarray."

He shifted slightly in his chair but said nothing. His eyes clouded as he digested what I'd said. I stood and offered my hand.

His eyes sought the major, who stared back stone faced.

Oskarsson regarded my hand and sighed. Then he gripped it. "I'm sorry too," he said around his swollen jaw. He wasn't used to any of this. "What did you hit me with?"

I let go of his hand. "Vietnam and a lifetime of practice."

He nodded as if that made sense. Even I wasn't sure what it meant, but it really didn't matter. I wasn't sure if young Mr. Oskarsson was a good guy or not, but I decided that he might have potential.

After the young man was ushered out of the room, Daniel showed me a small wry smile. "*Ya Ta Hey*," was all he said.

It was generic and ambiguous phrase. It could mean anything from *oh well* to *what the hell*. Suddenly, all I wanted to do was sleep.

TWENTY-SEVEN

We loaded our stuff into a stripped-down 707 with the words *Pineland Airways* along its fuselage. I wondered how many alphabet organizations had been cobbled together to make this operation happen and marveled at both the collusion and the secrecy. I studied the back of my hand just to make sure I really did exist.

I don't remember anything of the flight. I slept like a big rock. I awoke to what I thought was Bucket sniffing at my ear, but it was the fresh air from the open forward door. We disembarked, and Major Lewis ushered us into a small empty hangar.

He led us to a large, well-lighted map table. A satellite photo had been zoomed in to what I guessed was about fifty thousand feet. Borders and roads were overlaid in yellow.

"You are here," Lewis said, pointing.

The southern boundary of Gila Bend Air Force Base was about six miles to our north. The Pipe Organ Cactus National Monument was to our east. A little farther east was the Tohono O'odham reservation.

"You will meet Señor Montoya here." He pointed to a small blip on the map called Microondas. "We give you a ride to here," he finished with a tap on the map.

"How far a walk is it?" asked Daniel.

"About eight clicks," Lewis said.

"When do we start?" I asked.

"Whenever you want to," he said, "but I would suggest that you arrive in Microondas after dark. Sunset is at 17:41 today."

"How long to the dropoff?" Daniel asked.

"Forty-five minutes," Lewis said. "It's rough country."

Daniel glanced my way and shrugged. "Leave here at 14:15?"

"Sounds about right," I said. "That will give us time to be somewhere above this road"—I pointed—"just in time to enjoy the sunset."

"Very good," said Major Lewis. "I will be back here at fourteen hundred sharp. And your weapon is over there." He pointed to a nondescript gray case in the corner of the room. Rifle size.

"What about the Border Patrol?"

"They won't be patrolling anywhere near here this evening."

"Convenient."

"Yes."

He seemed to salute without doing so and walked out the door, leaving Daniel and me alone in the large, musty room.

We both studied the map as the quiet wrapped us. It pictured some of the most inhospitable country on the planet. Even so, it was part of a corridor for scores of people every month seeking a life in the United States. The derogatory term wetback referred to those crossing the Rio Grande. The only wet the people who chose this path experienced was the sweat on their backs as the relentless Sonoran sun did its level best to bake the life right out of them. A while back, I decided that I admired their grit and determination—they left families in Mexico they'd be sending money back to—but deplored the situation. No one should be an economic refugee, as so many from impoverished countries were. And they didn't walk here for free. The human traffickers on the Mexican side of the border charged two grand a person, or more, for passage and then nickel-and-dimed people the entire way. They came on buses and in trunks and crammed like sardines into the backs of trucks.

In Indian lore across almost all tribes, Coyote is the Trickster. It is no coincidence that the "guides" who are responsible for the safety of the travelers are called coyotes. At the first hint of trouble, they are gone, and the people are left to the whims of the desert. In many of those cases, it is a blessing to be found and apprehended by the U.S. Border Patrol, *La Migra*, as the illegal travelers call them. Jail and deportation is a better fate than a slow death by heat exhaustion and dehydration as your blood turns to mud and your brain to dust. Survival means another try at it. The two-legged coyotes have given the four-legged version a bad name for many years now.

Daniel straightened and stretched. I tapped the Tohono O'odham reservation on the map. "Got any friends there?"

His bronze face grew pensive. "I know a couple of the Shadow Wolves," he said. "One is my age. We served together in Laos. The other is the son of a man who served with me in Laos."

"The tracker guys who work the border over there?" I pointed to the east.

"Are you asking if they can help you get back?"

"It just crossed my mind."

"They are die-hard warriors, and their job is to stop anybody on the ground. I am not sure they would make any exceptions for a guy carrying what you will be carrying. Do not be fooled because they work for a government agency like ICE. They are very much on their own in the field."

"But you could ask, eh?"

"The US Immigration and Custom Enforcement. They are feds, just like *La Migra*. To the walkers and the mules they are *La Migra*, only they are Indians. If they come across your track, they will assume you are a mule because of the weight of your pack. They will come after you and will not quit."

"I've heard they could probably figure out which side I part my hair on just by cutting my sign."

"They are very good. Better than me, by a long shot," Daniel said.

"But you already know which side my hair is parted on."

"You do not have enough hair to part."

I decided not to sulk and instead follow my brother to the corner of the room, where he opened the rifle case.

I whistled in admiration. "M82?"

"M82A1," he said as he fit the gun together with satisfying chunk-chunk sounds. "This fifty-caliber rifle has taken out vehicles, radar installations, power grids, airplanes, and, of course, people. It has a stated range of eighteen hundred meters, just over a mile, but it will shoot with great accuracy farther than that if the wind doesn't interfere too much. It is a very wicked weapon."

"I'm guessing you know it well."

Daniel turned to me as he held the rifle. With his shining braid running down the middle of his back and his desert camouflage jacket, he was every inch a modern Dog Soldier. I was glad, as always, that we were on the same side.

"I know it too well," he said. "The only problem with it is that it weighs thirty-one pounds and is a son-of-a-bitch to travel with."

"I'm glad it's you carrying it."

"Fortunately," he said, "on this trip I do not have to carry much ammunition. And now," he said, putting the rifle away, "I'm going to make a call."

A call? I was surprised that there was a signal. The Ajo Mountains stood between us and Tucson. When I walked outside to join him, I noticed a small cell tower on the roof of the building we were in. I shook my head. Duh.

It came to me also that Daniel's little phone might also be able to triangulate with the communication satellites that were crowding the sky, just beyond the reach of everyday gravity. His technology was usually state-of-the-art military, sometimes prototypes of what wasn't even in the field yet. He didn't seem to be having any trouble with a signal. I took my phone from my pocket. It was standard issue and showed a weak signal, but at least there was a signal. I suspected that it might be mostly useless in Mexico. I had the international package with my contract, but now might be a great time to call my old pal Jasper Cronk.

Jasper was an expatriate surfer, raconteur, and force of nature. I'd met him in Nam. He and I were in different Special Forces detachments, but we'd hooked up when we'd volunteered for what became the POW rescue operation at Son Tay in November of 1970. As a mission, we got away with it—the worst casualty we suffered was a broken ankle—but we rescued no POWs. They weren't there, and our government had known that. We left behind many dead Charlie, who, it turned out, died because American politicians wanted something to crow about.

When we got back from Son Tay, I knew I was done. The fifty-six of us who went in there used up most of a lifetime of luck. After the raid, I had the lousiest Christmas of my life, but Jasper and I had discovered that we were good at keeping each other alive. We managed to end up in the same A-camps for the duration of our tours, had some adventures, and got to know each other very well. Our end-of-tour dates were very close. We spent the last four months on the dodge, avoiding the regular army very carefully because of a serious run in I'd had with a master sergeant. We took full advantage of the fact that in Vietnam, the left hand barely knew what the right was doing. I mustered out three weeks after he did. We got back together and spent time in Mexico where nobody cared that we were American veterans, nobody called us baby killers, and nobody minded that we were in dire need of nothing to do but breathe salt air and run barefoot on a long beach trying to recapture our arrested adolescence. After a few months, the beer and tequila wore off and I could sleep through most nights. I went home to Oregon. Jasper stayed. He said that he could find no reason to leave a place where his money went farther, the climate didn't require boots, the water was clear, the fish were plentiful, the surf was consistently good, and nobody asked about the war. I didn't argue with him.

I'd called him every year on *Dia de los Muertos*, Day of the Dead. It was this coming Tuesday, in fact. He probably wouldn't mind if I called early.

No answer. I wasn't surprised.

"Jasper," I said to the scratchy-voiced answering machine, "expect a visit. Short vacation, like the one we shared at Son Tay. Keep your ears open. See you soon."

That ought to pique his interest.

I went back inside and reviewed the contents of my pack. I was carrying my 9mm with five full fifteen-round clips; the three-fifty-seven with a hundred rounds of hollow-point magnum ammo; a thousand rounds of ammo for the CAR-15 that was broken down and packed neatly atop the ammo; an Air Force survival knife that I took out and put on my belt; a first-aid kit with sutures, morphine, sunscreen, and bandages; a small claymore with a preset igniter; three grenades; a white-phosphorus grenade wrapped carefully with tape; a small block of C-4 explosive with a roll of primer cord; a couple fuse igniters; a compact light-weight sleeping bag; a set of field binoculars; and my tourist disguise that consisted of a pair of shorts with a couple shirts. I made sure Willy's shoes were on top and judged the contents as perfectly capable of causing a diversion and, more important, liberating Willy. On a whim, I'd left the 10-guage in the truck at Willy's. Too bulky. The Special Forces motto, Liberate the Oppressed, rattled through my head. On this trip, all I would do was help one person. I was okay with that.

The CAR-15 had been my best friend during my tours in Nam. It was a Colt-modified sub-machinegun version of the M16, with a folding stock and a very short barrel. It was compact, very quick, and, in competent hands, a racehorse of a weapon. I decided to assemble it when we got to wherever it was that we were going. I was very hopeful that I wouldn't need it until then.

I glanced at my watch on my way back outside. Lewis wasn't due to show up for a few hours yet. I was not particularly sleepy but knew that if I sat still for a few minutes I could probably nod off for a while. There wasn't going to be much of that to be had over the next few days.

The sun in the sandy yard next to our hangar impressed me with its weight. The late October temperature, by the time we got out of the air-conditioned vehicle that would take us to where we'd be on our own, would be well into the nineties and still climbing. Sunscreen would be mandatory. Water would be the key to life or death.

It had been many years since the raid at Son Tay and one year less since I'd mustered out of the Special Forces. I had been on a couple operations with Daniel in those intervening years, but this one felt different. I hadn't focused on Willy during this build up. I found a relatively shady place where I could see for miles, sat down, and set my mind on her. It was almost a meditation.

I didn't pine, I didn't anguish—I just touched her spirit and let it be. I started a litany of support, like a mantra.

"I'm coming. Be ready."

The light sound of Daniel's boots in the coarse sand broke the spell as he approached. He squatted next to me, loose and easy.

"I will get back well before you do and will establish a contact on the To-hono O'odham rez," he said. "If you can get to a place called Gu Vo, on the east side of the Ajos, that would be choicely good. I will be as close as I can be."

I nodded, slowly coming out of my self-induced trance.

"If you cannot, you will have to improvise and get in touch however you can. Cell phone service is pretty much nonexistent on the rez, but there are pay phones still scattered around."

"And I should certainly avoid the Shadow Wolves?"

He nodded. "Avoid everybody. You will have no friends until you get to Gu Vo. And maybe not even then."

"I'm used to being popular. This will be hard."

"Being a pain in the ass is not being popular."

We were still, watching the distance shimmer. I thought of an old Hoyt Axton song and sang a couple lines.

Daniel laughed. "There are many kind men who guard this border, but they are not so kind to men like us. If your life needs saving, they will do their job. If you are smuggling, they would just as soon shoot you."

"I guess we're smuggling guns," I said.

"Yes. We are also smuggling the intent to kill a man."

The horizon wavered. "That's your job," I said. "I'm only in it for the girl. That makes me the noble one." I thought of Bucket looking at me that day Willy came to visit. "Or a complete idiot."

"I would not want to be between you and the girl. I sense great mayhem."

"Oh yeah. I've been thinking about the diversion part of the deal. I don't think that will be a problem. I can be very pesky."

"Yes, you can, but in a good way." He paused. "Mostly."

Noon came and went. The heat of the day was coming on. We went back inside and started drinking water. I studied the map some more. At about one thirty I folded it and put it in my pack. There were many details about the return journey that I couldn't know until I was standing in them. There were other details that, at the moment, were also hidden.

"You look perplexed," said Daniel.

"Planning is not my strongest suit."

"No," he chuckled, "but on the fly you are a genius."

"When it's just me, that's fine. This time I have somebody to worry about."

His eyes held me for a long time, his dark eyes seeing things that I would never see. He rested a hand on my shoulder. His calm and his deep and abiding connection to everything washed across me.

"Stay open," he said.

His inscrutable face wrote the span of our lives. The slow beating of his heart and the beating of all hearts bounded through my imagination. The measured breathing of everything in the world filled my ears. I touched Willy's living skin.

We heard a vehicle come up the road and growl to a stop outside.

"*Hoka Hey,*" I said.

The ride to the dropoff made me wish we'd walked. Across open desert, it was a torturous creep. The Humvee squeaked and rattled. We lurched. We shuddered. I tried to put it in perspective and feel gratitude for the ride. I'd be walking enough soon enough. The driver finally found a road and things smoothed out for the last fifteen minutes. I was grateful for that.

After unloading our gear, Daniel and I shook Major Lewis's hand in turn.

"Good luck," he said. "Señor Montoya will meet you in Microondas."

"How will we know him?" Daniel asked.

"He will know you. Follow the wash until it ends. Go straight when it does, and you'll gain elevation until you can see distance to the south. There is a border fence, but it is spotty at best. You should be able to see a couple lights in the village as it gets dark. Montoya will wait until twenty-one hundred."

As the Humvee rolled out of sight, I shouldered my pack and settled it on my back. Daniel did the same. He had the rifle lashed to the top of his.

"With that cross to bear, you might have trouble with doorways," I said.

He snorted as he studied my tie-dyed bandana neck-protector. "If you had hair, you would look like a hippie."

I pointed to the wicked Air Force knife on my belt.

"From the neck up."

We stayed at the east edge of the wash and proceeded as lightly as we could. A mile into it, the sweat was rolling. At two miles, the sun was an actual load upon me. Each time I breathed, the hot air dried the inside of my airway. At three miles, I could see where the broad wash started to transition into a shallow rise. Daniel was a few paces ahead, and he slowed to a stop. I came up beside him and was still.

"Tracks." He pointed.

I followed his finger to a faint line of human footprints across the coarse sand. He started again, and I fell in behind again. When we intersected the line of tracks, we stopped and knelt by them. It was a single set that came from across the wash in a slight arc and continued as the elevation climbed to the east.

"These were made last night," Daniel said. "See how those little insect tracks cross the footprint? That was probably early this morning."

"Archaeology of the recent past," I said.

"Exactly. The scouts who really know this stuff, like the Shadow Wolves, would know what insect made the crossing tracks and its behavior, so that they would have a much better notion about the time they were made."

He stood, and we followed the tracks to where they bent around a scrub of mesquite. We saw the broken twig at about the same time. Daniel squatted and studied the ground.

"He is wearing boots and sturdy clothes. I see no fibers," he said.

"And it looks like he knows where he's going," I added. There were no pauses or deviation in the line of footprints. "But he has a tendency to move to the left a little bit. Over time, that could really get him lost."

"White man pay attention," Daniel deadpanned.

We set off again and climbed the shallow rise. The sun sat low to our right and bled into the long shadows made by irregular washes and arroyos. Mesquite, creosote, groups of saguaro, and cholla were silhouetted like crazy dancers caught in mid-spin. The sky around it showed about every color in the spectrum of visible light. It was both forbidding and breathtaking.

The fence at the alleged border was a joke. We walked right through about a hundred yards of gap that looked as if there had never been a fence there.

"*Recepción a México*," I said.

We walked for another hour. The air didn't feel any different. I didn't either. I was in a place where feelings were a luxury. I would visit my feelings later.

We topped a small rise and looked down a long dry plain. I could just make out a road running perpendicular to our line of travel. As the horizon moved up to block most of the melting sun, I made out the faint smudge of a building's window.

"Must be Microondas," I said and pointed.

Daniel nodded as he drank from his canteen. "We hit it just about dead-on."

I studied the lights as darkness quickly wrapped the desert. The sun seeped into the horizon, leaving a psychedelic sky of oranges, purples, yellows, and pinks. I let myself stare for a couple minutes, watching its intensity fade. When my eyes readjusted, I looked back at Microondas. Lights winked in the distance.

"Not much going on there," I said.

"I wonder," Daniel said. "It may be a hotbed of intrigue and clandestine meetings."

"I reckon it is tonight. It can't be more than a few buildings."

"Shall we go check it out before we make ourselves known to Señor Montoya?"

"Capital suggestion."

We obliterated our tracks with scrubs of mesquite as we made our way to the road. We crossed the still-hot asphalt about two hundred yards east of the first lighted building and stashed our stuff in a very dark corner by an abandoned building where the dust was undisturbed, perhaps for years. I took the big knife from my belt and tucked it by my pack. There was no concealing it on my person. Sticking to the shadows, we advanced on separate paths through a scattering of adobe and aluminum buildings, some obviously in use and some obviously not. There was one neon sign. It said, *Open*, in blue and red. There was also a hand-lettered sign in the nearly opaque window that said, *Abierto*.

I met Daniel in the shadow of a dusty Diamond Reo still hooked to a lowboy trailer that had seen better days. Tie-down straps and chains were still neatly secured to both the cab and the trailer, so I guessed it was still a working vehicle. When I moved to the front of the cab, I could smell the engine. It wasn't warm, but it had been run as recently as yesterday, maybe even this afternoon. Four other cars, none looking able to haul Daniel and me, with our supplies, were parked haphazardly around the building.

"You feel like a beer?" Daniel said quietly.

"Do I look like a beer?"

"No. Your head is too small. But if you go in first and the place does not explode, I will follow in a couple minutes."

"Oh. White man goes in first to charm the locals and the Indian comes in when things are safe? Isn't that backwards?"

"Yes, Kemosabe. And it is about damn time."

I squeezed his arm and left him grinning like the Cheshire cat.

I checked the holster at the small of my back. The nine was riding comfortably. I pulled my Giants hat a bit lower. I'd left my Mariners cap at home. I was, after all, in disguise. The door opened easily. I smelled onions, grease, cigarette smoke, and the dust that came with constant air-conditioning.

It was a narrow dark room with a bar at one end and a pool table at the other. I felt the quick shift as the half-dozen people stopped whatever they were doing and turned to look. I didn't hesitate but went straight to the bar.

"Negra Modelo, *por favor*," I said.

The barkeep was a woman who could have been in her fifties, but she was probably in her forties, maybe late thirties. No one stays young in a desert border town. She had a strong Indian cast to her features and was packed into her T-shirt like ten pounds of mud in a five-pound sack. She moved behind the bar like a ship, slowly but with a ponderous grace. I put an American dollar on the bar as she brought me the brown bottle. Her smile was broken but genuine. I smiled back. I unwrapped the gold foil away from the lip and took a long drink. After the walk we'd taken that afternoon, the cold dark beer was like winning the lottery. I tilted my head again but left most of the beer in the bottle.

I turned to the room and played a game with myself, trying to decide if Montoya was here and who else there might be relaxing on a Microondas Saturday night. It was still early, but this was definitely the busiest place in town. It was also the only place in town. It didn't feel exactly right to even use the word *town*.

Two young guys sat at a table eating *frijoles* with *tortillas*. One was stocky and muscular, with dark ridges around his fingernails. The other was whippet-thin with the same mechanic's hands. Their coveralls had seen better days. The men would look at me from time to time while they were chewing. There were four bottles on their table, and the bartender swept around the end of the bar like a pulling guard carrying two more, which she put on their table. I marveled at her grace. She moved like a two-hundred pound ballerina.

At another table sat three young men drinking Dos Equis beer. They were dressed in jeans, T-shirts, and baseball caps. No Yankees and no Mets. I saw that as something in their favor. The guy facing me didn't seem particularly interested in me. I watched him without obvious attention as he watched his beer.

At the other end of the room a solitary man in jeans and a green twill shirt was shooting pool. His black hair was combed back, and he could have hidden a weapon in his mustache. His movements were crisp, and his aim was true. He rifled a shot into the side pocket as he watched me. I decided that I would not play pool with him for money.

I went over to a small table near the bar and sat facing the room. The door opened, and Daniel came in. Everybody looked. I did too, just to be one of the guys. As Daniel went to the bar, I stood and walked through the tables to the back. The mechanics watched me from the corners of their eyes. The young baseball fans stopped their conversation and watched me openly. I smiled at them but just got stoic stares in return. The pool player stood with his cue at parade rest.

"*Un juego?*" I asked.

He cocked his head at me slightly. "I thought you'd never ask," he said in perfect English.

I squatted and pulled the table lever. The balls dropped with a satisfying kachunk. As I racked them, Daniel came through the room to the table. He had taken off his camo shirt and was wearing a black T-shirt with a picture of Geronimo on it in silver. A red headband framed his face. I smiled to myself.

The pool player watched him. When Daniel arrived at the table, he offered his hand.

"You are Daniel," he said. It wasn't a question.

My brother cocked his head at me. "This is my brother Miguel."

"You can call me Mike," I said as we shook hands.

"You may call me Pablo," said Señor Montoya. "It's your money, your break," he added.

As I found a cue and studied my rack, Pablo and Daniel moved to the corner of the room and spoke quietly. I watched Daniel cross his arms over his chest. This was not a good sign. He stared at the three baseball fans for a moment and shook his head. I carried my cue over to them.

"What's up?"

Pablo was apologetic. "I am afraid that I need your help before we can continue your journey. Those three"—he nodded at the young Mexicans—"are coyotes of the worst stripe. I believe them to be waiting for a ride to Sonoyta for a job. I want to prevent them from getting there, but I also want to see who will be giving them a ride. I had truly mixed feelings when they came into the cantina. Yes, I am sworn to help you, but I would be failing my duty if I did not figure a way to thwart their activities."

"Thwart?" I said.

Montoya smiled. "My English comes from many hours of reading. I especially like Walker Percy."

"Ah," I said. "'Man has not the faintest of idea of who he is and what he is doing.'"

"Exactly," said Pablo.

Daniel brought us back to Pablo's request. "I guess we are in no hurry. Everything is set for Tuesday. Tomorrow is Sunday. How long will it take to figure out how to get inside?" he asked, looking at me.

I shrugged. "Hard to say. A day, probably. At least a few hours to walk around the property and see how strict they are."

"They are very strict," Pablo said. "But they are also very arrogant. It is their supreme weakness."

"Let's play eight-ball," I said.

Montoya brightened. "Yes."

After missing the eight out of politeness for a while, Pablo made a two-bank shot and buried the eight in the far corner. We shook hands.

He looked at his watch. "Perhaps we should retire to the outside smoking lounge," he said.

"You cannot smoke in here?" asked Daniel, waving his hand through the blue-gray air.

"Sure you can," Pablo said. "But I have a suspicion that it will be more exciting out there."

Daniel and I eyed each other. Our eyebrows went to similar elevations, and we followed Pablo Montoya outside into the warm Sonoran October night. His cell phone beeped. His brown face went silver-blue as it caught the light from the small screen.

"Excellent," he said as much to himself as to us. He closed the phone. "There is a truck coming with some uniformed men, who will take our border guides and their driver into custody. If we are very lucky, we may catch a bigger fish to fry."

"When this is done," Daniel asked, "how will we get to San Blas?"

Pablo smiled.

"We will go in my vehicle to an airstrip south of Sonoyta. From there it is a light plane ride to San Blas, unless..."

He was interrupted by the sound of a car moving at high speed, arriving from the west. We heard it slow down and then saw the headlights of a Ford as it turned in to the gravel around the cantina. Montoya checked his watch.

"*Dios maldito,*" he said and turned to us. "We must prevent that car from leaving, if it tries to before the uniforms get here."

I ran to where we'd stashed our packs. I came back with my .357. The Ford was idling, pointed east toward the long stretch of straight road.

"Where's the driver?" I asked.

"Inside."

"Okay, then. Stay hidden and cover your ears." I grinned into the darkness. Daniel sighed.

I walked up to the car and cocked the big pistol. I put two flaming rounds through the hood. The motor seized, hacked up its last breath, and shuddered to a stop. The noise the magnum rounds made was always astonishing. I sprinted west and around the backside of the cantina and what appeared to be a mechanical shop, probably the place where the two guys in overalls plied their trade. My ears rang like a big bell in a little room. The portable cannon I held in my hand had come through again.

I circled around the long building and came back toward the cantina in the alley between the machine shop and the warehouse I'd seen earlier. When I got back to where I'd started from, it was a completely different scene. Everybody who'd been in the bar was now outside. The three young coyotes were sitting as Daniel covered them with his Glock. The mechanics were leaning against the aluminum wall of the building, smoking as nonchalantly as they could. My attention went to a fat man, who was behind the bartender, using her as a shield between himself and Pablo's formidable pistol. I couldn't say for sure, but it looked like he might have a knife at her throat. I stepped up behind him, pressed the barrel of the .357 against the base of his skull, and cocked it. For him, it must have been deafening. I still couldn't hear a thing except a whine like an endless ricochet.

"*Tengo tu antención?*" I asked politely.

He sagged.

"*Caiga el cuchillo,*" I said, "*y déjela ir.*"

The knife clattered on the gravel, and the woman leaped forward, almost falling. Her considerable prow was heaving, but there were no tears.

"*Ahora, séntese,*" I said to the fat man.

He dropped to the ground like someone had hit him on the head. I wanted to let go a sigh of relief but didn't.

"*Pinche puto,*" the bartender hissed at the fat man. "*Gracias,*" she said to me as she held a hand to her throat.

I watched Pablo as I kicked the knife under a car. "This is your show," I said.

In the distance, tires sang on the warm asphalt. With any luck, it would be the cavalry coming to take these suddenly humble fellows off our hands. Pablo's *pistola* seemed to be in control of the situation, so I uncocked the .357 and slipped it into the back of my waistband next to the nine. I worried about my pants falling down.

A large green truck came off the road and slid into the lot, spraying gravel. It was a dramatic entrance. I melted back into the shadows to watch. I couldn't see Daniel, so I knew he'd done the same thing. As I watched the efficient transfer of the three young Mexicans and the fat man to the custody of the uniforms, I wondered what kind of cop Pablo Montoya was. He was deferential and respectful but also at ease giving orders. I didn't know much of anything about Mexican law enforcement hierarchy. I was thinking about that when a piece of gravel bounced off the back of my head.

"Dammit." I'd been killed again.

TWENTY-EIGHT

We rumbled east in the big Diamond Reo, now free of the low-boy left in Microondas.

"It will be fine," Pablo had said. "My *muchachos* in the machine shop will look after it. They are going to do some welding."

The three of us sat in the high cab, Pablo driving, Daniel in the middle, and me, being the widest, almost leaning out of the passenger-side window. Every window in the cab was open. I thought of the cold rain at home and of how Bucket seemed to love the snow they would surely be getting up at the H-Bar-H. Willy's laugh echoed briefly in my head, and my pulse quickened.

The countryside was dark. The only traffic we passed involved two buses. I leaned forward and asked Pablo about them.

"People who will try to walk into the US at some point this week. I'm sure there will be some very disappointed folks after our bit of handiwork this evening." He stroked the black bush under his nose. "It is the primary function of Sonoyta these days. They arrive from all over Mexico and Central America and stay in places where the spiders crawl and the bedbugs bite. They all have the dream. Making it across can be like winning the lottery. Almost all of them want to work and are willing to work hard. They do the things that Americans don't want to do, and for the most part, they do those things well. Most of them take great pride in working. It is what they do best. And after what they go through to get there, the work is a welcome respite."

"When you ain't got nothin', you got nothin' to lose," I sang.

"And everything to gain," Pablo said through his mustache. "It can be very much worth the effort for many families on this side of the border."

"That must be the Tohono O'odham reservation over there." Daniel pointed north.

"All of this country is Tohono O'odham country. For them, the border is an imaginary line that has become a major inconvenience. In the not-too-distant past, it was no big deal. *La Migra* did not bother them as they moved back and forth within their community."

"But the politicians on both sides of the imaginary line started bleating, and now they are hassled every step of the way," Daniel said.

"The walkers will do their best to avoid the Tohono O'odham, who are probably descended from the Hohokam, who used to have a vast and sophisticated civilization where Phoenix is now. In fact, Hohokam is probably a version of the name O'odham. There is no love lost between the walkers and the people on the rez. The mules, on the other hand, offer what amounts to big money to people on the rez for any number of illegal things, a place to stash the dope, a ride up to I-10, or simply a place to stay."

"When you ain't got nothin' … ," I didn't need to finish.

"What about the Shadow Wolves?" asked Daniel.

Pablo was quiet for a moment, lost in thought.

"That can be a very delicate subject," he finally said. "They work for the US government, but they are almost viewed as tribal police. I don't know about their day-to-day attitudes or, really, how they go about their business, other than when they cut fresh sign, it is come one, come all. What I do know is that if they find your track, you are not going to lose them. They are very tough, but I worry about them because the cartels have put bounties on each of the twelve men."

"And bounties on their family members too," added Daniel.

"That's a two-way street," I said, thinking of the next few days.

Nobody said much until we got to Sonoyta and turned south at the far edge of town. We passed nondescript warehouses and all manner of roadside businesses, motels, bars, abandoned hulks, and buildings with no identification whatsoever.

"One strange little town," I said.

Pablo sighed. "Yes. Its primary industry is border crossings. It is a strange mix of hope and despair."

And then I must have dozed because I don't remember anything until Pablo started downshifting. One light shined to our right like a diamond in a crankcase. We left the highway onto a dirt track heading toward that light and pulled up to a long, low aluminum building; the screws holding its skin on had rusted and dripped orange streaks. Pablo shut off the engine. At the same moment our headlights went out, the light that had guided us to the building went out.

"The gringo is here," said Pablo. "That is a relief. He is a good man and mostly very dependable, but he has too many, what is it, irons in the fire, so sometimes his priorities shift unexpectedly."

"Gringo?" I said.

"C'mon," Pablo said. "You will like him, I think. He is a very good pilot and, as Louis L'Amour might have said, is 'a man to ride the river with.'"

We hauled our stuff out of the sleeper and followed Montoya around the building. A single low-wattage bulb cast its weak light to the windows, but not really out of them. When we came to a stained white door, it opened. A shadow stood there.

"*Loco!*" Pablo said.

"*Pablito!*" said the shadow.

They embraced. As the shadow looked over Pablo's shoulder at Daniel and me, his dark face was oddly familiar. I saw his eyes widen and shine as they reflected the orange light.

"Holy shit!" he said as he almost threw Pablo to one side. "I'll be a blue-nosed gopher, it's Michael Ironwood!"

Suddenly I was encased in a bear hug that threatened to crush my ribs. As usual, he had no idea of how strong he really was.

"Hello, Jasper," I said and hugged him back, fiercely. He wasn't a large man, just under six feet and probably weighed 160. But he was made of whipcord, wire, and some kind of alloy that was probably top-secret stuff. My biker buddy back in Portland, Hogman, would call it unobtanium. No way could any one of us mere mortals find that strength.

We broke the embrace and held each other at arm's length. He had aged well and still had the same shag of sandy hair that flew every which way. His face had grown laugh lines at the corners of his eyes, but the rest of it was smooth and as tan as a deepwater sailor. The hard edge that I remembered in his eyes had mellowed some, but it still lingered, his invitation to all who met him to keep some degree of distance if you wanted to remain whole. Or maybe not everyone noticed the warning. It may be that I just knew exactly where to look.

"What the hell are you doing here?" he and I said in unison.

Laughter erupted among the four of us, and it would have been an oddly wonderful merging of worlds except suddenly I felt guilty about the enjoyment I was feeling while Willy was stuck hanging out with people who had no moral compass. I felt my face clamp, and the brief joy died.

"What's up, big guy?" Jasper asked.

I couldn't tell him. Reality wrapped me up, binding my tongue. I slid into a place where others couldn't go, where it was just me and what I had to do. I knew that I would touch Willy's face or die trying. There was no comfort even in my determination, though. I knew there would be no quarter asked or given.

When my silence stretched on, Daniel gently took Jasper by the elbow. "Show me the plane," he suggested.

I felt Jasper's gaze stay on me, but then I heard him and Daniel disappear into the darkness. I leaned against the wall and slid down until I rested on my haunches. Pablo Montoya squeezed my left shoulder, hoisted my pack, and followed after Daniel and Jasper. As I stared into the vacuum of my own mortality, Bucket came and sat quietly at my side, just as surely as if he had really been there. I heard his short whine as he yawned. His head pressed against my leg, and he licked my hand.

"Good boy," I said to the air. "You are such a good dog."

If there isn't a force that allows free travel of souls at the speed of imagination, I will eat my belt. I stood and followed in the direction of the other three.

The plane was an older blue-and-white twin-engine Beechcraft. It was beautiful. For a man who didn't comb his hair much, Jasper took particular care of his stuff. In Nam, the mud and blood didn't seem to stick to his equipment. He used anything he could find to keep his survival tools properly lubricated. They shined like dark and deadly jewels.

As I approached the plane, I heard Jasper say "... saved my life twice." He was probably referring to the controlled crash we'd made into the compound at Son Tay. Our HH-3 helicopter had clipped a stand of trees before landing and almost pitched several of us out the door. I'd grabbed Jasper by the straps on his backpack. Jasper and I fought side by side that dark morning and found a great rhythm, keeping each other covered and moving. Maybe we'd each saved the other more than twice. I still had trouble believing that we hadn't all been shot to rags. The last thing they'd expected twenty-three miles from Hanoi at two thirty in the morning was fifty-six berserkers to literally fall out of the sky and kill everything that moved and much of what didn't. As for Jasper and me, if Son Tay bound us together, and the patrols and firefights after it had cemented our friendship.

I knew that our current exercise would probably be similar, but the odds were much worse. I didn't think about anything in specific terms. The butterflies were doing complex gymnastics in both my head and my gut. I welcomed them. They meant I was still very much alive.

I was surprised that Pablo was going with us to San Blas. When I asked him about it, he just shrugged.

"I have some logistics to work out for Daniel's side of the party. We—um, make that Jasper—decided that he'd be your ticket back to the border."

As I settled into the passenger seat, I raised an eyebrow at Jasper. He smiled an old smile.

"You can take the dog out of the fight," he said, "but you really can't take the fight out of the dog." He paused for a minute, studying his gauges as the plane roared to life. "You decide how you want to play it, and I'll handle the local end. You're going to be extremely unpopular with a lot of people who make good money supporting the cartel. The honest people will love you but will not raise a finger in salute because they don't want to die. The only thing I would suggest is to get the hell out of San Blas as quickly as possible when you are clear of the compound. Let the countryside swallow you. There will be cops looking for you too because a lot of them work for the cartel."

I'd been thinking about this. "Get some black hair coloring, or a wig, and some clothes for Willy. Nobody in this country has ever forgotten a redhead," I said. "She's five nine and fit. Pretend she's your sister."

We arched out over the Sea of Cortez to follow the coastline south. The lights of Puerto Peñasco glistened as they slid beneath us.

"I have a small place in San Blas, right on the water, not far north of downtown. It's my surf camp. And home." Jasper grinned. "Another time you need to spend some quality time."

"I haven't surfed in a couple years. The water in Oregon is just too damn cold. I guess I'm getting more delicate as I age."

That brought a guffaw from Daniel in the backseat. "I think it is illegal to put *delicate* and *Mike Ironwood* in the same sentence."

"I think rough-hewn might be more accurate," Pablo chimed in. "But then, English is not my native tongue."

Jasper chuckled at that. "Your English is better than mine. And your Spanish is positively eloquent when you want it to be. Your Mayan is passable too."

"Thank you," Pablo nodded. "It is a gift."

The engine on the Beechcraft settled into a steady drone, and I wanted to let it lull me to sleep, but my mind whirred. Before I let go, I wondered how Willy and I were going to cover the ten miles from where we'd be down to San Blas. Making it on the sly was just another piece of the puzzle that was missing at the moment. As if he'd been reading my mind, Jasper spoke up.

"I will leave a couple bicycles where you can find them," he said. "It's almost all downhill."

"Two people on bicycles won't draw attention?" I asked.

"Well, sure, but just pretend you're a birder. There are lots of them along that road. Everybody wants to see a Berylline Hummingbird."

I thought about this. My instinct told me that the road would be a great place to avoid. When I'd studied the map, I'd realized that it would be a simple matter to set up a blockade. Crooked cops would certainly do that. Even the honest cops would because of the sudden drop in local population. It would be their duty to respond. I would have to figure a way to slow down their response time. I didn't like the fact that I would be unable to tell the difference between a cop who would simply be doing his duty and a cop who would just shoot me. It made sense to treat them all as crooked.

I liked the birder idea, but I didn't have the proper wardrobe with me. The seventy-pound pack was completely out of fashion, even birder fashion.

As if knowing I was about to argue about his idea, Jasper changed the subject. "Do you remember that regular army master sergeant who wanted to send us back north when we got back from Son Tay? You know, the guy you kicked the crap out of?"

I mulled this, reaching back past jagged edges of my memory. "He was the asshole whose job it was to see how many A-team guys he could put into harm's way. Big guy with a birthmark on his neck?"

"Yep. That's the guy. I saw him last week. I think he's become an alphabet boy, probably CIA. He didn't look any nicer. I don't know for sure, but I think those guys are running around here too. This Flores hombre has certainly stirred up some kind of hornet's nest."

Pablo leaned into the front from between the seats.

"His name is Grimes. He's on our side, but just barely. His boss isn't supposed to know what's going on, but nobody is supposed to know. I think those spooky boys are just gathering information. Señor Flores has created a lot of interest, worldwide, with his activities."

"They probably suspect something," I guessed. "Even Arthur Jepps, the FBI guy in Portland, suspects something. Everybody seems to be hovering around what Deems, the DEA rogue, has done to compromise everything. To have him slither over to the dark side is scary but"—I thought of how many guys in Nam, Vietnamese and American, had played both ends against the middle—"not unprecedented."

"When there is this much cold hard cash involved, human nature can show its ugly side," said Pablo. "The guy inside says that there is one room alone at the villa that has ten million dollars in it."

"Hooo," I whistled. "That's a big pile of cash. But I'm just in it for the girl. Besides, I have all the weight I can carry."

Daniel piped up from his seat. "Do not give me that," he said. "You could take the piano and stagger off with it."

Jasper laughed. "I have stories," he said.

"I bet you do," said Daniel. "We will have to compare them to mine sometime."

"I would like that," Jasper said.

I wasn't sure I would, but stories are stories. We are all the composite of our stories. It is who we are. Our stories carry the tracks we leave during our lifetimes. The most important of those tracks are in the hearts of our friends and our enemies. I thought of this Grimes character. His story would not shine a fond light upon me. But that was long ago and far away. Hearing that he was on the ground at the periphery of what Daniel and I were doing was odd. I wondered at the twists of fate that had put him here. There were a lot of lives hoisted up on this fulcrum, and coincidence seemed a weak excuse. My intellect, such as it was, acknowledged coincidence, but we look at the world through such a tiny window. What we don't see is surely larger than what we do see. Extrapolating a connection is endlessly fascinating, but I have learned to accept it, whatever it is and spend my time trying to understand what I do see.

"Where did you see Grimes?" I asked Jasper.

"At the ticket counter at the airport in Puerto Peñasco. He was going to Tepic."

"How did…"

"I know the ticket agent there, Eva. A lovely young lady." He grinned at me. "She told me when I asked her."

I smiled and shook my head.

A necklace of light strung the Mexican coast beneath us. I could make out a few jewels way across the Sea of Cortez where Baja slept in relative isolation. Finally, I surrendered to the song of the twin engines and let go of the world.

TWENTY-NINE

The airport at San Blas was a simple affair at the northeast edge of town. One runway ran west to east. If the wind was out of the north or south, as it was today, it made for an interesting landing. The sky to the east was only beginning to show some gray as we made our approach, but Jasper was already sweating through his T-shirt.

"Did you bring a fresh shirt?" I teased.

"Never fly with a pilot who doesn't sweat when he's landing an aircraft," he said.

I had heard this from pilots most of my life—from many people who care about and are good at their jobs, really. Fear is considered a bad thing, but fear is one of our best friends. It kept me alive through some very serious business. Acknowledging it, accepting it, and managing it make up whatever secret there is to avoiding panic. The body wants to continue. The mind just gets in the way, if it tries to go first. That's why the military is big on physical training and endless repetitive motion. If the mind can trust the body to keep itself alive, the mind can do what it does best, process information.

"You look lost in thought," Jasper said.

"Dichotomy."

He nodded. "The old same place," he said, borrowing from an old Firesign Theatre album.

"Yes," I said, examining my hands. "Things are starting to quicken."

Jasper taxied the airplane to the south side of the runway and shut down the engine.

"San Blas," he announced. "Perhaps one of the best-kept secrets of Mexico, the Land of Secrets."

With that, he hopped out of the plane and disappeared. I started to get out and stretch my legs, but Pablo put a hand on my shoulder to stop me.

"Wait, mi amigo. Jasper must get us through customs."

Jasper came back in about fifteen minutes, flipping a key on its ring around his finger. He climbed in and looked over his shoulder at Pablo.

"You owe me a hundred bucks. But I got hanger space with the deal." He tossed the key on the console and fired up the engine again, and we taxied back west.

After the four of us pushed the plane into the hangar, we unloaded the packs. Pablo left us with the plane and went off to find the vehicle that was supposed to be parked and waiting, somewhere to our immediate north. Daniel and I changed into our gringo tourist clothes. I put on khaki shorts and a brightly colored shirt. I stayed with the Giants hat. Daniel still wore the Geronimo T-shirt but swapped his headband for a hat that had an image of Kokopeli, the flute player, on it.

Pablo came back in a late-model Chevy pickup. There wasn't enough room in the cab for three of us, so I opted to ride outside in the warm air.

After we put our stuff in the back, I turned to Jasper. "I don't think the bicycles will work. There will probably be roadblocks, and I will still be dressed for battle. I don't know what the timing will be. Thanks for the thought, but I think we'd be sitting ducks."

"I thought of that too," he said. "Tell you what. I will leave the bikes on the far side of the river you have to cross. If the policia set up a block, it will probably be before that. When you get past that, it should be clear sailing into town. Come back to this hangar. If it is locked, this"—he held up the key—"will be right here." He knelt at the corner of the building and pried up a loose piece of asphalt.

He stood, and we embraced. As he stepped back, he extended his fist. "Here is to new good times."

"A toast for the ages," I said as our fists bumped.

He screwed up his rubbery face. "Aye, Laddie," he said in a deep Scottish brogue.

I laughed and vaulted into the back of the Chevy. As we pulled away, he was back in the hangar attending to his airplane.

THIRTY

We drove out of town until the road started to rise. The air smelled of eucalyptus and dust. There were few roadside attractions. About eight miles out, we crossed a small bridge, and I wondered if that was where Jasper had suggested that a roadblock might get set up. I banged on the window and asked Pablo to stop.

The stream was sluggish and shallow. Unless it rained, getting across would not be a problem. The underside of the bridge was heavy timber and concrete. I briefly considered blowing it up in the roadblock's faces after we were safely past, but that would put the surrounding communities in a world of hurt, and I vetoed the idea. I didn't want to crush anyone who wasn't directly involved in Willy's predicament.

We piled back into the truck and moved on. The road was good, and we passed mostly farm traffic. As the sky brightened, we turned from the main road onto a dirt track that wound its way up into the hills. Around a couple bends, we came to a broad gated driveway. There were two men in a guard shack. I could see at least one of them had a handheld radio.

Pablo slowed as we took a broad turn to the right. Through the trees I could catch quick glimpses of the two-story adobe and wood house that sat well back from the road in a swale that followed the road we had just traveled. I figured that we might be able to go straight down the hill and get back to the road without having to deal with the driveway. It would certainly be better cover. I would know more when I performed my due diligence recon over the next thirty-six hours. Knowing Willy was in there put slinkies in my stomach.

The road turned back to the left, and we took a right into a long narrow driveway. The rambling house sat up high and had a broad deck surrounding the front. I was eager to get up there and see what I could see. The closest neighbor seemed to be the villa down the hill, but it was hard to tell from where I sat in the truck.

Daniel and Pablo got out of the cab and stood, stretching in the morning sun. I joined them. A mild breeze ruffled the big eucalyptus trees and the sun, filtered through the leaves, warmed my chest.

"What's the weather supposed to do?" I asked Pablo.

"Sunny and warm," he said, looking at his watch. "Perfect vacation weather," he added with a grin.

We unloaded our gear and carried it into the house. No one had lived there for a long time. The curtains were drawn and the interior was dim, even with the bright morning just outside. Dust had settled over everything. Small rodent tracks dotted the kitchen floor. We disturbed little of it. The deck was much more pleasant. We sat at a wide weathered table and looked down the hill. The villa was just discernable through the trees.

Daniel opened his rifle case and began assembling the M82A1. I unpacked my CAR-15 and followed suit. We sat in companionable silence, just as if we were packing sandwiches for a picnic. The metallic sounds of precision parts clicking and chunking together was strangely comforting. I finished with the CAR-15 and set it aside. It did not gleam in the sun. It seemed to absorb all light. It was a Darkside weapon in the hands of a Good Guy.

"You figure his place about a mile down there?" I asked.

"Somewhere in that vicinity. I will tell you almost exactly in just a minute." He reached over and patted a small electronic device. "This will put me within six feet of exactly how far it is."

I reached over and picked it up. It was a boxy tube about eight inches long and three inches around. There were no manufacturer's marks on it.

"Snazzy," I said. I found a small switch. "Mind if I check it out?"

Daniel was intent upon fitting the scope to his rifle. His noncommittal grunt told me all I needed to know. I turned it on and looked through the eyepiece. There was some magnification but not much. I trained the crosshairs on a tree across the road. Nothing happened. I pushed the switch again. A small number appeared below the crosshairs. It said 50m. I repeated the process on another tree. I changed the field and tried to find a wall at the villa below us. Bingo. The display told me it was 1,350 meters away. Damn near a mile. I took a deep breath and let it out slowly. I tried to find something that resembled a courtyard patio. The magnification wasn't strong enough to be sure, but I found something that might fill the bill. I pushed the switch. The display read 1,365 meters. How about that.

"Pretty slick," I said as I put it on the table.

I was on my way to get my binoculars when Pablo came out onto the deck staring thoughtfully at his cell phone. He did not look happy as he walked past me without a glance and into the sunshine. He sat heavily at the table, leaned on his forearms, and stared down through the trees. Daniel and I both looked at him expectantly.

"What?" I finally said.

"They are hosting a *Día de los Muertos* festival at the villa on Tuesday."

We all sat staring down through the trees.

"Shit." A festival meant confusion—costumes, piñatas, singers and dancers, likely food and drink carried by servers—and bull's-eyes we didn't want as targets. Children, lots and lots of children. I think my choice of words was a good one.

After a few moments of silence, Daniel spoke.

"So, it will have to go down as early as possible, as soon as Señor Flores arrives on the patio." I noticed Pablo shift a little, as though there was something about that plan that made him uncomfortable, but Daniel kept talking. "He takes his breakfast there. He will be sitting at the head of the table facing this way."

"He has proven to be a creature of habit, almost obsessively so," said Pablo. "To our great advantage." He looked at his watch. "In fact, he should be there now—it's just past 8:30."

Daniel turned to the rifle and cradled it. As he held it and fitted his eye to the scope, it looked to be a part of him.

"Ah," he said.

I retrieved my binoculars and sat next to him. It took me a second, but I found the patio. There were a few leaves in the way, but I could see the breakfast table just fine. My heart stopped. Willy was also at the table, to Flores's left. She was wearing a white dress. She looked fine, but I thought her movements were rigid and unnatural for a woman of her easy grace. It was difficult to actually see her at this distance, so that may have been my imagination.

"Breathe, Michael. I can see her too."

"The pattern has been that she arrives at breakfast about ten to fifteen minutes behind Flores," Pablo said quietly.

My imagination was tumbling like a rock polisher. Each negative thought drew blood. My head was full of agates. I drew in a deep breath and let it out very slowly, focusing on what I knew to be true. I kept breathing until a clear image of Willy's smile stopped the spin cycle. Jealousy is a hard enemy who knows all of the buttons to push. I felt my mind clear and put myself in her place, where survival is the only option. She was smart enough to do what she had to do. I lifted my heart to her.

When my awareness returned to the three of us on the deck, I turned to

Pablo. "How close is the contact with your guy on the inside?"

Pablo cupped his chin. "He contacts us; I cannot contact him."

"The next time he does, please ask him to, somehow, tell Willy I'm coming. She's going to be in the crossfire. She needs to be ready, and she needs to be hopeful." I looked back down the hill and then back at Pablo. "I'm going down there to look around. I may or may not return after it's fully dark."

He nodded. Daniel sat up and laid his rifle on its side. "Mr. Deems is now at the table too," he said. "When he sat down, Willy got up and left. She walked fine. She is still intact."

"You thinking of Stockholm syndrome?" I asked.

"Yes. It happens. Survival is paramount, and extreme stress will do inexplicable things to people. But Willy's obvious defiance of the hierarchy down there is a good sign." He studied me closely. "And pardon me for indulging in what you call 'Injun mumbo-jumbo,' but I had a very clear vision that she is waiting for you. When you get close, she will probably be able to feel you, so be careful. It just depends on how close they watch her."

The warmth of the sun stroked across my back as I looked down the wooded canyon. Willy may be healthy right now—fed, uninjured, allowed to enjoy the sunshine—but I knew that whenever Flores realized she wasn't falling for him, he would resort to force. Maybe he wouldn't even wait till then—who knew when the crazy switch in his psyche would flip. And he had such a switch. My research on him painted a picture of subterfuge and deceit. He appeared regal and polite, but behind him was a bloody trail of boundless ego and cruelty.

"Do not try and see her tonight," Daniel asked.

He knew me too well.

"I'm serious. It would affect the plan."

Pablo sighed. "It probably would, yes," he said. "Still, if you can pull that off, go for it. But if you get her out of there tonight, you will still have to create your diversion in the morning." When neither Daniel nor I offered up any protest, Pablo continued. "According to the contact, her room is off the corridor leading to the master suite, which is on the west end, upstairs. They are installing electronics, but they are not operational yet, so there is a guard. He watches the money room and Willy's room and, of course, the master suite. The money is across the hall from her. Flores is at the end of the same corridor. His bedroom takes up that whole end of the upstairs."

THIRTY-ONE

I took off my Giants cap and replaced it with the floppy camo hat I'd used through my two tours in Vietnam. I reset my pack, checked my pistols, the canteen pouches full of ammo, and held out my hand.

"Might not be back this way, Pablo, but it's been great meeting you. I hope we all live through this. Maybe someday we can all sit around and have more than half a beer. If you ever get to Portland, come find me."

"I would like that," he said through his amazing mustache. His deep brown eyes were clear, and his handshake was dry and firm. "Look for the truck at the west end of town in Sonoyta. If the truck is there, so am I."

I handed him the Giants cap. "Keep this and wear it in good health," I said.

His gaze intensified; then he smiled and nodded.

Before I slid into the woods, I found a small pebble and carefully climbed the structure supporting the deck. I was very careful to make no sound and to not sway the deck. Daniel was still sitting at the table looking through the scope of his rifle. I launched the pebble and felt immense satisfaction as it bounced off the back of his neck. I could hear him laughing as I dropped to the ground, picked up the CAR-15, slung it around my neck, and melted into the trees.

Once under the canopy, I waited until my eyes adjusted. It was an easy walk down. I followed no trail and took care to leave no sign, no mark of my passing. My breathing was shallow and slow. I stopped every fifty yards or so to listen. I was hoping that a veteran Green Beret on a deeply personal mission was about the last person they expected to visit on such a nice warm morning. There was no margin for error. I was fairly confident that I could fight my way out of most anything I encountered, but this wasn't about me, and it wasn't just a recon to gather intelligence for an idiotic and counterproductive chain of command. I tried to keep my heart clear of feelings for Willy, but that was difficult. I missed Bucket, not only his nose and ears, but his easy camaraderie and unconditional friendship. I took deep breaths; I pushed myself. Sure enough, soon enough, my old training and the added maturity of being in my mid-forties had me deep into the focus I needed. I emptied my mind and let myself fall into the rhythm of the mission.

The only trails in the shallow canyon were those of small deer, dogs or coyotes or both. Small rodents had come and gone. No human footprints in the forest. I made it a point to look up into the tree branches because humans, unless they are birders, tend to not look up. In extreme circumstances, that can be fatal omission.

Every movement counted; every step was important. After about fifteen minutes, I came to the new-looking chain-link fence that likely surrounded the villa's property, and knelt to study it. There was no evidence of security measures. I crept along the perimeter, just inside the tree line. The terrain on the other side of the fence was open and easy to defend. There were meticulously maintained shrubs and flowers. Small trees were artfully spaced in weedless beds. Somebody worked the grounds here every day and had for years.

I reached a corner where the fence line turned west and got my first good look at the house. It sat about a hundred yards from where I crouched and looked sturdy, made from big timbers and adobe, maybe some stucco. I could make out what I thought to be the original building, from which the newer parts of the structure seemed to anchor themselves. It might have been a school at one time, or a small house in support of a bigger one. I heard a noise to my left. The front end of a wheelbarrow came into view. It was ancient and boxy; the noise came from its nubby metal wheel. It was full of bright-yellow flowering plants. The man pushing it might have been as old as the wheelbarrow, but he pushed it effortlessly. He reminded me a little bit of what Jasper might become as an elderly gentleman. He face was deeply lined and indescribably sad, framed by a shock of white hair that swept out of his straw sombrero and was tucked behind his ears. His plain cotton clothing was stained, but they were old marks; the cloth looked recently laundered. Worn rope sandals scuffed lightly through the grass.

He must have felt my eyes upon him because he stopped exactly opposite from me and set his wheelbarrow down. I did not breathe, and I shifted my gaze away. I tried to evaporate. I thought tree and earth. I thought air and the spaces between all of my molecules. I held my breath and lowered my face.

The old man came up and stopped, not two feet from the fence, and peered into the woods. I felt his milky brown eyes pass over me, but they did not linger. He seemed to reach a decision.

"I am old," he said in soft Spanish, "and my eyes and ears to do not work very well, but I know you are there. If you are the angel I have prayed for, I welcome you. If you are not, go away, because you will die here at the hands of these"—he paused and sighed—"people. *Vaya con Dios.*"

I waited until he was out of my line of sight before I slowly released my breath and took in a new one. It always amazed me how perceptive humans can be. I think we are all born with that sixth sense but lose it over time for many reasons. Warriors keep something like it going because it is so key to survival. I will never understand the physics of how you know you're being watched or how you sense the presence of something that shouldn't be there, but it is very real and very useful when you are also something that should not be there.

I continued down the fence line slowly and carefully. By the time I reached a small rustic shed where I assumed the old man kept his tools, my heart rate was back to something manageable. I made mental notes of the contents. There were rakes and hoes, a pitchfork, a couple shovels, watering cans, buckets, and a pile of stakes in a corner. On the workbench were wheelbarrow parts that might have been older than those on the one the old man was using. There was a familiar feel to the small room, a feeling I'd known since I was a child. I'd grown up with cattle and sheep and bison, but there was always a place like this that was dedicated to growing leafy things.

I went around behind the shed and was surprised by a large open garden area filled with flowers of every color. I knew none of the names, but the startling beauty of the plants was something to see. As I walked, I saw the old man kneeling in one of the beds, carefully tucking his flowers into the ground. I saluted his back.

I came to a place where the trees thinned and stayed a good twenty yards from the fence. The ground sloped into an arroyo that would collect and channel rain water around the property. I squatted at its edge. It was dry.

I moved back up to the edge of the trees and studied the house some more. Flanked with unevenly spaced windows, a door in the middle of the east-west wall marked where the second level of the building rose from the first. I put my binoculars on the windows. They were all curtained, except one on the second floor. I smiled to myself. That would probably be the money room, and Willy would be across the hall from there. I could also see where an upper patio began at the west end. I needed to check that out.

I went back to the edge of the arroyo and dropped into it, carefully obliterating my tracks with a short branch from a scrub bush. I was more in the open at the bottom of the watercourse but could make good time by walking this trail. I saw coyote tracks and was careful not to disturb them.

The arroyo ran fairly straight till it started to bend slightly to the north. I figured this would mark the end of the east-west fence line, so I left the arroyo, ever careful with my tracks. Sure enough. The fence wrapped along the west end of the property some thirty yards from the edge of the arroyo and about fifty yards from the end of the house. There was no cover between me and the large veranda. I looked back at the arroyo and followed its deepening cut until it fell off the end of the property, probably to merge with the small river that we'd passed on our way up the road.

I heard a vehicle coming up that road. It sounded like a small truck. I couldn't see it, but I heard gravel crunch nearby and the engine slow. I decided to sit tight and see what I could see.

Laughter erupted from the other side of the villa. I looked at my watch. Breakfast must be breaking up. I had not seen a single person, other than the old man. There were no guards at the perimeter. That bothered me. I scanned for cameras and saw nothing. I searched the roofline, under the eaves, everywhere I could see, and nothing. There were three spotlights along the entire length of the house, but what good would it do to light an area nobody seemed to be watching?

I could see the truck clearly now. Loaded in the back was what looked like a pile of bodies. Costumes. I breathed. There were clown faces, animal heads, grotesque masks, and all sorts of strange apparitions. A giant head sporting a vacuous open-mouthed grin with a big sheet attached to where the neck would be caught my eye. Two guys unloaded the cargo into the shade under the veranda. Between loads, they glanced around nervously. They did their work swiftly and couldn't seem to get out of there quickly enough. There was an official-looking guy with a clipboard who signed something and handed it to the driver, who was already moving the truck when the exchange was made. Gustavo Flores came out onto his large upstairs patio. Instinctively, I lowered my head a little and then scolded myself for moving at all. There was almost no chance that he could see me at eighty yards unless I moved. Humans have predator eyes, designed to pick up movement. We have a much harder time picking up still images in an expanse. Some people have the gift, but it is rare. I certainly didn't have eyesight that Daniel did. He could tell you details about things at a distance when I couldn't even see that there were things.

I watched Flores from behind a fragrant bush. There was a smugness to him that grated on me, but I kept that at bay. He seemed to be waiting for somebody. A few seconds later his head turned, and Deems joined him on the patio. I would've traded my entire collection of baseball caps to hear what they were saying.

After they'd spoken for about ten minutes, I swear Deems clicked his heels;

he left. What bidding of Flores's was that twerp about to go and do? At the sliding doors, he passed a stocky man in a dark shirt. Even from where I crouched, I could tell he looked angry and worried. Flores put a hand on his shoulder. The man didn't flinch, but he didn't relax either. Flores spoke earnestly. The young man nodded but remained wary.

After a minute or so, a young woman joined them. She did not look apprehensive. When she saw the man, she took on a subtle posture of victory. Suddenly, I had a very bad feeling.

Flores continued speaking, shrugging a few times, and then moved behind them. He slipped something from his pocket and quickly looped it around the man's neck. A garrote. The man fought for a few seconds, but the garrote has been an effective execution weapon for untold centuries. He was dead in less time than it takes to scramble an egg. The woman watching calmly, Flores pushed his victim to the railing and let him topple over the edge where the body landed half on the grass and half on the concrete below. Two men came around the corner of the house as if they had been waiting, gathered up the body, and took it away. The whole thing had taken less than two minutes. The giant head costume watched, grinning.

The woman stood quietly as Flores patted her shoulder. He leaned in and kissed her cheek. The woman, I think, wanted more but remained at military attention. She listened to what Flores was saying and left the patio. Flores sighed deeply.

Deems came back onto the deck. He nodded at Flores and they shared a short laugh.

Flores and Deems spoke for about five minutes when both of their heads turned and Willy and the young woman came out on the patio, followed closely by Jesús Chavez. Willy had changed from the white dress she'd worn at breakfast to her plain cotton shirt with jeans and boots. The woman nodded at Flores, touched Willy's arm, and left the patio.

My heart nearly exploded through my chest. A rush of adrenalin flooded me, and blood flushed my face. Sweat flowed like a river from under my arms. A very cynical corner of my mind told me that love will get you killed. I heard Daniel's voice saying, "Stay open." I took as deep a breath as I could and let it out as slowly as I could. I wasn't going to do Willy any good at all if I couldn't function properly. Ruthlessly, I forced myself into a cold place. Keep Willy alive. Wreaking as much havoc as I possibly could upon the men standing on the patio with her.

To my amazement and pleasure, I watched Willy step forward and slap

Howard Deems across the face. She hit him hard enough to force him a step back. I could see the back of his neck burn bright red from eighty yards away. He took a menacing step toward her, and Chavez moved forward too, but she held her ground. Flores put his hand on Deems's shoulder and appeared to speak sharply. Deems backed off, but I could see his quiver of rage.

Flores put his hand gently on Willy's shoulder, but she shrugged it off and said something to him with a quick shake of her head. Flores appeared angry now too. At a command from Flores, Chavez gripped Willy by the arm and jerked her toward the doorway. She resisted, but he was too strong.

An icy wind blew through me with an almost eerie calm. Colors brightened. Suddenly, I smelled the sandy dirt of the arroyo, the grass, a faint sour tinge of the greasewood growing behind me, and the exhaust of the truck that had brought the costumes. The buzz of insects and eucalyptus leaves rustling in the breeze filled my ears. My internal voices hummed.

Flores and Deems, two men strung together by mutual need and greed, still stood on the veranda. Deems earnestly spoke to Flores, who did not appear to be listening. Finally, he snapped something at Deems, who stood straighter and then spun on his heel to leave the patio. Flores put his hands out and leaned on the porch railing. He seemed to sag a bit before standing back up. He turned and left the patio as well.

I waited another minute—that patio seemed to have a revolving door—but no one else stepped outside. I carefully crabbed my way along the slope of the wash parallel to the fence, keeping my eyes on the house as I could. There were spotlights along the walls on this side as well.

The woods between the road and the fence offered good cover, and I was able to move more easily. I came abreast of the large patio where Señor Flores would have his last sip of coffee tomorrow, if all went according to plan. I thought of the line Chief Dan George's character had in *The Outlaw Josie Wales* when he said, "Hell is coming to breakfast." Yessiree.

I paused in the woods to study the wide ground-level patio. There were three sets of French doors along its length, a set of which looked like it led directly into a kitchen. One opened onto a stairway, probably connecting to the master suite—that would be the convenience Flores would expect. I couldn't make out any shapes behind the third, in the middle, so I'd have to count that as a hall or a room.

I sighed. It really was a nice place. It was a shame that I was going to leave it in a different condition. My primary issue, once I had Willy, was to make sure none of the innocents arriving for the fiesta tomorrow would run into any of my deadly games. For me, there is no such thing as collateral damage.

I wished I knew how to identify the man for whom I was creating a diversion. Having my own help on the inside would be a luxury. I wondered how he was planning on getting out and up to the house where Daniel and Pablo were. And I also wondered why the gruesome dismembering of Gustavo Flores would not serve as enough of a diversion. There was too much I didn't know about this whole thing. In that way it reminded me of my time in Vietnam. Special Forces back then too often operated on intelligence that the enemy also had. Many times out in the field, A-teams walked into an enemy who'd known they were coming. They'd even seemed to know the route we were supposed to take to get there. The survivors, like me, never followed those routes. My job had been to destroy the enemy, gather intelligence, and keep alive the other American and indigenous men in my group. They had all learned to trust me to do that. Technically, the other American, usually a radioman, and I had been advisors. But I'd also been the boss. Once we were out there, we freewheeled as best we could. I'd had absolutely no trust in the chain of command, which was illustrated by the story Jasper had mentioned concerning Grimes, who was now an alphabet guy. He was probably closer to where I was sitting than I expected or wanted.

I slowly made my way to the driveway and the first sign of guards I'd seen: a guard shack in the middle of the expanse of gravel. I estimated the fence's opening to be about thirty feet on each side of the shack. A swath of asphalt had been laid down for the wheels on the gate. It was actually two rolling gates, one for coming, the other for going.

I watched the guard shack. I could see a guy in there with nothing to do. He sat glumly with his chin in his hand. As much as I wanted to liven up his day, I went back into the woods. I crossed the road and got past the driveway into the trees on the other side. The guard never even shifted position. Maybe he was asleep.

I slowly worked my way back down the fence line. The flowers the old man had planted still looked happy. I wondered where he was.

I arrived at the place where I'd first come to the fence. I had no illusions about having left no sign at all, but after looking very carefully for signs of my passing, I could see none. I kept going until I heard voices, by the old man's shed. I slowly swiveled my head. They were coming from my side of the fence. Dropping to my hands and knees, I crept to the back corner of the shed. I stretched out on my belly and peered around the corner.

The old man was there, speaking to someone in the shadows. He was animated but was speaking quietly. He looked younger in his passion. I craned my neck to try and see who he was talking to. I made out a shadow. There was a familiar cadence to the voice. Suddenly, I knew. It was Daniel.

THIRTY-TWO: WILLY

"Oh, *señora*, you are so lovely."

The first dress I'd tried on was cut way too low, and I had laughed out loud. *Laughing is good.* The second white dress Angel had provided was much better but still fit tight enough to make me nervous. It created just a hint of cleavage. I wanted to wear my flannel shirt, but decided I'd better play their game for now. *I am not comfortable like this. Men generally misconstrue cleavage. They seem to think it an invitation. Maybe it is. Mike wouldn't let me catch him looking. But I've never dressed up for him.*

"I don't feel lovely. I feel angry and scared, and I want to go home."

"I felt that way when I first came here too. It will pass."

My face must have opened in wonder. "Where did you come from?" I finally managed. "Were you kidnapped too?"

Angel sighed. "No, I was rescued. After my mother died in the desert, I was grabbed off the street. I was being sent across the ocean, to work in a"—she faltered—"*casa de citas...*"

"A brothel?"

"*Si.* My brother convinced Señor Flores and Señor Deems to put a stop to it, and they brought me here. They saved my life."

Who was responsible for grabbing you in the first place?

"Who's your brother?"

"Chuey, Jesús Chavez."

I wanted to sit and put my head in my hands. Instead, I followed Angel out of the room and down the hall toward the broad stairway.

"Your English is very good," I said.

"*Gracias.*" She smiled. "Chuey taught me. He says knowing how to talk to Americans is really important for a Mexican girl, if she wants to"—she hesitated again—"improve her life."

I smoothed my brow and made a small noncommittal noise. Apparently, there was more to Jesús Chavez than he let most people see. *Ay, yi yi. I am adrift in a sea of lunacy. Steady. Breathe.*

The murmur of male voices put me on edge. When Angel and I entered the high-ceilinged room at the bottom of the stairs, the murmur stopped, and twenty eyes swept over me. *I am not a puppy, and I am not afraid.* These men were mostly polite, but there was an undercurrent as real as rock. I kept glancing down at my dress to make sure it hadn't changed to cellophane.

Gustavo Flores came over, smiling, his eyes curious and open. His faux intimacy crawled over me as he turned to the room. "Gentlemen. Our lovely guest is Willimina Hayes, a rancher from Oregon. We met years ago in Guatemala under sad circumstances. I'm hoping this is a much more pleasant time."

If the irony was not lost, it was invisible.

"I'm pleased to meet you all," I heard myself say. *I hope you all die in the way you fear most.*

Flores led me to various groups of men, all dressed immaculately. *Dressed to kill. My, my.* Introductions were polite and restrained, with several "hope you enjoy your stay" banalities. I forced myself to fall into the game of it. *How can I be so calm about this?* My anger seethed at a level I'd never suspected I had. The social patter seemed a survival skill. *I feel utterly ruthless. In another situation I might enjoy the recklessness of it. I can't be enjoying this. Can I?*

Angel watched me carefully and smiled appropriately when I made someone chuckle with something I said. *I really have no idea what I'm saying.* I also sensed Angel watching Gustavo Flores watching me as he led me around to various groups. Her face stayed calm, but her eyes brightened when she watched him. *Oh god. She's in love with him.*

A melodious bell sounded. Doors along the far wall opened, each by a man dressed in formal black.

The dining room was lavish with silver, linen, and china. Flores sat at the head of the long mahogany table. My chair was to his immediate left. Deems sat to his right, across from me. He was dressed less elegantly than many of the others, wearing a simple sport jacket and red power tie.

"You're looking lovely this evening, Miss Hayes," Deems said, his eyes dropping unconsciously to the hint of cleavage.

Jeez. Just took a shower. Now I need another one.

Pretending to look into his small marble eyes, I focused on the bridge of his nose. I put on my best phony smile and tried to keep my voice low.

"Please don't talk to me, you son of a bitch."

Flores interrupted with a smile that could've stopped a clock. "Willimina, I understand how you might be upset with Señor Deems, but please save your insults for after dinner when we are alone."

144

The idea of being alone with these two chilled me. *I might as well be in the high pasture, naked. Oh. In this group, what a terribly unfortunate image. Watch your step. Breathe.*

"Might be upset? Obviously, *señor*, you do not comprehend the half of it. But I will play by your rules as best I can. But only because I have to."

I sighed and looked around the table.

Perhaps because of the vehemence in the air at our end of the table, nobody acknowledged me. *My reckless feeling is growing. Probably not a good thing.* I smiled as brightly as I could, picked up my wine glass, and offered it to Deems in a toast. It took him a second to respond, his face blank with confusion. After he clinked my glass, I turned to Flores and offered my glass to him.

"To war, then," I said in a voice only they could hear. *Mike, you're not the only one who read that book.*

Flores smiled. "I am not without means," he said pointedly, but he was somehow pleased and excited.

Deems's look told me I was crazy.

I saw Jesús Chavez staring from the doorway, wearing a secret smile. His eyes briefly caught mine. There was no way he could have overheard, but he seemed genuinely amused. *What's up with that?*

The dinner went through four courses, and I just picked at all of them. I did enjoy two glasses of wine but was still uncomfortably full when the meal was over.

Flores took me by the arm and led me into a large salon. With the crowd present, I did not jerk my arm free. *Playing the game.*

"I have to meet someone briefly. Please wait here," he said. "I will return in a minute."

"Please, Señor Flores, I would really like to return to my room and go to bed. I am exhausted."

"I understand. I will only be a moment. And please call me Tavo."

As Flores left, Deems came over. *Cockroach.*

"Miss Hayes, if I were you, I'd go along with anything Flores wants. If you don't, the consequences will put you in Asia or the Middle East and a fate you can't even imagine. I don't think your idea of war would go very far in either case."

He's hooked himself into sex trafficking. I wonder if Mike has picked up on this yet. Maybe.

Deems saw Flores returning and left the room without looking back.

Flores was distracted. "Something has come up, and I must attend to it. I will ask Angel to see you to your room. I apologize."

I was much relieved and did not try to feign disappointment.

Flores put his hand on my shoulder. I did my best not to flinch. *Watch it. At this point, being polite will go further than your anger.*

"I will see you tomorrow at breakfast," he said and was gone. He nodded to Chavez on his way out.

Angel and I were walking toward the stairs when Jesús Chavez fell into step beside us.

I was curiously at ease with him. "My kidnapper." My tone was mocking. *What am I feeling, here? He reminds me of Mike. He's a murderer. How bizarre.*

Angel turned, mouth open. "Willimina said you were one of the men who brought her here."

Chavez shrugged. "*Sí.* I am a soldier, and I follow orders."

I wonder. I think you select the orders you will follow.

Angel's gait slowed. "You saw Guzman"—she tried to find the word—"put his hands on her?"

"*Sí.*"

"And did nothing?"

"He told Guzman that if he touched me again, he would kill him."

Ludicrous. I can't believe I just said that. It seemed defensive. I decided to just keep my mouth shut. *I need to get away from these people.*

Angel opened the door to my room. "Good night, Willy. I hope you sleep well."

Chavez's small smile was at odds with his eyes. *There are two of him in there.*

I looked back without speaking, following my own advice. *What is my face showing him? How would I know? My face feels disconnected.* As the door closed, before the lock clicked, I heard Chavez ask his sister a question.

"*Vamos a dar un paseo?*"

Something about a walk? I tried to think but was asleep before I could wonder much more about it.

In the morning, Angel brought me another white dress, but it was more casual and high-necked. I was grateful for that.

"Thank you. This one actually looks comfortable."

"I saw how the men looked at you last night. I thought this might be more…"

"Appropriate?"

Angel smiled. "Yes. That is the word. Thank you."

I'll be back to jeans and boots as soon as I can.

We went down the stairs to the patio off the salon.

"I have things to do. I will see you after breakfast."

The morning was warm. The tropical air, soothing. Flores came onto the patio dressed in light slacks and a blue shirt. He sat next to me, smiling like a man without a care in the world.

"*Buenos días*, Willimina. I trust you slept well?"

"Yes, thank you. Will I be able to go home today?"

Flores's smile broadened. "A few more days, my dear. We need to become more closely acquainted. If all goes well, perhaps that can be arranged."

I did not like the sound of "more closely acquainted" but said nothing.

Deems came to the table and sat down.

"*Buenos días*, Tavo. Good morning, Miss Hayes."

His voice wheedled. Something in me snapped. I abruptly stood.

"I'm very sorry," I said to Flores. "I am suddenly sick to my stomach. I will be in my room."

I turned and walked back into the salon. Upstairs, I surprised the guard in the hall and slammed the door to my room. I wished I could lock it from the inside.

I stayed in my room the rest of the morning, alternately pacing and lying down. I changed back into my ranch clothes but still couldn't get comfortable. Around lunchtime, a knock sounded on my door. I assumed it was Angel. It was Angel's brother.

"Señor Flores would like to see you."

His eyes were placid, but there was a tenseness in him that hadn't been there last night. My own apprehension began to grow. *There are riptides happening. Something has changed. And I think I feel Mike. He is close. I am done with their games.*

"What's going on?"

"*No se.* He told me to bring you to him."

We went down the hallway into a large bedroom. The bed was freshly made, and Angel was there, stuffing oversize pillows into their bright-white cases. Her smile was wan and couldn't reach her eyes.

"Angel, what's wrong?"

"Nothing, *señora*, nothing. Really."

I didn't believe her. Chavez just shrugged and urged me through the wide patio doors. Angel followed. Flores and Deems stood together in the sun by the railing. Chavez nodded toward the men. As Angel and I went to them, he stayed by the doorway. Angel touched my arm and retreated back into the master bedroom.

"Ah, Miss Hayes," Deems said. "I must say I enjoyed your wardrobe last evening much better. Your charms were much more"—he paused—"evident."

He leered.

Before I could stop myself, I stepped forward and slapped Deems across the face as hard as I could. After his involuntary step backward, he lunged at me, hand raised.

"Deems, enough." Flores's voice was used to commanding. Deems stopped, but his rage pulsated.

I would love to kick your balls through the top of your head. I am about done with this game. It feels good to tear it loose.

Flores stepped to me and rested a reassuring hand on my shoulder. I shrugged it off with heat.

"Your fantasy of charming me into your bed is not going to happen, so let's stop with these stupid games. Who the hell do you think I am? I want to go home. Now!"

"Do not push me, Willimina. That would be very unwise. I will take what I want when I want it."

His face flushed. I couldn't tell if it was embarrassment or anger. Maybe both.

Something just tore. It may not be mended.

Suddenly, Chavez was there, gripping my elbow. I tried to free my arm but could not. On the way through the bedroom, I caught his eye.

"I will go quietly. You do not have to drag me."

Chavez let go, and I followed him back to the room.

"You are very brave," he said at the door, "but very foolish. You are"—he groped for a phrase—"a duck in crocodile waters. I have never known Señor Flores to give up. On anything. He must like you very much, or he would have allowed Deems to hit you. Your fate is sealed. Only you can determine how much pain you have to go through. Angel says you are very intelligent. It is time for you to use that to survive as best you can."

"Giving in to Flores as he wants would be more painful than any alternative. I would rather die."

Chavez studied my eyes. "That is one of your choices."

I reached out and gripped his forearm. It was warm steel. "Is there any way you can help me?"

Chavez looked away. "My fate is also sealed. I can kill you very quickly and painlessly, if it comes to that."

His eyes were opaque. I turned and went into the room. I didn't remember even hearing the lock click.

THIRTY-THREE: MIKE

With infinite care, I made my way back into the trees and circled around to where I was behind Daniel. I pointedly stared at the back of his head. He didn't disappoint me.

"Michael, come on in and meet Carlos Carrera, master gardener and newest ally."

I tried to just appear as Daniel did so often, become visible all at once like some kind of apparition. I did seem to startle Señor Carrera, but Daniel knew exactly where I was.

He didn't waste any time answering the question in my face. "You do have to get her out of there tonight. Flores gave the order to give her Rohypnol with her dinner this evening. He has also confined her to her room. Apparently, she has done something to really piss him off."

The date-rape drug. Daniel was right. I needed to get her out of there as soon as possible.

"What will this do to your side of things?"

"My side of things has suddenly blown up," he said. "Pablo is beside himself. Our large-bore presents for Señor Flores have been put on hold."

I squatted and planted my backpack against a tree. I watched the trees march down to the arroyo.

"They must have cut some kind of deal."

"Something," Daniel said.

Señor Carrera stood to one side of us. He looked at me earnestly. "*Matarán a la mujer*," he said in his soft Spanish.

"Yes," Daniel said. "They will kill her. "Carlos here," he said, nodding at the old man, "says she is not the first captive they have had. Another American woman was here three weeks ago. And now she is nowhere."

"Do we know who she was?"

"Ever hear of Grabell Chemical?"

"Who hasn't?"

"She was Mrs. Grabell. The third Mrs. Grabell, in fact. She was the young, beautiful trinket to hang on Mr. Grabell's arm. Apparently, he really did dote on her. She was taken in Cancun."

"Ransom?"

"Paid. But there was no exchange. She is still missing."

"Would this be why somebody called you in the first place?"

"I do not know, but it is certainly possible."

I took off my floppy hat and put it on my knee. I regarded it as an oracle that would allow me to see everything I didn't know. It must have been broken because I leaned nothing. I put it back on my head. I smiled at Señor Carrera. He smiled back but clearly was still worried. He still didn't know what to think of the Indian and the gringo who were suddenly sitting in his garden like beetles on a beautiful woman's face.

"*Ayudaré si puedo,*" he said, telling me that he would help however he could.

"*Donde está su casa?*" I asked.

He pointed back up the arroyo. "*Dos kilómetros,*" he said.

"*Puedo llevar a la mujer allí?*" I knew I was asking a lot. If anyone got wind of where Willy was, he was as good as dead.

Carlos sucked in his breath. He measured me much closer than Mrs. Murphy, my first grade teacher, ever did. Finally, he nodded. "*Si, es bueno.*"

His hand, when we shook, was like a warm piece of wood.

"*Gracias,*" I said.

I turned to Daniel. "What does this do for the inside guy?"

"It keeps him inside for a while longer, I guess."

"What time is dinner?" I asked, jerking my head at the house through the trees.

"Usually around eight," Daniel said. "That has been the custom, or so I have been told.

I checked my watch. There were still almost six hours of daylight left. "Seeing as how I don't really exist," I said to Daniel, "I'm thinking that whatever happens this evening will not reflect badly on you or Pablo."

Daniel looked at me closely. "Are you thinking of making the world a better place?"

"Yep."

I looked at Carlos, who was looking thoughtfully back through the trees at the villa.

"*Quesiera ver su casa, por favor,*" I said. I would have to find it in the dark.

The old man raised his dark brown eyes to me. "*Vayamos,*" he said simply.

With that, he turned in a smooth motion and led the way up the arroyo, away from the shed. There were many tracks on the smooth worn trail, so I didn't worry about the ones we were leaving. After about eight hundred yards or so, a smaller path left the arroyo to the right and wound through the trees and shrubs. The air smelled heavily of eucalyptus, and there were birds of many shapes and sizes everywhere you looked. I'd swear they paid homage to Carlos as he led the way through the woods.

His house was solid adobe brick and mortar. The roof was thatched with palm, tied onto a framework of poles. The grounds around the house were immaculate and radiated care and comfort. I counted ten birdfeeders, filled to various levels with rice grains and some with seeds that I didn't recognize. The only word I could come up with for the impact of the whole place was enchanting. It was something out of an Audubon fantasy, with Walt Disney and, maybe, Stephen Spielberg thrown in for good measure. Daniel had a beatific smile on his face.

"This is so marvelous as to be unreal," he said.

I just nodded, removed my backpack, and put it against a tree with my CAR-15 leaned against it. Suddenly it had become obtrusive and utterly out of place. My pistols, however, stayed on my belt.

"Carlos," I said with deep sincerity, "*ésta es la casa más hermosa de todo el México.*"

In fact, it may have been the most beautiful house I had ever seen. It certainly wasn't fancy, and it wasn't richly appointed, but it was exactly where it was supposed to be and was lovingly cared for. I held out my arms and spun around, trying to encompass the whole place.

"*Una joya del bosque,*" I said. It was. It was a true jewel of the forest.

Carlos beamed like a proud father, which in a very real sense he was.

"*Gracias,*" he said with a twinkle in his eye.

Carlos asked if we were hungry, but we politely declined. The evening I had planned was best accomplished on an empty stomach.

"What's your plan?" I asked Daniel.

He let out a long sigh. "Pablo went to town to find Jasper. He is not hopeful that our original plan will resurrect itself. He is of the opinion that we should just clear out and forget that we were ever here."

I nodded, almost to myself. "Do you still have a ride back into the States?" I asked.

"Pardon the pun, but that is up in the air."

I considered this. Maybe we would all have to walk back. Suddenly, I was angry. I knew it wasn't productive, but the whole ludicrous sequence of events was for what? I almost hoped I would never know the whole story. But I knew better than that. I would have to know so I could leave it behind me.

On the other side of the argument was the simple fact that had nobody been spying on Willy, I would have never met her. At least, that's how it seemed. We'd been friends for a scant couple weeks, and now here I was, dressed for war, trying to get her away from a lunatic who meant to do her grievous harm.

Carlos came and stood before us. "*Debo ir. Mi trabajo no se acaba,*" he said.

I nodded. There was always work to finish.

Daniel went back to see if Pablo had returned. I grabbed my pack and found a small circle of trees at the edge of the arroyo that let me see the path without the path seeing me. I went through the ritual of making sure my guns were clean. I studied the explosives and made sure they held no obvious surprises. When I was satisfied, I sought a quiet place inside me and waited for dusk. I waited without expectation, breathing deeply, letting go of everything. I watched a millipede undulate across my left boot and continue on its way. Hummingbirds came and hovered in front of my face, wondering if it was an ugly flower and if there was nectar in my nostrils, their buzzing making the hair on the back of my neck stand out straight. Brush mice scurried past. I sensed, but never saw, something larger and cat-like and wondered if I was being watched by a jaguar. I heard the whine of a coyote and the hum of insects that, for whatever reason, left me alone. After a good while, I saw Carlos come back up the path and turn up toward his casa. The voices in my head begin to clear their throats. I knew they would rise to a chanting crescendo. When I told Daniel about this, years ago, his eyes grew very large, and he told me it was a great honor. The chanting had been a part of me since I was a child. Mostly, I ignored it, but it always came before a fight. Today, I regarded it as an old friend. Maybe I was losing my mind. That did occur to me from time to time.

THIRTY-FOUR

I crouched at the fence gate and studied the shadows. The two spotlights along the back of the house put out a fan of light that reached the fence. At the far end, where the master suite was, a floodlight threw a bright light clear down into the arroyo where I'd been earlier. The end of the house closest to where I was looked more promising. I went through Carlos's gate and crept along the fence line, trying to use the decorative shrubs as cover the best I could. I could smell the turned earth where he'd planted the flowers early this morning.

The shadow made by the bright light at the other end of the villa and the upper story of the house almost reached the fence. I relaxed a little in its welcome darkness. Even if I stayed in the shadow, I would be in plain view from the guard shack in the middle of the broad driveway. This east end of the house was where most of the traffic was, where all of the comings and goings took place.

Suddenly, I heard a rattling sound, a rollup door. A garage door. A long black Mercedes slid into view.

I launched into a crouched run. Except for the voices in my head, nobody yelled, there were no shots, and I was inside on my belly just as the door thumped to the pavement behind me. It was a long minute after door stopped until the light from the opener went out. I had enough time as I dove under the door to see three cars lined up to my right. There was a door on the far side wall. There was a refrigerator, and a workbench extended along the back wall where there was another door.

As the light clicked off, I started crawling on my elbows and was relieved that the lights were not motion sensitive. The concrete was smooth and smelled new, and I pushed off of it to stand. I heard the faint hum of the fridge. Even terrorists kept cold beer in the garage, apparently. I made my way so that I was between the first two cars; my eyes adjusted now, I knew they were another black Mercedes and a red Cadillac. The vehicle on the other side of the Cadillac was a dark-gray SUV.

The only light was in a switch by the door I guessed led into the house.

There was no sign of cameras. The lights were off-the-shelf. They must have felt very secure to be so cavalier about the business of staying alive. Maybe they just didn't care. Maybe, as Pablo had noted, they were so arrogant that they just assumed nobody would challenge them. Or maybe they were watching me right now, licking their chops.

I unlocked the side door, the one I figured went to the outside, but did not open it. Instead, I placed my hand on the handle of the door to the house, and turned it, and a heavy explosion rocked the building. The sound of small-arms fire quickly followed. I was through the door at a dead sprint, knocking kitchen people in white smocks aside like bowling pins, their faces open-mouthed with surprise. A man with his pistol drawn appeared in front of me. A three-shot burst from my CAR-15 stitched his chest, and he fell.

People yelled in Spanish. I took stairs leading to the upper level four at a time. There were three men standing in the hall. They all faced away from me, staring through the smoke that billowed from where I assumed the master suite was. My rifle barked short bursts, and they were down. The door I needed to open was locked. I slammed against it with everything I had and felt it buckle. I slammed against it again, and the door sprang open with a splintering groan, dangling from one of its hinges.

My eyes strained to see through the smoke. A tray of food sat before a wicker chair with what looked like a glass of white wine. I hoped it was untouched. A small shape crouched in the far corner of the room, between the bed and the wall.

"Willy," I said. "It's me, and it's time to check out of this dump."

She made a sound that was somewhere between a gasp and a sob. Then she gathered herself.

"It's about damn time. I wanted you here yesterday."

"Travel connections can be hell in Mexico," I said. "Wait. Only yesterday?"

Then she was on me in a hug so fierce it took my breath away. I gave her one good squeeze and pulled her to a corner where we couldn't be seen by someone in the hall. I gently touched her face, caressing the smoothness of her cheek. All I could see were her eyes. The first half of my adventure was complete. Now for the hard part.

I leaned my rifle and removed my pack. I grabbed Willy's sneakers from it. "Put these on," I said. "We have some country to cover."

"What about my boots?"

"I'll put 'em in my pack."

"Don't lose them. My father gave me those boots."

"Yes'm." I was busy with the WP grenade. I also grabbed one of the claymores. Willy watched with interest.

"Making room for my boots?"

I probably grunted something in response.

All of a sudden, I heard voices speaking English. "This is the room."

I put my finger on Willy's lips. She kissed it. Very briefly I wanted to laugh out loud. I could see her grinning at me through the smoke. Her eyes were red. Mine probably were too. I made a motion for her to stay put, and she nodded.

I edged to the splintered doorframe.

"Have you ever seen ten million dollars in one pile?" one of the voices asked.

"Nope, but I'm about to," the deeper voice said.

There came a clatter of automatic fire. It sounded like an M-16. I snuck an eye around the corner of the doorframe, careful of the jagged splinters. Two men stood there, dressed much like I was, battle packs and automatic weapons. The door across the hall was blown open, and I could see past them into the opposite room. There was a block of something stacked neatly in the center of the room, which was larger than the room we were in. If that was a pile of money, it was very impressive. I yanked the pin on the white phosphorus grenade and casually tossed it into the far room, past the men, where it landed with an audible thump.

"Incoming," I said.

Both men whirled. I stepped into one of them and made sure his jawbone snapped up against the nerve in his temple. He dropped like a load of doorknobs. With the second half of the same motion, I chopped the short barrel of my submachine gun down on the wrist of the second man. I felt it break. He didn't even have a chance to yowl because I used the last two seconds of the time I had to grab the mattress from the bed Willy had been sleeping on and stuff it into the opposite doorway. The grenade went off exactly when it was supposed to. The concussion rattled the walls, and the mattress burst into flames. White phosphorus does not kid around.

The guy whose wrist I'd broken looked up at me with hatred in his eyes. I recognized that hate. It was my old pal Grimes. For the second time in a few minutes I wanted to laugh out loud. Hell. This wasn't rock 'n' roll—it was fucking opera.

I don't think he recognized me, but it was hard to tell. I pulled a whip-wand from my belt and laid it sharply across the back of his neck. His eyes rolled up, and he sagged.

"C'mon, Willy," I hollered. "Time to un-ass this palace!"

I stuffed her boots into my pack, cinched it up, and swung it around my shoulders. I put my hands on her shoulders and fell into those green eyes.

"I do want to die with you, but not today," I said. "Stay close behind me while we're in the house and on this property. When we get into the woods, I want you to stay in front of me."

The heat from the burning money room was flowing into the hall like lava. The two Americans on the floor were stirring and groaning. I was pretty sure they'd wake up enough to stagger out of danger, but I really didn't care. I'd left Grimes in a condition similar to the one he'd left me in twenty-five years ago. The irony was sweet.

We got to the bottom of the stairs. I paused briefly. The expanse of back-yard was not appealing to me. We continued past the kitchen, now completely deserted. At the doorway into the garage, I made Willy stand away from the door and cautiously opened it. The main door was open, but only the SUV was gone. The Mercedes and the Cadillac were still there. I moved through the garage until I could see the guard shack. The sliding glass window had been shot out. I couldn't see the bloodstains that I knew must be there. I decided the door from the garage to the patio area would be our safest bet. The truck with the costumes had gotten in and out, so two people on foot could too.

When we got out there, we saw bodies everywhere. There were two or three of the kitchen staff in newly blood-spattered white coats, but there were at least six or seven men on the ground, scattered across the patio area. I did not see Deems among the dead. I suspected that had been in the Mercedes that had afforded me the chance to get into the garage. Where was the mysterious "inside guy" who had been passing information to Pablo? I also wondered about Jesús Chavez. Of all the men in this impossible array, he might be the most dangerous. A lot of his *compadres* were lying dead, but something told me he was very much alive and very much looking forward to seeing me dead as well.

I also didn't know how many men had assaulted the villa or what their affiliation was. Jasper thought that Grimes was CIA, and Daniel had mentioned that the Grabell of Grabell Chemical had paid a handsome ransom for the return of his wife. From what I'd heard Grimes and his buddy say, the money was their objective. But they would have needed more than two guys to move it. Now, they could probably use a shovel and a few sacks. Ashes are easy.

I would probably catch some kind of hell for reducing ten million dollars to a smoking pile, but it had been, to my way of thinking, exactly the right thing to do. That was money born of misery and greed and death. It appealed to my sense of justice. The misery and the greed and the death were not going away, but the reward for it was now merrily burning a hole in the floor of that upstairs room. It was a grim satisfaction to be sure, but it was satisfaction nonetheless.

I tried to think what I would have done had I been the lead on the small team that had assaulted the villa. I would probably have set up a command post in the arroyo at the west end of the property, where I had watched the little drama with Willy, Deems, and Flores play out. It was good cover and offered a quick way out. I would have a vehicle, or vehicles, at the bridge down the hill where the road crossed the small river. Radio contact would be crucial.

I was considering this when the unmistakable chuff of a bullet hissed past my head, followed immediately by the bark of a single shot from inside the house. I whirled and swept the room inside with a burst of my own.

"Back into the garage," I said to Willy.

We were too vulnerable to stay where we were. A line of splinters bristled the doorframe as we passed through it. Something struck my left arm above the elbow, but I paid it no mind. I took the claymore from my belt and considered it. These guys shooting at us now were American and were working stiffs just like me. They were also probably part of a covert team that was acting under the guise of some kind of perverted national security mandate. Willy was ready for most anything, wild hair pulled back, a sheen of sweat on her oval face, nostrils flared, with ice and fire in her green eyes. I made the choice.

"Okay," I said, "this is a claymore. When it goes off, it lays out a lethal spray of ball bearings at around four thousand feet per second. As it goes off, we are going to follow that wall of steel out into the driveway, past the guard shack and into the woods. Got it? Just stay as low as you can and move as fast as you can. Take this."

I handed her my air force survival knife. She hefted it like an old friend.

"Lay on, MacDuff," she said, studying our destination, "and damn'd be him that first cries, 'Hold, enough!'"

She looked every inch a Scottish queen in the heat of battle, and I was glad my name was not MacDuff. I wedged the claymore in the front bumper of the Mercedes that pointed out through the open garage door and tripped the fuse. The concussion of it in the small space ripped our ears. We ran like hell. Splinters flew from the plywood guard shack, and the trees gyrated from the impact of the steel wave. It was snowing leaves. We got to the trees, and I paused a step as Willy glided past me.

"Keep the fence line to your right," I urged. "Keep trees between you and the house. Wait for me at the corner, where there is a small shed. If you see an old man with kind eyes, he is your friend. His name is Carlos."

She slowed, looking over her shoulder at me.

"Go!" I said and waved her on.

She ghosted into the trees.

I turned back toward the house, which was still belching flame and smoke. Three men in fatigues had congregated in the driveway. One was attending to the second while the third stood watch. About every ten seconds his gaze covered the woods were I was, so I was very careful not to move, even though my left arm had started to throb and wetness seeped and pooled at my left elbow. The guy getting bandaged wore haggard like a hat. The wound looked like it was on his forearm, which could be anything. They were all much younger than me, probably in their twenties. They might have served in the Gulf War a couple years back.

The claymore hadn't damaged the front end of the Mercedes all that much. The grill was busted and scorched, but the bumper looked okay, not too twisted.

I saw a man in a sport shirt and slacks emerge from the smoke pouring out of the back door. He had what looked like a Mac 10, the infamous street-sweeper that the gangs on the north side of the border were so fond of. He crept down the wall toward the three soldiers. I thumbed the lever on my CAR-15 to single-shot, put the iron sights on him, and squeezed off two shots. He went down, his gun clattering to the paved sidewalk. At the sound of my rifle, the guy standing watch snapped his M-16 and fired a burst that tore through the trees to my left, uncomfortably close. When I didn't return fire, he chanced a peek around the corner and saw the guy on the sidewalk. He seemed to pause and turned back to the woods with a puzzled look. I didn't move. He said something to the other two, and they joined him at the corner looking at the guy I'd shot. Now they all looked into the woods. What was I supposed to do, wave? I stayed where I was until they were standing over the body. I took that opportunity to slide myself farther away from the fence and move down toward the shed, grateful for the darkness. I was pretty sure I'd given those guys something to talk about. These were American guys doing their jobs. I was guessing orders came from the CIA, but who knows how it was cobbled together. It was lucky for me to be able to send an unspoken message to the assault team, something other than what Grimes and his buddy might have to tell. It was, of course, very unlucky for the Mexican fellow. Such is war.

THIRTY-FIVE

I got to the corner of the fence where the shed stood quiet and unconcerned with the chaos at the house. The floodlights were out, and it was very dark, with weird flickers of light from the burning house. The fence gate was open. I didn't like that. I had expected to find Willy waiting, but she was nowhere to be seen.

I circled the shed. I could not chance a light to look at the ground for a sign. Finding exactly nothing, I dropped into the arroyo and began to follow it up the hill toward Carlos's casa. I'd only gone a hundred steps when I found Carlos lying in the path with a pitchfork sticking out of his chest. My heart broke, and a dark tide of anger seethed through me. I knelt by his body and used gentle fingers to close his eyes.

"*Vaya con Dios*," I said and bowed my head.

I stood and had to put a foot on him to pull the pitchfork from his body. I threw it as far as I could back down the hill. I didn't care who heard it.

I let the anger and sorrow flow through me until I could corral it and remove it from the now, though not the future. I knew it wasn't gone, and that it would visit me time and again after all this was done.

After a couple hundred yards, I saw a light up ahead. I slowed and crept carefully forward. A flashlight had been propped in the crook of a tree. Willy was standing against another tree looking at somebody I couldn't really see. My knife was at her feet. It had blood on it. There was also what looked like a nasty bruise starting to show on her left temple. I moved to the upper edge of the arroyo. I heard a man speak.

"Pick it up. Go ahead. You would love to cut me again."

"My father told me to never bring just a knife to a gunfight," Willy said. "Pick it up yourself."

"This arguing is getting us nowhere," the man said. "I am offering you a lifestyle that you cannot conceive of. I am the richest man in Mexico. Either way, I am going to have you. If you do not give yourself, I will shoot both of your knees and then, if need be, both of your shoulders. But make no mistake. I will have you. I have wanted you since I first saw you in Guatemala ten years ago, and I always get what I want. Always."

Flores paused as Willy considered what he'd said. "Now, I want to watch you take off your clothes." His voice was flat and thick.

Willy raised her chin. "I am glad that I cannot conceive of your lifestyle. Just shoot me, you bastard, because it's not going to happen."

I couldn't see it, but I felt the man shrug as he started to raise his pistol. I was lining up my shot when a curious thing happened. The man's head and shoulders seemed to lift away from the rest of his body, followed by a great plume of blood. On the heels of this magical transformation came a stunning boom. The lower half of the body collapsed in a pulsing heap with a sound like oatmeal hitting a kitchen floor. Willy sagged against the tree and turned away, beginning to retch. I couldn't blame her. My stomach was loose too. I rushed to her side and put a hand on her shoulder, but she brushed it away angrily.

"Don't touch me," she said. "I don't want anybody to touch me."

I squatted next to her as she convulsed.

As her quaking subsided, I said gently, "C'mon, we have to get the hell out of here."

Daniel appeared at the edge of the flashlight's pool of light. He was carrying the fifty-caliber rifle.

"That thing really makes a mess," I said.

"Hell gets another soldier," he said.

When she was able, Willy stood and smoothed her shirtfront. Her face was grey, especially in the eerie glow of the flashlight. With her hair sweated through and raked back I could really see the bruise that radiated from her left temple toward her ear.

"How's your head? Did he hit you?" I wanted to go kick his corpse, but it would ruin my boots.

"Yes, but it's okay." Willy stooped out of the light and came back up holding the knife I'd given her, now bloody. "And I got in my own round. With the help of the old man, when he diverted Flores's attention..." She trailed off, and I knew she had witnessed Carlos's murder. She cleared her throat. "Thank you for saving my life," she said to Daniel and turned to me. "You too," she finished.

She did not turn and look at the two pieces of carcass behind her. All of us avoided it.

I went to the flashlight and turned it off. The three of us stood in the darkness waiting for our eyes to adjust. It was not a comfortable silence.

When I could see the outlines of Daniel's face, it was time to go. The boom of the big rifle was surely bringing somebody. We moved out at a steady trot, up the path to Carlos's house. My heart ached to go past it. The birds would be fine, but the spirit of the grounds would fade to ruin. Mexico, more than any other place on earth, embraces ruin. I stopped suddenly and called Daniel's name.

"What?"

"We can't just leave him there for the coyotes," I said after telling Daniel what I'd seen.

Daniel sighed and looked heavenward. He knew I was right; he just didn't like it. Care of the dead was extremely important in his culture. It was also extremely important in the Special Forces culture. We owed it to our friends, our confidants, our allies that their bodies be treated with respect and not as a fast-food stops for scavengers.

"Okay," Daniel said. "We should wait back down on the main trail. If no one comes, we can go get him and bury him up here."

"If somebody does come?"

"Then we fight."

Willy was exasperated. "You guys are out of your minds."

"Probably," I said "but it is what it is."

Pablo was up at the road with yet a different vehicle. This time it was a beat-up Ford Explorer. We introduced him to Willy, and she was glad to stay with him. I tried to catch her eye, but she was having none of it. The joyous part of our reunion had been short-lived.

"The commando team is long gone," Pablo said. "And, predictably, the contacts I have are livid that they botched the money retrieval."

"When that shit hits the fan," I said, "you should duck."

His eyes were bemused. "I do not want to know," he said.

"Did the inside guy get out?" I asked.

"Yes, but he is still undercover. He left with Mr. Deems and Mr. Chavez. They are supposed to be on their way to Tepic."

I thought of the black Mercedes. "So, Deems is still trying to play both ends against the middle?"

Pablo nodded.

"You should suggest to your people that he has most of the money," I continued.

Pablo was aghast. "He has it?"

"No. He does not. Nobody does."

Pablo put his fingers in his ears. "Enough! I don't want to know." His mustache quivered. I could see Willy shaking her head on the passenger side. I couldn't be sure, but there might have been the faintest trace of a smile on her lips.

He looked at Daniel and me and shook his head.

"Go bury Señor Carrera, *hermanos locos*. Do what you must do. We will be here representing humanity with sanity."

Daniel and I moved back, stopping at the casita for the largest blanket we could find. We didn't speak until we got past the stinking pile that had been Señor Flores.

"The villa is burning. Some of that was you, I am guessing. You burned up ten million dollars." Even though he clearly hadn't expected anything less, there was still a note of incredulity in my brother's voice.

"Sure. Why not? That's the only thing any of those assholes understand. I suppose I might have figured out a way to get it into the local economy, but I was in kind of a hurry. I just wanted to give them all a black eye. In the heat of the moment, it seemed like a great idea. Besides, I had to spend that WP on something useful. Carrying those things around makes me nervous."

"Michael, Michael, Michael," he said in a sigh. "You are a piece of work."

We came, then, to Carlos. The ground beneath him was slippery with his blood.

"But I admire your logic," he finished.

The night held only the small sounds of furtive animals, probably drawn by the smell of blood. Every once in a while a crunch came from the burning house as the structure resettled. The wind was blowing toward the sea, so we could only smell a hint of the fire. Finally, I spread out the blanket. We carefully moved Carlos to its center and tucked it around him. We each grabbed an end and went back up the hill.

We buried him quickly but with deep respect. We used rocks to cover the grave and discourage the scavengers. The rocks were those that he must have painstakingly moved to border his gardens and pathways. Daniel chanted something that seemed to make the trees sing. I found it beautiful and envied him that certainty. I just tried to imagine the sound of all the hearts in the world beating, at rest and in peace, the frequency of Everything. All I heard of the voices was their deep and measured breathing.

In the glow of the Ford's dome light, a Mexican woman wearing Willy's clothes greeted me. In addition, she had a shawl wrapped around her head and shoulders. Coarse black hair fringed the edges. Her face, hands, and arms were a lovely brown. The transformation was stunning. Except for her green eyes, the disguise was complete. Any concern I'd had about pausing to bury Carlos was wiped away—Willy had needed to get into disguise before we traveled far anyway.

"*Quién es la mujer encantadora?*"

Pablo chuckled. "She is my sister Alejandra. We are driving to Puerta Vallarta to see our mother, Rosalba."

"What happens when we turn towards San Blas?" Daniel asked.

"We will be going to Guaymas."

"Who are the fellows in the backseat?" I asked.

"Not my problem," he chuckled.

Pablo drove us carefully up the road, away from the villa.

"Doesn't this go to Tepic?" Daniel asked.

"Eventually. But I would like to come into San Blas from the south, and we can do that going this way. Okay, I guess I care a little about who you are. You guys need to change your clothes, obviously. I think you should be hitchhikers who volunteered to pay the gas."

Daniel and I contorted ourselves in a careful dance, changing into tourist gear. Now that I was wearing a tank top, the wound I'd received was evident.

"Let me clean that up," Daniel said.

It was awkward, but he managed to swab it out while I bit my lip. He wrapped it snugly with gauze from my first-aid kit.

"We should stitch that up when we get a chance. I did not get all of the splinters in there."

I ignored that. "We're now presentable, but if we should get stopped, it's going to be very difficult to explain the contents in the back. What do you say about two rifles, four pistols, and other assorted party fun?"

"That is a problem," Pablo admitted. "I guess we'll just have to commit to not getting searched."

"Great plan," I said.

"Got a better idea?"

"Nope."

Willy remained quiet. I reached out and gently touched her shoulder. She did not brush my hand away, but she did flinch ever so slightly.

"You okay?" I asked.

"Better," she said. "But I feel like I'm watching a movie. I am lopsided and disjointed. I'm afraid I'll start screaming at any moment. The fear from these past days is muted now, but it is still here, waiting to take over. It doesn't feel any less; it's just farther away. I knew"—she sighed—"that this kind of world existed, but I never thought I'd ever see it first-hand. Everything has changed, and I miss my old calm."

"It will come back," Daniel said. "You have to trust yourself to find your place. Death is easy for the dead but much harder for the living."

"I'm sorry you have to go through all of this," I said. "And if you want to—"

"Incoming," Pablo interrupted. "There is a long line of traffic coming, and it is probably the *Federales* from Tepic responding to our little war. They will be suspicious of any vehicle they see."

He pulled the car over.

"You guys get down the hill with your stuff. I'll be changing a flat."

Except for Willy, we launched ourselves from the Explorer. I grabbed my pack and rifle while Daniel grabbed his pack and rifle case. Down the hill we went, causing a small avalanche of dirt. A few small bushes afforded us some cover. We looked back up at the obvious trail our rapid descent had made, but there was nothing to do for it now. We could also hear Pablo jacking up the Ford, and, eventually, we could hear the whine of many tires.

The vehicles continued past Pablo without pause, until they didn't. I heard one, likely the last in the convoy, slow. I grabbed my CAR-15, left Daniel watching for meteorites, and crabbed myself along the slope of the roadbed until I was behind the headlights of the new vehicle. Very carefully, I worked my way close enough to the road to see an olive-drab Jeep parked behind the Explorer. There was a fifty-caliber machine gun mounted in the rear deck with a man on it. I was impressed. Another man sat in the passenger side of the Jeep, but the driver was nowhere to be seen. I strained to hear voices, but the idling whine of the Jeep prevented that. Then, I saw Pablo walk through the headlight beams, followed by another man dressed in the same olive drab of the Jeep. Pablo was smiling. It seemed like he and the man knew one another. He said something, and the man laughed. They bumped fists, and Pablo squatted to investigate his "fixed" tire. The man moved back to his vehicle and said something to Pablo, who nodded and laughed. With that, the man climbed aboard, backed up enough to turn around, and roared off to catch the convoy, going through the gears like a Formula One racer. The guy on the machine gun was probably having quite a ride. I imagined him as a cartoon flag hanging on for dear life.

Daniel and I trudged up the roadbed slope with our stuff and tossed it in the back. "Who are you?" I asked Pablo as we settled into our seats.

He grinned at me in the rear-view mirror. "Maria Pablo Montoya Sanchez," he said and paused, considering. He looked briefly out the side window and puffed some air through his mustache. "I am a commander in the Mexican Navy," he continued. "If it was the American Navy, you would call me a SEAL, like your indefatigable brother. I am part of a relatively new effort to counteract the growing drug cartel problem in Mexico, which will get far worse. There is nothing to stop them. The money buys everything they need, including the freedom to operate without serious reprisal. The cartels will become, I'm afraid, the most powerful political force in Mexico. The sad thing is that they will vote with bullets, of which they have an endless supply."

"Do the cartels know about this? Do they know who you are?" asked Daniel.

Pablo's cheeks grew taut. "We're pretty sure they know something is up, but they do not know individuals. But that is just a matter of time. The ruling class in my beloved country is likely the most corrupt collection of politicos on the planet. We'll see what happens after this fiasco. The irony is that we had very little to do with it. It was supposed to be kind of a training exercise, to advise and see what is possible. Your CIA has, once again, thrown their weight around and screwed up the whole point of what we wanted to accomplish."

"What about Deems, the DEA guy?" Willy asked. "I told Flores that he was DEA, and they all just laughed."

"He was one of the catalysts for this. We figured we could use his example to show people on both sides of the border how powerful these cartels can become. They can buy anybody, given the right circumstances."

We rode in silence for a while, each of us finally having some time to process what we'd been through. Pablo found a road and made a right turn. Willy leaned against the window and fell into what appeared to be a deep sleep—I watched her head snap this way and that with the bumps in the road, yet she didn't wake. I tucked my jacket between her seat and the window to offer some protection the next time her head bounced back that way. She had probably not slept soundly for several days. I was glad to see it. Tenderness engulfed me, but I pushed at it. It was not the time or place to be Mike the loverboy. Too much had happened. We would both have to deal with that, eventually. Right now, I needed to be completely present. We were all depending on that.

I felt that I should be tired too, but I wasn't. I was back in a combat mindset, and sleep was important, but my mind was too busy for it.

"So, what now?" I asked the question to both Daniel and Pablo. "I mean, it's not like this is over just because we liberated Willy. The two assholes who got us into this mess are still out there. They have new motivation to make Willy's life hell, and I'm probably also at the top of their hit list."

"You should remember," Pablo said, "that Deems cannot go back to being an effective DEA agent. He probably knows that. His cover as a cartel mole is shot. He won't have unlimited access to travel. I would guess that as soon as the cartel replaces its head, there will be a strong inclination to go after Deems, who they will probably decide betrayed them. Maybe Chavez too."

I scratched the stubble on my chin. "So, the whole CIA fiasco we just witnessed is probably the last thing Deems wanted."

"Probably," said Daniel. "But he had to have known it was coming. That's why he was able to conveniently disappear before the shooting started."

"It's interesting that Chavez went with him. I wonder where his loyalty actually lies," I said.

After a mile, or so, Pablo answered. "Jesús Chavez is one of those enigmas wrapped in a riddle. He is highly intelligent, supports a network of youth football camps all over Mexico, and loves to kill people. In the cartel gang life, he is, maybe, one of the most feared men in all of Mexico."

I scoffed a bit. "Are we talking about the same guy? He looks like an ad for gangbangers."

Pablo nodded. "It's true. Think of it as one of his disguises. Apparently, he was close to his mother, who died trying to cross the border about ten years ago. She and the people she was with were deserted by their coyote, and eleven of the twenty died of thirst and starvation. *La Migra* found them about six days too late. He had a sister, but I know nothing of her."

"I'm guessing the coyote regretted his cowardice," said Daniel.

"Oh yes," Pablo said. "The revenge took many executions. That's how he got hooked up with Flores. His wrath was so devastating that Flores hired him, if for no other reason than to keep him close enough to watch. It wasn't long until he was part of the inner circle."

Willy stirred. "Chavez is loyal to Deems because he rescued his sister from a sex trafficking group," she said with sleep fuzzing her voice. "She was working at the villa as Flores' assistant. I think she was in love with him."

We all looked at her with our mouths open.

"How…?" I began.

"She was supposed to become my confidante, get me used to the idea that Flores would treat me with great respect and would not harm me, would even honor me. She told me she considered me to be the luckiest woman in the world. I liked her in an arm's-length sort of way. After I insulted Flores as best I could, I never saw her again. I hope she survived." Willy sagged against the window and went back to sleep.

I must have fallen asleep too, because the next thing I knew we were at what I assumed to be the south end of San Blas. The town seemed to be asleep, but there were traffic cones out and decorations along the uneven sidewalks. Early *Día de los Muertes* revelers were already walking the town. Pablo threaded his way through the narrow streets until we came to a frontage road that ran along a small marina. Boats of all sizes rested quietly on the smooth black water, some lit up, some dark. North of the marina we turned onto a dirt track. The change in the road awakened Willy, who groaned pleasantly and stretched. She rubbed her face with both hands and peered out the window.

"Where are we?" she asked in a sleepy voice.

"On the beach, just north of San Blas," Pablo answered.

"Where are we going?"

"Just guessing, but I think we're going to Jasper Cronk's surf camp."

"Very astute," said Pablo. "That's exactly where we are headed. We'll be there in about ten minutes."

"I hope he has food," Willy said. "I'm hungry enough to eat a whole cow, horns and all."

"Hooves?" I asked.

"Yep. Hooves too. I never got breakfast, lunch, or dinner yesterday."

"It is fortunate that you missed dinner last night," Daniel said. Your food was laced with Rohypnol."

Willy folded forward, gave a little groan.

"Mike was going to come get you this morning, during the confusion created by our killing of Senor Flores at breakfast, but we were tipped that you were to be drugged. So, we opted to move early. It was just circumstance that the other assault team attacked when they did."

"Who tipped you off?" asked Willy.

Pablo answered her question. "Doctor Relleas was passing information to my team," he said. "He was very worried that you would not survive the night."

"Doctor Relleas? I don't think he ever even spoke to me. I was just about to sit down to eat when the explosion happened. And you're saying that it wasn't you guys who set it off?"

"Nope. Mike was in there on his own."

She looked at me, eyes glimmering in the muted light of the dashboard.

"That explains a couple things I was wondering about, like those guys in the hallway speaking English. You'll have to tell me the whole story. "Do you think those guys got away from the fire?"

"What guys in the hallway?" Daniel and Pablo both asked. They weren't quite in sync, so it sounded pretty funny.

"Do you remember Jasper telling us that a guy we knew in Nam was lurking around town? Grimes is his name. He was actively involved in trying to get Jasper and me killed. He was a master sergeant working with the ARVN officer in charge of the indigenous at our camp. The ARVN officer was a Charlie spy. I was one of two guys who could prove it. That made me a walking target. Grimes delivered me orders to go on a recon. We weren't a hundred yards out of the gate when Charlie opened up on us. I lost two indigenous men immediately but managed to get everyone else out of there. We reacted well and survived. When we got back, I went to see Grimes. I lost my temper a little bit. He probably hasn't forgotten it either. He'd sent Jasper's patrol out too, but I caught them at the gate and told them not to go, that it was a setup. That same day we pulled our Special Forces men out of there. The army tried to find me for weeks, until I got out of there and flew home. I kept waiting for the other shoe to drop and wake up dead one day but was lucky—nothing ever came of it."

"Lots of stories like that in Nam," said Daniel. "We were the spooks. The regular forces did not know what to do with us. We were unconventional, which is quite the antithesis of the rest of the military."

"Sort of a shadow force?" Willy asked.

"More like a force in the shadows," I replied. "Our job was to teach the indigenous guys how to fight. I probably learned at least as much from them as they did from me."

"Truth," said Daniel.

"I've been thinking that the CIA guys, if that's who they were, helped my plan quite a bit. I think getting inside was much easier in the chaos they started. I should write the director a letter of thanks."

Pablo laughed. "Mike, I admire your positive attitude."

We rolled along the riprap road slowly. Up ahead, a light came into view.

"That should be Jasper's place," Pablo said.

The hair stood up on the back of my neck. The voices stirred. I always trusted the feeling.

"Stop the car," I said.

Pablo stopped the Ford, and we sat idling. He automatically turned off the headlights. Good man.

Daniel's eyes were hard on me.

"You'll have to humor me, but I want to go in on foot before we just assume everything is hunky-dory."

Daniel nodded. He had learned to trust my feelings too.

"Hunky-dory?" Willy asked.

I grinned at her but said nothing. I reached around and grabbed my pack and my CAR-15. I put the pack into the front seat between Willy and Pablo.

"There's a big knife, a couple grenades, and a .357 in there."

Pablo nodded.

"Pull back the hammer before shooting," I said to Willy. "You will have a much better chance of hitting what you're looking at."

She was no stranger to guns. Her eyes grew serious. She was suddenly afraid, but she was still in there. Her jaw set hard, and she was ready to do whatever needed doing.

Daniel got out on the other side, and we both clicked the doors closed. There was motion in the car as Pablo rummaged in the pack. Daniel and I moved carefully along the road. I could hear surf breaking to our left. I was sure there were tourists throughout this area and did not want to let any bullets fly.

"Meet you on the beach at the far end of the house," Daniel said.

We separated. I dropped down onto the sand, relishing the smell of the water and the waves. A moon graced the sky overhead, looking like a pale smile. The light from Jasper's place seemed to be in the courtyard in the middle of the structure. Like so many places in warm climates, the house itself surrounded a courtyard that became the primary living area. I loved the notion of it. When the weather was good I spent more time on my porch on the Willamette River than I did inside.

As my ears grew accustomed to the ambient sounds of the beach, I picked out a large motor idling on the water. I guessed it to be about three hundred yards off shore. After a short time looking, I was able to make out the long dim shape of a large boat pointed north. As I looked at the boat, I saw the flash of a paddle much closer. When I saw it again, it had moved farther away. I stood up and let out a long sigh. All I could do now was hope that Jasper was still alive. If Grimes had recognized me in the hallway before I whacked him, Jasper would certainly be at risk. I was assuming a lot from what I'd seen, but after a few minutes the engine of the boat rumbled, and the boat took off, heading north up the Sea of Cortez.

As I looked out to sea, I sensed Daniel to my right. I turned to see him standing quietly at the path leading up to the house. I went up and joined him.

"Apparently," I said, "Jasper's had visitors."

We found him in the small kitchen. He was lying in a pool of his own vomit and there was water everywhere. We cut the duct tape from his wrists and ankles and got the bleeding from his mouth and nose slowed down, but he still had trouble talking and breathing. When Daniel was satisfied that Jasper might live, he went to get Pablo and Willy.

"Just breathe," I said. "Talk later."

He kept trying to tell me something, and he probably thought it was important, but whatever it was could wait. There was misery in his eyes. Finally, he spat out a wad of something. He took a deep, shuddering breath.

"Bomb," he gasped. "Tripwire. Courtyard."

Just then, Daniel poked his head into the kitchen.

"Do not go traipsing through the courtyard," he said. "There is a claymore set up with a tripwire."

He was just so matter-of-fact. A guttural noise game from Jasper's throat, and he fell backward into the slop on the floor. He was trying his best to laugh.

"Hey," I said, "I know you would love to die laughing, but it is just too soon for that."

He stayed on the floor, still breathing raggedly. I looked at the room. To me, it was obvious that they'd used a water board technique on him. He had tape burns on his wrists and ankles, and there were bruises all over his arms. I helped him get into a kitchen chair that had been thrown into a corner. He rested his forearms on his thighs and put his head down between his knees. Slowly, his breathing evened and I could see him relax a bit. Every once in a while I put a hand on the back of his neck and squeezed softly. It seemed to work a little magic on Jasper, just like it did on Bucket.

Willy came into the kitchen and immediately started to clean up the mess. She didn't say a word. After a short while, Jasper realized that someone else was there and sat up. He took a deep breath, without any involuntary hesitations for the first time since we'd found him. He looked at Willy, who was intent upon her tasks. He leveled his eyes on me and raised an eyebrow. I nodded. He managed a small smile and stood.

"I'm gonna go clean up. I'll be back shortly to help."

Willy looked at him and smiled. She lit up the whole room. "Don't worry, I got it," she said. "It feels good just having something to do."

"Jasper, Willy. Willy, Jasper," I said.

They nodded to each other. Jasper gave me a meaningful look and beckoned me to follow.

We went out onto the beach. Jasper peeled off his T-shirt and shorts. He stood looking at the water. I took off my clothes too. We both stood there like birthday suit models.

"We were water-boarded in training, but there was nothing on the line. Those bastards have made me afraid to go into the water," he said.

"Can't have that."

"Nope." With a primal roar, he started sprinting to the sea, with me in close pursuit. We hit the water and dove through the small shore break. I watched Jasper very carefully when his face came up for air. He blew the salt water from his nose and mouth forcefully. I could see him fighting panic. After a couple breaths, he'd won the battle, I knew. His whole demeanor changed, and I was again treading water with the superb water man that I'd known most of my adult life. He was a surfer again, at home in the ocean. He spun around, facing out to sea, and with a powerful kick raised his body out of the water clear to his waist. His arm extended over his head and the middle finger of his right hand pointed to the sky.

"Fuck you!"

I chuckled as we swam to shore, but I was certain that there was more anger for him to express. Water had become, probably, the most important resource in Jasper's life. He loved everything about it. It was his connection to the world and had saved him from the demons we'd brought back from Vietnam. To torture him with it was to incur a wrath that I could barely imagine.

There was an outside shower at the north end of the house. Jasper stood under it for a long time, letting it run on his face. The waning night was warm and humid. The high grinning moon was still pale through the moisture in the air. I took my turn under the shower, rinsing the salt from my scalp. I turned and watched the never-ending play of moonlight and water. Jasper was studying the same thing.

"Did you recognize anyone?" I asked as I turned off the shower.

He sighed. "No. They were young, in their twenties, pretty well trained, but they weren't really warriors, at least the three guys who worked me over."

He paused, groping for words. "They were thugs. One of them had some kind of Eastern Seaboard urban accent and the other two were southern. They really enjoyed what they were doing to me. It gave them almost a sexual thrill, I think. It was sick. I think they wanted to get more creative, but the fourth guy, the one in charge, got what he wanted and ordered them to drop me and get out of there. When they saw what I assume were your lights, they took off in a hurry."

"What did he want?" I said, asking the obvious.

"Your name."

I was quiet.

"So I gave them a name."

I was quiet some more.

"John Elton," he said. "It was all I could come up with. If they'd had more time, they might have got more out of me."

"Like, maybe, Russell Leon?"

"I don't know. That water-boarding thing is pretty effective. You remember those training sessions."

I nodded. "They're gonna be pissed when they realize you threw them a knuckleball."

Jasper turned to me, his eyes dark and his face and lips swollen from the beating he'd endured.

"They weren't all knuckleballs. I remember telling them that you'd be walking back. They wanted to know where you were and where you were going. That's when I caved in and gave them something close to the truth. I wasn't kidding when I said the technique they used was effective. You get to a place inside yourself that you don't know. It's a place that I never want to visit again."

"How specific did you get?"

"I didn't know anything specific. By that time, I might have given them anything, made something up just to get them to stop, so it is good that I really knew nothing. But you can bet your last buck that they'll be watching the usual crossing spots. Pablo will have to come up with something creative."

I reached out and put my left hand on his shoulder. "Well, my brother, at least we got here when we did. They could have killed you."

He looked at me and smiled, but with his stiff lips it came off more as a grimace.

"I was in that place where I didn't mind dying if it would make what they were doing stop. I will have to swim every day to leave it somewhere behind me."

"But you do that anyway."

"The woman," he said. "She's why you came?"

"Yep."

"Is she the One?"

I didn't know what to say. Jasper knew me as well as I did. Perhaps not as well as Daniel, but close enough.

"From my side of the street, I'm pretty sure she is. But it's a two-way street."

Jasper radiated exasperation, but he said nothing more. I knew this conversation wasn't over.

Daniel and Pablo came out to where we stood. Jasper gave them the nutshell account of what he'd just told me, and Daniel told us he'd disabled the courtyard claymore.

"It is face-down under that small palm in the center."

Jasper nodded. "I'll have to find a safe place for it."

"Will it travel?" I asked Daniel.

"Yes."

"We could take it off your hands," I said to Jasper.

"By all means," he said. "Think of it as a party favor."

I went back into the house. The décor was right out of a sixties surf movie. I felt like a teenager again. Willy was standing looking at a framed photo in her hand. I came up behind her and looked over her shoulder. It was Jasper and me, probably sometime in 1971, sitting in front of a hootch. I tried to recall the picture being taken but couldn't. We were smiling around cigarettes, eyes squinting at the camera. We held our guns casually, but they were ready. They looked like extensions of our arms, which of course they were. It was after Son Tay. We'd only been in the same camp very briefly, so it must have been taken then. It was probably a few days before Grimes had tried to kill us.

Willy put the picture down and turned to me. We shared a long hug. Neither of us caressed the other; we just held on. She let out a long sigh.

"My entire life," she said, "is completely upside-down. I am not going to be the same person I was before this madness began. I just want to get back to the H-Bar-H and spend a week by myself riding the timber line and sorting through all this stuff."

"Can I come visit?" I asked hopefully.

She didn't answer immediately, but her hug tightened a little.

"Yes," she said finally. "But you are one of the things I need to figure out."

"I know. I'm not going anywhere."

She pulled back. "How can I know that?" Her eyes searched my face. "You could be dead in five minutes. Somebody could shoot you tomorrow, or the next day, or the next. You could just disappear and never be heard from again. You have very powerful enemies. I don't know how to handle that. I'm not sure I can."

"I don't know what to tell you. I am very good at staying alive, but I understand, I think, your dilemma. I live my life as it comes. I'm not a planner. You showed up in my life, and I can't imagine the rest of it without you in it. I know that's not really fair to you and your uncertainty, but it is what it is, and I'll have to deal with it, whatever conclusion you come to."

Willy stepped back from the hug and gave my chest a two-handed pat. "Let's take a walk."

We went back out to the beach. Pablo and Daniel were nowhere to be seen, but I heard voices around the corner, where I assumed the Ford was parked. We turned right at the tide line and walked up the beach in an easy gait. The sky on our right was a bright gray. To our left it radiated pinks, purples and golds that artists spent lifetimes trying to match.

"You must be tired," she said.

"I'm still running on adrenalin, I think, but I could certainly use some down time."

"How are we going to get back to the States?" she asked.

It was a reasonable question.

"I'm not exactly sure. I'm fairly confident that it will require walking."

"You mean we're going to sneak back into our own country? What about the border patrol?"

"At least a thousand people make it across every week, maybe more. And we will be much better equipped than they are. I'm more worried about the CIA than I am the border patrol. And we still have Deems and Chavez to worry about. Those guys will, most likely, have to go underground for a while, but they are not done with us, not by a long shot."

"Shit. This adventure stuff is a lot easier when you read about it."

I drew her against me and used my best Humphrey Bogart voice. "Stick with me, Sweetheart. I'll feed you peaches and cream from a glass slipper."

"Yuck," she said. But it made her laugh. Holding on to that levity, she said, "Race you back!"

She took off like a long-limbed hare. I fell into an easy lope behind her. She needed to run, to exert herself, to let her body assume control. I could barely imagine the stress she'd been under and the strangeness that the last several days had visited upon her. When the light of the house appeared, I kicked it up a bit and came alongside her. She grinned at me and found another gear. I lengthened my stride and timed my catching her to right as we got to the house.

Willy, laughing and looking just like herself, said she was going to find the shower. I told her I'd do my best to find her some clean clothes. Her underwear from home was still in my pack.

The guys were sprawled on the patio. "How is she doing?" Daniel asked. He was splayed out in a large wicker chair with a large glass of what looked like orange juice on the glass table in front of him.

"I think she's doing okay," I said. "There's a lot of stuff she hasn't processed yet, but I think she'll do fine."

"Let's look at that arm," Daniel said.

As Daniel rummaged in the first-aid kit, I regarded Jasper. "How are you doing? Your face looks much improved."

He tried to smirk at me, but it hurt. His lips were still swollen, and bruising had started around his nose and mouth. With his two-day whiskers, he looked like a peach that had lain on the ground in the hot sun.

"I will heal," he said. "You are stuck with your face forever."

This got a laugh from Pablo. "'Why did God make women so beautiful and man with such a loving heart?'" he said.

Jasper rolled his eyes. "I should have given up the name Walker Percy."

"Walker Percy would not mind," I said. "He's been dead for quite some time."

"Five years," said Pablo sadly.

Just then we heard a car coming up the access road. Daniel and I were up immediately, my arm forgotten, Willy's clothes certainly forgotten. Pablo stayed where he was but was very alert, watching Jasper. We were all watching Jasper.

A small maroon pickup came into view. Two surfboards were strapped with bungee cords in the bed.

"It's Maria," Jasper said. "She has come to fix us breakfast and to tease us into being dirty old men."

We all breathed, and I took this opportunity to ask Jasper about clean clothes for Willy. He pointed me to the bottom drawer of the dresser in his bedroom. She was just getting out of the shower when I got to the bathroom with the shorts and T-shirt I'd found and hastily covered herself with a towel.

I was dumbstruck at the physical impact seeing her had on me. I took a deep breath and looked away to clear her some space. It must have been utterly obvious. She smiled.

"I do want to make love to you again," she said, "but I want it to be in my bed, in full daylight, without a pistol hanging nearby."

I liked that she was thinking of us in such a future. A time without a gun close by felt so far away to me.

I left her there with the clothes. From the kitchen, the smell of frying chorizo nearly brought tears to my eyes. I couldn't remember eating anything recently and poked my head into the kitchen. There was a young woman in a T-shirt and shorts, a swimsuit showing through her shirt, arranging eggs, tortillas, and cheese, on the counter. Her legs were nicely lined with long firm swimmer's muscles, and as she turned to see who was there, I saw an open and honest face, with more Spanish features than Indian.

"You are Mike," she said with just the trace of an accent. "I recognize you from the picture." She nodded at the photo Willy had been looking at.

"Yep," I said. "And you are Maria." I stepped into the kitchen and offered my hand.

She clapped the flour from her hands and stepped over. Her hand was warm and small. She crooked her finger in a beckoning motion, and I leaned over. She kissed me on the cheek. There was a citrus smell to her that had an earthy tone with it.

"Cronkhead says you are famished," she said. "I will have breakfast ready in just a few minutes."

"Cronkhead?" I smiled.

"When he was teaching me English, Jasper was too hard, so I just called him Cronkhead. He did not seem to mind. Too much."

I excused myself to go and find good ol' Cronkhead. I felt that we had a small window of safety. We had to get back to the States as quickly as possible. I hated the fact that I didn't know where Deems and Chavez were or what they were up to. I also really wanted to see Bucket.

Pablo was just waking up from a courtyard nap in an oversized chair. He ruffled his mustache, stood up, and stretched his muscular frame. "Is that chorizo?"

It was a rhetorical question. Just then, Willy came through the archway that led to the courtyard.

"Breakfast is in five minutes," she announced.

"Is that grease on your chin?" I asked.

"Maria wanted me to make sure it was perfect. And it is," she said as she rubbed her chin.

"Don't really eat the hooves," I said to her. She snorted just like Daniel.

The food was glorious.

I was sitting in a large rattan chair digesting and undergoing Daniel's attention to my arm when Willy and Maria returned from a walk. Apparently, fixing breakfast had made them sisters. Maria came over and kissed Jasper on the forehead. Her fingers gently traced the bruises on his face.

"I have to go. You know how Mama is," she said.

Jasper nodded. I was too sleepy to even raise my eyebrow.

She looked at me. "I hope to see you again, Miguel. Take good care of yourself and of Señora Hayes." She regarded my recently bandaged arm, but didn't bring it up. Willy may have clued her in.

I smiled and gave her a thumbs-up. "Yes Ma'am."

"I can take care of myself," said Willy from the doorway, "but he has proven to be very useful of late." A smile colored her voice.

As Willy walked Maria out to her truck, Jasper stood and stretched.

"You guys sleep," he said. "I'll keep an eye out."

Pablo grunted something.

"Wake me if you get sleepy," Daniel said.

Morpheus came for me on padded feet. I never heard Jasper's response.

THIRTY-SIX

Bad dreams are not things to cast aside as "not real." The emotions are real even though the body is not threatened in the conscious plane. As I slept after breakfast, I dreamed a slide show of still images, each stranger than the last. I could almost feel the sparks in my brain as each image changed. There was no musical accompaniment, just a far-off wind that rushed through cold dry mountains. I saw my father and my mother. I saw Daniel and his mother. I saw Daniel and myself with our father. But there was something unsettling about each. I could not decide what because the images went by too quickly.

The speed of the images increased, but the clarity of each intensified. The subject matter seemed to be chronological. I saw the ranch and my old cow pony Spirit. I saw the trails we'd ridden around and through the Blue Mountains. I saw cattle and the cowboys, both white and Indian, who worked with us at roundup time. I smelled burning hair as the branding iron was applied and heard the bellows of cows in pain. Elk in a broad meadow. Elk hanging in a tree, whole and partially skinned. Pictures of high school whizzed by, almost in a blur. My father on his horse Blackie with his rope looped around the saddle horn. Bison in the upper pasture. Shots of Fort Bragg from the air. Boys in uniforms laughing. Asian women in a darkened nook with abundant décolletage. A helicopter lifting off from a muddy airstrip.

Then, things began to slow down, and I felt stirrings of fear. I saw a dead and bloated water buffalo and smelled the pungent gas that leaked from its body. I saw a decapitated boy lying in a rice paddy. Body parts festooning bushes. The head of a dog in the middle of a path. A young girl clinging to the body of her dead mother. A small man in black clothing at the instant a bullet slammed into his forehead. The sad deep-set eyes of an old man staring at what was left of his left leg. More body parts hanging from bushes and trees. A perfectly conical breast resting by itself at the base of a mulberry tree. Men with blackened faces huddled in the belly of a Sikorski gunship. A young Jasper laughing at me.

Suddenly it all changed to a sequence of dead men arrayed in all manner of positions, on their backs, on their faces, grotesquely twisted with rigor mortis, sometimes looking as if they were peacefully sleeping. They were American, Vietnamese, Montagnard, Korean, Australian, and some I could not identify. What they had in common was that they were all dead and had been killed by their own kind.

The dream changed from a succession of stills to a slow documentary pan. My internal camera swept across piles of dead in a field like Shiloh. Bodies from Vietnam mixed with bodies clad in ragged Butternut and Union Blue. Old men in olive drab on a beach screaming silently to the sky. I saw Lakota and Cheyenne. I saw Nimi'ipuu frozen to armored personnel carriers. I could smell the rot of it. I could hear the buzzing of the flies gorging themselves on decay and ruin.

Then, I saw myself in a long tan coat, hatless, hands thrust deep into the pockets, walking among the dead. I was searching for something or someone. I came to a small creek that tumbled over a short fall. At the base of the fall I could see something in the water. I squatted to look. Daniel was there, and so was Willy, in repose. The water did not touch them, but flowed around them, as if it were protecting them. As a great wave of sadness and despair overtook me, I looked through the waterfall and saw Bucket, ears up and tongue lolling from his dog grin.

"We all die," he said to me in my own voice. "It's the way it works."

I tried to speak but couldn't. Tears rolled down my face.

Jesús Chavez appeared next to me with the familiarity of an old friend, a black pistol in his hand. He shot through the waterfall at Bucket, but Bucket was already gone. He turned and grinned at me. I was trying to draw my gun and could not find it. Chavez laughed. Deems came up behind him. He was laughing too. Then the creek and waterfall turned to fire, and it raged around me. I tried to see Daniel and Willy, but they were gone. Deems and Chavez were covered with blood, and their laughter died away in the roar of the flames. I felt the heat on my shoulders, but the rest of me began to grow numb and cold. I was left standing in the fire but felt myself beginning to freeze. I tried jumping up and down to keep myself warm and couldn't. I felt weight holding me down. I looked and saw emaciated hands, curled and dried like curios, looped around my belt. It dawned on me that these were the hands of the people I had killed. I tried harder to jump and couldn't. I was turning into a vast tree, the hands running over me like bark. I heard Willy calling my name, and I strained toward the bell of her voice. The hands reached my face, and I shot up as if from a trebuchet.

I was back in Jasper's courtyard. I looked at Willy, close enough to smell.

Her face was taut with worry. Daniel stood next to me with his hand on my right shoulder.

I took Willy's hand and squeezed it. I looked up at Daniel.

"Pictures and a movie."

"How nice for you," he said. "Popcorn?"

"There was fire. I could've made corn pop."

"What was burning?" Willy asked. She let go of my hand and brushed something away from the corner of my eye.

"I don't know," I said. "Maybe it was just the air."

I shuddered at the thought of it and stood up to go to the kitchen. I needed water.

I drank a quart fast enough to make my eyes swim and took a deep breath. I looked at my watch, but the time didn't register.

"How long was I asleep?" I called to nobody in particular.

"About two hours," Daniel said from the archway into the courtyard. "Pablo and Jasper went to fuel up Jasper's boat. They are going to come get us, and we will move farther north, probably up to Puerto Peñasco. From there, we will play it as it lies."

I looked at my watch again. It was full daylight. I was feeling impatient.

"It's going to take us at least a week to get up there by boat," I said. "What about the airplane? I mean, come on, it's gotta be almost a thousand miles. If we average six miles an hour, that's a week."

Daniel came and leaned on the counter. "Pablo got a phone call," he said. "The police are looking for two gringos and a redhead. The *Federales* are still on alert too. And I got a text message a little while ago that says the CIA really wants to find us."

"Probably just to chat," I said.

"Like the chat those boys had with Jasper." Daniel smoothed the hair away from his face and. "Overland would be quicker, but traveling by boat should be safer. I think it is our best shot. You know as well as I do that hurrying through things like this will get you killed."

I knew he was right, but I could not shake my impatience.

"The CIA will find us, but I want it to be on the other side of the border. We will have to deal with them. Will your contacts be of any help?"

"I asked them to contact Jepps in Portland and apprise him of the situation. We are going to need all the help we can get."

Willy was leaning against the sink, listening intently. "Does any of this feel like a setup to you guys?" she asked. "I'm still trying to understand why all of this happened. Why did a government agency kidnap me and deliver me to a Mexican cartel? Because they wanted my ranch? Because Flores told them to? That seems like a real stretch to me. Why were you"—she looked at Daniel— "recruited to kill the leader of that same cartel, only to have it called off at the last moment? Why was the raid that blew up half of that villa staged at the very same time? I mean, who's pulling the strings here? None of it makes any sense. At least, not to me."

I looked at Daniel with a thin knowing smile.

"Cowboys," I said.

"Cowboys?" Willy echoed. Her eyes told me I was crazy.

"Cowboys," I repeated. "The American cowboy myth, anyway. The people on the end that is mostly invisible to us don't communicate directly very often. Oh sure, the FBI and the DEA have been known to hook up a little and share resources and notes, but neither outfit shows all of their cards. They like to be on their own, partly because it hides accountability but also because they like the freedom to improvise. The intelligence departments are similar to Special Forces in that regard, I think. They can be unconventional. They can use tactics that may be illegal or morally suspect, depending on who they are as people, as human beings."

"And do not forget the egos involved," Daniel said. "That is a large factor in games like this. When a situation dissolves into a pissing match, as this one seems to be heading for, it just becomes a scramble to see who ends up with the least egg on the face."

"Shit rolls downhill," I added, "and we're at the bottom of the hill. Not only are our butts on the line here, getting back home won't mean, necessarily, that we're done with this. We will need help from high places to get some very pissed-off people off our backs."

Willy was livid. "Games?" she sputtered. "They think this is a game? My whole existence has been thrown into turmoil, and you're telling me that these people consider it a game?" Veins stood out from her neck.

"Yes," I said. "And it is very important that you always remember that."

She looked at me with her mouth half-open, not knowing what to say. Her eyes were sabers and had the same determined set that I'd seen in the villa garage just before I'd lit off the claymore.

"It's hard to fight ghosts," Daniel said, "but it can be done."

"For the next few weeks," I said, "we will probably have to be ghosts. We will have no friends, other than each other."

Willy took a deep breath. Her shoulders lost their edge and rounded again.

Her hands relaxed. Her brow was still knitted, but her eyes lost the hardness of a few seconds earlier.

"You relax well," I said. "Where did you learn that?"

"Horses. I'm treating this whole ridiculous scenario like I would approach riding an unbroken horse. The horse would pick up on my attitude and respond in kind."

"Spoken like a true ranch girl," Daniel said, grinning at her.

"Coming from a ranch boy, I'll take that as a compliment."

Out on the water, we heard a whistle. It was familiar to me. Jasper and I had used it in Nam. Loosely translated, this version of it meant "all clear—gotta move."

We piled our stuff into the dinghy and Jasper rowed us out to his cabin cruiser. It was beautiful, with classic lines and lots of teak and mahogany.

"Where the hell did you come up with this?" There seemed to be no end to Jasper's ability to attract beauty into his life.

"This," he said proudly, "is an Elco forty-foot tri-cabin cruiser. It was built in New Jersey in 1931 and ended up in Mazatlán, where it sat for years, slowly rotting away. I got it for a song and spent six years restoring her as best I could. It'll cruise all day at eight knots and handles rough sea and the bad currents here in the Sea of Cortez very well."

We passed the packs up to Pablo and clambered aboard. I could feel the diesel motor idling through the clean teak deck. I helped Jasper haul the dinghy aboard and lash it in its place on the aft coachroof. It had *Maria* nicely scripted on its transom. I traced the lines of it with my fingers.

"Ever been an uncle before?" Jasper asked me.

I looked at him and smiled. "I was curious about that. *Ella es su hija?*" I asked.

"Yes. She was born not too long after you left here to go home to Oregon. Isabela, her mother, and I talked about getting married, but I just couldn't do it. But I promised her I would always be there for her and the child."

"Isn't that kind of like marriage?"

"I suppose so, but we never did live together. We are still friends and spend some time together every week. She doesn't like it when I sleep over."

"Because of what people think?"

"No. She is also very strong-minded and has a big heart, which is how she has established her place in her community even though she was an unwed mother. No, because of my dreams. She is afraid of my memories."

Willy's voice interrupted us. "Where would you like me to camp? I want to lie down and see if I can actually get some normal sleep."

Jasper pulled at his ear and smiled. "I don't really want to be presumptuous here, but I guessed that you and Mike could share the aft cabin." He pointed to the narrow ladder just under the bow of the dinghy we'd secured to the coach-roof. "It's not a lot of room for the two of you, Mike being a sizeable human, but it should work okay. I mean, it'll help that you seem to like each other."

Willy's eyes smiled at me. "Yeah. He's okay."

I mumbled something reciprocal, and Jasper showed her how to navigate the ladder and open the door, which he called a hatch. I stuck my head down there and was surprised at the size of the cabin. It was mostly bed, but there was a low-slung table with a lamp and even a small closet. Sailors would call it a locker. Another door was in the port corner of the forward bulkhead, and I assumed it led to a head.

Willy sat on the edge of the bed. "This will be cozy."

"I will try to be careful," I said, "not to overwhelm the space."

"I will do my best to be patient."

The boat surged forward, and I had to catch myself from falling on my head. I heard Willy laughing as I made my way forward to the pilot's cabin. Jasper was explaining the controls. I paid attention. We would all have to take a watch at the wheel. Pablo was at the chart table with a triangle and a pencil. I peeked over his shoulder. It looked, I said, like we were going to run the gap between Isla Isabel and Islas Marfas and hold that course until we had to clear Mazatlán and turn farther west before the final plot up to Puerto Peñasco.

Pablo ruffled his mustache. "Something like that."

We ran north until the light of the day started to fade.

After taking a turn at the wheel, Daniel was leaned back in his seat with his hands locked behind his head. "I believe I will go stretch out and get some shut-eye."

I took the helm for an hour or so. I was wary of sleep after my dreams, but I remembered how quickly Jasper had jumped back into the water after something much more serious than a nightmare, and I went back to the aft cabin. After working my way down the short ladder and angling myself through the narrow hatchway, I vowed that I would never again scoff at people who practice yoga. Decades of tai chi had helped me, though, and I was just beginning to congratulate myself on movement well done when my head slammed into an overhead beam.

"You okay?" Willy snickered.

"No," I said, rubbing the crown of my head.

I sat on the bed and pulled off my shorts and T-shirt. Pulling down the sheet, I very carefully slid in beside her as she lay on her right side facing the starboard bulkhead. She was naked. This produced a very predictable reaction, which poked her in the small of her back.

"Sorry about Mr. Happy," I said. "He just has a mind of his own."

She reached her left hand between us. "Wow, he really is happy."

I sighed.

She gave me an affectionate squeeze and withdrew her hand. "Maybe tomorrow. I know I said I wanted to wait until we got back to my house, but I don't think I can wait that long."

I sighed again.

"How's your arm?"

"It throbs like the rest of me," I said, poking her in the back again, "but is far less pleasant."

"We will look after both conditions in the morning," she murmured.

As I listened to her breathing deepen and felt the pulse of the diesel thrum through the boat, I was suddenly as happy as I had ever been in my life. I considered this and found it completely acceptable. I held the feeling close and knew that I would feel this way, somewhere in the labyrinth of who I was, at some level, for the rest of my life. The only uncertainty I had was how long that might be, but I decided that it didn't really matter.

When I awoke, the starboard porthole was brilliantly lit, and the port side was gray. I reached my right arm toward Willy, but she wasn't there. I heard water running in the head. The door opened, and Willy stepped out. I marveled at her body, lit to a golden glow on one side and shadowed on the other. She reached down and flipped the sheet from me. She studied me intently, and I responded. Neither of us said a word. Bending down, she crawled over me and straddled my hips. The heat of her engulfed me in its unique embrace. She buried her face in my neck then rose up. Careful of my left arm and shoulder, she dipped her head to kiss the bandage.

We locked eyes.

"First things first," she said.

"Yes," I agreed.

She began to move, and I went with her. It was gentle, then forceful, then gentle again. This continued as we climbed the mountain together and then leaped from it, soaring down long ridges and swooping through green valleys until we came to rest in a warm tangle of arms, legs, and lips. I had never before experienced anything even remotely like it. It was a brand-new country for me, but it didn't feel foreign. It felt like home.

Willy was the first to break our silence. "That was probably the most amazing experience of my life."

"I was just thinking the exact same thing." My voice was husky.

"I think," she said, "that no matter what happens, we just may be stuck with each other, for better or worse."

"In sickness and in health."

She reached her arms around me and hugged me with every ounce of herself.

"Till death do us part," she whispered into my ear.

I felt her tears on my neck. I hugged her back with a feeling as wide as the sea. She rose up and kissed the corner of my eye.

"Your eyes are leaking," she said.

"They're sweating," I said. "This much happiness makes them sweat. There just no place else for the happiness to go."

"Oh. Sweating. That's quite manly."

"Yes."

Her lips parted with a smile. "I can think of another place for happiness to go."

She showed me, and she was right.

"In fact, I think we'll promote him to Sir Happy. He's so much more than just a mister.

I was okay with that. You bet.

THIRTY-SEVEN

We ran northward for most of a week, taking turns at the wheel and sharing the galley duties. Willy proved to be good at the helm. Jasper sat with her a lot and ran scenarios past her. Her instincts were good. Daniel and Pablo, both navy guys, talked to her about weather and strategy and what to do in following seas, in diagonal seas, in heavy water, and anything else they could think of. She soaked it up.

I spent most of my time loving Willy, contemplating the ocean, reveling in the warmth, and trying to heal my arm. It was sore, but not swollen. I left the bandage off after the fourth day and gave the wound as much sun as I dared. It was still a bit angry looking and tender, but it wasn't hot to the touch. Motion was beginning to return to my shoulder.

I thoroughly cleaned my weapons and got the pack in order. Daniel and I went over the map that Major Lewis had given us back when we'd left the air force base. Willy sat with us too and studied it, asking questions about terrain and the availability of water.

"There is water," said Daniel, "but both the border patrol and the Shadow Wolves keep a very close eye on it. The only reason to go there is if it's life-and-death."

"Isn't the whole thing life-and-death?" Willy asked.

"Well, yes," Daniel said. "But there are varying degrees of how bad it is and how bad it can get. Michael and I have learned, almost"—he smiled—"where our limits are."

Willy looked at the two of us. "I cannot imagine where those limits might be."

"I would like it best if I never really knew. That way," I said, "I can always think of myself as a tough guy ready for anything."

Jasper turned from his place at the wheel.

"Michael will never find those limits because they keep moving. Just about the time you think he might be at the end of his rope, the rope magically adds a few feet to itself. To those that have fought with him and against him he is a legend in every mind but his own. It's just too bad that most of the guys who have fought against him can't add their two cents to the commentary."

"Hell, I'm no legend. I just like breathing."

But I had to admit that his vocal testimony felt pretty good.

"Michael does not fight alone," Daniel said. "He has a large force, sometimes at his command and sometimes as his leader. Sometimes, I hear them singing."

Willy's eyes got big.

"He's told me this before," I said. "I think what he means is that I have multiple personalities. He thinks I'm nuts."

Daniel laughed. "We have had this conversation many times. He will not accept my vision of it. We will go around and around about it forever."

"I just refuse to use myth and magic to explain myself."

Jasper surrendered the wheel to Pablo and came back to stand by us.

"What about the time you ran up that cliff face?" he asked in an almost accusatory tone.

Daniel's grin dwarfed the cabin. "I have not heard this story. What cliff face?"

Jasper loved this story. Truth be told, I loved it too, but for different reasons. He loved it because of the understandable skepticism people expressed when he told it. I loved it because I couldn't explain it. It was very dream-like, but I had absolutely no explanation for it, other than, perhaps, the world is not always as it seems.

"After Mike had his, um, argument with Sergeant Grimes," Jasper began, "we were both on the dodge, trying to stay out of trouble until we could get the hell out of the country. We were both short. It was where all of our training in being unconventional paid off. We volunteered to do training sessions in some very out-of-the-way places. About two weeks before Mike would fly home, we were in an A-camp up by the Laotian border working with some Montagnard guys. It was a good crew, and these guys were motivated.

"We were patrolling not far from camp when we ran into Charlie. They didn't see us at first, so we decided to set up an ambush. We ran through the forest along the base of a small escarpment, about thirty feet high. It was almost straight up and down. Mike had stayed behind to watch the enemy. I got the guys in place, and we heard a scattering of shots. Here comes Mike at a dead sprint with a look of utter concentration. All of us fully expected him to take cover where we were, but at the last possible second, he turned left and ran straight up the cliff. All of us watched him do it. Two NVA guys had rounded the corner behind him and saw him do it. They just stopped and stared with shock on their faces. Nobody fired a weapon. All of us, me, the Montagnards, the NVA guys, just sat there open-mouthed.

"Mike got to the top and melted into the trees. It couldn't have taken more than two or three seconds at most. The NVA guys just turned and ran the other way, hollering something about *Briaou* and *Khi-Trau*.

"Our Montagnards were stunned. Nobody said a word. We just looked at each other. Then, Mike reappeared at the top and just, kind of sliding and kind of free-falling, calmly came down the sheer cliff face on his butt. He landed softly at the bottom and walked over to us as if nothing out of the ordinary had happened. The indigenous guys wouldn't even look at him, and I must admit that I was also having trouble finding my voice."

"You guys looked like you'd seen a ghost," I said.

My memory of the event was different in only one important aspect. There had been little hand-holds going up the cliff, like short vines, every few feet. I used them to go up and used them again to come back down. Jasper claims that there was nothing on that cliff face, but I remembered distinctly. I remembered the feel of them in my hands.

I said as much.

"You say that," Jasper countered, "but there was nothing there."

"Sure there was, otherwise, how could I have done it?"

"That's the issue." Jasper laughed. "That's exactly the issue."

Daniel had his chin in his hand. "What did you hear while this was going on?" he asked.

I thought about it. "There is nothing definite in my memory, but there was a sound. I just don't remember what, exactly. I remember the smell, though. It was juniper, like home."

Daniel nodded and smiled slightly to himself. He stayed quiet.

"I have heard about *brujos* doing the seemingly impossible like that," Pablo said as he eyed me warily.

"I'm no *brujo*," I said. "It was really no big deal. Going up and down, it didn't seem all that steep to me. I was surprised when I looked at it again before we moved on."

"Did you see your hand-holds?" Daniel asked.

"No," I admitted. "I must have pulled them out on the way down." I had never spent much time thinking about running up that cliff. I knew it was perplexing, but I never questioned it. I didn't think we were supposed to understand everything. To me, it was just another instance of the world being vast and tiny at the same time. It all comes from a place that you don't explain because you can't. I am automatically suspicious of people who claim they have it figured out.

I felt Willy come up behind me. She put her hands on the tops of my shoulders and gave a squeeze. I caught her left hand and kissed it lightly. She rose up on her tiptoes and kissed the back of my head.

"You are full of surprises," she said.

"I have never been disappointed by any of Michael's surprises," Daniel said. "And I do not think you ever will be either."

I flexed my trapezoids, remembering the feel of Willy's small squeeze. A quick stab shot down my arm, but I was encouraged by its brevity. I smiled at Willy. "You have surprised me several times. They have been consistently pleasing, but that is no surprise in itself."

She actually blushed, which surprised me.

THIRTY-EIGHT

That evening I was sitting on the bed in the aft cabin trying to memorize features on the map of the border country when the thrum of the diesel motor changed its pitch, and I felt the boat slow to a crawl. I folded the map and went up on deck. There were no stars, and a steady south wind had come up. The temperature had dropped significantly. I could see city lights off the bow.

In the pilot cabin, Jasper was at the wheel with Willy at his side. Daniel and Pablo were huddled around the small radar screen.

They all looked at me when I came in. "Smells like rain," I said.

"There's a *chubasco* churning on the other side of Baja Sur," Jasper said. "The weather people don't know what it's going to do yet. But we can, at least, count on rain."

"Do they think it will become a hurricane?"

"It already has been a hurricane but lost some organization and is currently back to a tropical storm. Nobody knows for sure," said Pablo, "but there is a lot of moisture in it. Cabo San Lucas has water running in the streets. They have assigned the name Kiko to it."

"Isn't it kind of late in the year for hurricanes?" Willy asked.

Pablo ruffled his mustache. "The season officially runs to the end of this month, but yeah, it's late for a powerful one. I guess it mostly depends on water temperature," he said, "and this is an El Niño year, so the water has been warm. Back in September, Hurricane Ismael killed over a hundred people here in Mexico. Half of them were fishermen right here in the Sea of Cortez. I was running a rescue/recovery crew out of Puerto Vallarta when I got the call that involved me with the operation that quickly became the one Daniel was eventually recruited for. Two months later, here I am."

Jasper eased the throttle up a bit and the ride smoothed out.

"You should probably get your Mexican face on," he said to Willy. "We'll be ashore in about forty minutes."

She nodded and went aft to get her things together. I stayed on deck with Daniel.

"I have a strange feeling about this next hike," I said. "If we get separated, I want you to get Willy out of wherever we are and get her back to Oregon. If you don't know where I am, don't wait for me. Just go."

Daniel looked at me, his dark eyes unreadable. "If we are good and we are careful, no one will even see us."

"That's true," I said. "But I think there will be a lot of scrutiny. I think the cartel boys will be watching, and I know the CIA will be watching. Having Deems and Chavez still out there is making me a tad queasy. I think it will be a crowded crossing. Promise me that you will get her the hell out of there if things should go south."

"Mike..."

"Promise me, dammit."

He looked at me, and the years fell away from us. Suddenly, he was fifteen, and I was eighteen. A hundred shared images passed between us, all of them familiar and bright. A gust of wind blew his shining braid over his shoulder, where it rested against his upper chest, and the moment passed. We were again middle-aged men standing on the deck, each looking into a lifetime.

He nodded. "I promise."

"Thank you."

I reached out with my right hand and grabbed the inside of his right forearm. He gripped mine in return. We embraced quickly and strongly.

"Let's get home," I said.

We docked at a transient slip on the north side of the harbor, and Jasper and Pablo went to register with the harbormaster. Daniel, Willy, and I stayed with the boat. Willy had returned herself to the beautiful Mexican woman. She wore a maroon cotton top with a white shawl around her shoulders and a long cream-colored skirt with a zigzag pattern circumnavigating it. She was utterly lovely except for the wan look on her face.

"At least Jasper has good taste in women's clothes," she said, "because this wig is not pleasant. It's really hot."

Jasper came back with a sheaf of papers. He tucked them inside a cupboard to the left of the wheel in the pilot's cabin. He understood the "where's Pablo?" looks on our faces and smiled.

"He's gone to find a vehicle," he said.

"He has proven to be quite good at that," Daniel said.

"Do we have any kind of plan?" Willy asked.

Daniel and I looked at each other.

"Plan?" I said. "We need a plan?"

"The crux of it," Daniel said, "is to get into the desert without being seen. That will be more difficult than it sounds. From there, we will reckon our way to some place we can get a room and rent a car. When that's done, we will drive back to Oregon."

"And live happily ever after," I added.

She looked at me and shook her head, but not unkindly.

I helped Jasper secure and lock the boat. We stood at the bow and watched the lights play on the black water.

"Apparently, you are going up to the border with us."

He nodded. "I want to keep Pablo company on the way back, and maybe I need to make sure that you get started okay."

"What about the boat?"

"I think Pablito and I will drive back to San Blas. I will fly the plane up later and get the boat. Maybe Maria will want to come. We could take a couple weeks to get back, do some fishing and diving, and just unwind a bit. I have had some of my old dreams. I haven't had any of those in a long time."

"I'm sorry. This whole thing has triggered some of that old stuff."

Jasper looked at the sky to watch the swirl of cloud that was getting lower by the minute.

"When we got back from Nam," he said, "we both had post-traumatic stress disorder, but we didn't even know that there was such a thing. We'd had enemies on both sides, were strung out from stress, angry with authority, and deeply disillusioned. We drank too much, didn't know how to solve problems without force, and had no idea how to behave. Mexico saved us, gave us enough space and time to appreciate something as simple as a sunrise."

"There were some beautiful sunrises in Vietnam."

"True," Jasper countered, "sunsets too. But if you think about it, wasn't the primary beauty that you were still alive to see it?

"Reckon so," I said, thinking about it.

"We got to be kids again when we came down here and got to behave badly without much consequence, other than bad hangovers. Nobody bothered us. We were allowed to be ourselves and, eventually, the good resurfaced, and we were able to get on with our lives. But even now, all these years later, years of good life, that old stuff still shows up. Last night I dreamed about falling out of the sky at Son Tay, the sickening bounce when the chopper hit the ground, the fear, the adrenalin, the killing frenzy that followed. I sat straight up in the pilot's berth and slammed my head on the overhead. I guess all I'm saying is that all that stuff is still in here," he tapped his head, "and I don't think it ever disappears. Sometimes, it just pisses me off. Getting water-boarded last week didn't help either."

"I have walled a lot of it off," I said. "Part of me says that it is a terrible thing to be very good at killing people. Another part of me, because of what I do, is grateful that I am. Sometimes, I wonder about the quality of my character. How can I live with it? I'm glad that I can, but I get suspicious of how I do it. But until I know that it's broken, I'm not going to fix anything."

A horn sounded up in the parking lot above the dock. We looked up to see Pablo waving from a relatively new Lincoln Continental. We could see his grin clear across the fifty yards that separated us.

Willy was aft, standing by the coachroof of the cabin we'd shared. I hoisted my pack and went to her.

"I will never forget our time in there. When I am an old woman, I will remember the magic of it and will understand that it doesn't matter how or when, it just matters that it is."

I shifted my pack and took her hand. "*Hoka Hey,*" I said.

We stashed our stuff in the big trunk and climbed in. Jasper got in front with Pablo. Willy, Daniel, and I slid into the back.

"This is like a party room," Willy said from the middle.

"I am not going to ask where you came up with this one," Daniel said.

Pablo laughed. "I have a good friend who is a *bombero* in Cabo San Lucas. This is his grandmother's car."

"Do firemen make good money?" I asked.

"No, they are volunteers. He also waits tables for wealthy gringos, which pays pretty well."

"As long as the wealthy gringos tip."

He nodded. "Yes. The wages are minimal, but the tips are good."

Pablo dropped it into drive, and we left the harbor area. Within minutes, we were on Highway 8, heading for Sonoyta. The big car purred along. We rode in silence. The sky had lifted and I could see a few stars from my window. Willy put her head on my shoulder and rested her hand in the crook of my elbow. I put my left hand over hers. There was a lot of information passing between us, and I knew better than to interrupt it. I didn't have a lot to say anyway. I just marveled.

Eventually, we passed the turnoff to the airfield where we'd met Jasper. I looked out through the blackness and saw no light of any kind. Pablo stopped in San Pedro, told us to wait, and got out of the car. He'd been gone about a minute when a line of men carrying automatic weapons emerged from the low-slung building Pablo had disappeared into and surrounded the car. They didn't look our way; they faced away from us, like they were guarding us. I'm sure my eyebrows were held as high as Daniel's.

"Well," said Jasper, "I'll be a blue-nosed gopher."

Pablo came out of the building with a man in uniform. He had the look of a navy captain about him. Pablo saluted him smartly. The salute was returned. The officer looked toward the car and said something. Pablo nodded. The two shook hands, and the officer went back into the building. Pablo paused with one of the men, and they exchanged words. They bumped fists, and Pablo came and got into the car. The circle of men regrouped into a line and followed the captain into the building.

"What the hell was that?" Daniel asked.

Pablo hooked his elbow over the backseat and turned his face to us. "That," he said, "was my boss and my team. Apparently, we have become part of an international incident, and there are people on your side of the border calling for your heads. There are other people, equally powerful, who are calling for your protection and safe passage. The softest spot seems to be Microondas, where you came across, because it leads through the air force base."

"Are there cartel guys in Microondas?" I asked.

"It is very likely," said Pablo.

"So, we can't just go have a beer, maybe some *taquitos*, and head off into the night."

"That would probably be unwise." His eyes sparkled.

Daniel got out of the car, cell phone out. I watched him tap the keyboard. He turned in a half circle while he waited, and somebody must have answered because I could see him start talking. His body language became more erect. His face, shadowed by the oblique light from the building, betrayed no emotion.

It was a short conversation. Daniel snapped the phone shut and came back to the car. He got in, and we all looked at him expectantly.

"We will be met in the town of Why," he said, "with a car. From there, we're on our own."

"Well," I said, "that's something."

"Why?" Willy asked. "Where's that?"

"It's just north of the Organ Pipe Cactus National Monument, on Highway 85," I said, remembering the map. "From Microondas, as the crow flies, I think it's about thirty-five miles, but it's over some rough country."

"The rougher the country," Daniel said, "the less company we're likely to meet."

It was a quiet drive the rest of the way to Sonoyta, where we turned left and began to parallel the border, that line that shows so clearly on a map but is utterly meaningless in a wild place until you run into those who are committed to keeping track of it. After what I estimated to be about twenty-five miles, Pablo turned off the highway, coaxed the big car behind some scrub, and doused the lights. It was darker than the inside of a moose.

We got out and gathered our equipment from the trunk.

Willy removed her wig and stepped out of the skirt. Her jeans were damp with sweat.

"That's a relief," she said.

Then she looked at me pointedly. "You have my boots?"

While Willy completed her transformation, I shook Pablo's hand, and he gathered me into a quick hug.

"We said good-bye once before, but this one feels much more secure," he said.

"Practice makes better," I said.

The hug with Jasper took more time. "Keep that magic stuff alive," he said. "Your purpose has changed a bit these days"—he looked at Willy—"and I'm all for it."

Willy's good-byes were short and sweet. When Jasper told her to take care of me, she laughed. "He can take care of himself, but I will make sure he doesn't track mud into wherever we are."

"We will obliterate your tracks," said Pablo.

Jasper nodded his approval and that was that. We crossed the road and started up the slight grade toward the mountains we knew were there but couldn't see. We hadn't gone a hundred yards when it started to rain.

I stopped and pulled the poncho from my pack and gave it to Willy.

"We all need to keep our ears open for running water," Daniel said. "Until we can see more than ten feet, we will have to be extremely careful. After we can see a little, we only need to be very careful."

I laughed. "Redman make joke."

A pebble came from the darkness and struck me in the middle of the forehead.

"Paleface needs to be extremely careful always."

I heard a faint rustling as Willy shook her head inside the hood of the poncho. I changed the subject.

"What compass heading are you following?" I asked. "I reckon maybe I should be on the same one."

"Without stars," Daniel said, "the compass points will not help us much. But the GPS will."

"What would the Indians do?"

"First off, Indians would not be wandering around in the rain at oh two hundred. Truth be told, even warriors did not like traveling in the dark. Too many evil spirits and nasty surprises."

Daniel was out in front, Willy came next, and I was the follower, riding drag for the brand. I could not see my brother ahead in the darkness, and Willy was barely discernable. I had my CAR-15 slung over my shoulder. Suddenly, Daniel's voice rose above the incessant sound of the rain.

"Welcome home," he said.

Sure enough, the ragged fence we'd passed a couple weeks before was there in the darkness, posts at random intervals and unable to agree on a direction to point. It was an eerie thing, black-on-black in the steadily increasing rain.

Though I couldn't think where else I would want to be, I also didn't feel celebratory. The *Federales* were out of the picture, but not the cartel, who were much more dangerous. I wondered about the CIA and how the battles between the contentious factions at the political level were working out. The law said that I could not kill Grimes the next time I saw him, but I wondered how much that meant to me.

I also had a hollow spot whenever I thought of Howard Deems. I suspected that my dance with him was far from over. It rankled me that I had no idea where he was or what he was doing. I felt the same way about Jesús Chavez. I understood that he would kill me, or I would kill him. I was not going to spend the rest of my life looking over my shoulder.

I stopped abruptly when I realized that I was about to walk right into Willy's back. Daniel had stopped in front of her and was down on one knee. I put a hand on Willy's shoulder as I passed her and knelt next to my brother.

"Hear that?" he said.

I suddenly realized that I had been listening to the sound of running water for several minutes now. We were on the high bank of the broad wash we'd crossed when we'd come this way on the way south.

"We cannot cross it in the dark."

"No," I said. "From what I remember of the map, we can't go around it either."

"We wait," Daniel said, "for light."

It was an interminable wait. The rain was incessant. The huge drops pounded us with a million small hammers. The ground could not accept all of it and began to float in a peculiar way. The combination didn't create mud, exactly, but the finer particles pressed the larger ones together into an abrasive paste. For the moment, I was glad we were huddled together in a tight trio of bedraggled humanity and not slogging our way through it.

The sound of running water deepened in pitch and volume. I thought of all the creatures whose normal routines were being severely compromised by this rare desert deluge. We would have to stay alert to that. There would be a surface convention of all kinds of critters who usually stayed below ground but were now out because they were not built to live underwater.

After what seemed like forever I could see the shadow of Daniel's shape in front of me. Next to me, a dark pile that I knew to be Willy began to take form. I could barely see the edge of the slope that led down into the wash, but I could see the line of it before us.

When the invisible sun got high enough the three of us stared in amazement at the rushing torrent below us.

"It looks like the freakin' Mississippi," Willy said.

And it did. A broad brown torrent raced past us, carrying scrub trees and cacti. Balls of unidentifiable vegetable matter went by like tangled hair looking for a drain to clog. The body of a Peccary rolled past.

"Well," I said, "we can't cross the son of a bitch until the flood dissipates."

"We will have to follow it and turn north to cross when we can," Daniel said.

We slogged along the rim of the wash for a couple miles. The wash we were following was the southern terminus of what the map called the San Cristobal Wash. It ran northwest to southeast and, if I remembered right, petered out not far from where we were, at the western border of the Organ Pipe Cactus National Monument. If it was flooded badly there, we were effectively hemmed in. Even if we weren't, I was sure that we'd come upon several other washes, especially as we neared the mountains we had to navigate. Those washes would be steeper and their flows might be even more sudden and violent.

The rain began to abate, and though the sky above us grew lighter, the horizon was still roiling and black. Any rain uphill from us would keep the washes and arroyos supplied with water.

I was just starting to get used to the dryer conditions, when the wind came up. It was a serious wind, a wind with a purpose, a wind from the south that carried an angry snarl. It caught the edges of Willy's poncho and curled it up around her torso.

"Good thing you're wearing clothes under that," I said.

"What? You don't like to see me naked?" she laughed as she pushed it back down.

Daniel cut our flirting short when he dropped to one knee. Willy and I followed suit.

"I just saw what I think are headlights," said Daniel. "Dead ahead on the other side of this wash."

He had to shout to be heard over the wind.

I peered over his shoulder but saw nothing except brown water and open desert.

"We're still several miles from Highway 85," I said. "Who the hell would be out here in this weather?"

"That is certainly the question of the moment," Daniel said as he dug out his compact binoculars from a pouch on his belt.

"There!" Willy said and pointed.

Sure enough, a set of headlights shone out in front of us well to our north. They would be in view and then disappear, repeating this pattern.

"It does not appear to be a government vehicle," said Daniel from behind his binoculars. "It looks like a brown Land Rover."

"American plates?" I joked.

Daniel answered seriously. "Arizona."

"Those must be seriously good glasses."

He handed them to me. Sure enough, it was a dark Land Rover. It disappeared behind a low line of hills and then came into view again and stopped. A man got out and stood beside the vehicle. He too had a pair of binoculars. He also had what looked like a cast on his right forearm.

I thought about coincidence and rejected that immediately.

"I think I'm looking at my old buddy Grimes," I said. "The CIA has found us."

"There's another set of headlights," Willy said.

We looked to where she pointed. I handed the glasses to Daniel, who studied the new vehicle.

"Blue Japanese SUV," he said. "Maybe a Toyota. It is heading in the direction of the Rover."

About ten minutes later it joined the first rig and stopped. Four men got out. At the same time, three more men emerged from the Land Rover. This was getting interesting.

I slipped my pack off and got out my own binoculars. They weren't as powerful as Daniel's, but they were of good quality and brought the scene into focus. I couldn't make out faces, but I could read general body language. Nobody over there was relaxed. Two of the men from the Land Rover had rifles pointing in the general direction of the men from the SUV.

The blue car began to back up a little. There was a fifth person in it, unless it was driving itself. I was wondering about this when one of the men from the SUV drew a pistol and shot the two men from the Rover holding rifles. They never had a chance. It happened so fast that they'd had no time to react. The man with the cast tried to draw his weapon, but one of the other men from the SUV shot him. The fourth man from the Rover raised his hands into the air. The man who'd fired first raised his pistol and shot the last man standing as if he were on an execution range.

We heard nothing from where we were. We saw the muzzle flashes and that was all.

The one who had shot first was familiar. I was ready to bet the ranch that it was Jesús Chavez. And if that were true, the guy driving the SUV just might be Howard Deems. Somebody opened the back of the Rover and removed a package. It looked heavy. One of the men carried it to the SUV and stashed it in the back. The one I thought was Chavez stooped and picked something up off the ground, threw it into the back of the Rover and slammed the rear door closed. His companions might have been laughing.

I stowed my glasses and put my pack back on, gathered up my CAR-15, and stood up in time to see the distant headlights turning around. They began to drive back the way they'd come. I knew that it would be impossible to get there even if the ground were not a dangerous and slippery mess.

Daniel read my moment, knew that I wanted to fly and, with every ounce of my being, engage the enemy.

"Even an eagle could not get there quickly enough," he said.

The wind was starting to pick up sand. As uncomfortable as this was against my face, it was a good thing, indicating that things were drying out a little. The water in the wash was dropping before our eyes. Another few minutes, and we might be able to cross.

Willy came down to the edge, and I felt her regarding me as I stared impotently across the distance to where I felt I needed to be. The wind blew my hat off, and she instinctively caught it. It was brilliantly quick.

"Good catch, eh?" she said.

"Highlight reel."

"You have that look."

"What look?"

"Focused. I'm learning to recognize it."

I moved closer to her so she wouldn't have to holler against the wind. "Sometimes," I said, "I can be kind of distant."

She gave me a "yes, dummy, I know that" look.

"But that's you, and that's okay. You do what you do. I will learn more and do my best to deal with it. Sometimes, you can be very close, too, and I will deal with that as well."

I nodded and looked back across the wash. The water was now confined to only the deepest channel. Daniel came down the slope. He did not pause as he passed us.

"Double-time," he called back.

I motioned to Willy to follow him and fell in behind her, scanning the far side with my carbine at the ready. The wind buffeted us like linemen hitting practice dummies. When we reached the channel where the water was still moving, it was only a few inches deep, and we forged right through it. The bed of it was firm as we splashed across.

The other side was quite a spectacle of wildlife. Scores of insects, centipedes, scorpions, and tarantulas were moving apart from one another where the rising water had held them together. A sidewinder marked his esses along the ground, oblivious to the dozen little desert rats who were scampering to their own versions of safety. I'd seen the same kind of thing after a flash of fire had moved through the jungle, predators and prey and ancient mortal enemies, all sharing space without conflict while the common danger passed.

Daniel slowed his pace. There were still creatures scurrying, slithering, and crabbing by, but their numbers diminished with every stride we took. I can't say I was disappointed at not having to watch where my feet came down with every step.

Daniel shucked his pistol and held it at his side. I looked at my carbine and made sure the action was free of the goo that was all over our feet from running through the abrasive paste in the wash.

Eventually, Daniel help up his hand and we stopped. The Land Rover peeked over the small rise before us, only a hundred yards away.

Daniel moved off to the left and I to the right. Willy stayed behind me. I noticed that her right hand carried the big revolver I'd given her back at Jasper's. Good woman.

I tried to keep at least the roofline of the Rover in sight. I wasn't expecting trouble, but there were a lot of people dead because they had discarded their caution at a most inopportune moment. I looked to my left, and Daniel waved. I watched as he moved in toward the vehicle.

"Stay here," I said to Willy. "If any shooting starts, cock that thing and pick a bad guy. It's really accurate up to about fifty yards, but it kicks like a drunk kangaroo."

She nodded and followed me until she could see the whole scene. She waited there.

The man with the cast was Grimes, sure enough. Daniel knelt and put fingers on his neck. His eyes widened in surprise.

"This one is alive."

A two-way radio lay by his side, crackling intermittently with static. Daniel reached down and keyed it off. The markings in the sandy ground told me that Grimes had been groping for it.

I checked the others. They were not alive. The two men with M-16s were each shot twice. All four of those bullets had found heart muscle. Jesús Chavez, I was sure of it, was one hell of a shooter.

The last of them had pulled out his Sig .40, but had never got off a shot. He had taken two in his upper chest and one to his jaw. The wide-open wound had already attracted insects and would soon attract a lot more.

Daniel was cutting away Grimes's clothing. There were two blue holes in this upper chest. I slid my left hand beneath his torso to check for exit wounds. Both bullets had come through close together, leaving a gaping hole between his shoulder blades. The desert's efficient cleaning crews would find that in a big hurry. I went to the back of the Rover and was about to open the door when something stopped me. I wondered what and then remembered that Chavez had put something in there before slamming shut the tailgate. I wiped the dirty back window with the sleeve of my forearm and peered inside. I couldn't see anything. There was a blanket that would be very useful, but I didn't trust it. I opened the tailgate door very quickly and backed off a step. Nothing. Very gingerly, I picked up the nearest corner of the folded blanket and snatched it out, throwing it to the ground. A six-inch scorpion came out with it, tail erect and ready for trouble. With my foot, I scuffed sand at it, and it backed off, pincer and tail at the ready. I moved behind it and kicked more sand at it, while leaving it an escape route. I had no idea about their thought process, if any, but it used the opportunity to scuttle off in the direction I'd hoped for.

I picked up the blanket and snapped it open, giving it a good shake. There were no other unwelcome visitors.

When I got back to Daniel, he had Grimes's head cradled in his left hand and was giving him a sip of water from one of the water jugs he carried. As I approached, they both looked at me. I saw no flash of recognition in Grimes's face. Just as well.

I held out the blanket. "Let's get him on this."

We rolled Grimes onto his side and maneuvered the blanket around him. He gasped and coughed. A little blood frothed at the corner of his mouth.

"Am I gonna make it?"

"Maybe. It just depends on how bad you want to live."

Grimes sighed and coughed again. He looked at me. "You're the son of a bitch who broke my arm."

He had recognized me. I whistled to myself. "Yep. And we're still not quite square."

He looked puzzled at that. I offered no explanation.

"If you hadn't burned up that money, I wouldn't be lying here."

Now it was my turn to be puzzled. Then it came to me. "So you had to come up with another payment, bribe, or whatever you want to call it."

"I've made some bad choices recently," he said.

This was not the time for me to start listing some other bad ones from twenty-five years ago.

Daniel finished his bandaging.

"We are going to put you into the back of the Rover where you can call your CO," he said. "They will be in a much better position to get you the help you need, but for now, at least you are not bleeding to death."

We got him into the back of the Rover after folding down the back seats. Daniel left him the water jug and went for the two-way.

"I know you from somewhere else," Grimes said to me.

"Yes, you do. It was an A-camp near the Laotian border. You tried to get me killed."

Remembrance flooded his features. But he didn't get angry; he just looked glum and haggard and, well, shot. How could that be, I wondered. Where was his outrage?

Grimes spoke carefully. "I was working for the wrong chain of command," he said quietly. "You had every right to try and kick my ass. You were man enough to do it too. I'm sorry about it. I've been sorry about it for a long time."

I looked at him and marveled at how wrong a man can be when he holds a grudge. I reached out and found his hand under the blanket. I gave it a squeeze.

"Hatchet's buried then," I said. "Maybe we can find a way to make it better someday."

He looked at me with the faintest trace of a smile. "Hope so. But I have to get through this first."

"I have a question," I said. "Did you see the driver of the SUV? Was he a gringo?"

"That's two questions," Grimes said and tried to smile again. "I never really saw who it was, but you may have something there. He could've been a gringo. He had really close-cut hair."

I nodded. "Thanks."

Daniel came back with the little radio.

"We will stay around just long enough to make sure you make contact. We really do have to go. And do not forget to tell them about the blue SUV."

Grimes entered a key sequence, and the radio came to life.

"This is Muleskinner," he said. "I am in need of immediate medical help. The other three are dead."

Daniel had written GPS coordinates on a piece of paper he'd found in the glove box. He laid it on Grimes' chest, along with the Sig .40. Grimes looked at both of us and nodded his thanks.

Willy was there, doing her best to not look at the gruesome death on the ground. I finally noticed the vacuum sucking at us as the barometric pressure plunged.

"Batten down your hatches," I said. "We're about to meet a very angry mother."

It was interesting to watch it come. The wall of debris soon surrounded us. It was like being in a blender full of flying sticks and bits of cactus. I saw a small mammal whisk by head-over-tail. Large limbs of organ pipe or saguaro cactus whirling through the air had the potential to be vicious. The sound of it all was deafening. When we were kids, Daniel and I had been trying to cross a trestle when a train came. We'd been able to find a way under the tracks and let the half-mile of rumbling freight pass over us. This was louder than that. Then the rain came. Our blender was now underwater. It was difficult to breathe.

We sought shelter against a small rise, but the wind gusted probably to at least eighty, so we still weren't that safe. The wind drove the rain sideways hard enough to hurt when it hit my back. The grainy soil created a blaster effect that could strip paint. I put my arms around Willy and held on. I felt solid objects hit me. Most of them bounced off. Some of them, though, felt like they stuck, and the sting that accompanied those was very annoying. I had a vision of myself as a pincushion, or maybe an old ship encrusted with barnacles. I tried to imagine what this wind would do if it wasn't raining. The dust it would kick up would leave us utterly blind. Suddenly, I was glad it was raining.

I thought of Grimes lying in the back of the Rover awaiting help, knowing that it would be a long time coming. Until the weather broke, there would be nobody out in this.

After what seemed like forever, the wind began to abate, but the rain seemed to intensify. As I stood, my shirt felt stuck to my back more than with just rain; it felt like it was nailed in place. It turned out that it was. Daniel chuckled with amusement as he used his pocket pliers tool to pull out cactus spines one by one where they had tacked my shirt to the skin and meat of my back.

"I am so glad you are enjoying yourself." I winced with each yank.

"Did this guy sting you?" Daniel asked as he held a small scorpion wriggling between the jaws of his pliers in front of my face.

"How would I know? My whole back is on fire."

"You were the bulwark for both Willy and I."

I thought of a Paul deLay song. "Sometimes," I said, "it's not easy being big."

The temperature had plunged, and none of us were dry enough to stave off that chill. My government-issue jungle camo uniform shirt, which was a tad tighter than it had been when I first got it, felt only a little more appropriate now. I was still in a desert, but it was a wet one now.

The land began to rise and got flintier underfoot, much easier walking. We now paralleled most of the washes and arroyos as we climbed into a ragged cluster of hills. The canyons had become roaring torrents. They were short runs, waves really, down from the mountains and would empty as fast as they filled.

We finally crested a summit and looked east toward Highway 85 and, beyond that, the Tohono O'odham reservation. As I looked out at the country below us, I wondered how many border patrol people were hunkered in their vehicles blessing the rain for giving them an easier day than usual. As if to prove me wrong, I saw the dim gleam of headlights down on the highway. I guessed the road to be more than five miles distant, but in the faded, almost green, light, the headlight showed clearly.

Willy spoke for the first time in a long while. "How far do you reckon we are from Why?"

"Something less than twenty miles, as the crow flies. On foot, through these mountains, our route will probably be closer to twenty-five or thirty."

We started down. As I looked ahead I knew we'd be going up again soon. We repeated this pattern of up, around, and down for the next several hours.

The rain stayed steady, but we made good progress. Daniel would consult his GPS from time to time, but I think it was to confirm rather than to guide. He was born to find his way in the wild.

We saw no evidence of other people. The route we were taking was arduous enough to discourage travel. We crested another short pass and below us was a broad trail. It looked like a super highway from where we rested.

"This cannot be the trail to the Victoria mine." Daniel said, "We were past that miles ago.

"I'm hoping this might be one of the trails to Bates Well, as I'm pretty sure we're standing in the middle of the Bates Mountains. We've made good time, and that feels right to me. If it wasn't raining so damn hard, I'd dig out the map and look."

I heard a rustle, and saw Willy shaking open her poncho to create a shelter. "There's always a way."

Daniel and I squatted beneath her rain gear to study the map. The coordinates told us that I was right. Daniel pointed to what looked like a very steep drop to the Valley of the Ajo.

"I am pretty sure that is part of the pass we have been following. If we just keep on, we should be able to get to Why in a few more hours. I think it will be conveniently dark."

"Just like we planned it," I said.

Daniel looked at me. "You have never planned anything."

"In advance," I hedged.

While Willy smoothed her poncho, I watched the clouds, heavy and the color of bruised fruit. To our west, I saw occasional flashes of lightning, bright cracks in the rotten-eggplant sky.

Daniel stood looking with me. His fifty-caliber rifle case rested easily on his shoulder. Thunder rolled in from a distance.

"We should get lower," he said. "I have never been fond of lightning, in the mountains especially."

"I don't like it either," Willy said. "We once lost a very good horse to it."

The deep wash we followed was running steadily to the north with the ongoing downpour. After studying it for a while, Daniel suggested that we cross it as quickly as we could and work our way down on the other side.

It was thigh deep and powerful. We held on to one another and crossed. There were almost no debris, and the water was clear and clean. We found easier going after that, and we made good time.

Thunder rattled in the distance. We came around a sharp corner to a deep wash running west to east. Ahead of us we could see glimpses of the broad plain that we would have to cross to get to Why. Our trail, such as it was, started to peter out, and we could see where it disappeared at a sheer cliff face. We would have to cross the wash. From where we stood, it looked passable, and there was what looked like a way down to the valley floor.

"No time like the present," said Daniel.

He took Willy's left, and I took her right. The water was waist deep, but the current didn't seem as strong as the last one we'd crossed. We were about in the middle when I saw motion in a scrawny pile of mesquite and greasewood that had wedged itself between two thrusts of rock.

There was a young kit fox, soaked and bedraggled. She looked at me with pleading brown eyes. There was something in them that reminded me of Bucket, an intelligence that could not be denied. I squeezed Willy's hand and let go of it. She turned to me in surprise, and I motioned with my head at the fox. Willy smiled and went with Daniel.

I worked my way to the fox, who hadn't completely decided if I meant more trouble or safety. When I got to her, she decided that I was safety and willingly grabbed onto the arm that I offered. As I gathered her next to my chest, she was shivering so hard that she seemed to buzz.

Daniel and Willy had reached the other side and were out of the flow watching me. I was within ten feet of them when a wall of water five feet high came roaring around the corner, carrying everything it could before it. I had a split second to toss the little fox toward relative safety when it hit me.

I am a large, strong man. Surfing taught me that wild, moving water is always larger and stronger. I surrendered and let the wave take me. I did my best to relax and not panic. I tumbled. My pack turned me into a cam-like spinner that threw me around at an uneven speed. I was doing okay in the panic department, some small part of being upside-down was almost enjoyable, the way spinning on a carnival ride is. My wits seemed to be intact until my head slammed into a large boulder. I bounced against my left arm, and a lance of fire connected it to the sharpness in my head and neck.

Time did not exist. The power of the water stayed steady and maybe even increased. I went through a series of long drops, each ending in a jarring impact that drove precious air out of my lungs. Some vague flicker of mind knew that my carbine was gone, but I felt the pistol at my back.

Suddenly, a terrible pain raked along my ribs and around across my back. I stopped moving with the water and the pressure of the flow drove me deep under. I was snagged on something very sturdy. I felt the buttons on my shirt straining and tried to get my hands in a position to rip them open. My left arm was tangled with my pack, but my right, free of the responsibility of carrying the CAR-15, got there and ripped at my shirt. My right side was suddenly free, but my left was not. I felt the spasms in my diaphragm telling me that I would soon try to take a breath of something, anything.

I got my feet around to something that I could push against with my legs. I felt my shirt rip, and then I was back at the mercy of the flood. Without the pack, I was lucky enough to shoot to the surface, where I caught a very brief lungful that was mostly air.

Suddenly, I was falling. It might have been forever. Maybe it was. I don't remember landing.

THIRTY-NINE

I came to slowly and wished I hadn't. Every cubic inch of me either burned or ached. The voices had formed a circle and were chanting in my head. They seemed insistent. There was a great weight crushing my chest and an insistent tickling in my nose. I struggled to move, to try and sit up, and could not. I opened my eyes. At least I could do that.

A dark-haired man sat on my chest. His pock-marked face smiled at me in a way that told me he enjoyed pulling wings off of small living birds. The tickling in my nose was the six-inch blade of his knife. "Thank you for the pistol, *señor*," he said. "Do you have anything else for me?"

There came laughter from my left. I couldn't turn my head, but I placed that to be about six feet away. I felt a sharp sting at my nose.

"Oh, *señor*, you are bleeding."

He actually giggled, as did his unseen partner. I knew I wouldn't be able to speak, so I didn't attempt to engage in witty repartee. I quickly arched my back, hoping that all my levers were intact. I was instantly thankful they were. The man on top of me went sailing over my face and landed on his own. He probably still had his knife. The man to my left was digging into his belt with a very surprised look on his face. I closed the distance between us and watched my right hand drive a thumb into the side of his neck. My fingers curled around his Adam's apple and made a fist. There was a sullen pop, followed by much gurgling and wheezing. His right hand forgot about the gun in his belt and flew to his throat, vainly attempting to repair the irreparable as he sank to his knees in the wet sand. I turned to the first guy, who was trying to get to his feet. He did still have his knife, but it was lodged in his right shoulder. He also had a pistol. My Glock 19. The knife in his right shoulder was occupying his left hand while he was trying to get the Glock out of his belt with his suddenly weakened right. I launched a kick into his right knee and felt it give. He fell on his right side, which probably ruined his chances for getting the knife out.

He whimpered like a coyote with its leg in a trap. I laughed grimly to myself. That's exactly what he was, a coyote. If he was here, that also meant that the people he was ferrying were, hopefully somewhere close. I went and picked up the Glock.

"Mine," I croaked.

All at once, I was very dizzy and had to sit. The adrenalin rush was passing, and I felt cold rain on my back. My vision became unfocused, and my head hurt like a clothes dryer full of broken glass must hurt. Between bursts of clear vision and blurred images, I tried to check out the state of the left side of my chest. There were two deep gashes that started near my nipple, raked downward across my ribs, and wrapped around across my back. The wound was bleeding freely, but I could see it starting to clot. I was more worried about my head.

Gingerly, I probed my skull with my fingers, which hurt like hell. There was swelling, but nothing had ballooned. As near as I could tell, the bone was intact, but I was probably concussed, maybe severely.

I took a deep, ragged breath and looked at the bozo who had been sitting on my chest. He was lying on his stomach, utterly still.

I cleared my throat. "Hey, *pendejo*. Wake up and smell the blood. *Despierte. Huela la sangre.*" I thought this was quite clever and cackled briefly. What a comedian. I should book a gig in Las Vegas, only a few hundred miles to the north.

He did not stir. I tried to stand but fell over about halfway up. This did my head no favors, and I lay in a fetal position for a few moments, watching bright lights flash where I knew there were none. Raindrops hit the sand. They did not get sucked up immediately; each one bounced minutely as the surface tension broke and reformed. Water is such an amazing substance. Suddenly it was hysterical that I was laying in one of the driest places on earth having almost drowned. I really wanted to laugh. Instead, I began to shiver.

There was a siren in my head, punctuated by the deep percussive clang of a pile-driver. The voices were improvising with the noise, doing some kind of ancient scat. I crawled to the inert form I'd heaved from my chest.

"*Pendejo!*" I slapped his foot. Nothing.

I crawled again and gripped his shoulder. It took all the strength I had to roll him over.

The knife had cut through his shoulder, somehow missing bone, and was now lodged in his throat, where it had severed his carotid. Most of his blood was now soaking into the wet sand.

"Sharp knife," I said to the sky as I rubbed at my nose. My left nostril was split about an eighth-inch. This made me sad. The Indians I knew would secretly think I'd been branded a liar, or worse. I tried to get angry about it, but I just couldn't. I was overwhelmingly sad. I saw Bucket's mischievous eyes and felt Willy's heart beating against my own. I remembered the eyes of the little fox on me. I heard Daniel's voice but couldn't make out what he was saying. It sounded like *focaccia*, but that couldn't be right. What would bread have to do with anything? I gave up and watched the rain spiral down.

I must have passed out again, because the shivering woke me. I felt an odd sense of urgency. I was forgetting something important. My abdomen tightened, and I sat up. The two bodies hadn't moved, and my concern came to me. Coyotes. Coyotes meant people. I had to find them and make sure they were okay. The enormity of it was daunting. I would have to stand. I would have to move. I would have to find my strength. I would have to be responsible.

I would have to stop shivering.

The rain was lighter now, and the sky felt higher. It was still a roiling mess of gray. I tried to guess at what the temperature was and didn't like my estimates. My shirt was still tangled with my pack at some snag back up the mountain. In it were a couple T-shirts and my small thermal blanket. I picked up the two pistols and walked back to where the wash came down to the valley floor. It was a much-reduced waterfall coming off of an overhang that was twenty feet high. The landing area was mostly sand, but there were gnarly rocks and small piles of heavy debris that had come down with the flood. I must have missed everything except the ground. Gratitude flooded me. I wanted to see more of where I'd come through but could not see up past the overhang. Maybe it was just as well.

I stuck my head under the flow of water and washed the blood out of my hair. The gashes on my chest and side were no longer bleeding, but they were seeping. I wished for something to bandage myself with, but if wishes were a horse, I could have ridden to Why.

I caught a flash of motion to my left. I looked that way and saw nothing. I was not completely convinced that I had really seen something. My vision was still coming and going. I thought I'd seen something white moving against the tumbled rock at the edge of the first slopes of the mountain. I put the extra pistol under my belt to the left of the buckle. Gripping my own pistol, I faded into the rock myself. I figured that my muddy pants and my tanned skin might be able to blend with the surroundings. I wondered, though, about the giant flashing neon beacon of my head. There was no hiding it.

But now I was on the hunt. I felt the old concentration return to me little by little. Something had moved, and I was going to find out what it was.

I slowly worked my way to the base of a cliff that rose thirty feet. Large boulders had tumbled from it over the millennia, and these afforded good cover. I spent a lot of time listening, even though I had to do so through the ringing in my head. Finally, I came across human tracks in the sand. They were small, and indicated at least three people.

I kept them in sight but did not follow them exactly. I stayed to the outside of them, keeping them on my right, trying to melt from one boulder to the next. I was breathing more easily, and the noise in my head had dulled to a distant roar, like an angry sea heard from inside a beach cabin. I missed my voices chanting to me. I inched ahead, using all the craft I could muster and presently heard hushed external voices.

"*Dónde sé fue?*" one voice said. She sounded like a teenager.

Another young voice answered. "*No sé. Creo que es un fantasma. ¿Has visto cómo se movia cuando mató nuestros guías? Ningun humano es asi derapido.*"

I liked that the youngster thought I was so quick, but then a third voice spoke, softer, a little older, a little more based in reality. "*No, él es humano y él es lastimado.*"

"*Silencio. Él le oirá,*" said a much older male voice. It was a kind voice, but it was used to being obeyed.

"*Escuche a su abuelo,*" said the voice who knew I was hurt.

An uneasy silence descended, broken only by the falling of the soft rain and the trickle of water coming down the wash. I moved behind the voices and carefully leaned against a rock about thirty feet away, looking at their backs. There were two young girls, very pretty, just entering adolescence, and a young woman, also pretty and perhaps in her late twenties. My eyes weren't working well enough to detect any family resemblance, but I had to assume that there was. Maybe the older woman was a big sister or an aunt. She could even be the mom, for all I knew. Their loveliness struck a chord in me that jarred sharply with the two men I'd met back where I'd landed.

The old man was dressed in what once had been a fine suit. Like everything that had been out in this weather, it was bedraggled and stained. It was easy to imagine his dirty, wet white hair combed neatly and laying like silver filigree against the collar of his jacket.

I tucked my pistol into my belt and spoke in a calm voice. "*No soy un fantasma.*"

I had to be honest with myself and admit that I felt like a ghost.

They all whirled, and the two young girls made little yipping noises. The woman threw a hand to her throat, and her lovely face blanched white, but she did not make a sound. Her eyes searched my face. The grandfather also had fear in his eyes, but there was a resolve there too. I did my best to smile and spread my open hands to each side of me.

"If you touch them, I will kill you," said the old man in perfect English.

I looked at him and bowed my head briefly before holding his gaze. "I am the least of your worries."

I considered their predicament and wondered aloud.

"You are in the United States illegally, your 'guides' were both cruel killers with severe antisocial tendencies, and your companions are lovely young women." My voice took on an edge. "What did you think would happen? I'm guessing that you are waiting here for someone to come and provide passage to somewhere. I'm sure you have made a deal, but I am also sure that whoever you trusted will break your heart and that the safe passage of these women will not be as you imagine. I think you began to suspect that all was not as it seemed when you had to set out in the terrible weather. I am also very curious as to why a family of your obvious means"—I made a point to look at his suit—"had to resort to an illegal border crossing."

He looked at me for a long moment. The woman started to say something, but he held up his hand, and she quieted.

"*Señor*," he said, "our business is not your business, but your intuition is… surprising." He brushed his wet hair from his eyes. "I will tell you this, but you must promise on your honor, that you will keep it to yourself."

I nodded. "I promise, as long as it is the truth. If I discover a lie in it, my promise vanishes."

He studied me again for a couple of heartbeats. We came to some kind of agreement. The wind moaned around the corner every once in a while, and the rain spiraled in answer. I waited.

"My name is Chimalma Hector Benedicté Acalan," he began. "My daughter, Helena"—he nodded at her—"was married to a powerful man named Rudolfo Luiz. It was a marriage that I did not approve of, but I gave my blessing because our once-proud family has fallen on hard times, and this man was very wealthy. To shorten this long story, I will just say that Rudolfo was murdered a few months ago by a despicable man named Gustavo Flores."

I think my heart skipped a beat, maybe two.

"Flores owed Rudolfo a lot of money. Rudolfo was gunned down in his driveway. Thank God Helena and *las niñas*, the twins, were visiting me in Guadalajara."

"So," I said, "when Flores was killed, you all became targets."

His eyes got big. "You know about this?"

"Yes," I said after a while.

I thought of the little fox's eyes as I'd plucked her from the snag in the middle of the wash above. She'd been worried but determined. If not for her, these people would be utterly doomed. Señor Benedicté would likely be killed and his family would be forced into god knows what kind of life. I was willing to bet my life that they would not end up as maids or field hands. Their fates would be back rooms, colored light bulbs, forced drugs, and a long line of insistent men, whose ideas of intimacy involved using other human beings as masturbation aids. A nagging vision of Howard Deems would not leave me alone, and I wasn't sure why. An old anger settled in my middle and although my head was still ringing like a payphone, I noticed that I was no longer shivering. If I had anything to say about it, and I did, these people would survive this and, at least, have a chance to climb back to a life as a family. I thought more about this and came to a decision. I wished Willy was here standing next to me. At that very moment the casual squawk of a great blue heron came from somewhere above us.

"Where are you supposed to be going?" I asked Hector.

"Phoenix," he said. "At least, at first."

"I think," I said, "that you should go to Oregon and get as far away from these people as you can."

Hector looked at me like I was crazy. It was a look I am used to.

"I cannot break my word, *señor*." He was horrified.

I went to him and caught his sleeve. "Walk with me a bit."

He came with me reluctantly, looking over his shoulder at the loves of his life. There is an old saying about "reading from the book." It was my turn to read. When we were out of earshot, I turned to him.

"*Señor*," I began earnestly, "your daughter and her children are in grave danger. These men to whom you have given your word will kill you and sell your *corezones* into a profane slavery. These men are not worthy of your honorable word."

"How do you know this?"

"It has a lot to do with the characters of the men who led you here. When they found me, I became their toy." I pointed to my nose. "Call it a very strong hunch. I am willing to bet my life on it, and I do not do that casually."

He looked at me deeply for the first time. His eyes were liquid brown, with small gold flecks. I could see his uncertainty. I could smell his fear, but there was courage there too.

"Ask yourself," I said, "why you are here right now. Why are you not already in Phoenix, warm, dry, and safe? Why are your granddaughters shivering with cold? Why is your daughter so deeply frightened? At a profound level, everyone knows what is happening. Will you let it continue because you gave your word as a gentleman to men who are not?"

"If a man does not have his word," said Hector, "he has nothing."

"True enough. But a man who sacrifices his life and his family when it could be prevented is a fool. You were ready to fight me to protect them, so I know you have great courage. You need that courage to protect them now."

There it was. His eyes searched mine. He turned to look at the women huddled by the boulder and turned back to me.

"You know this danger to be true?" he asked.

"In my bones."

"There will probably be more than one. How can you stop them?"

"I may be a little banged up, but I am not without resources."

"*Alguien está viniendo!*" cried one of the twins.

Sure enough, the sound of a vehicle moving over rough ground became obvious to me. Thank goodness for young ears and a head that was not ringing. I thought of the great blue heron call that had come from above us and threw back my head and did my best to make the sound of an eagle calling to his mate. It came out pretty well. Hector and the girls looked at me, shocked at the noise. I put my hand on Hector's shoulder.

"We have friends above," I said.

"So I am trusting a crazy person," he said as we walked back to his family. He barked a short laugh. "It is in God's hands now."

"What is your name?" I asked the twin who had heard the vehicle.

She looked at her mother, who nodded.

"Gabriela," she said and looked at the ground.

"Gabriela, your hearing has saved us all."

"My name is Gisela," said the other twin, "and I heard it too!"

I smiled, but neither one of the girls would look at me. I guessed their ages to be about twelve. They were in that stage where their girl shapes were changing to woman shapes. I'm sure it was a tumultuous time for them. Men looked at them differently and treated them differently whether they recognized it or not.

I turned to Helena, their mother. She had been watching me watch them. Whatever she saw in that seemed to have made her less wary of me. Her eyes didn't exactly smile at me, but they were more open than they had been.

"Take your daughters," I said to her, "and find the best hiding place you can. Your father and I do not need to know where it is. Do not come out of it until you hear me make the eagle call again. There will be gunfire, and there will be blood. Do not let the girls see any of it. They do not need more scars. I know they saw me kill those two men, and I am very sorry about that."

"We will do as you say. Please protect my father. He is a brave man, but he has lost much of his strength. I know he does not look it, but he is nearing eighty and has spells of tiredness."

"Eighty!" I whistled low. "You're right. I thought he was much younger."

The sound of the vehicle was getting closer.

"Go now," I urged Helena and the girls. "Do not come out until you hear the eagle."

"I think I know a place," she said.

She gathered the girls. They had moved a few paces when she turned to me again.

"*Vaya con Dios,*" she said.

"*Gracias,*" I said and turned back to where her father was. I did not want to know where they were going.

I found Hector crouched behind a boulder, peering around it. I crouched next to him and handed him the extra pistol. It was a thirty-eight revolver of some mysterious origin. There were no manufacturer markings and no serial number that I could see.

"Do you know how to use this?" I asked.

Hector nodded and took the gun. He opened the cylinder and saw that it was fully loaded. He handled it easily, and I felt a glimmer of hope.

"My brother and—" I searched for a label for Willy and was surprised that I didn't have one—"my woman are somewhere above us. They are armed and will cover us from wherever they are. There will be very little conversation with these people. When they see the bodies, they will be wary and ready to shoot. Do not reveal yourself unless you have to. They will be professionals, so respect their skill."

"What will you do?" he asked.

I was honest with him. "I'm not sure, but I am very good at making it up as I go."

His eyes grew large. "You really are crazy."

"You can thank me later."

The day was growing late, though I didn't know exactly how late because my watch was gone. I wished for sun because it would be in the eyes of the enemy unless the mountains blocked it.

When the vehicle came into view, I was disappointed. It was not a blue SUV. It was a gray late-model Chevy van that had been jacked up to make room for big wheels with big knobby tires. It looked like a surfer's rig on steroids. It drove slowly through the end of the wash and stopped. I guessed that they had seen the bodies and were figuring out what to do. They were also probably on the phone relaying this new development. I hoped there was no signal out here, but on this side of the mountains it was very flat and a cell tower could be picked up from miles away. Until I knew for sure, I had to assume that they were in contact with someone.

The van lurched forward as they turned and went into a small gully so that only the top half was visible. This pattern repeated as they came slowly toward us. Finally, the van crested from the last of the endless undulations of desert and drove up to stop at the bodies of the men I had killed. I felt no remorse whatsoever for the taking of those two lives. It was a dead spot in my emotional landscape. I thought back to the villa and felt nothing for those men either. The ringing in my head had taken on an almost surreal quality, a rising and falling that reminded me of a cartoon symphony with an ancient choir, but my body felt relaxed and ready. I felt the familiar connection with long ages of fighting men who'd come before me and will continue long after I am gone. There was an edge to it that wasn't exactly fear, although that was part of it, but was more a kind of anticipation. The old phrase "it is a good day to die" flowed through me and settled me into a calm place that made seconds somehow longer. I hoped it wasn't a complete illusion. My usual voices were there too, their chanting mingled with the ringing, creating a very strange internal deluge of noise. I got back to the now.

Three men got out of the van. Two were Latino and one was a gringo. They were all wearing baseball caps. One of the Latinos held what looked like an AK-47. I caught through the open sliding door what I thought was a flash of movement, so there was at least one more occupant in the vehicle.

The gringo walked slowly to the bodies, his eyes relentlessly scanning the tumbled landscape that led up into the mountains. They moved past the boulder where Hector and I were hiding. He said something over his shoulder to the other men and squatted next to the corpses. He studied them for quite some time.

The three men fanned out a bit and were studying the ground. They were looking for tracks, of which there were many.

"Shoot whoever gets out of the van," I whispered to Hector.

He nodded.

When the three men passed us, I stepped out behind them. I followed them for a few paces, putting myself between them and the van. The gringo and the second Latino were between the one with the AK-47 and me. I raised my pistol. It was time to get the dance started.

"Drop your weapons," I called in my best voice, the one I used to stop charging bears in their tracks.

It froze them for only a second. The man closest to me had his gun out and whirled. I shot him twice in the chest. He went down. The man with the AK-47 simply exploded. That's the only way to describe it. He burst like a water balloon and was scattered across the damp sand. The thunder from Daniel's rifle rolled down from the mountain.

Something burned my neck as I shot at the gringo. I aimed for his chest but hit him in the shoulder. He deftly switched his gun to his other hand, and I fired at his chest again. This time I hit him in the hip. Apparently, my Glock had suffered some damage during my wet pinball ride. It was either that or I had suffered the damage and couldn't shoot straight. He went down, but his pistol was still in his left hand. I fired twice more, and he lay back on the ground.

There was a yell behind me. It was a girl's voice. There came two shots, each from a different gun. I turned to see Hector slump to the ground, holding his middle. I stepped back so I could see the van. A fat Latino man held a wildly struggling young girl by the waist as she kicked at his legs. He turned from Hector and hit her in the head with his pistol. I shot him, and he whirled toward me, forgetting about the girl who fell to the ground. I shot him again. He was too big to miss, but I wasn't confident about exactly where the bullets were going. He went down like a sack of rice, and his gun fell from his slack fingers. I ran to the girl, who was still trying to fight, even through her dazed state.

She looked to be about ten years old, skinny but lithe. He face was clouded with pain and fear but held a determined look that could only be called fierce. She was Indian, but I had no idea of what tribe. She might be Tohono O'odham or Apache or even Yaqui. She wasn't pretty in the classic sense, but there was something about her face that commanded attention. I put a hand on her head, where the fat man had hit her with his pistol. She was bleeding from a knot the size of a duck egg.

I picked her up, and she stiffened but stopped struggling. I carried her over to where Hector sat, slumped against the boulder we'd hidden behind. He had a sad look on his aquiline face.

"I fear I am dead," he said to me.

I opened his shirt. He'd been shot high in the abdomen. I reached around behind him, feeling for an exit wound. There was none.

"Hell," I said, "you're only eighty. You have years yet to honor the ladies. Breathe as deeply as you can."

He smiled an indulgent smile.

"Thank you, *mi amigo*, for your vote of confidence, but I feel things slipping away. If I do not survive this, please look after my family."

"You have my word, but do not suddenly get old on me and give up."

The young Indian girl stirred. Her eyes fluttered open, and she regarded me with a hard stare.

"Hello," I said to her. "You are safe. No one here is going to hurt you. Do you speak English?"

She looked at me through a haze of anger and fear. "Bite me, you big honky," she said. She could have been from New Jersey.

I tried not to laugh. Hector hid his smile.

"Respect this man," he said as sternly as he could. "He just saved your life."

She listened to him and heard the pain in his voice. "You are hurt," she said as she got to her knees and looked at his wound.

The tough girl vanished, and she put a hand on his shoulder. I knelt down beside her.

"We have to get Señor Benedicté to a hospital as quickly as we can," I said. "And we should have your head looked at."

"You should probably have your head examined too."

I was framing some sort of retort when I heard running footsteps behind me. I rose from my crouch and turned, bringing my pistol up.

It was Willy, and she was at a dead sprint. She wrapped me in a percussive hug so strong that it took my breath away. I eventually managed to squeeze back.

"You're getting my shirt wet," I finally said.

"You're not wearing a shirt."

"Oh. Yeah," I mumbled into her hair.

She hugged me tighter. I hadn't thought that possible.

"Oh, gag me with a fork," came the girl's voice behind me. "Get a room!"

Willy let go a little, and she looked around past my shoulder. She gave me a final squeeze and stepped back. I could see Daniel examining the bodies of the first two men I'd shot. He nodded his head. I nodded back. He went to where the AK-47 had flown when the fifty-caliber had hit its holder. He picked up the gun without looking at the man he'd killed. I saw him sigh. I didn't blame him.

"And who might you be?" Willy said to the girl.

"I am Elina."

I turned to Willy and wanted to kiss her raised eyebrow. She went over to Hector and knelt next to the girl. She also looked at the hole just beneath Hector's chest.

"My name is Willimina," she said to both of them, "but please call me Willy."

Hector was looking at her with an expression that was probably similar to the one I'd worn when I first saw her. He might be pushing eighty with a bullet in him, but he was still very much a proud heterosexual male.

I resisted the urge to slap my forehead. I had completely forgotten about the old man's family. I threw back my head and attempted the eagle cry again. It came out better than the first one.

"You are getting quite adept at that," Daniel said as he walked toward us.

Elina's eyes were huge. "Are you a shape-shifter?" she asked, edging behind Willy.

"No, he is not a shape-shifter," Daniel said to her. "He is a great warrior who commands respect, both in this world and in the other."

I wanted to roll my eyes, but they hurt.

Elina got closer to Willy and hugged her hip, Willy's arm draping around her, as Daniel studied her face.

"You are Apache," he said. It was not a question.

Elina became the little girl that she actually was, if just for a moment. She nodded and dropped her eyes. Then she raised them back to regard my brother.

"You are of the Northern Plains. All you guys look alike. Are you a Shadow Wolf?"

Daniel smiled at her. "I am Nez Percé, *Nimi'ipuu*," he said, "and I am not a Shadow Wolf, although I talk with two of them regularly."

"I want to be a Shadow Wolf when I grow up," Elina said.

Daniel gave her his look that strips away everything but the essence of who you are and could be extremely unsettling. Elina tried to meet his gaze and did, mostly, belying the notion that Indians don't hold eye contact. They certainly do when there's a reason for it.

"You just might," Daniel said after a good long while.

I left them to their conversation and went to find Helena and the girls. I met them where I'd last seen them and steered them away from the gruesome mess that Daniel and I had made.

"Your father has been shot," I said to Helena. "He needs a hospital."

She gasped and ran to where she saw people standing.

Gabriela had tears in her eyes. Gisela took her hand, and they followed their mother. I skirted around several boulders and found myself staring down at the gringo I had shot. He had been tall, with a look of competence about him. Now, he was just long. I'd hit him with all four of my shots. The fatal shot had hit his head, probably the last one as he fell from the one in his hip. I knelt and went through his pockets. I found no ID, but I did find a lone key with a paper clip hanging from it, threading one of the angular holes in its top. There was a worn and faded number stamped on it: 206. As I stood, I slipped it into my pocket.

Standing from the kneeling position made me light-headed, and I paused while the pins and needles in my extremities and the ocean sounds in my head faded. When I cleared, I tried jogging back to the wash. Not a great idea. But I had one more pocket to check. I found the guy who'd died not by my hand but by his own knife and felt in his pockets. Sure enough, I found my watch. I was delighted to find it still working.

I was strapping it on when a strange horn sounded. I looked up and saw that the van was running and had its lights on. I looked around at the carnage the last hour had witnessed. I was glad that I wouldn't have to clean it up. That would be for the desert to do, and it would do it very efficiently. I walked slowly toward the van. It would be good to sit for a while.

FORTY

Daniel drove east. It was a tortuous maze of gullies, washes still wet from the storm, sinks where the washes ended, mesquite, and the ever-present cacti. He took it slowly for everyone's sake, especially Hector's. Finally, we turned north onto Highway 85. Before we rolled into Why, Daniel stopped at a place only he would remember, and we stashed all of the weapons in the desert. There was no point in driving around with them in a van that probably had a terrible reputation among both law enforcement and local people. I was completely surprised to see my pack in the pile. Daniel must have found it on the snag and brought it down off of the mountain. I thought briefly of grabbing a shirt but couldn't quite translate thought to action. I was woozy and disoriented. The whacks on my head were now beginning to present their evidence.

It took only about five minutes to make contact with the people Daniel had been talking to in a steady stream of acronyms. The military loved acronyms. It seemed as if you could convey volumes of information without uttering a single English word.

I stayed quiet while Daniel conferred with an efficient-looking young fellow wearing jeans and boots that somehow still looked like a uniform. As the story unfolded, his eyes got bigger and bigger, and he whipped out his cell phone and began to bark earnestly into it. Soon after that, an Air Force ambulance arrived and Hector was gently transferred to it. Helena and the girls went with him.

As it sped off toward Tucson, I found Daniel talking into his cell phone. I tried to interrupt him, but he kept waving me off. I wanted to tell him to call Pablo so that when Hector, Helena, and the twins were deported, there would be somebody trustworthy, somebody who cared about their story, to meet them and intercede with whatever authority they were afoul of. Finally exasperated with my impersonation of a mime, he took the phone away from his ear.

"I am already talking with Pablo," he said impatiently and put the phone right back up to his ear. He also, pointedly, turned around to continue his conversation.

Hey, I thought, who was the big brother here anyway?

I went back to the van. Daniel had parked it behind an old gas station. There was no brand. The sign just said *Gas-o-line.* A jeep with a couple uniformed men was parked in front of the van, blocking its exit. Willy and Elina were nowhere to be seen. I looked in the van for anything that might be mine. There was nothing. The guys in the jeep eyed me warily. The young man Daniel had been talking to was absent. As I went to the jeep, the bulge of the nine-millimeter in my pocket felt huge. I made a point to keep my hand away from it.

I nodded to the driver. "Did you see which way the woman and the kid went?"

The older of the two looked at me like I was a museum specimen. It was not a sneer. He was not disdainful. If anything, he was reserved and respectful.

"They went to find a motel, I think," he said. "There's one just down the street. And pardon me, sir," he continued, but was struggling with it, "with all due respect, sir, shouldn't you find a doctor and have yourself looked at?"

My face must have registered surprise. I was sure that my head was misshapen, and there was the gash across my chest and ribs. The newest wrinkle was the apparent crease from the gringo's bullet across my right shoulder. There might be another one on my neck. I decided that I needed to find a shirt.

"Thanks for the thought. I guess I'll get there when I can.

There wasn't much of a town. I was sure it was a community, but as a town, it wasn't really there. There was a motel sign ahead, and I went toward that. The streets were still damp, but the drizzle had stopped. The air smelled wonderfully clean. When I got there, the office was dark, but there were about ten rooms arced around a small parking lot. The lights were on in one of them, and its door was slightly ajar. I peeked in.

Willy was nowhere to be seen, but Elina was watching the TV from one of the twin beds. I didn't want to scare her, so I knocked very lightly. Still, she jumped about two feet off the bed and somehow ended up in the corner, her big dark eyes open like two hobbit doors. Her hands were at her throat.

"I'm sorry. It's just me, the big honky."

A brief smile crossed her face and was gone. She regarded me very seriously. "It is okay. I have been pretty jumpy lately."

I heard water running from the bathroom as I sat in a bile-green chair by the window and put my face in my hands. I wanted to ask her how she came to be in the van and where she lived, but I couldn't put the words together.

"Are you okay?" she asked.

I thought about the question. Right now, it was a hard one to answer.

"Not really. I feel pretty weak. But more important, are you okay?" In the light of the room, I could see her jaw had been broken and set poorly.

Her face closed a little. "I'm fine."

Her posture spoke volumes. I wanted to reassure her, but I didn't know what to say. The water in the bathroom stopped. Willy came through the door. I tried to smile at her but felt myself falling sideways. I was powerless to stop it.

I woke up on the floor. My head was that dishwasher full of broken glass. Willy's face was a mask of concentration as she wiped my face with a cool, wet cloth. The Mexican sun had accented her freckles and lightened her hair. Her eyes searched mine, seeking who and where I was. I tried to put something into mine, some reassurance, some acknowledgement, some kind of fire, but in hers I saw no recognition of any such thing appearing. I saw worry there, which worried me.

"Can you help me get you up on the bed?" she asked.

It seemed like a reasonable request. "Is that a proposition?"

It was a fleeting smile, but it gave me some strength. Willy gathered herself into a squat and gripped my wrists. I was able to sit up, but that's as far as I got. I tried breathing deeply, and my head cleared a little. Our next effort got my butt to the end of the bed. The world started to spin, but I held my ground and gripped my knees.

"Elina," Willy said, "get all of the towels from the bathroom and fill the trashcan with warm water. Throw a bar of soap in there too."

"Got it," Elina said.

I heard running water again.

"Wouldn't it be easier if I made it to the bathroom?" I thought it was a reasonable question.

"The question is, can you make it to the bathroom? I can't carry you."

I answered her by attempting to stand. It was wobbly, but with Willy's strength supporting me, I made it. Elina had filled the plastic trashcan with warm soapy water.

"Thank you, dear," Willy said to her. Now go keep an eye peeled for Daniel. He will need to know where we are. If anybody you don't know shows up, pound on the door."

"Can I help?" Elina asked.

"Not with this," Willy said and closed the bathroom door.

It was a cramped space for one. With the two of us, it was downright claustrophobic. The shower was straight out of the 1960s, a fiberglass one-piece stall with a showerhead that came all the way to the back of my neck. Willy had me stand while she sat on the commode. Very matter-of-factly, she undid my belt and my pants fell off my hips. The pistol made a loud thump when it hit the faded linoleum. She stood, edged herself around behind me, and started the shower.

"Get in there."

"Yes'm."

The water hit me, and I felt the sting of it in my open wounds and scrapes. It felt wonderful. I was alive. Willy put the trashcan full of soapy water in the sink and took off her own clothes. She got into the shower with a soapy washcloth.

"Turn around," she ordered.

I did, and she went to work on my back. Whatever lethargy I'd been feeling disappeared almost immediately. She scrubbed my open wounds with a vigor that made me gasp. Soon I could see blood swirling around my feet and down the drain. I must have grunted.

"Sorry about this, but a lot of these are a very angry red. We really need to get them as clean as we can. You will need butterflies at the very least and probably stitches. I wish we had some antibiotic salve, or something."

"Rum works," I said.

She scrubbed harder.

"Turn around."

I did, and she got a very close look at the parallel gashes across my chest. The water sprayed against my back and stung. I looked down, past her breasts, and saw that the swirling blood had abated a great deal. When she started scrubbing my chest, I knew that was temporary. I gritted my teeth.

"This may be the only time in my life," I said, "that when, in such proximity to your naked self, Sir Happy isn't leaping skyward and proclaiming his joy."

When we got out of the tiny shower, Willy dried my torso as stoically as she had scrubbed me. When she got to my waist, she handed me the towel.

"You can finish the rest of you. My hands would probably tremble and you'd get the wrong idea."

Putting my pants back on was not a pleasant experience. They were gritty, stained, and still damp. If there had not been a ten-year-old on the other side of the door, I would have put off putting them on for as long as I could. It reminded me of high school football when you'd go down to the locker room and pull on that damp, twisted, cold jock strap.

When I stepped into the other room, I felt much better. I sat, again, in the green vinyl chair.

"You are not going to fall over again, are you?" Elina asked. "That was creepy."

"I will do my best to stay upright. Can I ask you a couple questions?"

She stayed still, but I sensed her squirming on the inside. This girl did not like questions. She looked at Willy, then back at me. Finally, she nodded.

"Okay. I'll start with something really easy. How did you come to be in that van?"

She looked to Willy and seemed to collapse in on herself a little. Willy reached across the short space between the twin beds and took her hand.

"It's okay," Willy said. "He really does need to know. I could tell him what you told me, but it would be better if you did. He really is a kind man."

Elina looked at me skeptically. I got the distinct impression that kind and man were two words that she did not readily associate.

"I thought you said easy," she said, looking at me.

"The other question I have is easier," I lied.

She sighed and looked at the TV. It had been switched to mute so the talking head with hair that looked like a helmet was just silently moving her lips.

"My aunt and uncle in Lukeville sold me to those..." Words failed her.

"*Pendejos*?" I tried to be helpful.

She brightened.

"Exactly. They said they were going to take me bowling at the lanes in Ajo. I love bowling. They tried to hide it, but I saw the gringo give my aunt some money. I do not know how much. My aunt's cousin was the fat guy you shot."

"So, you went from there to where I was in the desert?"

"No, we actually did go to the bowling alley in Ajo."

"Did you get to bowl?"

She looked at me as if I had two heads. "No." She shot Willy an "is he really this stupid?" look.

"I never even got to go in. The blond-haired guy hopped out with a package and was back in a couple of minutes. Then we headed to where you were. Garcia, the fat one, would not leave me alone. The others just laughed."

"Okay," I said. "Here's a hard one. What do you want to do now? I guess, legally, we're supposed to turn you over to whatever passes for children's services here. They'd make sure you have food and shelter and try to find you a home. It's what they do. It's a difficult job."

Elina's look could have stripped paint from a locomotive. I saw Willy squeeze her hand and let go.

"Been there, done that," Elina said. "I will not do it again. I would just run away."

There was a slight quiver in her voice, but there was steel there too.

I looked at Willy, who looked back at me and shrugged. I turned my open palms up and rested them on my knees. My decision was easy. I wondered how many laws I was ignoring.

"You haven't told me what you want to do," I said to Elina.

"I want," she said, running her small hands through her tangle of black hair, "to go to Oregon with Willy and you and live on Willy's ranch. I can work. I know horses. I can cook." Here she paused. "Sort of. I have not really wanted something in a long time. But I do know that I want this."

Willy and I looked at each other. A superhighway of information and acceptance moved between us at well over the speed limit.

"It's okay with me," Willy said. "We can work out the details later. I really do think it best to get her out of here."

I nodded and studied Elina. "Okay, but you have to promise me that when things get dangerous, you will do exactly as I say, no questions asked."

I was amazed as hope washed over her features. With hope in her eyes, she became quite pretty. A tumbler moved somewhere inside me, clicking into place. I had no idea what it meant, but it was deep and reverberated through places in me I'd never met before. This girl was ten, going on fifty, maybe older. I thought of that little shivering fox back in the Bates Mountains. It was a marvel that I did not understand, but I knew also that understanding it, right now, was of little importance.

Elina left her place on the bed and jumped into Willy's lap. She quivered like a puppy. Willy hugged her and looked at me over the top of Elina's head. Her eyes were dark green, big, and wet. I think she had just felt a tumbler move too.

"Thank you," Elina said with a choked voice.

"You are welcome," I said to them both. And I meant it. At the moment there was enough welcome in me to accommodate a small planet.

I heard tires crunching on gravel. The pistol appeared in my hand as I moved to the edge of the window. A late-model Chevy station wagon had come into the parking lot. Its headlights were on, and I could not see the driver. Whoever was in there doused the headlights, opened the door, and stood in the uncertain light. It was Daniel. I slipped the gun back into my pocket and was out the door.

He watched me walk to the car. "It seems that a little spring has returned to your step and that you have left Zombieland."

"It's still kind of touch and go, but I haven't wanted to eat anybody's brain for at least fifteen minutes."

"I brought a decent first-aid kit to knit you back together. I do not know about anyone else, but I am tired of looking at what is under your skin. Besides that, I do not want you to ruin the clean clothes I brought. I also retrieved our gear. And I have called Agent Jepps. He tells me that your buddies Deems and Chavez have fallen off the radar. I told him of your suspicions regarding what we saw this morning, and he was gravely interested in that. He did some checking through the CIA and called me back. This is a big deal and involves—"

"Human trafficking," I cut him off.

"Yes. And it reaches into high levels of law enforcement."

"Deems," I said.

"Apparently, he had carved quite a lucrative little empire using DEA investigations as a smoke screen. He set up a two-way pipeline, moving women and boys from Mexico and the United States to Asia and the Middle East. Jepps thinks that the money you burned up was Deems's buy-in with Flores.

"What about the CIA confrontation this morning?" I asked.

"It was not nearly as much money, but Deems is strapped right now and trying to recoup his losses."

"So, the pile in the villa wasn't the ransom money for Mr. Grabell's wife?"

"Jepps didn't think so. He thinks that got split up and laundered somehow."

"I think I know where some of it is."

Daniel's eyes widened.

"I think, tomorrow, before we finally head north, we should go bowling in Ajo."

"You really did take a whack on the head."

"Several," I told him about the key.

"We should just give the key to the FBI and let them handle it."

"That's fine. But there's another reason I want to go to the bowling alley."

Daniel's face was a question mark.

"Bowling."

I needed stitches at the impact points on my chest and where the deep grooves made the transition to my back, just past my ribs. Daniel moved the curved needle quickly and confidently after coating my skin with a local anesthetic and paid extra close attention to my left nostril. He was smiling as he sewed it back together but said nothing. The sensation of thread, however fine, moving through my skin was something I would never get used to. The local only worked when the needle pulled one way. I had to visit many favorite places to get through it, but at last the surgery was done. Willy patiently made large butterfly bandages to pull the rest of it together. Elina used her cool, deft fingers to press the edges of my wounds as close as she could while Willy applied the butterflies.

"You are going to have to avoid anything strenuous for as long as possible," Willy said to me when she was done. "Knowing you, that will need to be longer than a few hours. If you don't, this whole origami exercise will come apart."

There were also a couple of places on my head, and on Elina's, which required attention. I was more worried about the inside of my head, but there was no bandaging that. The jeans and light flannel shirt Daniel had brought fit just fine, and I felt complete for the first time since my ride down the mountain.

Willy had also rented the room next door, so Daniel and I moved into that. We said our goodnights and Willy, and I shared a long hug, much to Elina's disgust. I knelt down and looked at Elina. "You don't do hugs, do you?" It was more of a statement than a question.

"Nope."

"Okay. But I'll warn you right now that I like hugs. You may have to learn how."

Her eyes bored into mine. There was defiance there, but also a yearning and, maybe, a little humor. "We will see, Big One, we will see."

I was careful not to ruffle her hair or do anything that might cause her to withdraw. I wanted to show her some affection but decided to figure out what would work best for her before I chanced insulting her.

Daniel was waiting at the door to our room. "I think we should reconnoiter a bit before turning in."

"Yep."

Daniel took the shadows toward the south. I stopped briefly at the car and rummaged in my pack. Daniel had somehow found the CAR-15, broke it down and stowed it. This made me very happy. I found my Giants hat, crushed and soggy. I put it on anyway. Pablo must have snuck it back there when I wasn't looking.

I moved off to the north, scouting both sides of the highway. The town had rolled up its sidewalks. I was glad of it. The big storm had moved on, and the sky was awash with the Milky Way.

When I got back to the motel, Daniel was already in the bathroom. I carefully undressed, crawled between the sheets, and was asleep before my brother turned off the water.

FORTY-ONE

I was up with the sun. Outside on the walkway, Elina was already sitting in one of the cheap plastic chairs she'd dragged from her room. She had on a new orange T-shirt Daniel had brought her and her pair of faded blue jeans. Worn moccasins I hadn't noticed yesterday wrapped her feet. They were handmade and the beadwork was missing in places. She nodded solemnly at me. "Good morning." Her face was like stone.

"Good morning, yourself. Are you always this cheerful in the morning?"

"Usually less so. I am thinking this morning is pretty good."

I gave her my "the world is an amazing and beautiful place," smile and her face softened but did not break. I decided to go with the big guns.

"I'm thinking that as we head north, we should stop at the bowling alley in Ajo." I let it hang there before dropping the hammer. "And bowl a few games," I finished.

Her brow furrowed briefly. "That would be good," she said and paused, measuring me. "Why are you doing this?"

I was caught off guard. "Doing what?"

"Being nice to me."

Her face was basalt. I held back the urge to tell her that her view of the world was tragically skewed by her experience and that not all people, men especially, were out to use her for their own advantage. We might have that talk someday but not this morning.

"Because that's the way I am," I finally said.

She turned and looked at me like I had two heads. I was starting to get a Zaphod Beeblebrox complex.

"But you kill people. You are that way too. How can you be a nice person who kills people?"

My normally glib tongue stuck to the roof of my mouth. I hoped that when I opened my pie-hole to answer, whatever came out of it would be honest. Leave it to a ten year-old Apache waif to ask a question that I had avoided nearly all of my life and had never really answered.

"That's a really hard question," I said, buying time.

Elina squinted at me through the morning sun and waited.

"I am a warrior. I fight the Bad Guys. Sometimes I kill them before they kill me or hurt somebody I care about. It is a part of me that I don't think about very often."

That was, pretty much, what I'd told Willy in my living room a few weeks ago. I didn't like the fact that it seemed to be my stock answer.

"You killed Garcia without even blinking."

"Yes. He had just shot my friend Hector and hurt you."

"But Hector was not really your friend. Willy says that you had just met him, and you did not even know me. How could you care about me when I was a stranger to you?"

I marveled at this youngster who was nailing me to the wall as if I were a deer hide.

"I thought it was wrong that he had a weapon and you did not. He was a Bad Guy."

"What if you saw a man hit a girl in the grocery store? Would you shoot him?"

My head throbbed. "I would most likely say something."

"Like what?"

"I don't know. Just something. You ever hear the expression "reading from the book?""

Her blank look gave me the answer.

"When you "read from the book," you are telling someone what is right. You are talking about the way it is and the way it should be. If I saw a man hit a girl in a store I would read him from the book."

It took a second, but her face loosened when she got it.

"Willy says you are a protector. I am not sure you are a thinker, but I am okay with the protector part."

Suddenly, my brain was very small, and I lost the perspective of Elina as a child and me as an adult. I was staring into the eyes of an ancient spirit. I might have heard a far-off rhythmic singing, a chanting from a darkness I had been familiar with since the moon was young. For an instant, I could see the rhythmic rise and fall of hands on a drum. I smelled the curling smoke from a small fire in a large black space. Then the door to my room opened, and Daniel stood in the sun. Today he was sporting a red headband and a plain black T-shirt. He shaded his eyes and looked at the two of us.

"Looks like an inquisition."

"Yep. She needs to know stuff."

"So do you, Big One, so do you. Good morning, Daniel," she nodded. "I have questions for you too."

"It's a long ride to Oregon."

"I have never been to Oregon." She slid off the chair. Her jeans made a whispering sound. "I am looking forward to it."

With that she opened the door to her room and disappeared inside.

I caught my brother's gaze. "Yikes."

Daniel laughed. "I think your life has taken an interesting turn." Then he got serious. "You will have to follow the rules with Elina or risk a kidnapping charge."

"This isn't against her will."

"So say you. A government agency might claim that does not matter. We should discover who has legal custody and jump through all of the hoops."

"Her aunt just tried to sell her into a life we cannot imagine. I think the human law should take precedence over an arbitrary government law."

"Yes, of course, but in a court that means nothing."

I sat in the chair Elina had just vacated. She had been exactly right. I needed to know stuff too.

Daniel walked over to the station wagon and leaned against it. He pulled out his cell phone and was soon in earnest conversation. After about twenty minutes of me staring into an undefined distance, he walked over and handed the phone to me.

"Jepps," he said.

I put the phone to my ear. "Arthur? What's up?" I was still hearing the drum.

"Michael," he began, "I have some bad news for you that I think you should know about before you get back to Portland." He paused. "Your house burned down all the way to the river early last week. I'm afraid it's a total loss. The fire bureau says it was definitely arson."

It took me a couple of seconds to remember to breathe. "Total loss?" I said dumbly. "Everything?"

"Your friend Hannarty tried to rescue your Harley, but the flames beat him back and it went up with the house. I'm sorry, Mike."

"That son of a bitch," I seethed.

"Who?" Arthur sounded like an owl.

"Deems. He has to be the one."

"Don't you have other enemies?" Jepps sighed.

"Not at the moment," I said. "The rest of them are dead."

That wasn't really true, but through my growing anger, it felt really good to say. I stood up and began to pace down the walkway along the mostly-empty motel. I had put hundreds of hours getting that house back into shape from the hulk it had been. It was my refuge, my nest, my home. I'd put hundreds more into rebuilding the motorcycle. My friend Hogman had put a new cam in it just last summer. It was my pride and joy.

"Mike?" Jepps said into my ear.

"I'm sorry, Arthur. It was just sinking in."

"Daniel says you'll be back in Oregon tomorrow. Please call me when you get here. Whoever burned your house won't stop there. You're on his list, and Miss Hayes may be too. And be careful at the bowling alley. Our people will meet you there, but the other side might have it staked out as well."

"Roger that. You need Daniel again?"

"Nope. Call me when you get back."

We clicked off, and it was all I could do to not throw the phone as far as I could. The house was gone, the Harley was gone, but that was just the tip of the iceberg. My father's desk was also gone. I was very glad that the .36-caliber Navy Colt was in my office desk. The beret I'd had on the wall was gone, along with my laptop, my old Martin guitar, my clothes, and all of my photographs. There was some stuff at the office but not much. My guns might be okay if the safe had survived. I shook my head, trying to clear it, but that was a mistake. All it did was scream back at me.

Where else was I vulnerable? Willy, certainly, and Bucket too. Daniel as well, but Daniel would watch out for himself. Elina was part of it now, even though I had no idea where that was all going to land.

I spent the next half hour on Daniel's phone. I called my insurance guy, a couple neighbors, and, finally, Hannarty.

"Yo, Mike," he said. "I'm sorry about your house. It went up so fast that nobody had a chance to save anything. I tried to get the bike out, but the paint and thinner and all that went off, and I couldn't get to it. Singed my damn eyebrows."

"Thank you for trying. Do eyebrows grow back?"

"We'll see."

"Any evidence? Any anything?" I asked hopefully. "Is the safe still standing?"

"The fire guys say that the accelerant was very sophisticated, high-end stuff. Whoever it was knew what they were doing. Your safe must be in the river, which may be okay."

It weighed seven hundred pounds empty, so it was probably still sitting twenty feet down. It was airtight.

We said our good-byes. I walked over to where Daniel was watching the sunrise and handed him his phone.

"It's all gone. All of it." I didn't know what else to say.

Daniel reached out and squeezed my right shoulder. "*Ya-Tah-Hey.*"

Depending on the tribe and the context, it's a phrase that can mean anything from a "what the hell" shrug to "good morning" to "may the sky bless you." I guessed that he'd offered me the blessing. I was grateful.

Willy and Elina's motel door opened, and Willy stood blinking in the low morning sun. Her hair showed as much gold as it did her deep red. "What's wrong?" she asked.

I told her. She came over and put her arms around me. I didn't hug her back immediately and felt her stiffen and draw away a little. After a couple heartbeats, I decided that anytime this woman hugged me, I was going to hug her back, even if I was on a morgue slab, so my arms came up around her, and I held her against me. Over the top of her head, I saw Elina standing in the doorway. Instead of looking pained, she had a small smile as she watched us. Vaguely, I wondered about that shift in her behavior.

"You smell good," I said into Willy's right ear.

"You feel good. I'm so sorry about your house. Stuff is stuff, but I know the desk meant a lot to you. You can stay with me for as long as you want."

I squeezed her tight and let her go. "Thank you. My insurance guy says I can probably rebuild it. He's working on a settlement. We should be able to start pretty soon. At least we got to make love in it for one day."

Her eyes caught the sun like emeralds. "We really do need to have a long private conversation," she said.

I kissed her lightly. Her lips tasted of mint. I noticed that Elina's expression had gone back to neutral. "Yep. We do have some stuff to figure out."

It didn't take long to get our stuff into the station wagon, and then we all followed it. Willy used Daniel's phone to call home. She got through to Rosa, and things were fine. Aurelio was working full days from both horseback and the ATV. A couple Nez Percé fellows from Daniel's ranch Iron Wood were still camped out and working, which didn't surprise me. I was sure Daniel had made it abundantly clear that this was more than just a helping hand. Willy also warned Rosa that there was a ten-year-old coming for a stay of undetermined length. From Willy's laughter, I guessed that Rosa was delighted with that news.

She also passed along a hello from me. After they said good-bye, Willy closed the phone and smiled at me.

"Bucket says howdy and wants you to get home soon. Whenever he's not working, he sits and stares to the south for long periods of time. He and Aurelio have become great pals. Daniel's men think he is something more than just a dog and treat him with great respect."

"If I bought into all the mumbo-jumbo, I would tell you that he has visited me several times on this trip. She's right about Bucket being a special dog, though."

Daniel had yet to start the car. I didn't ask. I'm sure he had a reason.

My watch told me it was just before eight. The sun had been up about an hour, and the heat was already palpable. Evidence of the storm had vanished except for the green that was beginning to glow from the mountainsides to the south. I wished we could make time to wander out there and watch things bloom. It would be spectacular in its own quiet way.

"What day is it?" I asked everybody. The adults pondered. Elina spoke up from the backseat.

"It's Tuesday. You people should pay more attention."

"Tuesday? Really?" I turned and hooked an arm over the seatback. I felt the pull from stitches and tape. "You're right. We need to pay more attention. Daniel, make a note of that."

"So noted. My phone says it is the fourteenth of November," he added, looking at me. "If you had a phone, you would know that."

"I thought Indians knew all that stuff just by breathing."

"We know where the sun is. The rest of it does not matter."

"Unless you have to coordinate with white people."

"*La Migra*," said Elina just as an unmarked Chevy pickup pulled into the parking lot. They stopped right behind us.

Daniel checked his watch. "Pretty good. They are right on time."

He got out of the car. I turned to Elina. "How did you know it was *La Migra*?"

"They are Shadow Wolves. Most of the time they are not in fancy cars with lights, like the border patrol. They are much more clever."

She had answered my question without really answering it. I looked at Daniel talking with two men dressed in desert camo. They were very well armed. I got out of the car. The morning heat was almost a physical presence. One of the men had round facial features similar to Elina and stopped speaking when I joined them. I nodded to them both, and they stared back without really looking at me.

"My brother," Daniel said, nodding his head at me. "He needs to know as much as he can."

The Apache-looking fellow looked directly at me for a heartbeat and went on.

"No one is going to miss this child. Her father drank himself to death, and her mother is dying of diabetes and is still drinking. The kid has been living with various relatives around the rez since she was six. Her siblings are grown and long gone. I do not think she has ever met them. The child people in Sells are overwhelmed, and I do not think she is on their radar."

"How do you know this? She is a lost kid, and you are a busy man."

He measured me for a few breaths. I waited.

"I have had contact with the family she was staying with in Lukeville. They recruit mules down south and have mysterious cash flow. I do not think they are related on the maternal side, which means she was at the end of the trail, family-wise."

I digested this. There was more to the story. The other man was studying me closely but not obviously. I'm sure he had registered the stitches and tape. Daniel was watching everything. From the corner of my eye, I could see Elina's face at the window of the station wagon.

"She wants to do what you do when she grows up," I said. "She wants to be a Shadow Wolf. I get the sense that it is more than just a child's phase. And," I added after a breath, "she is the oldest ten-year-old I have ever met."

There was a silence that I let continue. Daniel had pounded into me, over our lifetime, that when discussing serious matters, Indians do not speak just to hear their own voices. I had just said my piece and was done. Now, it was someone else's turn.

The round-faced man reached into his shirt pocket and pulled out a card. I took it. It was an ICE card with his name, Frank Morehead, and a phone number. I put the card in my pocket and reached out my hand. I knew it was a white-guy thing to do, but hey, I'm a white guy. Frank smiled and shook my hand.

"I am Mescalero, and she is Lipan," he said. "I will tell the tribe she is in good hands."

"I would appreciate that. And will wait for the rest of this story."

The other guy gave me his card too. His name was Robert Begay. He said nothing as they nodded at Daniel and rejoined their dusty late-model Chevrolet. The diesel clattered, and they were gone.

"Thanks for that," I said to my brother's somber face.

"Of course."

"Let's go bowling."

We were tooling past the main body of Ajo when Daniel looked at me.

"Got that key?"

I fished in my pocket briefly and handed it to him.

"We just need a brief stop."

With that, he cranked the car into a StopNGo store just off the highway and drove through an alley to where a dusty blue Volvo was parked behind the store. The key was handed off without a word being spoken.

"A Volvo?" I asked. "You would think they'd at least use an American car for these clandestine events."

"Just goes to show you how sneaky they can really be," Daniel said.

"I thought we were really going bowling," Elina said. She sounded very suspicious.

"We are," I said. "We really are. The rest of this is just a convenient sideline."

"You are a goofball."

Willy gave me a look that said the same thing.

The bowling alley was on a corner where Rasmussen Street crossed the highway. Daniel pulled into the large parking lot and suddenly stopped, not yet in a space. I followed his stare to a dusty blue SUV with Arizona plates. There was nobody in it. We pulled around to the other side of the building and parked. There was no shade. The Volvo was parked in the front. There were two other cars in the lot, both of them nondescript Fords. That was more like the FBI I knew.

"Is that the same SUV we saw in the desert?" Willy asked.

"Impossible to know," I said. "But it's a coincidence that I do not trust."

Daniel had his phone out. "Have you run the blue SUV in front?" he said into it.

"It's from Tucson," came the scratchy replay, "registered to a leasing company."

"You guys go on in," he said, "while I take a turn around the building."

I looked at both Willy and Elina. "Might as well see what's up. But let me scope out the inside first."

I walked through the glass front doors as casually as I could. The only person I saw was an employee standing behind the counter that ran along the wall to my right. He looked at me with hopeful eyes.

"Maybe you could help me. When you rent a locker here, how many keys do you get?"

"You get one," he said, "and the house keeps one. You looking for those other guys?"

Was I that obvious? I absently fingered the stitches in my nose. "Yeah."

"Lane twelve."

I started to turn around but turned back. "If anything bad starts to happen, get out of sight and call the cops."

His eyes got big. "What?"

I gave him my "are you deaf?" look. "Just pay attention. *Prestar antención*," I added for good measure.

I went to the far end, went down a couple steps, and peeked around the corner, down the long stretch between the lanes and the lockers. Two men were standing in the middle of the run. A locker door was open, and there was a square package sitting on one of the tables. One of the men was the guy from the Volvo. The other looked familiar, and it took me a minute to place him. It was the guy I'd seen at the H-Bar-H when Jepps had come to collect the stash that Deems had left to try and frame Willy. I hadn't liked him then, and I didn't like him now. The back of my neck tingled, but I saw no reason to interrupt them. It was their ballgame, and I didn't expect to pitch today.

I slipped back up the steps to the front desk.

"Got a pair of thirteens back there?" I asked.

His worried look turned into a smile. "You bet. How many games you want?"

"Hang on a sec. I'll be right back."

I went back out the front door to wave to Willy and Elina. Daniel was back with them.

"Jeez," Elina said when they got inside. "It is about time."

I grinned at her and resisted the urge to ruffle her hair. "C'mon."

When we gathered our shoes and went down to the lanes, the two men were nowhere to be seen. The locker was closed.

"Where's the back door?" I asked Daniel as we looked through the rows of heavy balls.

"Around back, Kemosabe."

He let me give him a look before he pointed to the far corner at a doorway that looked like it led to a bar. I hadn't seen it, which bothered me a little, but I shrugged it off.

"The alphabet guys have their package," I said. "I guess we're off the clock for a while."

Daniel cradled a battered black ball, slipping his fingers in and out of the holes.

"Close enough." He sauntered back up the line of lanes.

After rummaging through several racks I finally found an old beat-up Ebonite that almost fit me. I went and joined our jolly little crew. Elina was already up, ready to bowl, her body at ease as she aligned herself. She glided to the line and let her lime-green ball roll with a fluid motion that belied her small stature and age. The angle looked good, and the ball hit the pocket, but left a six-ten split.

"I was robbed!" she cried, but she was smiling. Her smile changed her whole face.

She missed the spare by a whisker. "Stupid pins," she laughed.

"I haven't bowled in twenty years," Willy said.

She stepped up and rolled a strike. Her unabashed dance was a wonderful thing to see.

Neither Daniel nor I fared as well. Daniel had a natural hook to his, missed the headpin, and left him a little picket fence on the right side. He made the spare. Worried about ripping my stitches and tape loose, I had no hook at all, and the ball crashed into the right side, leaving a cluster of pins on the left. This delighted Elina.

"Big One. You do not have to throw it so hard."

"I will try and remember that, Little One."

We finished the first game. Elina had the best score with a 131. Daniel was next, Willy third, and I came in last with a 117.

We settled into the second game, each of us feeling a mixture of competition and camaraderie that we all reveled in. It seemed that I hadn't been at this ease since before I found Willy's truck in the middle pasture.

I had just picked up my ball for my turn when I heard a voice behind us.

"Now, isn't this a nice family picture."

I turned and there was the former, I assumed, special agent and head of the Portland office of the Seattle-region DEA, Howard Deems. He was smiling. I was not. Next to him, with his gun drawn and pointing at me, was the FBI guy I hadn't liked. I liked him even less now.

Daniel, sitting in his chair at the scorer's desk, went into his own calm "it is a good day to die" place. Deems raised his pistol to point it at the back of his head. I gave him my "don't move" look. The whir of the bowling machinery in the background was suddenly very loud. Willy and Elina were hardly breathing.

Deems looked thinner and smaller than the last time I'd seen him close up. His eyes had lost some of their arrogance but had maintained their cruelty. There was also something else, something I'd not seen before, a depravity that communicated an eagerness to express that cruelty. He'd given up all pretenses about functioning in a civilization. He no longer cared about anything other than causing pain, grief, and despair for his own gain. For an instant, I almost felt sorry for him.

"As much as I'd love to stay and chat," he said, "I fear I must be on my way. I would love for you to watch what will happen to your lovely woman"—his gun moved from Daniel to Willy—"but I will have to leave that up to your imagination. Truth be told, I actually prefer it that way. Not knowing, in this case, will be worse than knowing. She's a survivor. She'll probably learn to enjoy her new profession."

"You," he said to Willy, "come up here and bring the girl with you."

There was a quiet moment.

"Now!" he barked.

The FBI man had a little smirk on his face that enraged me. I heard the singing start. I felt the drums become an insistent distant pulse. I felt Willy look at me, but I did not look back. My body began to disappear, and my heart swelled to twice its normal size.

Willy and Elina began to move past me toward the steps when a curious thing happened. Elina paused and pulled the bottom of her orange T-shirt up to her face. Both of the men looked, their guns moving slightly in the direction of their gaze. At that instant, the bowling ball in my hand launched at the head of the FBI agent. Suddenly, he had sixteen pounds of battered Ebonite in his face. Strike. When it collided with his head, it made a sound that I will never forget.

Daniel threw himself backward, taking the small chair with him into the wall of lockers. He was now out of Deems's line of fire. Willy, Elina, and I were not. But something in Deems broke. He turned to run. I flew to the top of the counter above, gathered myself, and dove at his retreating feet. He turned and fired, but I felt the pressure wave pass over me. Then I was on him. He tried to shoot again, but I had his gun hand against the floor, and the bullet cut an ugly groove in the carpet. I felt bones in his wrist break. The gun came out of his hand, and I rolled him away from it. Grappling with him was like trying to hold on to a coil wire as someone starts the engine. He had nothing to lose. But I was large, and I was very strong. I was also extremely motivated. I had no thoughts about what I was doing. I smashed his ribs with the heel of my hand as my left thumb found his carotid at the left side of his neck. He was suddenly quiet, but I did not let up. A vast reservoir of blackness was upon me as I bent to my task.

All of a sudden the singing and the drums stopped, and I felt hands at my shoulders, urging me away. There was crying. Through it all, a small quiet voice was suddenly very loud.

"Big One," it said. "Do not do this."

I saw my brother's hand place itself over mine. His skin was cool. He put his fingers under my palm.

"Big One," the little voice came again.

"Michael," Willy's voice was a chord like the Milky Way above the Sea of Cortés.

I let go and fell over on my side, still wanting to squeeze the life out of Mr. Deems. But there was a peace upon me too. My head throbbed with the painful timbre of a thousand drums. The sound of breaking glass was loud and cut at the backs of my eyeballs. I felt hands upon my face and smelled sagebrush and water. I let it all go and fell into a long well. The last thing I remember before I was engulfed in silence were the eyes of a small fox, who said thank you and good-bye.

FORTY-TWO

I woke up smelling an odd mix of disinfectant and industrial laundry soap. I looked at the world from a very long way away, like seeing through a backward telescope. My head was full of cotton, and my mouth was full of mud. It took me a full second to remember my name. I was relieved to find that amusing. I slowly realized that I was under some kind of bizarre sedation and was probably in a hospital. I tried to open my eyes, but couldn't. I tried to reach my hands up to feel around my eyes, but I couldn't do that either. This concerned me.

Daniel's voice came through what seemed like a long ceramic tube. It was calm and, maybe, a little amused.

"You are in a bed in a clinic at the Gila Bend Air Force base. Your eyes are taped to limit their movement because you have some loose stuff rattling around in your head, but you will be okay. Your hands are restrained because you kept ripping the IV out of your arm. Willy and Elina are off having breakfast. They were here all night, talking to you, reading stories, talking to each other, and making sure at least one of your loose bits knew they were here."

I let this sink in. I tried to speak, but my throat was closed. I felt Daniel's hand on my chest.

"Hold on. It is Thursday morning. Deems lived through your onslaught. We got you off of him just in time. Had you not let go, you would have sent him to his ancestors. I do not know where he is, but he is seriously damaged. The FBI guy did not survive the night. Jepps flew straight down here as soon as I called him. He is with Willy and Elina. You solved two huge problems for him, and he has run excellent interference for you with the local cops. As soon as you can sit up, we are free to go home."

"I'll need a couple minutes," I croaked. "There's still a bunch of me missing."

"What?"

I tried to clear my throat and manage the claustrophobia that was creeping over me like spiders in the moonlight. I felt Daniel's hand slip behind my head to hold it up as he put a cup to my lips. The tepid water smelled of dank pipes and fluoride, but it was still fit for the gods. I sucked it down until there was no more.

"Get my hands loose."

There was a Velcro sound and a releasing of pressure I hadn't known was there, and I raised my hands to my face. What felt like gauze was wrapped around my head, covering my eyes. Whatever drug they'd given me had put me in a place that felt like none of this was happening to me. I was a disinterested person watching a film. I didn't like it.

"Hang on," Daniel said. "I will go get a nurse and see if we can get that stuff off of you."

I felt the air move against my skin as he left the room. I let out a long shudder and leaned back against the pillow. While I waited, I put a hand under the hospital gown and felt the new stitches and bandages. Whoever had sewn me up again had not spared any thread.

My head was better. The incessant ringing was far away, and my brain didn't feel like ripe guacamole. I really wanted the drug to wear off. The detachment I felt was unnatural and wrong.

I was sitting on the edge of the bed with my feet on the floor when Daniel came back with both a nurse and a doctor. The nurse smelled of lilac, and the doctor smelled of soap. Daniel smelled of Daniel.

"Mr. Ironwood," the doctor said, "you should lie back down and rest some more, at least until the anesthetic wears off."

I wasn't ready to stand, but I wasn't ready to lie back down either.

"Get this stuff off my eyes," I said. "I need depth perception."

Daniel and the doctor must have shared a look because I heard the doctor sigh and shortly felt hands unwinding the gauze and taking the pads from my eyes. The light was intense.

"Do you feel any dizziness?" the doctor asked.

He was in his forties, I think, about my age. He was lean and had a face that looked like an eagle. It wasn't his beak, so much; it was more the quality of his eyes, piercing and bright.

"Not at the moment. What the hell is this strange drug you used to put me under? The ringing is still there, but it's farther away."

"Ketamine. It can have some odd effects, but it is a very useful anesthetic, especially for head injuries like yours. It is also used to treat symptoms for other, um, circumstances."

I considered this.

"Because of the way it detaches you from yourself?"

"That's a good way to put it, I think."

"Okay. Maybe I will lie back down for a little bit. Do we need this thing in my arm?"

"It's only rehydrating you," said the doc. "There are no drugs being delivered."

I was okay with that, except for the itching in the crook of my elbow. I let myself drift and lost all contact with the world.

Voices woke me. They were talking about me.

"Indians do not lose their hair," Elina was saying.

I swallowed. "What about scalping?" I said. "That's losing your hair."

It was one of the few times in my life I'd ever heard Daniel actually giggle, but a giggle it was.

"That is gross," Elina said finally.

I felt Willy's hand on my forehead and opened my eyes just in time to see the blur of her chin as she kissed me. Her lips were dry and soft. I wondered if dogs derived the same pleasure from a caress. I gave a little bark and a happy whine to test the theory.

"Good boy," said Willy.

Daniel and Elina laughed.

"I am thinking that he is on the road to normal," Daniel said. "Normal for Michael might be taken as lunacy in most people, so we had best get him out of here before he is locked away by the Brain Police."

"They might just want to study him," Elina said. "He might make a good specimen."

I shot her a look. Her face was still, but her eyes shined like a disco ball.

"Someday," the doctor said, in farewell, "you will have to deal with not fighting as a way of life. You will have to face what gives you the edge in combat. Part of you is still curled up in a muddy foxhole. Yeah, yeah, yeah," he continued as I started to protest, "you don't really see it. Yet. But it is inevitable. There's a guy down the hall who is in the same place. He's very lucky to be alive and is not entirely out of the woods yet. Your choices have been better than his because you're not on your way to the brig. But you will eventually have to face the same demons."

"His name wouldn't be Grimes, would it?" I said, grateful to move the spotlight from myself.

His eagle's eyes snapped even more sharply. "You know him?"

"It's a long story."

He led me down a short hallway. I motioned to Daniel and he fell in step with us. A uniform with a Federal Marshall shoulder patch sat at the end of the hall on a folding chair. He looked bored. The doctor nodded to him as we approached, and he nodded back.

Grimes was pale, thin, and looked like an advertisement for surgical tubing. When Daniel and I first walked in, he seemed apprehensive, but relief flooded his features as he recognized us.

"You survived," Daniel said.

"So far," said Grimes. "And I wouldn't have without you guys. Thanks, again."

"Aw, shucks," I said. "The guys who shot you, was one of them wearing a Yankees cap?"

Grimes pondered this, his waxy face frowning as he went back to the event. "Yes. I believe he was. I had my gun in my hand and was still not quick enough. He was amazingly fast. I kept waiting for him to finish it, but he never did. I don't know why."

I didn't either. Chavez must have been in a hurry and let his arrogance assume Grimes was finished.

There wasn't a lot to say, but it was good to see him breathing. I'd spent so many years remembering him with an acidic taste that it was good to let the anger go. I hoped that he was in a similar place.

"When you're done with whatever happens next, look me up if you ever get to Portland. I'm in the book."

He eyed me warily, but he said, "I just might do that," and shook my hand.

Willy and Elina were out by the station wagon. Arthur Jepps had left for the airport. Apparently, he'd run out of time to see me.

"Elina has something for you," Willy said.

I looked down at Elina. She looked apprehensive but determined. She looked up at me and crooked her finger at me.

"Come down here, Big One."

I knelt on one knee, and she threw her arms around my neck. I stood up with her in my arms as she wrapped her legs. It was like hugging a hummingbird made from charged wire.

"Thank you," was all she said.

It only took a few seconds before it became obvious that she wanted me to put her down, so I did. It's hard to tell when Indians blush, but I thought Elina's face might be a little darker than usual. Again, I resisted the urge to affectionately ruffle her hair. I still hadn't come up with some casual way to show her the affection I had for her. I also wondered about discipline. I had no illusions about her strong personality. I was sure that there would be times when she would challenge everything I said.

I suddenly caught the strangeness of my thought process. I was already having fatherly notions. I looked at Willy. She looked back at me. Her eyes said: "I know, I know. Get used to it."

Daniel came through the swinging glass doors of the clinic, talking on his cell phone.

"For an aboriginal guy," I said, "you sure spend a lot of time with modern technology."

He shot me a look. "Yes. But I have far fewer scars. I never forget that I am not a tank, or a surface-to-anywhere missile."

He had me there. I didn't forget, really; I just focused very tightly.

FORTY-THREE

We drove north until we reached I-10 and turned west. The country was alternately bleak and green. Sharp hills and mountains, with spreads of gold, red, and green desolation gave way to vibrant oases wherever there was water. The rain that had come through while we'd been walking north was gone from the surface but was settling nicely into the reserves beneath the scalded desert. The only indications of it were a multitude of greens and wild splashes of bright color that spread across the flats to the mountains.

"What put you onto Deems as a human trafficker?" Daniel asked me as we rolled through the day.

"I guess it was the money. Two things about it, really. What did he need it for and where did he get it in the volumes that came to light as we went along? He wasn't moving large quantities of dope. He had access to it. That stuff he planted at the H-Bar-H proved that, but he didn't have enough to generate that unfortunate pile in the villa. Process of elimination said it had to be people. And the most lucrative avenue in that business is moving young people, both girls and boys, for the sex trade. But I wasn't completely convinced until I saw him in the bowling alley. There was just some smell about him that hammered it home for me."

The inside of the car grew quiet, each of us lost in our own thoughts. Daniel was driving, and I rode next to him. Elina was behind me, with Willy next to her.

I finally broke the comfortable silence. "You thinking Vegas, Tonopah, Reno, Susanville, Lakeview, and home?"

"Sounds about right. Those Ochocos will look pretty good."

I heard a grunt of agreement from Willy.

"You talk to Randy?"

Daniel stretched an arm behind his head. "Yep." He shot a sidelong glance at me. "We could sure use your help for a month, or so. I mean, if you can still remember which end of a horse you should be looking at when you are aboard."

"I'll split him with you," said Willy. "I could use an extra hand too, so I can catch up on what I've missed for the last two-and-a-half weeks."

It was nice to be wanted. I think. Actually, it sounded like work.

We went through Laughlin and hooked up with US95, where we veered north toward Las Vegas. US95 is also called the Veterans Memorial Highway. Its two-lane blacktop cuts through a vast plain of desolation, which I found fitting for a veterans memorial. The doctor back at the clinic had been mostly right. There were places in me that I'd never been and never wanted to visit. Those places had kept me alive and, for now anyway, I figured that was a pretty fair trade.

The romantic and patriotic notion of soldiers is the province of misguided poets, political rhetoric, and modern media. The elephant in the room is that killing is always an ugly business, no matter the cause. In a firefight, both courage and cowardice are drawn from the biological need to stay alive and the equally strong desire to keep alive your brothers-in-arms and the people you are protecting. For front-line people, day-to-day is a study in hurry-up-and-wait. It's a job, and even if you do it to the best of your ability, that rosy sunrise may be the last one you ever see. It is the ultimate commitment. It has nothing to do with romance.

We stopped at the north end of Vegas, bought a cheap Styrofoam cooler, and filled it with stuff for the long ride home. I took over the wheel and drove to Tonopah, where I took the turn to the west. We blew through Reno and caught US395. We made a bed in the back of the station wagon for Elina, and Willy took over the wheel. We followed the tunnel of light the headlights made in the high-meadow dark. There were remnants of new snow, but the road was clear. Willy sure wasn't wasting any time. Her driving was smooth, competent, and fast.

"I'll get us there from here," she said. "I have a serious case of Horse Barn Syndrome."

I dozed in front on the passenger side while Daniel dozed behind me. The miles rolled on and on. I felt Willy's presence beside me, but we were content to just be there without talking. I marveled at the complexity of our new relationship. The deepest part of it evoked an undeniable notion of family within me. She was fast becoming a best friend, lover, sister, and teacher, all sculpted into a vibrant companion. I felt a deep gratitude for the way my life had undergone this sudden change. I reached over and gave her an intimate touch where the crease of her right leg met her torso. She dropped a hand from the wheel and squeezed mine. I treasured the moment. I gave her upper thigh a pat and withdrew my hand.

"I think I'll keep you," she said.

"Consider me kept."

The car was a womb. I listened to the road noise, a rush of tires on pavement and air parting around us, tucking us into a blanket of white noise. Finally, I slept.

I awoke to the back end of the station wagon slipping. Willy gathered it up without trouble, and we kept going. The sides of the road were covered with white, and the snow blowing through our swath of headlights made it seem as if we were going a hundred miles an hour. The big wet flakes hit the windshield and immediately dissolved.

I stretched as best I could, feeling the stitches and the tape pull against my skin. "Ow," I said.

"Wimp," said Daniel from his perch in back.

Willy laughed.

We stopped for gas in Lakeview at the only twenty-four-hour station in town. Daniel paid. What little money I'd had was scattered across a wash somewhere in the Organ Pipe Cactus National Monument. The wind cut through my flannel shirt like cold steel.

"Have you heard what 31 is like ahead?" Daniel asked the attendant.

"Talked to a guy who came down from Paisley about an hour ago. He said it was okay but getting worse."

I looked at Daniel. "We got chains in this thing?"

My brother shook his head and looked at the kid.

"We should have the right ones," the kid said.

He squatted down and read the tires. "Yep," he said. "Be right back."

He passed Willy and Elina as they came back to the car.

"You want me to drive?" I asked Willy.

"No. I got it. I kinda like being the damsel in control instead of the one in distress."

"Can I ride up front?" Elina asked.

"Sure, Squirt, you bet," I said.

"Do not call me Squirt. That is gross."

When I thought about it, I realized that it was.

"Okay. You know, I think Elina is a pretty name, but I just realized that I don't know your whole name."

She looked at me, deciding if she would share the secret of her entire name. "I am Elina Blackfox. I do not have a middle name like you Americans."

"Aren't you American?"

"I am Apache."

I held out my hand. "I am Michael Ironwood. I am very glad to meet you."

She looked at me, her face somewhere between pride and exasperation. "You really are a goofball," she said, but her small hand gripped as much of my big hand as it could and squeezed.

Daniel put on his worst British accent. "Blackfox? Would that be of the Lipan Blackfoxes?

Elina's giggle was a short cascade of notes that reminded me of a winter wren. She put her hands on her hips and pointed her chin. "Oh yes, that would be we," she said in the same terrible accent.

"Are you sure," I said to Elina, "that you're really ten and not a thirty-year-old midget?"

"Pretty sure, Big One." She stuck her tongue out at me.

We climbed into the station wagon.

The road was okay. Willy made the best time she could. This was high desert, over four thousand feet in elevation. We passed through several snow squalls, each one heavy enough to reduce our visibility to nearly nothing. My watch told me it was 3:35 a.m. We'd be back at the H-Bar-H by sunrise.

We went through Paisley and got about halfway to Summer Lake when we had to stop and put the chains on, which is most always miserable. Elina got out and helped for a little bit because she wanted to learn what it was about. As soon as she figured it out, she rejoined Willy in the warm car.

"Pretty good snow for November," I said after Daniel and I had each done a wheel.

"Pain in the ass. Four-wheel drive with good tires makes a lot more sense."

"Hey, Tonto, you picked it out." I pointed at the car.

"Best I could do, given the circumstances."

I nodded, and we both slid into the backseat.

"Pretty bad out there. You sure you don't want me to drive?" I said to Willy.

"Sexist pig," she snorted.

I shut up and tried to rub some feeling back into my hands.

We clumped and chattered past Fort Rock and ascended Picture Rock Pass. At the top of the pass, the sky cleared, and the stars were dazzling. Willy turned off the headlights and slowed to a crawl along the packed snow. It was breathtaking.

We took off the chains when we got to La Pine and Highway 97. It was still snowy, but the road was mostly just wet. From there it was through to Bend and on to Prineville. As we started climbing up the McKay Creek road into the Ochocos, the sky was a bright pink with peach and deep lavender swirling through it like astral syrup. The ponderosas and lodgepoles stood guard all the way to the Mill Creek Wilderness. When we turned into the long driveway and passed the H—H sign, Willy could barely contain herself. The road was full of snow, but the Chevy wagon pulled us through it, probably shoved by the sheer weight of Willy's will. Horses greeted us from the small pasture that led to the house. When the house came into view, Willy stopped the car and just stared. Tears ran down her cheeks. Elina looked at her in wonder.

"I was born in that house. And if it wasn't for those two galoots in the backseat, it might have been taken from me."

Elina looked back at us, an understanding slowly dawning in her round face. She looked back at Willy.

"It is a beautiful house."

And it was. But even more beautiful was the shape loping towards us right down the middle of the road. I got out of the car and ran through the snow.

Bucket stopped and sat, watching me come. I slowed until I stood about six feet from him. We regarded each other for maybe a breath or two and then melded into a warm tangle of arms and legs, hands and paws. He pressed his head hard against my chest as I rubbed his back and scratched his belly.

"Good boy. You are such a good dog."

He whined, croaked, and groaned in an excited dog monolog. He sniffed through my shirt at my bandages, commenting at each new smell. I heard the car creeping up behind us. We moved aside to let it pass. Daniel had the window rolled down.

"Bucket," he called. "Your bipeds are back."

When the car stopped in the yard by the shop and Daniel got out, Bucket went through another round of dog speak, dancing between Daniel and Willy until he couldn't stand it anymore and sprinted circles around the car, snow flying everywhere. He'd made about five loops when he noticed Elina. He stopped in front of her and stared. She stared back. He went up to her and bowed into his downward-dog pose. Elina smiled.

"Hello, Bucket. Willy has told me about you."

He lowered his butt to the ground so that he was lying there with his head up. She looked at me, and I nodded. She dropped to one knee in front of him and tentatively stroked his head. He licked her hand. I went over to Elina, knelt down next to her, and put my arm lightly across her shoulders. Bucket looked at me and then back at Elina, studying her face. She ruffled his ears. He gave a little yawn and licked her hand again.

"You have soft ears," she said.

He stood up and sniffed her hair, her face, and her neck. Bucket shook himself and came over to me with a light in his eyes.

"He says you're a keeper," I said to Elina.

She wanted to say something smart, clearly, but stopped herself. "He's a keeper too."

Her smile was different than what I'd grown used to over the last few days. There was a tenderness to it. I put my hand on her shoulder.

"You will meet a lot of new people in the next few weeks. If you get too shy or lonely, go find Bucket. He knows exactly what to do."

"I am used to being alone," she said, looking down at her wet moccasins.

"There's a difference between lonely and alone," I said. "Sometimes, you can get lonely in a room full of people."

She nodded, thinking about it. "I know."

The rest of the morning was a whirlwind. Willy was everywhere. The Ruiz family was overjoyed. Aurelio appeared to be well but admitted to being still sore sometimes. He shook my hand but said nothing. He didn't have to. David came to me and gripped my hand.

"*Gracias*, Mr. Ironwood," he said. His eyes were luminous with feeling. Not letting go of my hand, he brought me over to his family.

"This is Adriana, *mi corazón*. And this is Adolfo."

The young boy's face was serious as he offered me his hand. I shook it firmly but couldn't help smiling. Adolfo forgot his serious face and flashed a quick smile in return. He looked to be about eight or so and like he was dressed for school. Of course, I thought, it must be Thursday morning.

"And this," David continued, is *mi pocita querida*, Beatriz."

She stayed behind her father's leg and peeked around his hip at me. I smiled and nodded to her. She must have been about five and regarded me as seriously as her brother had.

"Thank you," Adriana said, and now she was shaking my hand. "Willy means everything to us."

I didn't know what to say. She meant everything to me too. I just nodded and tried to match her sincerity with my own.

Rosa had been standing behind the knot of people, taking it all in. Finally, she came to me and wrapped me in a hug that seemed to go on forever. I hugged her back. There was no self-consciousness in it, and I felt her soul envelope me.

"Miguel, Miguel, Miguel," she said against my chest. "*Usted es un buen hombre.*"

"*Gracias,*" I answered. "The work is almost done."

She broke the hug and her eyes searched mine. "The danger is not fully past?"

"No. But we are close."

Willy introduced Elina to everyone. "She will be staying with us, and I would like you all to welcome her as part of the family. She has had some serious adventures with us and is a very brave young lady. She also has a wicked sense of humor, so watch out."

Elina held up well under the scrutiny, her back stiff and her face solemn. "Hello," was all she said.

Bucket came up and nudged her. A quick smile lit her face. Her hand trailed to his head, and she softly stroked his ears, which said more to everybody than any more words could have.

Later, when the hubbub had died down and Willy and Elina were getting the empty-for-too-long out of the house, Daniel, Bucket, and I took a walk up toward the lower pasture.

"This isn't over until Jesús Chavez is dead," I said. "I don't think I have to hunt him. I think he will come to me."

"I think you are right. Are you thinking of traps you can set?"

"I think the only trap I can set is me accepting being the bait. He will come, and I think he will come when you are not around. He's smart enough to know that he cannot defeat us both."

"That means he's watching. What about the Willy and Elina?"

"I don't think they are on his radar, other than being objects to use and discard. He may see Willy as a gambling chip, but I don't think he cares one way or the other about the little one. And yes, I think he's watching."

"Speaking of her," Daniel said, "she did very well this morning. I think meeting that many people at once was brand-new to her. She may have some memories of tribal gatherings but not for a long while."

"Yeah. I've been thinking about her mother. Have you noticed anything in Elina that points to Fetal Alcohol Syndrome?"

Daniel shook his head.

"I haven't either. That tells me that her mother was not drinking when she was carrying her. If that is true, isn't it rare, considering what Frank Morehead told us? The stereotype says that drinking starts early and continues unabated until disease and an early death."

Daniel sighed. "It is the norm for so many of the people, no matter their tribe. Genetically, we are all similar, and the incidence of alcoholism is chronic.

You just cannot argue it. But what people forget when they think 'drunk Indian' is that we are all individuals and make choices. All I am saying is that maybe her mother did not start drinking until after Elina was born. Maybe she just started making bad choices after the birth and not before. She could have been very young."

"Whatever the reason," I said, "I'm glad that Elina got her start with a full deck. She will make her own choices."

"Speaking of that, I am hoping she will want to go with me to Iron Wood. It might do her good to see a bunch of Indians without alcohol dependence. I do not think she has seen much of that. I think it may be why she so admires the Shadow Wolves."

We walked along through the snow, listening to the crunch of our boots.

"Maybe, I will take her there and come back as quickly as I can, only as a ghost. Chavez will think you are alone, and Elina will be out of harm's way."

"Yes. That is a good plan. See? With you around, I don't have to make plans. I just have to react."

Daniel looked at me and shook his head. "I am going to start calling you Atom Smasher."

I must have looked blank.

"You are like a nuclear reactor. At critical mass, enemies seem to shrivel and vanish."

As we walked, I marveled at how at ease we were but also at how we still kept scanning the landscape for minute details, assessing, supposing, rejecting, and accepting. Being aware of where we were was such a deep instinctive part of us. It was in the very core of us; it was as involuntary as breathing. We were born with it. The military had honed it to a razor's edge, but we started with it long before they got their mitts on us.

We made it to the lower fence of the lower pasture and stopped. A flatbed truck was at the high end, most of a mile away. A man was dropping bales of hay across the snow for the cattle that were wintering after roundup. Unlike the buffalo that Daniel raised, cattle would not dig through the snow to find grass.

"I think that is Aurelio pitching bales. I cannot tell who is driving. It might be my cousin Barry Two Cloud."

I squinted into the sun. "I think you're right. But even I can't see the driver."

"Your eyes are older."

That was hard to argue. We watched the truck for a while, until we started to get restless. We climbed the fence and started walking up the pasture.

"What did you think of Elina lifting her shirt at the bowling alley?" Daniel asked.

I'd been thinking about this. "I think it was pure instinct. She knew they would look and that it might give us the split second that we needed. She really doesn't have any protective notions about breasts yet. And just because it was instinctive doesn't make it any less brilliant."

We walked along in silence. The truck's engine was more audible now. It was starting to come down the hill to us.

"I think she is properly named," Daniel said. "In Apache culture, I am pretty sure that Elina means 'intelligent.'"

We met the truck in the middle of the property, not far from where Willy had been abducted. It was Barry Two Cloud driving.

I hopped up on the flatbed with Aurelio, and Daniel got into the cab with his cousin. The light work felt really good, and I got to assess the superficial damage that was trying to heal under my shirt. My jacket was open and Aurelio must have caught a glimpse of my bandages.

"How bad it is?" he pointed.

"Stitches and tape. Nothing serious."

My head was clear and sharp, so I wasn't lying to him. When we got to the gate, I hopped down and handled it. Barry Two Cloud kept the truck moving, so I had to run to catch up. I vaulted up onto the flatbed and stumbled a little into Aurelio. I heard laughter coming from the cab.

"Paybacks are hell," I promised with a smile.

We got back to the house. Elina was sitting in the kitchen eating a sandwich. "I'm going to get fat. I have never seen so much food."

"Leave some for me. Where's Willy?"

"She said she was going to the barn."

Daniel sat down at the table. "Can I have a bite?"

She drew her plate to her and put her arms around it. "Make your own sandwich."

I headed out the door into the yard between the house and the shop. Bucket trotted up to me and bumped me with his head.

"Work," I said.

He cocked his head at me and fell in behind me at my right side. When I went into the shop, he stayed at the door.

Willy had put on clean jeans and a denim shirt. Over that she wore a green down vest. Her hair was pulled back into a ponytail. She looked utterly relaxed and happy as she curried Annabel, her favorite mare. When she saw me, her grin was a sight to see.

"I don't want to ruin your day," I said, "but we're not completely done with everything yet."

Her grin did not fade. "I know. But I'm home and we are together and my intuition tells me we're going to be okay. Life is good."

And death is easy, I thought.

I filled her in on what Daniel and I had talked about. She listened intently but never stopped her work with Annabel. When I was done, she put her comb down and looked at me.

"I should start calling you Mr. Cheese, or Mr. Bait."

"Just as long as you don't call me Master Bait, I'm okay with it."

Willy rolled her eyes and led Annabel to her stall. "I will feel better, if Elina is out of harm's way until this is really over."

"Me too."

Willy linked her arm through mine as we walked back to the house. I wanted to whistle with pleasure. I had been worried that Elina wouldn't want to go to Iron Wood with Daniel, but she was excited to do it. They'd decided to leave in the morning, right after breakfast.

We went down to the Ruiz house for dinner that evening, and it was truly a feast. The steaks were butterflied and cooked in the Mexican style and there were butter beans and baked potatoes, and canned peaches for desert. Afterward, I put my hands on my belly and gave Rosa as big a smile as I could muster. She responded with a gracious nod of her head. Daniel, Elina, and I cleared the table, and Inez, David, and Adriana washed everything up. Willy and Elina were in a warm corner by the fire, talking.

Aurelio offered cigars, and Daniel and I each took one. He also offered brandy, which we both declined. He looked at us with his eyebrows up as we followed him out to the porch.

"I'm still working," I said and left it at that. Aurelio nodded with understanding.

"I wondered about that. We are still in danger, then."

"For a while yet," Daniel said.

"I don't think you or your family are, so much," I said. "Even Willy is probably no longer a target, but I most definitely am, so anyone near me is at risk. I am hopeful it won't be for very long. I thought about going back to Portland tomorrow, but Daniel and I have decided to set and bait a trap here. It's a gamble. Willy knows what's going on."

We smoked and talked. Aurelio enjoyed his brandy. I watched Bucket out at the top of the yard that separated the Ruiz house from Willy's. He was sitting up, alert, but calm. After a while, I excused myself. I caught Willy's eye as I left, and she nodded.

The walk to Willy's was cold and crisp. Stars popped up high when the fast-moving clouds scudded past. It seemed like it would snow if it got the chance. Bucket heard me coming but stayed where he was.

"You are such a good boy. C'mon." He followed me to Willy's where I left him at the door into the kitchen. Daniel would let him in the house when he got there.

"Work," I said and went inside. When Willy, Daniel, and Elina got back, I was sitting in the kitchen cleaning my guns. Nobody said a word.

FORTY-FOUR

I lay there listening to Willy breathe, watching the window begin to turn gray. I was restless and sore. The bed was too small. I heard Bucket snort.

Very carefully, I got out of the bed and pulled on my pants, making sure the cold pistol sat comfortably at the small of my back. Willy stirred but did not wake. I was pretty sure that with the extra room, in her own bed, she would fall into an even deeper sleep.

I let Bucket out. He padded off through the snow like he was on a mission. I wondered about that. I added fresh kindling to the coals in the kitchen stove and got a small fire going. While I waited for coffee, I pulled on my boots and looked out across the yard at my truck. It was parked exactly where I'd left it three weeks ago. The snow on it followed the round lines of the body and the straight line of the truck bed. Except for the gun safe sitting on the bottom of the Willamette River and whatever I had in my office in Multnomah Village, it was all I had left.

I was still wondering about Bucket and the purpose he'd shown when I'd let him out. I grabbed my jacket from its peg in the mudroom off the kitchen, threw it on over my bare torso, and followed his tracks through the snow. They led around the face of the shop and on around the barn. I stopped when they showed that he'd broken into a trot when he cleared the far end of the building. The tracks led across a wide lot where Willy kept the horse trailers and the extra features for her tractor. There were also rows of stacked firewood, a hydraulic log splitter, and a pile of slash wood that would be cut up and be put to any number of uses. Bucket's tracks went between the two horse trailers and looked like they headed into the woods beyond.

I broke into a trot myself. A distant singsong chant started in my head. It was not the insistent dark voice that presaged combat; it was more like a celebration or an honoring of something. Part of me tried to recall when I'd heard it before, but I couldn't put my finger on it. Maybe these voices and sounds were so ingrained in me that I'd actually given up any pretense of sanity and had gone around that bend in the river where all behavior and rationale became unpredictable.

I got to the woods and slowed. I heard Bucket snuffling ahead. I called him. He came into view from where the ground dipped down toward a streambed and came about halfway to me. His ears were up, and his eyes were bright. He wanted me to follow.

He stayed ahead of me and literally pointed at a confusion of tracks at the edge of the snow-filled streambed. I squatted and studied them while Bucket sat beside me and let out a deep growl followed by a short whine. I ruffled his ears.

"Good boy."

I had seen tracks like these once before in my life. I'd been about fifteen and Daniel about twelve when we had stumbled across them high up in the Blue Mountains. Randy Grey Wolf had been teaching us to track, and at first we thought he'd been playing a trick on us. We'd run back to get him and showed him what we'd found. They were four inches long and each toe had a distinctive claw mark. It was a short stride, and each heel print looked something like a sergeant's stripes. Randy had knelt by the tracks, much like I was doing now, and let out a low whistle.

"You boys have found something very rare these days," he'd said. He'd stared at them for a long time.

"What are they, Uncle?" Daniel asked.

Randy looked at us with respect in his eyes. "Wolverine."

I was looking at the same tracks here in Central Oregon ranch country. It was beyond rare, especially here. The last sighting of these fierce and reclusive creatures I'd heard about had been several years ago up in the Wallowas, near Joseph in Oregon's far northeastern corner. What made it even more special was that I was looking at the tracks of two animals, probably a mating pair. I sat back on my haunches and marveled. I guessed that they had been made last night. The chanting in my head continued unabated. I felt it in my chest and along my arms. It was telling me to let them be, to let them go about their business, whatever it was. Their presence put every chicken, calf, goat, and dog within a hundred miles in jeopardy. Willy's big henhouse was close to the Ruiz house. These tracks did not appear to go anywhere near there. This was a puzzle I mulled over all the way back to the warming kitchen.

When I got back, I fed the fire and enjoyed some coffee. Daniel came in and poured some for himself. He went to the eastern window and squinted out at the new day. The land rose into the low clouds like an artist had erased it. He stood, with his mug steaming, under the framed photo of Willy's father.

"Do you have any photographs of our wild youth?" I asked. "Maybe something with Pop? Our mothers?"

"Yeah, somewhere." He knew exactly what I was talking about, my lost photos. "I will dig them out and have some copies made."

"I would really appreciate that."

"David ran a trickle charger on both of our trucks," he said, looking out the other window.

I sipped coffee. I could feel it trickle-charging me.

"What the hell would a pair of wolverines be doing here in the Ochocos?"

Daniel turned to look at me with eyes as big as the plates up in the cupboard.

"Wolverines? Are you sure?"

"Yep. Over in the woods, yonder." I nodded my head toward the barn. "Follow Bucket's tracks, mine too, for that matter, and they'll lead you right there."

He cocked his head. "I am guessing you heard something. You have that look in your face."

"What look?"

"The far-off but focused look you get when you hear something you refuse to acknowledge."

The look I gave him told him everything he needed to know. He nodded and sipped more coffee.

I heard a toilet flush somewhere down the hall. It was time to create some breakfast. After rummaging through the refrigerator, I decided that I had what I needed for a frittata. There was bacon too. I wasn't much of a biscuit maker, but there was bread so toast would have to do.

Elina came down the hall, dressed in her grubby jeans and a T-shirt that was too big for her. Her face was freshly scrubbed, and her black hair was tucked behind her ears. She was very interested in what I was doing.

I set a bowl on the counter. "Here, kiddo, break a half dozen eggs into this bowl and whip 'em up till they're all blended together. Put a little cream in there too, milk if there's no cream."

Daniel started grating some cheddar onto a plate. He knew where we were going. I lay bacon in a black iron skillet, and we were off and cooking.

About five minutes after I'd turned the bacon and started caramelizing some onions, Willy came into the kitchen, rumpled and soft. She offered her sleepy face for a kiss. I was happy to oblige.

"Put a shirt on," she said. "Your stitches are making me itch."

She took the tongs from me. "I'll handle the bacon."

After throwing on a shirt, I built the frittata carefully and layered on the caramelized onions with the cheese.

"Master Cheese," Willy said.

My sip of coffee almost came out my nose.

As the frittata finished in the oven, Daniel and Elina went out to move Daniel's stuff from the station wagon to Daniel's truck. Elina didn't have any stuff.

On the way out the door, Elina was excited and beamed at Willy.

"Big One found some wolverine tracks." The door slammed behind her.

Willy's eyebrows went up into her hair. "Really? I've never heard of any sightings here and I've been here my whole life, except for the time I was in California. We'll have to really make sure the henhouse is secure."

"Yep. It's a puzzle. The tracks don't seem the least bit interested in the chickens, which I find odd. But if they stay around, they will surely bother the chickens."

"Elina needs clothes," Willy said, changing the subject as she drained the bacon on paper towels. "She needs to get signed up for school, which will be interesting. She needs shoes and boots. She needs everything."

"How," I said, "will she handle school? I can't imagine it not boring her to death. She is so advanced."

"She still needs to learn stuff too. And she needs the social part for sure, I think."

"She is an Apache warrior living in a ten-year-old girl," I said. "The first kid who gives her grief is probably going to be in for a huge surprise."

"I've been worrying about that," Willy said. "How do you teach a child, who doesn't think of herself as a child, that her first instinct may not always be the right thing to do? That's the part she needs to learn."

"Have you talked to her about it at all?"

Willy sighed. "Yeah. Briefly. She says she knows she has to go and says she will, but I'm not convinced she's bought into the reality of it. And the other thing is, the school is going to want to know who she is. We don't even know that. We have to figure out how to become her legal guardians."

"This is all new to me. A month ago I was just a guy living contentedly on his houseboat with his dog. Today it's a completely different ball game. I don't know even the first step. What I do know is that the Indian Child Welfare Act has the potential to make things problematic for us. But the first step, I don't really know what to do."

"I do," Willy said as she stood on her tiptoes, wrapped arms around me, and kissed me on the neck.

"Hmm?" I hugged her back.

"Saying 'I do' would be a good first step."

"You mean…"

"Yes."

"Isn't marriage when two people decide to spend the rest of their lives together," I said, "based on what they know to be true and commit to an agreed fidelity and partnership?"

"Well, yes." Willy said.

"I've already committed the rest of my life to you. In my mind, I am already married to you."

"Yes," she said. "But if we registered it with the state, it might help with Elina."

I chewed my lip and pondered this. I felt Willy stiffen a little at my silence. I responded to that by deepening the hug.

"I have no problem with any of it."

"What do you mean you have 'no problem' with it?"

Uh-oh. I was afraid I'd just felt a bear trap close on my head. I blindly forged ahead.

"I mean that I'm more than willing to do whatever it takes to make it work. Whatever it is."

"Whatever?" Willy had backed out of the hug and was standing in the middle of the kitchen with her arms folded across her chest.

"Wait a minute," I said. "If you and I getting married is the most sensible thing to do, then let's have breakfast, go down and find a justice of the peace and get it done. Unless, of course, you want to go down before breakfast."

She didn't crack a smile. Her eyes were slits of hard jade. "Sensible?"

Daniel and Elina came through the door and stopped.

Willy spun on her heel and stacked plates on the drainboard. I went to the oven and pulled out the frittata. It looked perfect. Using a couple spatulas, I slid it out of the skillet onto the butcher-block cutting board. I grabbed a long carving knife and split it like a pizza.

"Are you guys fighting?" Elina asked.

Leave it to her to wad subtle up and throw it out the window.

Willy looked at me with something like pleading in her eyes, but it wasn't pleading. It was an uncertainty I'd never seen before.

"No," she said to Elina's question. "Not really, it's just…I don't know."

I watched her eyes well with tears.

"I don't know," she said again and left the kitchen in long strides. I heard her bedroom door close.

Daniel and Elina got their plates and helped themselves to the food. Before she started eating, Elina looked at me.

"I think this is where you go in there and apologize for whatever stupid thing you said."

"But I don't know what I said. One second we were fine, and the next we were not."

"Boy," Elina said with her mouth full, "this is really good."

"You should do something," Daniel said, "even at the risk of being wrong."

I heaved a sigh and went down the hall. I gently tapped on Willy's door. I heard a muffled voice say, "Go away." I tapped again. Nothing.

"I love you," I said to the door. It remained stoically silent. Then, magically, it opened a crack. A puffy eye peeked out.

"What did you say?"

I felt like scuffing my feet on the floor and running, but I sailed ahead anyway, remembering the adage about old dogs and new tricks.

"I said, 'I love you.' I realized that I've never said that. I've never said it to anybody. Well, except Bucket. And I was drunk. But I wanted you to know that and that I'm sorry for whatever I said. This is all new to me. I don't know…" I finished lamely and resisted the urge to stuff my hands into my pockets.

"It's new to me too. The intensity of it. The rightness. But it's scary too. I've lost two loves to early graves, and they didn't put themselves in harm's way like you do routinely. Loving you scares me spitless, but I can't help it. Every fiber in me tells me it is exactly what I should do. But this has happened so fast that my heart is spinning like a ceiling fan. Sometimes my brain has trouble believing my heart and keeping up."

I felt like I'd had ten cups of coffee, but I had yet to pour my second. "C'mon," I finally said. "Let's have something to eat."

I kissed her on the nose, which she wrinkled at me. Her eyes were open again and deep. I decided that if she ever proposed to me again that I should probably just accept it and not trot out my intellectual fool. The emotion surrounding the concept had me worried. Until Jesús Chavez was out of our lives, I needed to be focused and calm. I explained this to Willy as we ate.

"There are two of us now," she said. "That should make a difference. I am no longer your client—I'm your teammate. And, by the way, I've saved that check you tore up and left on the counter. You didn't have to do that."

"Yeah, I did. When it became personal, I had to tear up that check."

"How in the world do you make a living?"

"To tell you the truth, I don't really think about it. I just do what I do, and things seem to work out."

Daniel and Elina came into the kitchen. She had a tattered jacket on over her T-shirt and a pair of worn sneakers on her feet. She looked from Willy to me and back to Willy.

"You guys are okay, then?" she said.

Willy went to her and gathered her into a hug.

"One thing you have to realize. We will always be okay. We will argue, and we might fuss a little, but we will always be okay. You can count on that."

"I am counting on it," Elina said. "And please thank Inez, again, for the sneakers and jacket. They are broken in just perfect."

"We'll get you your own stuff, whatever you need, when you get back," Willy said.

"I just thought of something," I said. "You will probably sleep in my old room while you're at Iron Wood. In the bottom lefthand drawer of the desk in that room is an old baseball. Would you bring that back for me? There should also be a small sheath knife in there too. Would you bring that too?"

"Sure." Her face was puzzled.

Daniel looked a bit puzzled too but stayed quiet. "We should hit the road," he said instead. "While we are gone, would you take the station wagon to the FBI office in Bend? I would like to be clear of them for a while."

I nodded. "We'll do that today. I also want to drop in on Nancy Kelso briefly."

Daniel hugged Willy and kissed her cheek. He clapped me on the shoulder and gave me a meaningful stare.

"See you."

"Yep." I knew that when he went to ghost mode I wouldn't see him until he wanted me to. I looked at my watch. It was about eight. I figured he would be back and on the prowl around five this evening.

Willy and I flipped a coin to see who would have to drive the station wagon. I won, so I got to drive my truck, following Willy to Bend.

It was a quick, uneventful trip. We got to the office and I walked in with the keys to the Chevy wagon while Willy waited in the truck. It had served us well. The receptionist in the office was calm and efficient.

"What are these for?" she asked as I lay them on her desk.

"Your car, in the parking lot," I said with a smile.

"What are you talking about?"

A man had come out of his office and was standing behind her, looking hard and official.

"May I help you?" I don't think his heart was in it.

"Nope. Just dropping off the keys."

I went back out the door as quickly as I'd come in. Sometimes, things just work perfectly. He came storming out of the office just as the elevator doors closed. I believe he did see me wave. When I got to ground level, I heard him pounding down the stairs above. I ducked out the front door and went around the corner of the building where I'd parked the truck. I clambered in and watched my red-faced pursuer come out and look at the parking lot. I'd parked the truck facing east so the sun would reflect off the windshield. I knew he couldn't see us. I watched him give up and go back around the corner. I counted to sixty and idled slowly out of the lot and merged with traffic.

"What was that all about?" Willy asked.

"Allowing the teenager in me full reign. Just a bit of fun at the expense of Authority."

"What did you do?"

I told her, and she did her best not to laugh. "You're nuts,"

"Yep. And you'd better drive because all of my identification is still somewhere in Arizona. I didn't want to have to explain anything to some alphabet guy when he asked me to identify myself. Where's the nearest cell-phone store?"

I pulled over, and we changed positions. Willy drove to one of the stores that sold phones with prepaid minutes.

"You could have told me sooner that you didn't have your driver's license."

"Could you loan me a hundred bucks?" I asked.

"You're an expensive date."

When we got back out to the truck with my new chartreuse phone, the first thing I did was call Daniel.

"This number will work for a while," I said when he answered, and hung up.

Next, I called the Bend FBI office.

"Federal Bureau of Investigation," the front desk woman said.

"Has your boss calmed down yet?"

There was some sputtering, and after a few moments his strong voice came on the line.

"I'm tracing this call," he said in his best menacing tone.

"Great. Call Arthur Jepps. He'll fill you in. Bye."

I clicked the phone off and slid it into my pocket.

Willy clapped her hands. "How old are you?" she laughed.

"It varies," I admitted.

We were about halfway back to Prineville before we spoke again. It had been a comfortable cruise, each of us lost in private thoughts.

"This is a great truck," Willy said.

"Yes, it is. It's not only my prized possession, it's one of the few possessions I have left. This truck and my guns are, pretty much, it."

"You have me," she said.

"You're not a possession. You are my best pal and the love of my life."

Willy made a satisfied noise low in her throat.

We stopped for gas, and I got out and looked around. It was a fine day with high overcast and splashes of blue. The temperature was probably in the forties somewhere. Mount Jefferson's white shoulders dominated the western skyline. I studied the parked cars I could see, not from a sense of foreboding, but more out of habit. Willy paid the attendant, and we were on our way again.

I adjusted my position so I could see the mirror on my side of the truck.

"How long has that black Trans Am, three cars back, been behind us?"

"I'm not sure," Willy said. "Maybe since the gas station."

"Keep an eye on it."

"You think it's following us?"

"Don't know. I saw it parked across the road when we were getting gas. If it is following us, it has been since we left the ranch. See if you can get a plate number."

We motored past the Les Schwab Tires headquarters and slowed as we came into the main part of Prineville. The two cars between the Trans Am and us peeled off to the right. It stayed back rather than coming up on us. I didn't like that.

"Oh-eight-two, TYU," Willy said. "Oregon."

"You have good eyes."

"Runs in the family. My dad could count the hairs on a rabbit's butt at a hundred yards."

"Swing by the cop shop, and we'll see what he does."

Willy continued down Third and turned right into the police station parking lot. I watched the Trans Am slide past, and got out of the truck. Walking out to the sidewalk, I watched it turn left a block ahead. I walked to where I could see down the street it had turned on. The Trans Am was nowhere to be seen. I shrugged and went back to where Willy was standing by the truck.

"Gone."

"What do you think?" she asked.

"Hard to say. I don't have any bells or whistles going off in my head." I didn't want to admit that I'd been waiting for the drumming to start.

It was Saturday. Nancy Kelso was in the office but not in uniform. She wore blue jeans and a red sweater with black sneakers. Even in civvies, she looked every bit a cop.

"Just came in for a little while to catch up on some paperwork."

"Can you ever really catch up?"

She rolled her eyes at me. "Sometimes. Computers have made it easier and harder at the same time. So"—she paused, eyeing both of us—"you're back safe and sound."

"More or less. But we're still paying attention."

"What brings you to me?"

"A couple things. Have you heard anything about that tweaker kid who shot Aurelio Ruiz and the DEA sprang from the county jail?"

"I've heard nothing. He disappeared into thin air. What else?"

"Can you run a plate for me?"

Nancy looked at Willy. "Cheeky, isn't he," she said with good humor.

"But he's honest."

"Sure," Nancy said. "But what's in it for me?"

"Knowing that you've served your community and maybe an arrest."

"Good enough."

Willy gave her the plate number, and we sat waiting while Nancy accessed the database. It didn't take very long.

"Stolen in Madras day before yesterday. What's up?"

"It followed us into town from the 76 station about eight miles out. It had probably been following us all day. It turned left on Elm about fifteen minutes ago."

"Excuse me a minute," Nancy said and went to put out an APB.

Willy leaned over to me. "What are you thinking?"

"Just supposing, really. Chavez won't risk being seen, and the kid who shot Aurelio has been bugging me. At first I thought that Deems had just iced him, but that never settled. I'm thinking the kid is still useful as a buffer and a scout."

"But Deems is in custody in a hospital somewhere."

"You're probably right, but we don't know that for sure."

I looked at my watch. Daniel was probably on his way back from Iron Wood. As if on cue, I began to hear distant drums, coming and going, like the sound of tree limbs on a breezy day.

"Where did you just go?" Willy asked. "Suddenly, you were very far away.

"I don't know," I said honestly. "You'll have to get used to it," I said as I saw the concern on her face. "I mean, I'm almost used to it."

Nancy Kelso came back. "The word is out. Every car out there is looking, county and state too. If it moves, we'll see it."

"Anything reported stolen in the same general time frame?"

Five minutes later Nancy was back with a printout. "Five," she said, handing me the list. "Got anything particular in mind?"

"Maybe," I said and looked at the list.

What I was looking for turned out to be number four. It was a 1988 F-150 four-wheel drive, stolen in Redmond about an hour after the Trans Am was taken. If my hunch was correct, Jesús Chavez was in that truck somewhere on or near the H-Bar-H. While Willy and Nancy chatted, I went out on the front steps and called my brother.

"Spook Service," he answered.

FORTY-FIVE

When we got back to the H-Bar-H, the mid-November sun was starting to wane. The air had turned colder and the sky had decided to scowl with the threat of snow. I figured there were a couple hours of daylight left. It was time to make something happen.

"I'm going to take the truck up to the top pasture and do some hiking."

"I'm going with you."

I started to argue with her, but the hard edge on her face told me that it would be futile. Bucket gave me the same guff. He was up in the back of the truck before we even got outside. I had my Glock in its usual spot and the .357 mag in a holster at my hip. I considered my shotgun but didn't want to carry it. The CAR-15 stayed in my pack as well. For all I really knew, this would just turn into a hike up the hill and a walk back in the dark.

We left the truck at the top of the high pasture, not far from where I'd tossed Deems's tracking device. I wondered how the snakes were doing in their collective wad. I was not real fond of snakes, and they didn't like me much either.

"How tough would it be to follow the road loop from the timber?" I asked Willy.

"Doable, but it gets pretty steep. There's a game trail that sort of parallels the road cut."

I nodded and started up the hill. The drums were still far away, and the singing was nowhere to be heard. Bucket went ahead without a sound. He knew what he was doing. As we walked, I pointed to a set of tracks off to our left.

"The wolverines are up here."

Willy said nothing, focused on her footing.

We'd gone about a mile when the hair on Bucket's back stood straight up, and he growled deep in his chest. The drums in my head stopped, and I felt a jolt of fear travel down my spine. The wind was blowing across our track. I never heard or sensed anything before a blinding pain gripped my left arm. I went down hard from the weight of it. Willy stumbled and fell against me. At the same time, I heard the double report of a pistol and the *wuff* of bullets as they passed over me. Had I still been standing, they would have both dead-centered my chest. One of the wolverines had clamped his or her jaws onto my elbow and the sheer muscular weight had pulled me to the ground. I barely caught a glimpse of the stocky black and brown body as it bolted off into the trees. I struggled to get my gun out and ready to bear, but Chavez was there, standing twelve feet away, his pistol pointed at me. From my position, the barrel of it looked as big as a ten-gauge shotgun. I heard Bucket breaking through the underbrush as he chased the wolverine.

"Oh, *señor*," he said, "you are bleeding. Do not worry—I will put you out of your misery."

I thought how familiar that sounded as he sighted on my forehead. My world had gone completely silent. I didn't even hear the wind. Willy screamed, "No!" and launched herself across me just as Chavez fired. I heard the *thock* of the bullet hit her and the air go out of her lungs. She landed across my body and lay there, inert. I awaited the second shot, but it never came. I looked up to see Chavez staring at something off to his right. It was Bucket running for all he was worth right toward us, with the wolverine in hot pursuit. Chavez leveled his gun at the dog and was about to fire when he howled in pain. The mate of the chasing wolverine had taken a bite out of his left hand and was running off with one of his fingers sticking out of its mouth like a grotesque cigar. Chavez screamed and ran back along the game trail we'd been following. I was still trying to get one of my guns out, but Willy's weight was making it difficult. By the time I got the big revolver out, Chavez was out of sight.

I gently rolled Willy off of me. Her breath came in quick gasps, but her eyes were open and clear.

"Go get that son of a bitch," she said.

"I'm not leaving you here with those wolverines around."

"They don't want to kill us," Willy gasped. "They saved our lives."

That, of course, was impossible, no matter how it seemed. I looked at Bucket, who was quivering with his exertion.

"Good boy."

Suddenly, Daniel was there, kneeling in the snow next to us.

"Listen to the lady," he said. "Go get him. I will take care of Willy. You go. His truck is down where the road meets the fence line. If you go straight over the hill, you will get there before he does."

I touched Willy's face. "Don't you die on me."

"That would be a switch. Go."

As I took the first stride up the mountain, the drums came back at full force and almost knocked me down. It was the whole damn tribe of voices. I just fell into it and let it carry me up over the top and down the other side. I knew Bucket was loping along beside me. I saw Chavez below me, clutching at his mangled left hand. I didn't slow down. I ran right at him. I didn't care if he heard me or not. I drew back the hammer on my big revolver.

He heard me coming and turned sideways. I shot him through the lungs. It spun him around, his gun flying off into the snow. As he crumpled, his hand instinctively reached into his jacket. I shot him again, through the hand and into his chest. He made a great sucking sound and fell in a heap. I advanced slowly, watching his hands very closely, marveling at the precision with which the wolverine had taken his fingers.

Arterial blood was welling into the snow. He looked at me, angry at himself for being afraid, angry at me for killing him, and angry that his death was just as he had lived.

"I will see you in hell, *señor*."

"If you do," I said, squatting about six feet away, "you'd best run."

Before he could answer, his eyes became unpolished agates. I watched him for what seemed a long time, willing him to sit up so I could shoot him again. Bucket finally came up and licked my hand where my own blood dripped into the snow, breaking the spell. He looked at me reproachfully, like he knew there were more important things to do. And of course there were.

Bucket trotted back along the hillside toward Willy and Daniel.

"Pardon me for being human," I muttered to his rear end and hurried to catch up. My breath came in great heaves, so I guess I must have been running pretty hard. My arm did not hurt. It was blessedly numb.

Bucket stopped briefly and looked back up the steep hill we had just run down. At the top were two dark shapes, watching us. I swear they were grinning. I raised my arm to them in an awkward salute as they melted into the trees and were gone. This life was turning out to much stranger that any of the stories I'd heard as a kid around a campfire. There was a single loud clap of a hundred drums, and then it was just Bucket and me standing on a hillside in the Ochoco Mountains, at the back end of the H-Bar-H, under a rapidly darkening sky. A few snowflakes started to swirl as the dog and I started moving again.

Willy was sitting up, holding her jacket across her lap while Daniel worked on her back. She was pale and probably in a state of shock.

"The bullet is lodged under her left scapula," Daniel said. "We need to get her to a hospital, but she is not in grave danger, unless the shock goes out of control. As near as I can tell, it completely missed her spine. She is a very lucky lady."

"I can do something about the shock, I think," Willy said, taking as deep a breath as she dared. Her mouth set in a grim line. "Luck is a very relative concept," she added.

I squatted in the snow. "Thanks for saving my life. Fireman's carry. Let's go."

My left arm had started to wake up and was an issue at first, but we found a position I could live with. Daniel knew better than to offer to carry her. It was more than just a macho thing—it was deeply personal on so many levels. He knew that if I couldn't finish, I would ask him to take over. He also knew that wasn't going to happen.

"Boy," I said after a while, "it's a good thing we're going downhill."

Willy sighed into my ear. "Just shut up and shift gears."

"Ooh. Grumpy."

She bit my ear. I shut up. I could hear Daniel chuckling softly.

When we finally got to the truck, Bucket hopped up into the bed without being told. I wrapped Willy in the big fleece blanket I kept behind the seat and put her in the middle. Daniel drove. I cradled her against me and juggled the phone to call Jepps.

"Your wayward fugitive is dead."

Jepps sighed. "I figured it was just a matter of time. What is that old movie line? You're easy to track. Just follow the trail of bodies. Where is he?"

I explained the general location.

"You'll have to be interviewed and make a statement, but there's no real hurry on that."

I told him about Willy and let him know where we'd be for a while.

"I'll send a team up to take care of the body, The Crook County M.E. will have to be involved, and the OSP.

"Can't you just let him rot for a while?"

Jepps barked a laugh without mirth. Before he hung up, he told me that Thad Krieger had busted the kid in the Trans Am. Shots had been fired, and Thad had not been hit. The kid was in the hospital under lock and key.

I put my cheek on the top of Willy's head and tried to absorb all of her pain. When we got to Emergency, I put Bucket in the cab, and things happened very quickly. Willy went into surgery, and my arm was scrubbed out and sewn back together. I watched it all but felt like it was happening to somebody else. I found it kind of funny that my stitches had stitches.

They worked on Willy for over two hours. When the doctor came out, she gave me a tired smile. Her name tag said Carmichael.

"She'll be fine. A couple weeks of rest and she'll be up and able to do light work as much as she wants to, but probably not from horseback. In about six weeks, she'll be as good as she's going to get for a while. Good as new?" she shrugged. "That's pretty much up to her."

"Where is she?" I stood up.

I think she wanted to divert my attention but realized it would be futile. "Come on."

I followed her down a dimly lit hall, and she ushered me into a room with an east-facing window.

"She should sleep through the night."

I touched her arm. "Thank you, Dr. Carmichael."

She nodded, yawned, shook my hand, and left. I dragged a chair to Willy's bedside. Before I sat, I kissed the top of her head. Even after the surgery, there was just a hint of sagebrush. I settled into the chair and got as comfortable as I could.

Daniel appeared in the doorway. "I have the dog. We will keep a sharp lookout."

We smiled at each other.

"Another chapter," I said.

He grinned. "Another verse."

I must have fallen asleep because when I blinked he was gone.

FORTY-SIX

A subtle change in her breathing awakened me. Maybe it was her legs stretching. I snapped awake, full and complete. My arm ached. The first hint of morning lit the window, and Willy's eyes were rolling beneath their pale lids. They fluttered open and struggled to focus.

After a moment or two, they found me sitting at the bedside. They were very green in the gray light. My good hand instinctively found hers and cradled it gently. She squeezed back and offered a wan smile.

"You're here," she said with a cracked voice.

"Always."

"*Always* is a very big word."

I nodded. "Yes, it is."

We were quiet then, awaiting full sun.

THE END

EPILOGUE

Willy and I married on Thanksgiving Day in the yard between her house and the Ruizes'. Aurelio walked her down the aisle. Willy wore a pale green dress that took my breath away. Her hair was broad and full and danced on her shoulders. Rosa stood as maid of honor. Daniel stood up for me. Bucket was Best Dog. Elina and Beatriz were ring bearers. Thad Krieger showed up, as did Tom Hannarty, whose eyebrows were growing back, and Arthur Jepps with his wife. Nancy Kelso came too, with her husband Kevin. Pablo Montoya and Jasper Cronk flew up in Jasper's airplane and gave the small crowd an exotic flair. The ceremony was short and sweet. The food was fabulous. There was added good news: Pablo told me that Hector Benedicté had pulled through his surgical ordeal and was seriously considering visiting Oregon.

I wore black jeans and a beaded, deep-green shirt that Daniel had given me, saying it had magical powers. I did not scoff. The wolverines who had saved our lives had me completely rethinking my whole relationship with the Universe. I can still see the bright eyes of that bedraggled kit fox that changed my life's course so that Elina became a part of it.

The ancient rhythmic voices in my head have stayed mostly silent. Sometimes, I think I hear them yawn, but that may just be the wind.

We filed the papers to adopt Elina. The State of Oregon is on board, but we have yet to hear anything official from the Mescalero tribe, of which her Lipan people are now a part. Daniel has been in touch with Frank Morehead, who doesn't foresee much trouble, as long as Elina is active with the Nimi'ipuu people and culture. Daniel will certainly see to that. But the wheels turn slowly, as they must.

Willy healed quickly and was working from horseback within three weeks of taking Chavez's bullet for me. For our honeymoon, we went to Portland to see about getting my houseboat rebuilt. The insurance company said we can start on it right after Christmas, and I am scrambling to get plans approved. Tom Hannarty oversaw bringing my gun safe up from the bottom of the Willamette. Everything inside was dry and intact. I'd forgotten about a photo of

Jasper and me that I'd stuck in there, so I still had one left from those tours in Vietnam, a blessing to be sure.

Howard Deems has vanished into what Daniel calls the Spookland Jailhouse. Somebody knows where he is, but Daniel cannot, even with his contacts, trace him. This concerns me because I know that if he ever gets out, I'm one of the first people he will visit. I'm pretty sure it won't be cordial.

Willy and I have still to work out the nuances of our marriage. We decided to share two houses instead of just one. I will spend time in Portland trying to earn a living. My office is there, and so are most of my clients. Willy is a rancher through and through. Her permanent address will always be the H-Bar-H.

In the meantime, I am a husband, a father, a pack leader, a working hand on two family ranches, and a currently unemployed private cop.

I'm okay with all of it. You bet.

ACKNOWLEDGEMENTS

I would like to thank my friends in Oregon and all over the country for putting up with my obsession. You know who you are. I'm sure you grew weary at times listening to my bubbling babble and my whining. But there are other people to whom I should express my gratitude for helping me understand what I was trying to do and offering their own hard-earned wisdom and experience. These mentions, like the rest of my life, have no particular order and if I forget anybody, I owe you a refreshment of your choice.

My friend Craig Ryan, already in the middle of his own complex project, took the precious time to read an early draft and claimed to like it. But he did say: "Your villains are crap." As usual, he was right about that and the other suggestions he made. I had to take it back into the man cave for some serious surgery. Thank you, Craig, the patient lived.

My lifelong friend and musical pal, Gil Sanchez, helped with the Mexican Spanish used throughout the story. *Gracias, mi amigo.* If any of it isn't right, it's my fault.

Kristin Thiel, editor extraordinaire, took a thoughtful scalpel to the vast wad of words I gave her, fixed my meandering tense, and coaxed the story out of the woods. Without her careful work, I might not have been able to pretend I knew what I was doing.

Thanks to Jessica Glenn, Jessica Hardesty, and everyone at Mindbuck Media for their experience, knowledge, and extreme patience. They knew from the get-go that I was marketing-challenged and guided me through the painful process of selling both myself and the novel. Next time, maybe my skin won't feel like it's inside-out.

I also want to mention Kim Stafford, Craig Johnson, and Brian Doyle, for the marvelous stories they tell and for their encouragement and advice. Each offered a perspective that allowed me to keep a tenuous grip on the reality of writing and marketing something as immense as a novel.

There is no way I can adequately express my thanks to Andra Watkins, who really started me thinking that maybe I could survive the birth of this story so that it might breathe on its own. And Michael T. Maher at Word Hermit, thanks for taking a chance on this old hippie guitar player.

My offspring, Jess and Ben, thanks for putting up with the old man and not laughing too hard (at least not in front of me) when I stopped making sense while trying to be hilarious.

Now, we come to Laura, my best pal, confidante, and the love of my life. Without you, my dear, none of this would be likely, maybe not even possible.

-Jim Stewart; Portland, Oregon; 2015

ABOUT THE AUTHOR

Jim Stewart started his journey in the Midwest, went through his formative years in New England, and made it to the West Coast just in time to try and figure out what was happening in Vietnam. Music and writing kept him mostly sane. He lives in Portland, Oregon with his wife Laura. A lifelong writer of poetry and short fiction, *Ochoco Reach* is his debut novel.

REACH

CPSIA information can be obtained
at www.ICGtesting.com
Printed in the USA
FSHW011255061218
54290FS

9 780990 859338